Seven
Malas

Seven
Malas

a love story

JOHN LESLIE LANGE

Seven Malas: A Love Story
Published by Arjuna Press
Boulder, CO

Publisher's Cataloging-in-Publication data

Names: Lange, John Leslie, author.
Title: Seven malas : a love story / John Leslie Lange.
Description: First trade paperback original edition. | Boulder [Colorado] : Arjuna Press, 2019. Also available as an ebook.
Identifiers: ISBN 978-1-7324730-0-3
Subjects: LCSH: Spirituality—Fiction. | Metaphysics—Fiction. | Yoga—Fiction.
BISAC: FICTION / Literary.
Classification: LCC PS370-380 2019 | DDC 813 LANGE–dc23

Cover design by Victoria Wolf
Front cover photograph and head shot by Julie Kruger Photography

Gamble Everything for Love used by permission of Coleman Barks is from The Essential Rumi, New Expanded Edition, copyright © 2004 by Coleman Barks.

QUANTITY PURCHASES: Schools, companies, professional groups, clubs, and other organizations may qualify for special terms when ordering quantities of this title. For information, email johnleslielange@gmail.com.

*This novel is dedicated to The Divine Feminine in all her forms,
but most especially to my mother,*

Pauline Leslie Lange

Author's Note

This is a work of fiction. The characters that populate the story are fictional, and as author, I take full responsibility for everything they say or do or feel.

* ~ * ~ *

For love is the magic
That changes music to rubies,
Weaves silver through poems,
And sets fire to dreams.

~ James Wilder

* ~ * ~ *

* ~ * ~ *

A *mala* (Sanskrit:माला; mālā, meaning garland) is a string of prayer beads commonly used by Hindus, Buddhists, and some Sikhs for the spiritual practice known in Sanskrit as *japa*. It is usually made from 108 beads, and these beads can include wood, seeds, bone, precious metals, or precious and semiprecious stones. Malas are used for keeping count while reciting, chanting, or mentally repeating a mantra or the name or names of a deity. They can be simple, inexpensive items or beautiful pieces of jewelry.

* ~ * ~ *

The First Mala

Stolen Moments from Another Lover

~~ *The Gods Looked Down on Us* ~~

The gods looked down on us
and said,
"You are our favorite children.
So why so sad?
Have we not given you
the sunlight
and the moonlight
for your love games?

We created you
to fill our ears with laughter.
To fill our hearts with longing.
To fill our souls
with the sweet music of your sighs.

Your job
is to love one another.
Get to work."

~~ * ~~

Chapter One

~ * ~

Amazonite

The October sun spilled a pool of golden warmth into the center of the atrium. It bathed the gray stepping stones and the white crushed rock of the winding pathway through the Zen garden. It washed the dusty red leaves of the Japanese maple and the low, mounded greenery of the evergreen shrubs. It filled the place where the water would have been, if the designer of the atrium hadn't run out of money or ideas and left a miniature bridge to span nothing but concrete floor. And it invited James Wilder to pass that way, to turn his pale face up to the sun like the faded leaf of a plant withering in darkness.

As he stepped into that puddle of light, he noticed a woman coming the other way. She was tall, with ebony hair that fell to her shoulders like curls of shiny silk. She wore a maroon sweater, a turquoise necklace, and slacks that shimmered like quicksilver. As she drew closer, his eyes traced the classic lines of cheek, lips, and jaw, a marble bust of the goddess Aphrodite come to life. They met in the center of the Japanese bridge, over the dry concrete lake, and just as she passed, "Aphrodite" turned her head and glanced at him. Her gaze met his, and he stumbled sideways, shocked out of his foggy torpor by the unexpected electricity of eye contact. Her eyes were as blue as the Colorado sky. He turned to watch as she continued through the atrium and disappeared into an office at the far end. After a moment, he pulled himself together and arrived at his biweekly session with Theresa, his hypnotherapist.

"How're you feeling, James? You seem a bit...disheveled today." Theresa looked like the Buddha would have looked if he were a short, Hispanic woman in her fifties, with graying hair pulled back in a bun. Her brown, round face emanated kindness and serenity, and her almost-perfect English was flavored with the tropical hints of some tiny country down in Central America.

"Yeah, I'm OK...good really," James replied, his breathing a bit labored. "Hey, I just saw this woman. Killer blue eyes, dark hair... she went into an office down at the other end of the atrium—" His words must have sounded as disheveled as he looked.

"Oh, that's Willow. She's some sort of therapist here in the building." Theresa noticed his expression and added as kindly as she could, "I hear she's engaged to a nice young man, and they're very happy."

Of course she was. Women that gorgeous are rarely alone, and besides, even if she were, he'd have no chance with her. Theresa was treating James for cancer, part of a program of alternative-medicine treatments that he'd cobbled together when faced with the horror of his more conventional choices. He was skinny, feeling sick, and his prospects were uncertain. Throw in a fresh divorce and two young, part-time kids, and he had no extra bandwidth for anything, much less a goddess with sky-blue eyes.

James pushed Willow out of his mind and lay down on the couch. It felt soft and warm and familiar, and he willed himself to relax. He started breathing the way Theresa had trained him: long breaths in, and long breaths out. "You've got a death-grip on life," she'd said when she first met him. "Let go. Breathe. Life is a gift. Don't crush it. Let it unfold."

He closed his eyes, and Theresa began speaking in a soothing monotone. "You're lying on a warm bed of rose quartz. Its healing energies flood your body with light…warm, liquid light, washing through you, as you float weightless.…Look up into the night sky above you; see a galaxy of white diamonds spinning slowly…dripping golden sparks that fall toward you, splashing into your body like drops of rain into a still pond…dissolving the dark energy of the cancer…neutralizing it."

James felt his fatigue and his stress, even any awareness of the boundaries of his physical body, wafting away on the currents of Theresa's words. He could see the galaxy spinning above him. He could feel the golden light flow in and, for a moment, fill the enormous void of depletion that hollowed out his deepest core.

After the session was over, James thanked Theresa and walked out into the atrium. He was still a bit disoriented, so he took his time wandering back to his car. As he passed by Willow's office, he noticed a small table outside the door with a few color brochures and a stack of business cards. Out of curiosity, he picked up one of the cards. Like her, it shimmered—an effect she'd created by hand-decorating each card with blue glitter and streaks of gold and silver paint. It read, "Willow Leaf, Massage Therapist," and underneath were her phone number and email and work address. *Willow Leaf? Really? There's a story here*, he thought. He looked at the other cards. Each was unique, an exquisite, tiny, handcrafted masterpiece, and after a moment's deliberation he decided to keep the first one he'd picked up. It felt like a talisman, a reminder that beauty existed, even in his lonely, gray world. He stuck it in his wallet, next to the picture of himself with his kids, at the beach in happier times, and he headed out to the parking lot.

It was about noon when James arrived home. Rocco greeted him with licks to his face, his whole body wriggling with excitement, like James was Santa and the Easter Bunny and his favorite chew toy all rolled into one. James had rescued him from a shelter as a consolation prize for the kids when divorce split their world into two lesser halves. Rocco was a mutt, a mix of many random liaisons that left him with the intelligent face and tricolor coat of a border collie, the medium-sized body of something a bit larger, and long legs that loved to run.

Rocco was smart and knew James's moods better than any wife. He loved the kids and watched over them like his flock. Mostly, he filled the empty hours when they were with their mom and James's house echoed with loneliness. James tried to get out with him every day, whether it was sunny or snowing, hiking the trails that wound through the open space in Boulder. Rocco was a good runner, and there'd been a time they ran two, three, even four miles together. But these days, with James feeling weak from the cancer, they were only walking.

They headed to the Bobolink Trail, a mile from James's house. The Bobolink wound along South Boulder Creek, through thickets and cow pastures, and ended three miles away, near Marshall Mesa, where other trails took over. To the east, pastures and housing developments speckled the dry, rolling prairie that flowed all the way to Kansas. To the west, beyond more pastures and wetlands and cottonwood-lined ditches, the foothills of the Rockies rose up like the eroded walls of an ancient, giant castle guarding the snow-covered peaks of the Front Range. The city of Boulder nestled against those walls; an expensive little Colorado town of university students and engineers and scientists, real estate agents and psychotherapists and rock climbers, cyclists and yoga teachers and world-class athletes.

James parked the car, and he and Rocco started down the

Bobolink. The air was cool but warming as the afternoon approached, and small puffs of clouds sailed overhead in the crystal October sky. Rocco zigzagged, nose to the ground, reading the doggie newspaper. They came up to a couple of women, chatting as their dogs chased each other through the tall, dry grass. Rocco strained to join them, so James let him off the leash to play. The women smiled, and one said, "Such a beautiful day."

James agreed, and they chatted, the dogs racing and darting around one another, burning energy and enthusiasm. James noticed one woman staring at him while the other talked, and suddenly she interrupted to say, "Has anyone ever told you, you look like David Bowie?" It was 2006, and David Bowie's face had been everywhere in the public consciousness for decades.

"Yeah," he smiled. "All the time. Only he's got one blue eye and one brown. Mine are just brown."

James laughed inwardly at the familiar joke. He'd heard the comparison before. Other than the fact that he was much taller, his face wasn't as thin, and he had a conventional haircut, yeah, he looked just like David Bowie. Or Robert Culp or Anthony Perkins or their cousin from Cincinnati. For some reason, he had a face that people wanted to attach to a name. He even had someone in New York say to him, "You're somebody, aren't you? I've seen you on TV, or in the movies. You're somebody." James had just grinned and held his finger to his lips, as if he were going incognito and the other guy was sharing his secret.

A friend said it was the bone structure. And damned if he didn't look a bit like Bowie, if the light was just right and his expression just so. One time at New York's LaGuardia Airport, it actually got him on the plane before everyone else, the gate agent treating him like he was her fantasy rock star. He got free peanuts and drinks all the way to Houston, where he was meeting with the treasurer of a large energy company. After work, James and his customer had gone out for a beer, and the bartender had told the treasurer that he looked like Elvis, so maybe it wasn't just James.

He talked with the two women a bit longer. Then Rocco and he continued down the path, another day in the life of a divorced, lonely, sick father of two and his dog.

That night, his kids came over—the weekly exchange he did with Elizabeth, his ex-wife and the mother of his children. Annie was ten years old and Chris was seven. Beautiful blond kids who took the best from Elizabeth and him and made it better. They came with their bags of clothes, backpacks of school books, and homework. Rocco greeted them like long-lost littermates, jumping and wriggling and wrestling. He and Chris tumbled across the floor in a tangle of barking and laughing, and Annie teased Rocco with a new toy.

After the chaos of transition settled down, James fed the kids a dinner of chicken, stir-fried veggies, and brown rice. They ate at the bar in the kitchen, with Chris sneaking bites to Rocco and Annie scolding him like the big sister she was. Later, James helped Annie with her math homework. Then all of them, including Rocco, snuggled up in a dog pile on Chris's bed while Annie read the bedtime story. They were working their way through *The Lord of The Rings* and were right at the part where Sam finds Frodo after he's been bitten by Shelob, the giant spider, and Frodo's in despair, thinking he's lost the One Ring. That's how James felt later that night, alone in his own bed, staring at the ceiling and wondering how he'd lost the One Ring of his life: his direction, his purpose, his power. His marriage. James sighed, and tried desperately to sleep, but his mind gnawed at the past like Rocco with a bone. How was it possible that two people who'd been so madly in love, who'd inhabited the same kaleidoscopic realm of plans and hopes and dreams, were now so intractably at odds? The centers of their respective universes had stayed the same, their kids, but everything else had fractured into two separate realities that clashed like broken glass from different mirrors.

Elizabeth. His greatest joy and best friend when they were in their midtwenties and life was good, probing the boundaries of possibility and partnership in the Big Apple. He'd been a junior investment banker on Wall Street, paying his dues with long hours and short weekends, and she'd been an artist, juggling motherhood and nannies and hanging out with other artists and actors and activists in the East Village. On the surface, it looked like they were knocking it out of the park. Unfortunately, Elizabeth had eventually reached some sort of limit, whether of patience or love or understanding, or all of the above.

"You've become a tool of The System," she accused.

"Yeah, well someone had to," he defended. "I see that *you're* not too proud to benefit from "The System"! And sure, thanks to *his* hard work, they were doing OK, but didn't she understand that by the measuring stick of New York City and Wall Street in particular, they hadn't made it yet, hadn't stacked away the "fuck you" money that all the young bankers fantasized about? But perhaps even worse was that she no longer found him interesting, and she had a particularly stinging way to make that evident.

"You're boring! All you do is work!"

Yes, he was aware of that because, guess what? Someone had to! *He* was the guy rising before dawn to get from their comfortable Upper West Side apartment down to Wall Street, descending into the garbage-strewn, piss-stinking tunnels beneath the city, enduring the screech of metal on metal as the subway cars ground their way past stop after stop to where he could finally emerge and walk the six blocks through rain or sleet or subzero wind or stifling heat to his office. And *he* was the one who had to fold his long frame into the cramped space of his trading "desk," knee-to-knee with hundreds of other traders, had to stare through bleary eyes at ten computer screens and monitors, and had to juggle twenty phone lines, all the while shutting out the ambient roar of the trading floor. So, of course, when he got home, usually after the kids were in bed, all he wanted to do was sit quietly, enjoy the silence, and be boring.

But maybe the problem was also that he'd felt like a fraud from day one, trying to fake it in the world that greed built, and Elizabeth knew it. He had the brains, the math skills, and the work ethic but not the blind lust for money, or the dullard's need to flash the bling, drive the Porsche, or brag about a golf game. James couldn't give two fucks about golf, or Rolexes, or what car he drove, and somehow the gods of greed recognized his reluctance to trade his soul for currency. Nevertheless, he'd insisted in wallowing in mediocrity for ten years, never quite making it, and he and Elizabeth struggled, fighting over differences big and small, until they gave up on their illusory shot at "fuck you" money. James quit his job and moved his family home to Colorado. It was too late. They got divorced anyway. And soon after, while flailing around for new footing, he'd been diagnosed with cancer, an ironic "fuck you" from fate. And lying in his bed, alone, James stared at the undeniable truth, written up there in the shadows on the ceiling. At how the change between him and Elizabeth was irrevocable, and how neither of them was the same person they'd been at the beginning, back when the world was fresh and green and young.

A year went by, a year in which James remained firmly stuck in the swirling drainpipe of grayness, loneliness and divorce that was his life. His encounter with Willow receded into memory, and she resurfaced only rarely when he would open his wallet, see her card, and smile. And then one afternoon, when James was downtown on the Pearl Street Mall, a woman handed him a brochure. It advertised a weekend yoga retreat at the Arapahoe Yoga Ashram in the mountains west of Boulder. He'd never heard of the ashram and didn't know anything about yoga, but the brochure promised good food, private cabins, and a free massage treatment along with the yoga. What the hell, he'd figured. He was alone in the world, for all he knew probably dying young, and the money he'd saved for a rainy day—well, it was raining.

James arrived at the ashram Friday evening, got checked into his log cabin in the pines by Parvati, a young woman with glasses and a white turban. She took him over to the dining hall, another large log building where everyone—disciples and guests—ate family style at long tables. The food was delicious, all vegetarian and flavored with Indian spices. It was loaded with "*shakti* and love," per Parvati's description. Whatever *shakti* was, it was damn tasty to a guy who'd been cooking his own meals for far too long.

After dinner, James relaxed on a couch in the common room, flipping through a book of Sufi poetry. A fire crackled in the fireplace, the couch was soft, and the poetry had wit, rhythm, and a sense of deep, deep beauty. He felt his jittery stress easing its grip a bit as he lingered over one poem in particular:

> *Gamble everything for love,*
> *if you're a true human being.*
>
> *If not, leave*
> *this gathering.*
>
> *Half-heartedness doesn't*
> *reach into Majesty.*
> *You set out*
> *to find God, but then you keep*
> *stopping for long periods*
> *at mean-spirited roadhouses.*
> *~ Rumi*

Yeah, he thought. *That's me. Stuck at a mean-spirited roadhouse.*

"Hello, James? I'd like to introduce a classmate from your workshop." The voice was Parvati's, but all he saw was a goddess materialized from the mists of memory. Tall, with thick black curls to her shoulders, and blue eyes that sparked echoes of electricity.

"Hi, I'm Willow," she said, smiling. Her voice resonated at a low frequency, like a perfect chord drawn from some stringed instrument.

"I know who you are," James replied. He reached into his wallet and drew out her card, a bit worn from riding in his pocket for the past year. He held it out to her, and she took it with both hands, like it was something rare and precious, or maybe dangerous. She looked at him, her eyes asking questions, but James said nothing. He'd carried that card for over a year and taken it out from time to time to marvel at its beauty. In his memory he'd see again her face, feel again a faint spark of the electricity that had shocked him awake when those sky eyes met his, but he'd never dreamed he would actually meet her in person. She sat down next to him on the couch and they chatted, background noise to the real conversation that was going on in the subtext.

Who are you? Why do you have my card?

I can't believe you're real.

There's something about you that intrigues me.

As the night wore on, she moved closer, shoving her stocking feet under his thighs, as if to keep them warm, and he told himself it didn't mean anything because she was a massage therapist, comfortable with crossing personal boundaries as if they didn't exist. He asked her about her name.

"Why Willow Leaf? Were your parents botanists?"

"Nope," she smiled. "Hippies. I was born in a teepee up in the mountains. I have a sister named Aspen and a brother named Rowan."

"And let me guess. Your dad's name is Basil and your mom is Petunia."

"No, silly!" She burst out laughing. "George and Doris."

"That explains a lot."

They laughed and talked for what might have been minutes or hours, until someone walked into the room and said there was an amazing meteor shower happening outside in the night sky.

"Shall we?" Willow asked, her eyes telling him to say yes.

"Of course," James replied. He staggered a bit getting up, as if in crossing back into the timestream of the present he had to find the stepping stones. He offered Willow his hand. Hers was warm and soft and yet very strong, the hand of someone who spent her workday rubbing oil into knotted muscles and tweaked limbs. They stood in the dark under the moonless sky, lit only by pinpricks and streaks of light across the blackness. Above them, meteors zoomed over the treetops and skirted mountains, leaving traces of magic in the frosty night air. Neither James nor Willow was wearing a jacket, so she wrapped her arms around his body and held him close, as if in doing so she could capture whatever heat he radiated.

"I love the stars," she whispered, her breath warming his cheek. "Do you know the constellations?"

James pointed out a few. "That's Orion. See the three stars of his belt? He was a great hunter, and over there are his hunting dogs, Canis Major and Canis Minor. And that's Cassiopeia—kind of a W shape—takes a bit of imagination. She pissed off Poseidon, proclaimed herself more beautiful than his sea nymphs."

Willow hugged him even more tightly. "Brrr! Never piss off the gods!"

No indeed. They clung together under the stars, picked out a few more constellations, and even made up a few of their own, the only rule being that it had to be the name of a god or goddess. "See those over there?" she said. "That triangle with the bright star above it? That's Durga, waving her sword before she kills the buffalo demon."

James had no idea who or what she was talking about, but he was game. "Oh yeah? See that area over there? With the four bright stars and the cloud between them? That's the Beatles, and that cloud of stars is Ringo's drum."

"Really? The Beatles?" she asked, laughing. "When did they become gods?"

They stood under the sky, laughing and picking out ever more egregious imaginary constellations. He found Elvis and Led Zeppelin, and she pointed out Vishnu and Lakshmi. They exclaimed every time a particularly bright meteor or group of meteors interrupted their game, and he felt peace and warmth in her embrace, as if he'd become immune to the cold. He would have gladly stood there all night, but finally she said she was freezing and had to get to bed.

"What cabin are you in?" she asked, her teeth chattering.

"Uh, the one down this path about a hundred yards. It's called the Hanuman Cabin, or something like that."

"Mmmm, Hanuman, the monkey god." Her laugh had the deep patina of fine, tarnished silver. "Suits you."

"So I remind you of a monkey?" he asked.

She laughed, and gave him a very long hug, her warm lips brushed his cheek, and then she left him in a daze of heat and pheromones, her scent lingering upon his sweater and skin.

James staggered down the path to his cabin, trying to make sense of the miracle that had unfolded since he'd drawn her card from his wallet. Was any of it real, or was it just a fevered dream triggered by intense loneliness? And why did she ask what cabin he was in? Was she going to seek him out? Impossible! Yeah, but the whole night so far had been beyond impossible.

He crawled into his bed, his cabin cold with frosty autumn air. Perfect sleeping weather. He fell asleep dreaming about her—the way her body felt against his, her lips on his cheek, and those beautiful eyes. He slept deeply and woke refreshed, feeling better than he had in months.

He didn't see Willow at breakfast and quickly convinced himself that the previous night had been an impossibility, an anomaly, a black swan event, something more than three standard deviations from the mean that would never ever happen again in a million years. She'd had a momentary lapse of sanity, and the cold light of morning had sobered her up.

And then she came to yoga class. In later years, James would remember nothing about that class except Willow. Her smile that whispered of inner secrets, her beautiful black, curly hair framing her face, the way she stretched, reaching for her toes. She practiced totally absorbed in her movements, flowing gracefully, her eyes closed or half-closed the entire time. James flopped around, awkward and out of synch in a foreign dance where he didn't know any of the steps. By the end of class, he felt drained, still weak from the cancer trying to take over his body.

There was a fifteen-minute break between yoga sessions, and the morning sun was flooding in through a long window at the end of the room, spilling a golden puddle of sunshine onto the wooden floor. James lay down in the middle of that puddle, his eyes closed, soaking in the warmth. His thoughts were drifting far away when suddenly he felt someone rubbing his feet. He opened his eyes. It was Willow, smiling down at him. The black swan had arrived again.

"Sleep well last night?" she asked.

"Best sleep in years," he replied, grinning.

"I dreamed of falling stars all night. It was magic. Thank you."

"Thank me? What did I have to do with it?"

"I don't know. Something." She shrugged. "You showed me the celestial dance. Your words. What are you, a poet?"

Was he? A poet? Cancer and divorce had cracked open his shell, and in the last year he'd discovered poetry, mystic Sufi poetry to be exact. The verses of Rumi, Hafiz, and others had leaked in like seawater to change the essential chemistry of his reality. Suffused in the rhythm and mysticism of their words, he began to see magic and beauty in the world around him, when he looked carefully enough. He heard the gods' whispers, when he listened closely enough. He was like a man who'd lived his entire life floating high and dry on a raft on a deep blue sea until a rogue wave tossed him into the water. Like that man, his life had been limited to two dimensions, defined by the length and width of his raft. The gift of misfortune was that now he knew there was a third dimension, depth.

And James began to write his own poetry, filling journals with little droplets of pain and loneliness and longing that coalesced on the page into simple sentences, then verses, then longer works that spoke of realms imagined and loves desired. But he hadn't shown his poems to anyone. He was just learning, accreting language and music like a snowball rolling downhill, adding layers of ice crystals and specks of dirt and pieces of twig and leaf. Maybe he would end up a giant snow boulder of poetry and art, or maybe he would break apart into slush, another failed experiment of the gods.

"You've got amazing hands," James said, propped up on his elbows as she massaged his feet and ankles.

"I love touch. So much healing can come from just a touch."

"Then you're in the right business. I feel better already."

She laughed, and he joked brightly about inconsequential things, and she laughed some more, her face silhouetted against the sunlight pouring into the room.

After more yoga, they went their separate ways and promised to meet for lunch. She'd scheduled a facial. James went back to his cabin for a nap.

Lunch was more goodness served at the long tables of the dining hall, and afterward they decided to hike up the nearest hill. The day swirled between the clouds of late fall, threatening snow flurries, and the sun broke through with rays of frosted sunshine. They wore sweaters, and she had a woolen scarf.

"Look!" she exclaimed. "My scarf matches your sweater!" Actually, her scarf was woven from the exact same yarn in the exact same color as his sweater, a coincidence that was more than that. It was confirmation that the gods were up to something.

James had lived a life dominated by rational thought. Cause and effect, the scientific method, linear analysis. But lately, while reassembling his working model of the universe that had been smashed by the twin hammers of cancer and divorce, he'd discovered new truths. Like how a rip can suddenly appear in the fabric of dull reality allowing in synchronicities that aren't just coincidences, signs that are actually signs, and messages from strange ambassadors that clearly speak for the gods. How else to explain why he'd carried her card in his wallet for a year, why he'd chosen that particular weekend to do something he'd never done before, and why she'd done the same?

After the hike, she sat across from him on the edge of the hot tub, warm in her bikini as October snowflakes drifted from the sky. Her body was every bit as perfect as he'd imagined, and on her finger, a large diamond glowed. His happiness deflated as it reminded him of the reality of her status.

"When's the date?" he asked, nodding at the rock, his voice casual and his gaze steady.

She sighed and looked down at the water. "Dan doesn't want to set a date yet. Says we still have so much to figure out beyond just a commitment to each other."

"Huh. Just living together then?"

"No. I live with a girlfriend. We share a condo. You? Ever been married?"

"Once. Crashed and burned three years ago." James nodded without any reason to. "Yeah...."

The cold wind sent a low, rustling sigh between the pine trees, and the late afternoon sun peeked out from behind the clouds to set the sky on fire. Willow slid down into the hot tub to warm up. She sank completely under the water in the middle of the tub and resurfaced, tipping her face up, slicking her hair back into a ponytail. She moved through the water and sat next to him, chest deep, her shoulder and hip touching his. James watched the sunset in silent bliss, every nerve in his body stretching out toward her like flowers bending toward the sunlight.

That evening in the dining room, they sat surrounded by the half-seen specters of other humans. Again, Willow chose to sit so that she was constantly in contact with him—her hip against his, her hand brushing his forearm. It was as if she'd claimed his body as part of her personal space.

After dinner they moved to the couch in the common room, in front of the fireplace. If there were other people there, James didn't notice. They were disappearing into their own little world, the bubble of pure electric vibration that cocooned them like a cloud of dancing atomic particles zooming around and through them in a huge, warm, unified field of attraction. They took turns reading aloud from a book of Rumi's poetry. As James held the book, Willow wrapped her hands around his forearm, occasionally massaging his muscles. She was sitting cross-legged next to him, her side against his side and her knee in his lap. James breathed in her closeness, the heady scent of essential oils distilled from flowers rising from that place on her neck where her hair stopped, and bare skin began. If he had leaned sideways just a little, he could have buried his face in her hair.

That night, he escorted her to her cabin, a dorm she shared with three other female guests. They walked hand-in-hand, in silence. At the door she gave him a long hug. Her cheek rested against his, and he imagined he could feel her heart beating against his chest. Every cell in his body demanded that he kiss her lips and crush her body to his, but he didn't. After a huge sigh, she gave him one last squeeze and went inside.

James felt his way down the dark path back to his cabin, seeing the cold night sky as a slightly lighter shade of star-speckled black behind the silhouettes of the pine trees that towered over him. Why hadn't he kissed her? Why hadn't he taken the chance? Even as he asked the question, he knew the answer. He didn't want to force her to remember her obligation to another man, a man to whom she was engaged to be married. He wasn't ready for her to choose between her fiancé and him, between history and potential. It had been only a day since he'd handed her her card, and that wasn't enough for him to trust in the future. As long as he never pushed that question to the fore—this dance, this connection, this stolen ecstasy from someone else's dreamlife could continue. As James stumbled down the uneven path, he whispered out a prayer, a plea for mercy, to the gods.

"Please, please, please give me a break! Please, just this once!"

It must have been a dull evening in heaven, because the gods decided to toy with him for a little while longer.

James stripped off his clothes and climbed under the frosty sheets of his bed. He took one last look at the simple wooden door of his cabin. Would she come? He listened, and for a moment he was sure he heard someone coming down the path, but it was just the wind stirring the branches of the pines. James grinned to himself and turned off the light. Like she would ever do that! But hey, it was the final night of the retreat, and what had already transpired between them was way beyond anything he could have imagined, so who knew what else could happen?

James fell asleep quickly, and she never came, at least not in the flesh, but her memory slept next to him, wrapped around him, her breath on his cheek, and the scent of exotic flowers from her hair filling his nostrils with jasmine and orange blossom and wild rose.

Chapter Two

~ * ~

Silver

The next morning, it was breakfast, more yoga, and then time to head home. It was a gray day, with low clouds and the threat of snow hanging over the treetops. The misty air was heavy with the damp scent of the pines, and James could see his breath as he hugged Willow goodbye in the parking lot. Again, Willow held him for an overlong time, and again, he didn't want it to end. Apparently, neither did she.

"I really enjoyed our hike yesterday," she said wistfully. "Maybe we can get together down in Boulder and do it again?"

James smiled at her, trying to not look as sad as he felt. "Sure. What's your home number? I'll give you a call."

He had little hope that once she left the bubble of the weekend and got back together with her fiancé, she would have any interest in some random guy she'd met at a yoga retreat. The weekend had been a wonderful escape, but it was over, and any continuation of the fantasy just seemed impossible.

She gave him her digits, they hugged again, and then she climbed into her car. It was a little, nondescript gray sedan, a Toyota maybe. What made it memorable were the plastic flowers she'd taped to her radio antenna. They were white daisies, with a few green leaves to make them look more real. James touched them and grinned at her.

"I guess these help you find your car in the parking lot, huh?"

She laughed, waved goodbye, and drove off down the gravel road, all the color and connection and magic of the weekend trailing after her like tin cans tied to the bumper of newlyweds.

James tossed his bag into his car and headed down the hill, back to blacktop and reality. As he drove, part of his mind mechanically negotiated the twists and turns of the canyon road that led down to Boulder, but his awareness clung desperately to the sights and sounds and sensations that were already dissipating like a dream in the first moments of waking. He strained to hear Willow's voice again and grasped at every mental snapshot of her face. He delved into the places in his body that had buzzed with electricity. He struggled to embed the scent of her perfume into his memory. Finally, as he pulled into the cul-de-sac that fronted his house, he let it all go.

He parked in the driveway, got out of the car, and looked up, already exhausted. This was his life, right here, a big, ugly house that needed work. Dried out, cracked wooden siding that had to be replaced. A front yard with a dismal patch of dying grass and some scrubby low junipers. A small blue spruce that he'd planted like a flag when they'd moved in, proclaiming, "Colorado, I've come home." He took a deep breath and unlocked the front door.

Inside, the open floor plan featured a large living/dining room space with vaulted ceilings and a fireplace, a dated kitchen with pressed-wood cabinets and dull tile, and a stairwell to the second-floor bedrooms. There wasn't much furniture, the holes in his decor reflecting the relationship that had been torn out by the roots when

Elizabeth left. The empty spaces were gradually refilling with usable stuff he'd found at thrift shops, along with his own comforting man-cave possessions: his fossil and mineral collection; a watercolor painting of a Caribbean beach with palm trees; a large TV for watching movies and football. But still, almost two years later, there weren't enough lamps, no dining room set, and divorcehood echoed from the empty cabinets and mismatched pots of his kitchen.

James dropped his bag on the floor and went next door to retrieve Rocco, who'd spent the weekend under the care of his neighbor, an elderly woman grateful for the company. Rocco danced and pranced as James thanked her, and they returned home, where James cracked open a bottle of beer and collapsed on the couch with Rocco's head in his lap. Rocco stared up at him with those adoring, doggy eyes, and James scratched him behind the ears. His thoughts drifted to Elizabeth. Had remodeling the house really been a problem? Or was it simply the last arena where the gladiators drew blood, where the combatants themselves had signaled "thumbs down" on their marriage? In any event, within six months Elizabeth had moved out, to create a life with "less resistance." Stuck with "their" house, James had to do whatever his energy and pocketbook allowed, which, after the financial catastrophe of divorce, wasn't much. He'd hired a contractor to put in two skylights in the living room and replaced the awful shag carpeting in the bedrooms. That was it. Resources depleted. Painting, however, was something he could do himself. He'd started with the living room, covering the horrible, original builder-white-painted walls with a soothing celadon green that changed subtly under the new skylights to silvery blue or aspen-bark gray. And that was good. More light and more color made him feel better. Intuitively, he needed to surround himself with vibrancy after the shabby, soul-sucking drear of his days on the Wall Street trading floor. He needed beauty.

Encouraged by his experiment with color, James had moved on to the front hall of the house. He'd read somewhere that a red wall facing the entrance of a house was good *feng shui* for prosperity and health, and he'd started that project. But the sudden arrival of cancer had thrown a huge block of "resistance" into his plans, and he'd only completed half.

James sighed and took a sip of his beer. Maybe today was the day. Did he want to get up off the couch and finish the wall? It was just a little thing, and he could be done in three hours. No, he decided. He didn't want to start painting. He just wanted to sit there, with Rocco, and not do anything at all….

* ~ * ~ *

He let a couple of days pass and then sucked up his courage and called her. He left a message on her answering machine, sure that he sounded like an idiot. To his surprise, she called back a few hours later and said of course she'd go for a hike. She suggested climbing up Flagstaff Mountain, a decent trail in the foothills above Boulder. That night it snowed a good six inches. Winter had come, and with it, cold sunshine under a sparkling blue sky.

James met Willow at the trailhead. When he pulled into the parking lot, all nerves and excitement, she was leaning back against her little car, letting the sun bathe her face. She smiled as James and Rocco walked up, the shade of her blue eyes matched by her wool jacket and headband.

"Who's this?" she asked, bending down to pet Rocco. He gave her his customary licks and wriggles.

"That's Rocco, the wonder dog," James replied. "He's an amazing hiker."

She and Rocco bonded for a moment, and then they started up the hill. James let Rocco off leash, and he scouted the path ahead, sniffing every tree trunk and bush.

The snow was pristine, without a footprint. The trail wound up the hill between trees and occasional large boulders and outcrops. As they hiked, the snow crunched underfoot with the sound it makes when it's dry and cold. In places, the long dead grass of summer pushed up through the surface. Here and there, tracks of tiny forest creatures left a record of nighttime adventures in search of food, shelter, or whatever the little furry guys were doing at night. Occasionally, larger tracks crossed the trail—deer, fox, rabbit. In one spot, the perfect imprint of large, outswept feathery wings placed a fatal exclamation point at the end of a series of tiny footprints—some mouse or vole or ground squirrel that ended up an owl's dinner. James felt deeply present, his senses sharpened as he took in the acute details of the world around him. But mostly, he took in Willow. How she walked, her laugh, the way she would look back at him as she climbed around a boulder or threaded her way through tree trunks. Every move she made, every flicker of expression, even the smallest utterances of sound, were etched into his awareness like a tattoo.

They came to a level, open meadow where the snow sparkled under the bright-blue sky, and Willow grabbed James by the hand and dragged him out into the middle. She pushed him down onto his back to make snow angels. James felt a bit silly but did it anyway.

"Haven't done this since fourth grade," he said.

"Then it's about time," she replied as they lay head to head in the snow, feet pointed in opposite directions, their ears so close that if he turned to look at her and she turned toward him, they'd kiss. They flapped their arms and legs, creating arcs of snow wings.

"Careful getting up," she warned. "We don't want to ruin them."

She came to stand next to him, smiling at their artwork. Two flying angels, head to head, frozen in flight, as transitory as "I love you" scribbled into the wet sand of a beach. Rocco sat on his haunches, his head tilted comically to the side as he looked up at them.

"Maybe the birds will appreciate our talent," James said as a large hawk glided high above, catching the winter thermals rising up the side of the hill from sunlight reflecting off the snow. "No one else is gonna see these."

"Maybe," she smiled, her eyes sparkling. "Or maybe someone will wander by and think they were made by lovers."

"Imagine that," James replied and met her gaze.

What the hell was going on? She seemed totally into him, and yet the ring was still on her finger. James had looked for it before she put on her gloves. Last night she'd probably been wrapped around her fiancé, making sweaty love while he, James, struggled to find sleep in his lonely bed. He tried to drive that image from his mind. He couldn't imagine that any man lucky enough to sleep with her every night wouldn't want her as much as he did, wouldn't devour her again and again before he sent her off to dreamland with a smile on her face. And yet, here she was, with him.

They continued up the hill, past pine trees and outcrops, through dark patches where the sun was blocked by thick branches overhead, and across clearings where the sparkle of light off the snow was blinding. At times they would stop to admire the view, but really so James could catch his breath. Theresa had said that the body's fight against cancer took the same energy as running a marathon every day. If that was true, then James was outdoing himself, even with their pauses to rest. Finally, they reached the top, the crest of the ridge that looked out over Boulder and came to a fork in the trail. A sign pointed westward toward "Artist Point."

"Let's go!" said Willow, who led him by the hand.

Artist Point was a sunny outcrop on the west side of the ridge, with a clear view all the way to 14,000-foot peaks covered with snow. Below them spread an upland valley with trees, meadows, an occasional cabin, and a road winding toward the far mountains. Hawks rode the thermals, soaring in great spirals without flapping a wing. Out in the distance behind the snowy peaks, a line of clouds promised weather later in the evening. But for the moment, the sky overhead was blue, the sun was bright and warm, and the wind was a gentle breeze. They cleared the snow from a flat boulder that faced west and settled in. Rocco explored the outcrop, peering over the edge.

They chatted, and James didn't register a word of it. How long they sat there, he had no idea. He was like a rabbit trapped in the gaze of a cobra, mesmerized by those eyes, enthralled by the music played by the gods on their snake-charmer flutes while they laughed and took bets on how long he could hold out under such temptation. Her gloves were off now, and he could see the marquise diamond sparkling in the sun, held against her finger by the band of platinum. It was beautiful, a diamond worthy of this woman. And like a ring of power, it kept him from grabbing her and kissing her hard on the mouth.

James tried to imagine her fiancé. In his mind, he had to be a man-god befitting a woman-goddess—tall, dark-haired, handsome and athletic, oozing cool and bad-boy charm. James visualized him bending his knee as he opened the ring box and offered himself to her, confidently searching her face for signs of delight and happiness, giving himself a mental high-five when she smiled and said yes. *What the fuck am I doing here?* James asked himself again. And yet, he couldn't walk away. This was so much more than a dream. He'd thought about this woman for a year, placed her inside a glass box on a high pedestal, without hope, without assumption that he would ever even talk to her, and here she was on a sunny day, miraculously sitting next to him on a flat rock at Artist Point—engaging him, eager for his smiles, for his attention, even now touching his arm with her hand, the one wearing the ring that sparkled in the sun.

Later, he'd remember small details: meltwater dripping from a red berry on a bush next to their boulder; the piercing, clear cry of a hawk as it soared above them; the distant chug of a truck's engine as it ground its way up switchbacks across the valley. But most of all, he'd remember the play of sunlight on ice crystals in the snow around them like a billion brilliant marquise diamonds. Maybe those were his jewels to offer her—this day, this experience, this magic memory against the one static diamond she wore, perhaps already drained of its power.

It was getting late, and they walked back down the trail, laughing and slipping in the softening snow heated by the afternoon sun. Rocco chased a few squirrels, which always escaped up into the branches and perched there, scolding him with their chatter. Down at the cars, they hugged again, and James headed home, his heart both lightened by the memory of her presence and heavy with the prospect of the inevitable when she came to her senses and ended this—whatever *this* was.

Later that night, with Rocco curled up at his feet, James sat at his desk playing with words. His thoughts were tangled in his emotions like fish in a net, just when he needed clarity. Maybe he should try casting words onto the page like bones tossed by a soothsayer, and see what wisdom they revealed? He'd spent his working life as an analyst, charting a careful path through financial obstacles scouted in advance, but this post-divorce, cancer-ridden reality was different. Uncharted, and perhaps unchartable. He'd have to take gambles, follow hunches, watch for signs from the gods. James felt exhausted, but he was eager, too. There was something oddly exhilarating about marching blindly into the unknown.

~~ *Two Ants* ~~

Two ants
were walking down the road one day,
and one announced,
"I'm going left at the fork."

The other ant,
surprised,
said,
"But our way lies to the right!"

The first ant smiled sadly,
and said,
"My heart knows that that is true,
but my head
has a mind of its own."

~~ * ~~

Chapter Three

~ * ~

Carnelian

James spent the next few days immersed in the stuff of normality. Getting the kids to school, work, errands, then picking the kids up. But no matter what he was doing, his thoughts drifted to Willow. In any rational world, they would've never met at the ashram. In any rational world, she would marry Dan, and they'd buy their little house behind the white picket fence and start popping out babies. But the gods do not inhabit the rational world. They are irrational and restless and easily bored. Willow and James provided an opportunity for some mild entertainment, so they kept the pot boiling.

Four days after the hike to Artist Point, a letter arrived. James wandered out to the mailbox and there, nestled among the bills and the advertisements, was a magic envelope, addressed to him in colorful handwriting that reminded him of high elvish script from

The Lord of the Rings. She'd decorated it with her trademark swirls of metallic paint and glitter, just like her business card. James felt an adrenaline rush that roared through his body and ricocheted off the dark block of deep fatigue inside. He picked up the envelope in both hands, like it was Holy Communion, and raised his eyes to the heavens.

The gods were all leaning out of their balconies in the sky, eager to see his reaction, and he did not disappoint. He fell to his knees and begged, literally begged, without a care that his neighbors might see, without even words—just pure aching desire and need pouring out of his chest like light and smoke that rose in swirls to form giant symbols up in the clouds. His message, written in god language, started with "Please!" and went into a bunch of feelings not easily translated into human speech.

James hurried into the house and sat down on the couch, a sharp steak knife in his hands. He slit the end of the envelope carefully so that he wouldn't ruin the art on the front. He slid out the letter. It was a single piece of a rosy-beige stationery covered by elvish writing on both sides. His heart pounded in his ears as he read. About how their meeting at the yoga retreat had been amazing and unexpected. About how the hike to Artist Point had seemed like magic. And about how she felt an incredible connection to him that made time stand still when they were together. There was more, much more, and he must have screamed himself hoarse, because when he came to his senses, his throat hurt, and his eyes were watering.

"All right!" he shouted. "You got me!" And James pushed all of his chips into the center of the table. He would "gamble everything for love," as the poem had commanded. He sat down at his laptop and composed the most poetic letter he could manage, with the gods leaning over his shoulders, offering suggestions as to what phrases to use, laughing and high-fiving and paying off bets. James shared that he, too, felt the incredible connection between them. He wrote that she was the most stunning woman he'd ever seen—which was why he'd taken her card and carried it with him for an entire year, without hope of ever meeting her. He agreed that their meeting had been like a step outside time to a magical place. He printed it all out on a sheet of Japanese rice paper that he'd saved for a special occasion, rolled it up like a scroll, and tied a piece of ribbon around it, blue to match her eyes. He looked up the return address on her envelope and drove over to her home. Turned out she lived only a mile away, in a ground-floor condo that backed onto open space near the Bobolink Trailhead. He'd driven by her home almost daily for the past year without knowing.

She opened the door and seemed surprised to see him.

"Hi, I got your letter," James said as he handed her the scroll. "Here's my response."

He held her hand for a moment while their eyes met, and then he turned and walked back to his car without another word. Back at home, he wandered around the living room, wondering what she was thinking. He didn't have to wait long. The phone rang.

"James, I've got to see you. Can I come over?"

"Sure," he replied. "I'll be home."

She came over after dinner, after dark, and walked into his house and straight into his arms. She hugged him desperately, as if the elegant yacht of serenity that had anchored her long hugs at the ashram had slipped its own moorings. She was wearing a soft silk sweater and jeans and the scent of wildflowers in her hair.

James had a fire going in the fireplace, lit candles on the coffee table, and music playing on the stereo. They migrated to the sofa, not talking, just holding each other. For hours. This time, he buried his face in her neck, breathed in her heat and her scent. He kissed her on the lips, and she kissed him back. He pulled her body up against his and felt her need even through her clothes. And at some point, she pulled away and studied his face.

"You're a work of art," she whispered, caressing his cheek.

Really? What did she mean by that? James smiled back at her, waiting for an explanation, but she just sighed and pulled him closer. A thousand questions crowded his mind, and he pushed them all away. He didn't want to question anything. He just wanted to bask in the glow of this unexpected glimpse of perfection, this rip in the fabric of reality that allowed in warmth and color and sensation. He lost himself in the rise and fall of her breath, the smooth skin beneath her sweater, the softness of her stomach and neck and breasts. Her hands slipped beneath his shirt to caress his chest, and her fingers lingered in his hair as he kissed her throat. All night they cuddled under the soft, woven blanket that he pulled from the bottom shelf of the coffee table, their soundtrack the snapping of the logs on the fire and the sensuous music of Sarah McLachlan, Van Morrison, and Loreena McKennitt. And that was enough.

When they finally rose from the couch, the first light of dawn was frosting the ice-encrusted windows with swirls of orange and pink like a translucent cake. They stood facing the sunrise, wrapped in the blanket, his face half-buried in her hair, his arms around her. She leaned back into him, sighing as if fighting an upwelling, unwelcome emotion. Reluctantly, they watched their night together dissipate with the darkness and felt the onrushing reality of daylight.

"I have to go," she said, turning her head and kissing him. Those were the first words either of them had spoken in hours.

James watched her pull on her coat and hat, pick up her mittens, and start out the door, only to pause and look back. Was it to remember his face? Imprint a memory of a night she'd never see again? She smiled wistfully and left.

Disoriented, James wandered into the kitchen. He felt as if he'd just surfaced from a deep-sea realm where hours and minutes and day and night and even breathing were meaningless and unnecessary. He was sure that Willow was the pinnacle, the epitome of everything he wanted in a woman. Of course, he hardly knew her, but that gave him plenty of blank canvas to paint in whatever colors his mind could project. And that was OK. The canvas came in a very pretty frame, and some colors were already splashed here and there from their three days and one night together, like her scent when they were standing outside under the stars, and how it was subtly different when she was closer, breathing into his hair. He knew the outlines of her eyes and lips and face, and he knew how her tongue moved when they kissed. He'd seen the small raised mole behind her right ear, just below the hairline, and was learning the little noises she made to express desire or contentment. But what he didn't know was why she connected with him. What did she want? What did he offer her that her fiancé wasn't providing? She'd revealed nothing that gave him any clues. She remained an enigma, a perfect beautiful fantasy woman, perhaps conjured by a dream.

Chapter Four

~ * ~

Lapis Lazuli

After Willow left that morning, James somehow got himself to work. He was useless, his mind stuck back in the time warp of the previous night, and his partner was having none of it.

"Dude, what's with you today?" Eliu Klein asked, pulling at his curly, prematurely gray hair with both hands. His brown eyes were wide with the stress of juggling too many priorities, and one eye was twitching. They were in the tiny conference room of the office of "Wilder and Klein Custom Builders," their fledgling company that specialized in residential construction. Eliu was the contractor who had put in the skylights at James's house. They'd started talking, and it turned out that Eliu was looking for a white face to be his partner and front man. Boulder was a progressive place, but as Eliu liked to say, he was the only black, Jewish builder in town, and the predominantly white, Protestant customer base still subconsciously preferred to deal with their own kind. James had come on board, and he handled the financial and marketing side of the business while Eliu handled the actual construction. The son of a Jewish beatnik who'd married an African American woman back in the days when such things just didn't happen, Eliu was used to having to deliver perfection in order to compete with "good enough," and his standards were high. Their clients and potential clients were waiting on the huge stack of building permits, architectural drawings, and proposals that covered the table, and James wasn't delivering perfection.

"Sorry, man, just a bit out of it," he said, even as he knew how lame that sounded.

"I hear you, man, but I need you focused. We've got a lot to do here!" No doubt Eliu was thinking James was distracted by some aspect of his ongoing fight with cancer, and James felt a twinge of guilt for letting him think that way.

"Hey, what happened with the Rodriguez guy?" James asked, changing the subject. "Did you pay him off?"

"Yeah," Eliu sighed. "Hated to let him go. The guy's just a hell of a worker. But we can't take the risk." He shrugged and hurried out the door.

James turned to the document pile, his thoughts lingering on their conversation. Miguel Rodriguez had been a key member of the framing crew. Hard-working, punctual, always cheerful, and very good with tools. But his paperwork had come up wrong with the government. His Social Security number had been fraudulent, which meant that he was probably in the country illegally. Confronted with the news, Miguel had broken down, begged them not to fire him, but they'd had no choice. It was such a shame. Miguel had been one of their stars and was sending money home to Mexico every week to support a family. They'd given him a severance, but that didn't change the fact that life was not fair. James turned his attention back to the paperwork and forced himself to concentrate. For the rest of the day he analyzed spreadsheets and edited proposals, and then went home.

Even though he was exhausted, he couldn't relax. He wandered aimlessly around the house as he waited for the next step in his mating dance with Willow. Their simple little *pas de deux* of attraction had evolved into a more complicated, erotic tango, and as with any tango, drama was sure to follow. Luckily, his kids were with Elizabeth for the week, so his dysfunction did not directly spill over onto them.

James didn't hear from Willow that night, so he went to bed and slept like a dead man. He's been awake for thirty-six hours. The next evening after dinner he was reading on the couch when the phone rang. He picked it up.

"Hello, is this James?" A man's voice.

"Yes. Who's this?"

"James, my name's Dan, and I'm calling you about my fiancée, Willow. She's here on the other line with me, and we're asking you to respect our relationship and stop interfering." Dan sounded pissed but restrained.

James's pulse accelerated. So, this was it! The showdown, the opportunity for Willow to make a choice. Her past or her future. He took a deep breath and spoke with a calmness he didn't feel.

"Dan, I understand your position, but I'd need to hear that request from Willow."

"Listen, I'm telling you that's what she wants!" Dan's voice rose to a squeak and he was breathing hard, his composure cracking. "We're engaged to be married and that should be enough! You need to just leave us alone!"

"Again, Dan, I sympathize. I really do, but this is about Willow's choice. If she wants to marry you and wants me to go away, I will, but I need to hear it from her."

Dan's voice strained with frustration. "OK, Willow, tell him!"

Crickets. There was no sound on the other line.

"Willow!" He was pissed. "Tell him you're done with this!"

James heard Willow's sigh, and her dispirited voice said dully, "James, we can't see each other. I'm marrying Dan."

It didn't sound convincing or enthusiastic, but she'd said it.

"OK, Willow, if you're sure that's what you want?" His own breath was catching in his throat.

A silence as long as one of her hugs.

"Willow!" Dan hissed into the phone.

"I'm sure," she said lifelessly.

"OK then. Goodbye," James said, and hung up. He was shaking so hard, a punch to his stomach would have been welcome. But that was it. Done. She'd chosen Dan. James got up from the couch, went to the fridge, and pulled out a beer. Cracked it open and drank a long, grounding swig. The incredible, unbelievable, improbable, impossible fantasy was over, just as he'd always suspected. Negative thoughts battered his mind like the wave-tossed planks of a shipwreck against rocks. Willow choose him? That could never happen. Getting exactly what he wanted? The gods wouldn't dream of it. Sure, they'd let him taste that sweetness, but never more than a mouthful, never the whole meal. He'd pushed all his chips to the center of the table, gone all-in on a wild-ass bet, and come up broke, tapped out. Time to leave the table.

James chuckled humorlessly to himself and muttered aloud, "You stupid asshole!" He drank the rest of his beer and went to bed, hoping that sleep would help him hit the reset button on life—again. Hoping that when he woke up, he wouldn't have this ache in his heart from the empty space that Willow had briefly filled. Hoping that daylight would somehow wash clean the shroud of yearning and frustration and disappointment that hung over his life, make it less opaque, less gray.

James got through the next week, burying himself in work and taking Rocco for walks. He felt defeated, his energy drained from his spirit. Even Rocco seemed subdued, reflecting back to him the vibe he was giving off. At his next session with Theresa, James tried to talk about it, but his words escaped like fireflies from a broken jar.

"It was like magic! Like we stepped away from time, and it was just her and me! I forgot I had cancer. I forgot everything!"

"James," Theresa said gently. "Remember when you came in here a year ago, all flustered over her, and I told you that she was taken?"

"Yeah, but she sure doesn't *seem* taken now! You should have seen us! We were like, *joined* energetically! How can she spend the whole night with me and at the same time believe that she's going to marry Dan?!"

"Love's complicated," Theresa replied. "It's rarely black and white. Human beings are complex, and their motivations even more so. What makes you think that attraction between two people has to make any sense?"

"That's exactly what I mean! I have no idea why she and I…but we do! It's like nothing I've ever felt before! God, I sound like an idiot!"

"No, you're not an idiot. You're just in a very stressful place right now, and you're all alone. Do you have anyone you can really talk to? Any close friends?"

"Well, when I was married, Elizabeth was my best friend." James paused, took a breath. "It was just the two of us. I guess I was working too much."

"And now?"

"No." James shook his head. "No one I'd ever really…*talk* to, not like this. I mean, what would I talk about? My divorce? My cancer? I'd be *that* guy. Mr. Bummer. But with Willow—"

Theresa sat silently, giving him space to say what he needed to say, to release what he needed to release. Finally, James ran out of words. The fireflies had all escaped the jar.

"It's just that I'm so…fucking…lonely," he finished, his voice a whisper. The whisper hung in the air between them, flapping its fragile wings in a silence that stretched uncomfortably.

"That's good, James. That's good," Theresa soothed. "You've expressed your feelings. Now, let them go."

James fought for control, desperately plugging leaks that spurted forth from the fracturing dam holding back his emotions.

"So, do you write in a journal?" Theresa said after a moment, seeing his struggle. "Get things down on paper?"

"Sometimes," James said, swallowing hard, "I write poetry."

Theresa smiled. "Good! Poetry is feelings distilled into words. Write poetry. It can help you process and release that energy."

James nodded, but he already knew it didn't help. His words expressed how he felt, sure, but didn't negate or relieve any of the feelings. But—everything was OK. He'd fought back the despair, patched up the dam, and they could move forward to hypnotherapy. Until next time.

Finally, the weekend arrived, and Annie and Chris charged through the door, with Rocco barking a welcome and jumping, and bags spilled everywhere. Another turn at fifty-fifty parenting.

"Chris was feeling a bit under the weather yesterday, so please keep an eye on that," Elizabeth said as she handed over his backpack of books and toys.

"Will do," James replied as Annie hugged him around the waist and Chris wrestled with Rocco.

A bit later, Annie went next door to play with a neighbor, and James took Chris to do some errands downtown. Chris's blond head bobbed along beside him as they walked into the grocery store. For the moment, life did not suck, and they were on a mission to score some ice cream.

"I want chocolate chip cookie dough," Chris said, his open face lit up with excitement. "Ben and Jerry's. They have the best! And I like the cows."

"OK, little buddy, you get chocolate chip cookie dough, and I'll get Phish Food. And we'll share."

"And Annie wants Cherry Garcia!" Chris added with unusual selflessness.

"That's a lot of ice cream! How are we going to eat all that?"

"We'll manage," Chris replied in a serious tone, parroting back one of the lines that James always used on the kids. James laughed as Chris pulled him toward the frozen foods section. Suddenly, a shot of adrenaline rocked James's body as he noticed Willow in the produce department. She was staring at him from about twenty feet away, from the other side of a colorful display of fruits and vegetables. James kept his cool, nodded, and continued down the aisle toward frozen foods, but he also saw the guy she was with. Average height, glasses, longish, curly hair, sunken chest, totally absorbed in a cantaloupe. On the face of it, not the man-god James had imagined. Reflexively, he wondered what a woman like her was doing with a guy like him. Then James scolded himself for being so shallow. Who was he to judge her choices based on appearances? He knew *nothing* about their relationship. Maybe she just loved the guy, for whatever reason. Bottom line, she'd chosen Dan. The reason didn't matter. A few minutes later, as he and Chris walked out of the store, James imagined he could feel Willow's eyes burning a hole in his back.

At home, James fixed dinner with an ice cream party for dessert, and the week passed, each day a little easier than the one before. The magic was dissipating, loosening its grip on his heart, his head, and his stomach. The razor-sharp edge of focus—the little tingles and sparkles that had been so prevalent when Willow was constantly in his thoughts—faded, and life returned to ordinary and dull in a familiar, comforting way. Annie and Chris went back to Elizabeth's house for their week with her, and James settled into his lonely routine of workdays, solo hikes, sessions with healers, and meals for one. Then, ten days after Willow's final goodbye, the phone rang again.

"Hello?"

"James, I have to see you." Willow's voice sounded anxious, eager, even desperate.

What? She wants to come back? What about Dan? Had she left him? Would she stay this time? All of these thoughts swirled like the heavy blood that pounded in his ears, drowning out whatever she said after. James took a deep breath, steeling himself for the energy required to dive back in.

"OK."

"I'll be over in an hour," she promised and hung up.

James tried to recreate the magic of that first night together. He scrambled around and picked up the socks from the floor, straightened the pictures, ran the vacuum. He had the candles lit and the fire in the fireplace snapping and crackling. Sarah and Van and Loreena were stacked up and ready on the stereo.

She walked in the door, shed her coat, and came straight into his arms. "I missed you so much!" she breathed into his ear and kissed him. Instantly, they were launched back into the fantasy realm of their previous night together. He led her to the couch, where they lay down, face to face, lips to lips. As she caressed his cheek with her left hand, James saw that she still had the ring. He waited for an explanation, but she said nothing. He let it go, sure that anything that invited reality into the moment would pop the iridescent soap bubble in which they floated. She rolled up on top of him and opened his shirt. She kissed his chest, lingering on the spot right over his heart, and then sat up and raised her arms over her head, her eyes offering an invitation. His hands needed no urging, and her blouse came off easily. Her breasts were perfect, small, shaped like a French sculptor had loved her. He pulled her down and she sighed, as if whatever specter that haunted her was leaving her body. He wanted her badly, so he started to unzip her pants, but she reached down and captured his hand.

"Not yet," she whispered. "I can't."

As the night deepened, the heat and light from the fireplace died down, and the candles sputtered. The air grew chill, and they lay pressed against each other under the blanket, suspended in an exquisite purgatory between desire and surrender. At some point they slept, their skin warmest where they were in contact with one another.

The next morning, James opened his eyes to see her sleeping face inches from his own. *Resting Beauty*. A great title for a poem or a sculpture or a painting. He lay there watching her breathe, her face a study in classic lines and contours. A gift to all who looked upon her, like a Botticelli Venus.

~~ *Resting Beauty* ~~

Resting beauty,
like a pebble tossed into a quiet pond,
creates a ripple,
a perfect circle,
nature's most simple geometry,
and yet, it can rise up,
a tsunami of consequence,
that alters shorelines,
changes landscapes,
washes away the good and the bad,
and only the resilient
remains.

~~ * ~~

Their night together ended like their previous one. She rose from his embrace, refused coffee and breakfast, kissed him as she dressed, and left him alone in a cloud of pleasure notes and sadness.

Chapter Five

~ * ~

Citrine

After Willow walked out that morning, she left a message on his answering machine that she needed time to think, and she asked James not to contact her. For a change, he put an optimistic spin on that bit of news. He figured that if she was thinking about it, there might be a chance that she'd leave Dan for good. But then the days stretched out one after another, without any word, and he began to lose hope.

One night, James went to a party thrown by Eliu. As a rule, James wasn't very good at parties, and that night was no different. He ate a few chips with hummus, sipped a beer, chatted with a few coworkers, and felt painfully out of place. All around him were healthy, normal people discussing their kids and jobs and whatnot. Most were couples, friends of Eliu and his wife, living their easy, romantically dull lives in the security of knowing that they weren't sleeping alone. James stood by himself not talking to anybody.

After a while, he noticed a tall, skinny woman with a wild mane of red hair, staring fixedly at him across the room. *Here it comes*, he thought. He was wrong. She crossed the room to give him a message. "Where's the red? You have no red."

"Excuse me?" he asked.

"You have no red. Your root chakra. No red energy. You have no red."

James mumbled a thank-you for her news and carefully extracted himself from her intensity. Red energy? Root chakra? As a conversation starter, it was a little weird. But this was Boulder, and when it came to crazy New Age stuff, there were more feather merchants and crystal wavers in this town than you could shake a rattle at. But maybe she had a point. After all, cancer had given him permission to drop all preconceptions about what might work and what might not. The Western medicine approach to treating his cancer was so scary that he'd already run screaming (figuratively) from the doctor's office and turned to alternative medicine, so who was he to be skeptical? He was feeling pretty drained, so maybe his root chakra really was shot.

James decided to consult his best friend, Kat, who dealt with this stuff all the time as an energy worker and massage therapist. Kat and he had dated, briefly, back when he was first divorced. Their friendship had miraculously survived the experience, and when he was first diagnosed, she'd helped him explore the alternative medicine scene. She'd since moved down to the Caribbean, but from time to time they still talked on the phone.

Kat had been there to guide him when he'd had one of the most amazing experiences of his life. It had happened when he was new to the world of spirituality. His meltdown after the divorce had been the catalyst, and like many devastated recent divorcees, he was casting around for new footing, a new context, a new way to understand the world, as his old reality had crumbled beneath his feet. Kat had introduced him to meditating, and he'd started a practice of slow, deep breathing in the evening before bed, sitting in a dark room, watching patterns of light wash behind his closed eyelids. There was usually nothing dramatic, just waves of subtle purple against the blackness. The waves ebbed and flowed to a rhythm that was different from his heartbeat. It was slower.

One night as he sat there, eyes closed, breathing, he saw a spot of light in the distance, growing as it approached out of the blackness. As it got closer it resolved into a caramel-colored, faceted jewel, rectangular shaped with the long dimension in the horizontal. It zoomed toward him and smacked him right in the middle of his forehead.

"Holy shit!" James had said aloud and opened his eyes. What was that? Had he fallen asleep? Could it have been just a dream?

Settling back in, he'd restarted his breathing, and before long was back in the groove. This time, two points of light appeared in the distance, side by side, and zoomed toward him. They resolved into two identical, round, faceted stones cut like diamonds. The one on the left was that same caramel, caffe latte color, and the one on the right was pale blue. The facets glittered with sharp, defined edges, and the two stones smashed right into his forehead just as the first stone had. OK, he knew he wasn't asleep this time, so he immediately called Kat.

"Wow, James! You just downloaded some serious energy from the universe!"

James had no idea what she meant, but she assured him that it was significant and a good thing. Soon after that, he started to hear the gods' whispers.

So, this night, after his encounter with the red-haired messenger, James again called Kat.

"Tell me about chakras," he said into the phone. "This crazy lady said I had 'no red' in my root chakra. Sounds like gibberish to me."

"Don't be such a skeptic," Kat scolded. "Chakras are energy vortices in your body. There's seven of them, and they have different colors depending upon the type of energy that flows through them. Red energy is your basic life force, and the root chakra is right between your legs."

"Between my legs?"

"Yeah. Your chakras stack up your body like a rainbow stoplight: red, orange, yellow, green, blue, indigo, violet, all the way to the crown of your head. And the higher you go, the higher the energy vibration is. Your crown chakra, with violet energy, is your connection to the gods. But you better go get that root chakra checked, cowboy."

She arranged for him to have a session with one of her Boulder friends, a psychic and energy worker whose name was Gia. When he showed up at Gia's doorstep, he was greeted by a huge sculpture of a penis. Not just any penis, but a giant, six-foot-long curved dong painted in lifelike colors and sporting a bushy vagina at the base. Or maybe it was a statue of a bearded, pink caterpillar standing on its head with its mouth open, but it sure looked like a giant penis to him. No doubt the neighbors loved it.

James rang the bell, already regretting his decision to come, when Gia opened the door. She was a pretty, unexpectedly normal-looking woman with dark hair and red lips. Early thirties, he reckoned.

"Come on in," she said, and James followed her inside.

The house was a standard suburban home, but there was a definite theme to the decor. The penis statue outside the door must have been her trademark, because there were about a dozen of them inside, ranging in size from the giant door guardian to tabletop models. All of them sported a gaping vagina surrounded by bushy black hair at their base. James said nothing but followed her into the kitchen. In the breakfast nook, instead of seating for four, there was a massage table set up.

"I work with red energy, which can be activated by sexual energy," she said. "Take off your clothes, and lie face down on the table, under the sheet. Call me when you're ready."

She left the room. James took a deep breath, stripped down, and got under the covers. His face was in the face cradle, and it was pretty comfortable. OK then.

"Ready," he called.

He heard her come back into the room, padding around in her bare feet. He could see her toes through the face cradle as she stopped near his head, placed her hands on his back, and started breathing deeply, as if meditating. James studied her toes. They were pretty, her nails painted a dark blue.

She moved around to the foot of the table, keeping her fingers on his back. She pulled the sheet down to his waist, then he heard her oiling up her hands. She started to massage his lower back, just like any massage he'd ever had. So far, this seemed very conventional. He settled into it and became drowsy.

After a bit, he noticed that her breathing was becoming more pronounced and her strokes were getting longer, coming down further onto his back and even onto his buttocks. And she was working up a lather, her breathing becoming more excited, her hands running up his sides and onto his shoulders, and then down his thighs and up onto his butt. The sheet seemed to have been pulled all the way off. In the interests of scientific curiosity, James decided to go with the flow, see where this went. After all, what was the worst that could happen?

She was panting now, pushing against the table with her hips, and it was rocking. She groaned.

"Hey, are you OK?" he asked idiotically through the face cradle. The subtext in his question was, "What the fuck?"

"Red energy is life energy, sexual energy," she panted back. "I'm using my sexual energy to restart your life energy."

With that, she crawled up onto the table, straddled him with her hands on his shoulders and her pelvis grinding against his ass. From the feel of her skin against his, he realized that she was naked from the waist down, or at best wearing only a thong. He lifted his head up, but she pushed his face back down into the face cradle.

"Lie still," she commanded.

The table was really rocking now as she pumped and groaned and squeezed his shoulders and neck with her hands. Finally, she climaxed with a long, satisfying release, her hands locked around his throat, her pelvis jammed up against his tailbone. She collapsed against his back, and James could feel that she was still wearing a top. After a few moments, her breathing returned to normal, and she got off of him and stepped down to the floor.

"You can get up now. Put on your clothes," she said matter-of-factly.

James lifted his head and watched her walk out of the room. Yep, naked from the waist down, and she had a beautiful ass. He pulled on his pants and was buttoning up his shirt when she came back into the room.

"Coffee?" she asked, and they sat and talked as if nothing had happened. She told him about her energy work, how she was also an artist, and how she felt that male and female sexuality was a continuum, hence the statues with both male and female genitalia. James joked that he was glad she hadn't come at him with a strap-on, and she just smiled.

"Maybe next time," she deadpanned. Somehow, he wasn't sure she was joking.

OK, time to leave. James paid her and headed home.

"Kat," he said into the phone, "That was the strangest massage I've ever had. In fact, I'm not sure that she shouldn't have paid me, the way she got off."

Kat just laughed. "Gia's a trip, but she's legit. I'm sure it helped. And knowing you, I'm sure you enjoyed it!"

Kat, as a former lover, knew how much he loved sex and the female body. And as a friend, she understood perhaps better than anyone how his mind and his heart worked. This interaction with Willow was like a distillation of every neurosis, every tic he'd ever had in his dealings with women. A soup that had all the vegetables:

anxiety, insecurity, self-doubt, lack of self-esteem, projection, and impossible expectations, all simmering to a perfect dish of crazy. How was it going to end?

* ~ * ~ *

He'd just dropped the kids off at Elizabeth's and was making himself some comfort food, a bowl of brown rice and stir-fried veggies, when the phone rang. It was Willow.

"Can I come see you tonight?"

"I thought you needed space."

"I did. Now I need you."

James sighed. "Willow, this is kinda hard on me…."

"Please? I really miss you."

He thought about telling her no, but the gods vetoed that response. He'd begged them to give her to him, and they were not about to take her back. He said OK and sat on his couch waiting for her. No fire in the fireplace this time, although he did open a nice bottle of red wine he'd been saving. She walked in the door, and he handed her a glass.

"Let's talk," he said and led her to the couch. "What's going on?"

"It's nice to see you, too," she grumbled. "No kiss? Just a glass of wine?"

"What is this, a booty call? I hear nothing for ten days, and suddenly you need to see me?"

Willow started to cry. "I'm so confused. I want to marry Dan. He's been so understanding and patient with me. But I feel so connected to you, even though I hardly know you! God! What do I do?"

James took the glass from her hand and set it down on the coffee table. He pulled her into his arms and kissed her. She kissed back through wet, salty lips. She kissed as if she were starved for kisses, and every kiss was as hungry as if it were the last kiss on earth. As for James, Gia must have ignited his red energy, because he was bursting out of his pants. Somehow, they helped each other undress, their clothes discarded on the floor like their fears and inhibitions and frustrations.

She lay back on the couch, and his mind took a snapshot of that moment in time. Her wet, glistening eyes, her tearstained cheeks. Her mouth, slightly open in anticipation of what was coming next. Her hair, sprawled wildly against the cushions. Her body, a thing of beauty, pale, with curves in all the right places, soft, open, inviting.

She reached for him, and suddenly he couldn't breathe. He lowered himself onto her, and her hands guided him to the right spot. She wrapped her legs around his back as they pushed and pulled and groaned with agonizing pleasure, moving as one organism. Their first orgasm came quickly, a release that had been building since the first night they'd met. Their next one came more slowly, more poetically, as they savored the sensations like the wine they finally sipped between kisses. James listened for the gods, strained to hear their commentary, but for once they were silent.

Chapter Six

~ * ~

Rose Quartz

At some point, they migrated upstairs to James's bed, with just a candle for light. Their physical desire had passed, and he had questions. She was still an enigma wrapped in a mystery, and he needed to find a way to ask her, without asking her, what she wanted from him. And since he didn't directly ask, she didn't directly answer.

"Tell me something about you," James whispered in the candle-light. "Something I wouldn't know just by making love to you."

"What more do you need? And why does it matter?"

"I don't know. Give me something."

"Mmmm. I like older men." She nuzzled his chest.

"Hey, I'm not old! I'm only thirty-nine!"

"That's really old! I'm six years younger than you!" She nibbled his nipple, and he squirmed away.

"I already know that!" James said. "Tell me something…hard to tell. Something you wouldn't tell anyone else."

She remained silent for a moment; then very softly, so that he almost couldn't hear, she whispered, "I had an eating disorder when I was a teen. My mom put me in the hospital."

"Wow. You're so beautiful! Can't imagine you like that."

"See? You look at me, and all you see are my looks! You think I have no problems?"

"No! I didn't mean that!"

"It's OK. I'm used to it. People look at me, think they know me. And *everyone* looks at me…even when I was a little girl."

James thought about that as she lay in his arms. Beauty, a curse as much as a blessing. He pictured her as a little girl, trying to understand why everyone treated her as if she were the keeper of something precious that they could share if only they could get close enough. How was he different? Was he any different? Was it possible to see behind the persona of physical perfection and see the person?

"Hey, I'm sorry—"

"That's OK. You asked me to tell you something personal. Something…hard. Now it's your turn." She rolled over and stared him down with those blue, blue eyes. "Go on. Tell me something *I* wouldn't know just by making love to *you*."

She'd turned the tables on him, or maybe he'd turned them on himself.

"Well, OK. Umm." He thought for a moment. "I don't have many friends."

"Why not? Are you a jerk?" She grinned in the dim light.

"No! I mean, I make friends easily, but…I don't go very deep, I guess. Just the way I am, ever since I was a kid. I don't know. My dad was in the army, we were always moving, from post to post. Always the new kid, figuring out the lay of the land, you know, sorting out friends and enemies, then moving on a few months later."

"Ah, my cousin was an army brat. Tough life."

"Yeah. It was what it was."

"And your mom? What was she like?"

James shook the cobwebs off his memories of Mom. They'd never been close. She'd been a beautiful, dark-haired, well-bred woman of the fifties who breathed fire and ice, smoked cigarettes, drank cocktails, and danced at parties. Like her officer husband, she'd had little bandwidth for cuddling and warm fuzzies when it came to her kids.

"She passed away when I was sixteen," was all he said.

"Oh, I couldn't bear that. I'm very close to my mom," Willow said with sympathy. They fell silent, deep in their own thoughts, and his drifted through the dusty corridors of memory. Back to when his mom fell sick, and they shipped him off to all-male boarding school. He'd been a stranger in a strange land, a castaway on an island of lost boys. Not a place he liked to frequent, but he was there now. He'd just entered puberty, a skinny, big-footed puppy with size 12 feet and weighing a buck ten wringing wet. He'd studied and slept in hallowed, brick-and-ivy buildings where the shadows of his ancestors had studied and slept. He'd played sports on vast green playing fields and in musty gymnasiums where their flickering ghosts threw balls, ran, and tackled one another. His classes had been taught by old codger teachers who towered over him with their cadaverous faces as they tormented him with strange Latin phrases and shook their heads. "Hopeless—just like his father," they said. He was bullied and alone, and yet he never felt homesick. Sports was the only thing that had made sense in that bizarre, *Lord of the Flies* world, and over the course of four years, James had grown and filled out and fought his way to the top of the pecking order and played on the football and lacrosse teams and anchored every relay in swimming. It didn't matter to anyone but him, though. No cheerleaders in short skirts and ribbons, no parents in the stands. Even in sports, he couldn't shake his aloneness.

"My mom loves Dan." Willow's whisper, so soft that it almost slipped by him, pulled his awareness back, briefly, to the sputtering candlelight and the soft sigh of their breathing.

In the morning, she kissed him and tried to get up from the bed, but James held her. "Am I going to have to wait another ten days before I hear from you again?" he asked.

She looked away and wouldn't meet his gaze. "James—" she started, then didn't finish.

Disappointed, he let her get up. They were entrenched in a pattern that had no resolution. At the door, she turned.

"Please be patient. Let me go through my process. I'm trying to understand why we...we do this. Dan's very important to...to me, and to my family. But I'm drawn to you, connected to you somehow. You feel like my soul brother, and I feel so...helpless. Please, please, please, be patient while I figure this out." She smiled sadly, blew him a kiss, and left.

Soul brother? What the hell did that mean?

"Honor your poetry," Theresa said at their next session. "These are your truest feelings, expressed in your best words. Print them out. Put them in a book or something, separate from your other writing. Make it special. If you physically honor these, your mind and your heart will do the same."

Somehow, her words seemed like a permission that James had been waiting for, and he knew just what to do. He retrieved a scrapbook from a dusty cardboard box of random stuff that had belonged to his mom. It was covered with red leather that had been embossed like crocodile skin and had clear plastic sleeves. She'd wanted to be an artist, but the only thing that had made it into the book was a small watercolor of a flower. James kept her little painting in the first sleeve and added copies of his poems that he printed out on cream-colored card stock edged with gold filigree. Already he had a few poems that he deemed good enough for the book. Theresa was right. His poetry did feel different this way, like crystallized emotion with its own identity separate from his. He wondered what his mother would have thought if she could have seen them. Surely, her spirit knew, with the clarity of the afterlife, what he was feeling. "This is for you, Mom," he thought.

The days went by, and James busied himself with his job and his kids, and when he was alone, with the painting project. Filled with more energy and optimism, he finished the red wall in the front hallway. It was a deep, Moroccan red, and in the middle, facing the front door, he hung a beautiful, gold-framed painting of an aspen grove in dappled sunlight. He started on the rest of the front entrance and the stairwell to the second floor. Those walls would be a light, buttercream color. Painting became a creative process where he composed poetry as he worked. And miraculously, by bringing in more light and color, the house began to feel more like a home.

As for Willow, he gave her space to go through her process, and it seemed ten days was as long as she could last without spending a night with him. A recurring pattern, as regular as the cycles of the moon. She'd come over to his house after dinner, but only when his kids were with Elizabeth, and they'd devour each other—sometimes on the couch, sometimes in the bedroom. They'd communicate mostly through touch and sensation, like two blind, mute lovers who knew each other only through their skin and their mouths and their sex organs. Somehow, they both knew that too much verbal intimacy could only lead to separation and heartbreak. Instead, they'd make excruciatingly beautiful love all night long, then exhausted, she would depart. No breakfast, no update on her process, no change in the forecast. Cloudy and foggy with a chance of infrequent but intense sexual activity. Christmas came and went, January followed, and February was slipping away into March.

Then one sunny but cold day, while hiking with Rocco up Mount Sanitas, a steep, popular trail at the edge of town that climbed up the foothills, James ran into Willow and Dan coming down the mountain. James stood aside as they passed, and Dan ignored him because, of course, he'd never met him, but Willow looked right at James and walked by with a sheepish smile. James watched them go, then turned and continued up the hill. He was near the top and felt like he wanted to scream. That night, seated at his desk, burning with emotions that demanded release, he wrote the words he needed to say to her.

~~ *Stolen Moments* ~~

The night flees the coming sun,
just as you flee from my embrace.
Stolen moments
from another lover.

Do you miss me now?
Are you with him again?

This crazy dance of forbidden love
will make us both insane.
Is it worth the cost?
Is there a way to win?

I walk the earth in search of meaning
and find only a rock
against which to beat my head.
This is the insanity of lovers,
heedless of the cost in pain.

Can you see me now?
Or are you tied to him
by a promise made
in another life?

There is no good way to end this.
Pain or pain, you decide.

~~ * ~~

The next time she came over, James didn't mention the encounter on Mt. Sanitas, but their lovemaking had a tension to it that manifested in a coupling that was almost a wrestling match, a contest of wills played out with physical intensity. By the end of the evening, though, they'd settled back into their familiar pattern of sexual exhaustion while they clung to each other like two castaways on a lifeboat. And then she rolled over to dig through her purse.

"Whatcha looking for?" James asked.

She handed him a photograph. It was her, standing in the sunshine, laughing.

"Here, I want you to have this," she said.

Something shifted in him. Suddenly, he couldn't do this anymore. He sat up and handed her back the photo.

"I don't need a photo of you, Willow. I know what you look like. I've memorized every feature on your face. I know how you smell and how you taste and how you feel against my skin. What I need from you is a decision. Please. It's time. Him or me."

Willow's face fell. She took back the photo, holding it limply in her hand. On the coffee table, the candle sputtered in a sudden draft. It was late, and there was only an inch of the stub left to burn. She started to tell him that she was still going through her process, but James cut her off.

"Willow, I don't believe for a minute that you're going to marry Dan. If you were, you wouldn't be here with me. But regardless, both he and I need you to make a decision. I love you! I need you, not just every ten days, but every day. I want to have a normal life, *with* you, where we eat meals together, lie around in each other's arms, and watch movies. Create a home together. Hang out with my kids! This thing we're doing…it can't continue. Too much damage. You need to decide."

"But James, I can't leave him. I haven't…decided that."

"Please. Him or me."

James locked eyes with her, not smiling, feeling his heart pounding in his ears, his soul in a barrel going over Niagara Falls. He was drawn to this woman at his deepest level, was connected by some mysterious force beyond comprehension, but she didn't seem real to him. For all he knew, she could be a hallucination, a dream, an elaborate escape his mind had created to give respite from a lonely, gray existence. His sympathy for her life dilemma of too much beauty had dissipated in the face of his own dilemmas. Her life was not his life, and he felt stretched to the breaking point. He was exhausted, his energy drained by the stress of not knowing where this was leading, feeling like he'd already spent too much at the roulette table and he was finally ready to cut his losses.

"Him or me," James repeated.

Willow said nothing, just searched his face and saw that he was serious. Slowly, she got up and put on her clothes. His heart sank, just as he had always known it would have to, but that didn't ease the hurt. As if sleepwalking, she reached down and picked up her purse, put her photo back into it, and walked to the front door. She pulled on her jacket without looking in his direction, almost as if she had her eyes closed. She stood for several seconds without moving, and then opened the door.

Naked, James got up from the couch, wrapped the blanket around himself, and walked over to her. He didn't reach out or touch her, just stood there, feeling her withdraw from him energetically, like the roots of an electric plant being ripped out of his body. She walked down the front steps one at a time, shaking as if she would collapse at any moment, and paused when she reached the bottom, with her back to him. She swayed back and forth for what seemed an eternity. He kept thinking, *Turn around! Come back to me!* but said nothing. He was witnessing her choice in slow motion.

She stood there on the icy front path, and then slowly started to walk down the driveway to her car. He watched her unlock the door, get in, and then drive away. The night air against his naked flesh only added to his numbness. He turned, went back inside, and closed the door on an infinite number of alternate realities that had countless versions of him continuing in limbo with Willow, enjoying her body and her kisses until the inevitable end. The gods whispered among themselves, sadness palpable in their unintelligible murmurings. James knew what they were feeling but just didn't feel it himself. He was too numb.

He lay down on the couch and turned onto his side, his head on one of the decorative pillows. Her scent, the scent of essential oils distilled from wildflowers, pervaded the fabric. He breathed deeply, closed his eyes, and imagined her lying there next to him, his face buried in her hair.

~~ *The Wood Elf* ~~

I was walking one day,
lost in thought, pondering Love,
when Hafiz appeared,
and told me about the wood elf.

"She's a mythical lover,
a mirage.
You might see blue eyes peeking
from behind a tree,
gone in a moment,
the hint of a smile.

You'll look for her,
follow deep into the forest,
but not find her.

And then,
when you least expect it,
at the edge of a pond
she will sit down beside you,
an apparition,
a sudden presence manifesting.

And if you are lucky,
she will kiss you,
and haunt your dreams,
and disturb your meditations
with visions of her face,
and the memory of her lips.

You will want to know her,
know why she has chosen you,
but she will never tell.
For she is a wood elf, and they
keep their thoughts locked up
inside their mystic hearts,
the shyest of the shy.

And then one day,
she will come no more,
and you will search the forest
for a hint of blue,
but all you will find
is the reflection off the pond,
and the whisper of the wind,
like her fingers,
gently brushing the back of your neck,
one last time."

~~ * ~~

The Second Mala

A Tombstone Angel in a Midnight Churchyard

~~ *Smoke in a Bottle* ~~

Love's a special type of magic,
ephemeral,
hot,
cloudy,
a shapeshifter of many forms,
like smoke in a bottle,
a jar filled with fireflies,
or buzzing static,
the kind
that makes your hair stand up.

It can be a thunderbolt,
blue lightning
that smacks you right between the eyes,
a shock so strong
that speech fails,
muscles collapse,
and you are jolted out of time.

Or it can tingle
at the edge of your mind,
an itch that can't be scratched.
Something about her
catches your eye,
draws you closer,
like a bee to a flower,
buzzing this way, and that,
until finally you settle
on the sweetest petal
for a fatal sip of nectar.

Love scrambles your compass,
makes your guiding star
fall from the sky,
redraws the map
to your greatest treasure,
and changes the gods
you pray to.

It's a drug so addictive,
you'll surrender your soul,
sacrifice your body,
and rewire your mind
for just another kiss from its lips.
It's smoke in a bottle.

~~ * ~~

Chapter Seven

~ * ~

Blue Sea Glass

When James was initially divorced from Elizabeth, the first woman to swoop in on him was someone he'd known at business school. Anne was a successful executive, living in Chicago. She had her life figured out, and the central focus was her career. Never married, she had a role for men to play, and it did not involve love or relationships in the traditional sense.

She came through Denver on business and after a few drinks put him through his paces as a lover, assessing if there was any potential there for entertainment. There wasn't. James was green and had been sleeping with the same woman for twelve years. He was equally clueless when it came to just what they were about. After spending a few weekends together, she dumped his sorry ass, and he protested, saying he loved her or some such drivel. She stopped him in his tracks with as much kindness as she could muster.

"No. No you don't. And I don't love you. Besides, I don't need a man in my life. They're messy. Leave their stuff all over the floor. I like my space." Subtext: *You suck as a lover, and you're really not very interesting as a person.*

"But what about us? I thought you, you know, we had something we could build on."

Even as naive as James was back then, he didn't really believe it was love, although he felt obligated to say something. After all, they'd slept together! She just looked at him, judging whether she could give it to him straight.

"Tell me, James. Did you have fun?" she finally asked.

"Yes," he replied.

"Did you learn something?"

"Yes."

"So what's your complaint?"

His jaw dropped. He was speechless as the clouds parted, the angels sang, and truth dawned. He didn't have to be in love to have sex with a woman! He could just like her, enjoy her company. With women, he'd always confused love and sex and friendship. They were like the three-headed dog that guarded the gates of Hell—try to kiss one head and the other two heads would bite your face off.

Anne and James went their separate ways, she to chase the next no-strings-attached lover who could offer a higher level of sophistication, and James, armed with his new knowledge, to start his remedial studies in women, relationships, and sex. She'd brought him a piece of the puzzle, and he'd found the place where it fit.

For the next year, as James transitioned from monogamous husband and full-time dad, he honed his skills in the dating world. He became very good at the attraction game as he swam in a sea of divorced women as wounded and insecure and desperate as he was.

"The relationship you had with Elizabeth, that purity of hope and plans for the future, and that clean slate—you'll never find that again," Theresa had said. "The women available to you now will have torn edges, places where their souls have been ripped by the pain of divorce, just like you. Finding sex will be easy. Finding love and trust and intimacy, not so much."

It was true. *Love* became an exotic word from a strange foreign language. He had no idea what it meant anymore, so he settled for *attraction*. He continuously dated at least three women at the same time as he desperately sought reassurance that he wasn't a total loser—that he was still desirable. At some level he felt vaguely guilty, as if he was doing something wrong, but he rationalized his behavior by being completely open about it.

"I'm a single guy, just out of a long-term, monogamous relationship," he'd say to a potential girlfriend. "And I'm going to do whatever I want, with whomever I want, whenever I want, and if you're OK with that, then we can date." Somehow, enough of them were OK with his legal disclaimer, even the part in the fine print. He'd be with Alice Monday night, then Cathy on Thursday, and spend the weekend with Carla. He was like the hub of a wheel, able to have an intimate relationship with all of the spokes individually. And the wheel of intimacy and sex and love drama would go round and round with him at the center, and sometimes a woman would get attached and possessive, and she'd tell him she couldn't take it anymore and she'd leave, but there'd always be another one to replace her.

That was when the gods must have lost patience because, suddenly, at thirty-seven, James was diagnosed with cancer of the prostate, a disease that usually hits old men. James had no idea what that disease was. The surgical urologist, a bespectacled, soft-around-the-middle, balding man, cleared away his ignorance.

"Your prostate is a little organ the size of a walnut that sits below your bladder. The urethra, the tube you pee out of, runs from your bladder through the prostate and down through the penis. We go in, cut out the entire prostate and a large enough margin around it to catch any escaped cancer cells. We reattach the bladder directly to the urethra, and you're in the hospital for three, maybe five, days.

Back at work in a couple weeks." The surgeon's foot was jiggling as he sat at the little desk in the examining room. No doubt he was already late for his next three-minute appointment.

"Um, OK, you cut it out, but…isn't that a lot of plumbing you're messing with? What about side effects?" James felt panic begin to rise up inside him.

"Well, sure, there's some important nerves that run right through there, next to everything. We accidently cut those, and you're permanently impotent. No more erections."

"Ouch! And how often—"

"Well, statistically it happens about 40 percent of the time. It's a complicated surgery. But I've managed to bring that down to about 34 percent. I can fit you in next Thursday." The surgeon got up to leave, secure in the comfort he'd offered with his 34 percent failure rate.

"Wait!" James said, his breathing labored. "Any other side effects?"

The surgeon paused at the door. "Fifty percent chance you'll be incontinent the rest of your life. But they've made great improvements in adult diapers. Most people won't even know you're wearing them." He left.

James sat there stunned as his new reality sprouted and grew like a poisonous mushroom. Impotent and incontinent…at the age of thirty-seven! No more erections…no more sex. Even worse, no longer a way into the magic of connection with another person, another heart, another soul that he still believed was somewhere on the other side of sex, if he could only find the lost treasure map to it. He was already off-balance, a cast-off male recalibrating his relationship with women, with family, with life. And now this! Who would want him? A broken spare part. Damaged beyond repair.

James left the surgical urologist's office, never to return. His oncologist had said that prostate cancer was slow-moving, so maybe he had time. Maybe. James sought out alternatives: a naturopathic doctor and a macrobiotic diet; acupuncture and vitamin supplements and Chinese mushrooms; herbal infusions; hypnotherapy; Native American energy healings, chanting, and meditating with crystals. Knowing nothing, he was open to anything that claimed efficacy in battling his disease. Cancer had given him permission to drop any preconceptions about what might work and what might not. He had only himself to rely on, his own first-hand experiences to test claims, to judge results. He was betting his life on the hope that there had to be a better way. And that way had led him to Theresa and to the yoga retreat and Willow.

And now, two months after Willow had walked out his door for the last time, he wasn't doing very well. His acupuncturist said his kidney energy was overstimulated and his liver energy was shot. Theresa said his aura was filled with tears. Mary Two Bears, his Native American shaman, told him his spirit had gone into shadows. And his naturopathic doc expressed concern over his blood tests and loss of weight. When one gets a consensus like that, it's best to pay attention.

James had no idea what to do, so of course, he called Kat. She invited him down to St. John for a visit. As friends. Annie and Chris were with their mom in Florida for spring break, so James was free to go for two weeks.

Kat had been there at the end of his hub-and-spoke days, along with two other women. One, a bright, sexy divorcée named Susan, had figured out that she deserved more than what James was offering, and she'd traded up to a rich real estate developer with land in Steamboat Springs. The other, Lisa, had married an insurance salesman and moved to a bland suburb of Denver. Kat had gone to the Caribbean and had found a job as a massage therapist at an eco-resort on St. John. She lived on-site in one of their tents on raised wooden platforms nestled in the foliage above the beach.

Kat never took much damage from James because she'd known right from the start what he was up to and didn't invest much emotional capital. She'd been the roommate of a woman he'd been dating.

They'd discussed him, and somehow, the other woman had given Kat permission to check him out. Kat seduced him one night, talking him into giving her a back rub when her friend wasn't around. Things got a little heated, and James was surprised but not surprised when she rolled over and pulled him down.

Kat was pretty in an unconventional sense, one of those women you have to look at more closely to see the true, very real beauty. Brown eyes and brown hair cut short, average height. Didn't believe in makeup and didn't need it. Slim hips and wonderful, perfectly firm breasts that pointed upward. She had a son somewhere else, and he was struggling with addiction issues. She was in her late thirties and had birthed him when she was very young and unmarried.

Their greatest connection back then had been intellectual. The sex was fun, but the best parts were the long talks they had into the wee hours of the night, about life and the universe and God and science. She was smart, Phi Beta Kappa smart, curious, articulate, and interesting, but she'd never been to college. She came from an impoverished background in Kansas, her father a plumber and an alcoholic, her mother a beautician. Kat could have been someone who accomplished great things, given the chance. And they probably also could have been great partners, given the chance.

When James stepped off the plane in St. Thomas, he was immediately immersed in the thick, humid air of the tropics. The warm breeze stirred the miasma of leaves, rotting fruit, ocean smells, and jet fuel that filled his nostrils, and the end-of-day heat was like balm to his body.

Kat met him inside the terminal. The first words out of her mouth were, "You look like shit."

Yes, he did. Truth was, he felt even worse. Theresa had said that the body is the outward manifestation of what's going on at the deeper levels of one's being—at the emotional, mental, and spiritual levels. Given how depleted James felt, it was no surprise that he looked awful. He had dropped down from a skinny 180 pounds to a gaunt 165. At over six feet two inches tall, he was a walking skeleton.

Kat looked tanned and luminous. She gave him a huge hug and kissed his cheek. James grabbed his small bag filled with T-shirts, swimsuits, flip-flops, and snorkel gear, and they headed to the parking lot to grab a taxi to the ferry. The ferry ride was magical, a sunset voyage at high speed across gentle swells to the neighboring island of St. John. James could feel himself starting to sink into a less-stressed state of being. By the time the ferry docked, the sun had gone down, and the harbor of Cruz Bay was lit up as if for a party.

They met Kat's friend, Mr. Fred, a local entrepreneur who drove a garishly painted taxi truck. Mr. Fred was black, about fifty, with glasses and a straw hat. He also sported a large gold chain with a solid-gold eagle pendant spreading its wings. In his soft voice, he invited James and Kat to grab spots in the back. It was open-air seating for twelve that also featured a roof over the seats, which was a good thing because just at that moment they were hit with an early evening sprinkle of rain. The trip to the eco-resort took about twenty-five minutes, around grinding switchbacks up the sides of the steep hills that comprised St. John's coast. Kat told James that the typical car on St. John was a jeep and had to have its transmission replaced every two years.

By the time they arrived at her tent on the grounds of the eco-resort, he was pretty tired, and he lay down in her simple bed. She lay down next to him and put her arms around him. She knew, intuitively, what he needed, and as he let go, he felt all the pain, the frustration, the confusion, and the rejection leave him, first from his shoulders that tensed up as he tried to fight the upwelling emotions, and then from the rest of him as he lost the battle for control and huge, tearing sobs shook him to his foundation. She asked no questions, just held him, soothing him with that gentleness that comes naturally to open-hearted women, and when he was done, she wrapped herself around him like a bandage for ten hours while he slept like a baby.

Chapter Eight

~ * ~

Moonstone

In the morning, as the light began spreading over the ocean, James got up and looked around. The tent was a simple structure of waterproof fabric to waist height, with insect netting above that. It was stretched over a basic but sturdy frame of two-by-fours, and the whole thing was built on a wooden platform that was joined by elevated walkways to other tents. The beach was just a few hundred feet away, down rickety steps. Tree branches overhung the walkways, and leaves and rotted fruits and lizard droppings littered the wooden planks, making them slick in places.

James and Kat grabbed their snorkel gear and headed down to the beach. They were on Little Maho Bay, which faced west away from the rising sun, so the waterline was still in shadow as the sun rose on the other side of the island. The water was warm and calm and clear over a pure white, sandy bottom. James waded into the shallows, saying a prayer of thanks to Grandmother Ocean. It was a ritual he'd started doing years earlier whenever he first entered the water on vacation. Somehow, it always seemed like coming home. His prayer was more a feeling of reverence and gratitude than words, but it was real, and the water was soothing.

James sat down and slid on his light fins. Spitting into his mask, he washed it out to create a fog barrier, then slipped it over his face. He adjusted the snorkel so that his breathing was unimpeded, and then looked over at Kat. She was still putting on her gear, and he was eager to get out into deeper water, so he decided to swim out a little way.

He'd taken maybe five or six strokes and was about fifty feet from the shoreline when he noticed a huge shadow off to his right at the edge of his underwater vision. The direct sunlight still had not risen over the hill in the center of the island, so the water remained in shadow. James looked closer. Was that a coral head over there or a sunken boat? It moved and was coming steadily toward him. He'd never seen anything so large moving underwater. He wasn't frightened, but any lingering sleep fog was immediately banished.

The shape resolved itself into a wide-winged creature headed straight for him, flying majestically through the water like a giant pterodactyl. James couldn't believe his eyes—it was a manta ray, here, in the Virgin Islands! He popped his head up above the water and tried to shout to Kat through his snorkel, but she couldn't understand a word. James put his head back in the water and watched the magnificent creature glide through the water right below him. It was at least twelve feet across, or twice as wide as he was tall, and if he hadn't been frozen by the shock, he could have kicked once and reached down to touch it as it glided past. Too late, he turned and tried to keep up with it, but it swam effortlessly away like a giant bird flapping its wings in slow motion. Sadly, James watched it recede into the murk of the shadowed water, and then he swam back to where Kat was finally ready to go. It was his first time to St. John, and he'd been in the water less than four minutes. Grandmother Ocean had heard his prayer.

"A manta!" he babbled. "A manta ray just swam right under me! Holy shit!"

"You lucky, lucky bastard!" Kat exclaimed. "I've been here for a year and never seen one. You're here for thirty seconds, and it swims right up to you. I hate you!"

James was so excited he was hyperventilating. On other snorkeling trips he'd seen spotted eagle rays with wingspans of six or more feet, but they looked tiny compared to this giant.

"I've heard about this guy," Kat continued. "Others at the resort have reported it. But pretty rare around here actually. Apparently, it likes to sweep the beaches early in the morning."

They chatted a bit more about his luck, mantas, and what more they could possibly see to match that, and then they calmed down enough to put their heads back in the water and discover what else Grandmother Ocean was offering that day. They snorkeled around the point into Cinnamon Bay. There was no reef, but the rocky boulders and outcrops along the shore had plenty of marine life going on. They were entertained by beautiful fish, some small barracudas, and a random octopus. As always, James was filled with a feeling of pure delight as he glided through the gentle waves of the bay. His years on the swim team in high school had helped him develop an intimate feel for the water, and he knew how to control his body with just the tiniest movements. Add unlimited natural beauty and a warm turquoise sea, and he was in heaven. After their brief swim, they beached themselves on the soft sand of Cinnamon Bay and admired the view.

"Man, you live in paradise," James said as they soaked up the early morning sun, which was finally high enough in the sky to clear the hilltop.

"Yes, life does not suck."

Kat was topless, as was her wont. For her, it was just how she preferred to swim when there was no one around. James certainly had no complaints.

They lay there for a few minutes, two friends just relaxing and enjoying the peace under the coconut palms, their skin dappled by the sunlight that filtered through the fronds and warmed them. The water in the bay was calm, only occasionally disturbed by a sudden rain of silver minnows jumping from the water as some larger fish chased them beneath the surface. A few brown pelicans flew down the shoreline in formation, and one peeled off to dive beak-first into the shallows for a meal. Kat nudged his foot with her big toe and broke the silence.

"So, lover boy, why'd you allow yourself to get so bent out of shape by this Willow person?"

"It's complicated," James replied.

"Bullshit. You built her up to be something she wasn't. You're hopeless!"

Kat was right. His ideals about love and relationships had crashed and burned with his marriage. He had no idea how to be in love, or with whom, or why. Willow had been proof of that. To move the subject off of him, James asked her if she was seeing anyone. She ignored his question.

"Let's go make breakfast," she said, and hauled him to his feet. "Gotta fatten you up, Hansel. You're too skinny to eat."

OK, that wasn't an answer, or maybe it was. James just didn't know how to read the tea leaves.

They hiked up the short path through the jungle to the resort, skirting the cactus and shrubs and understory foliage of the Goat Trail that climbed over the point to Little Maho Bay. Back in her tent, she whipped up a gorgeous breakfast of coffee, scrambled eggs with island vegetables and onions, and fresh papaya. For the first time in a while, he felt refreshed and optimistic about the day to come.

After breakfast, Kat had a schedule of massage appointments to work through, so they agreed to meet for lunch. James could hang around the tent, maybe go take a yoga class at the central pavilion, or hit the beach. He watched her change clothes, and she did it with no self-consciousness or bother. She simply took off her bathing suit, used a wet towel to wipe away the sand that had collected here and there, and pulled on dry clothes. No makeup, of course—Kat had decided long ago to not engage in that particular war with beauty. But she put on earrings made from the feathers of some colorful bird and wore a long, beaded necklace, which he would later learn was called a mala.

James wondered if Kat considered herself a beautiful woman. He *hoped* she thought of herself as a beautiful person. She glowed with an inner light. He could see it in her eyes, those windows into her deepest being that sparkled with humor, frankness, and sharp, sharp intelligence. When she locked those eyes onto his, he knew she could read his thoughts. That same light also emanated from the rest of her being, as if she were not of this earth. It was subtle. When he remarked on how luminous she'd looked at the airport, he'd thought it was because of her delicious tan, but as he gazed at her in the tent, her bare skin caressed by the sun streaming in through the skylight in the roof, he could see that she glowed from within, as if she carried some secret fire inside her.

In that instant, he experienced one of those moments when time stops, takes a photograph, and plants it in the forefront of one's awareness. It was suddenly obvious how gorgeous she was, inside and out, and his heart ached with regret as he looked at her. Too bad he'd met her when he did and was so self-absorbed when they'd been involved.

"I saw you," she said as she finished dressing.

"Saw me what?"

"Looking at my butt."

"It's a nice butt."

"Yeah, just don't get any ideas."

She kissed him on the cheek and set off down the wooden walkway wearing shorts, flip-flops, and a halter top, a cloth bag slung over her shoulder, her ass swinging unapologetically from side to side as she walked away from him that morning, the picture of relaxed island elegance. Years later, that's how James would see her, forever etched in his memory.

Chapter Nine

~ * ~

Green Sea Glass

James wandered up to the pavilion, an open-air space where the resort hosted meals, yoga classes, lectures on the local ecology, and after-dinner movies. It was built high up on the hillside so that it had an unobstructed view of the ocean to the north, the west, and the south. Its high thatched roof provided shade at that hour to the yoga class.

He watched with interest as the teacher led about two dozen students through a flowing series of poses. He noticed that very few of the students were men. What was it with yoga and women? The class looked very challenging. There were a few moves he recognized from dipping his toe in the water up at Arapahoe Yoga Ashram, but mostly stuff that was new to him. He resolved to give it a try with Kat next time she had a free moment that coincided with class. He headed down to the beach to get in an open-water swim.

The bay next to Maho is Francis Bay. A perfect curving beach of white sand on the south end and rocks that had merged into a turtle grass bottom on the north end. James started at the south end and motored with steady strokes across the deeper water, seeing the sandy bottom thirty feet down, feeling the thrill of not knowing what was swimming out there just outside his vision. Sharks haunted the edge of fear as improbable but not impossible, just like the manta had been. But he never saw Jaws. Just some pompanos, the occasional needlefish cruising an inch below the surface like a sharp-nosed submarine, and a few stingrays stirring up the bottom as they flowed like large rippling leaves across the sand.

As the bottom sloped up into sea grass at the north end of the bay, James entered turtle country. Sure enough, he swam over a moderately sized green turtle, the flippered cow of the sea, placidly grazing below him. A little farther along, he met a pair in about fifteen feet of water. They flapped slowly away, unhurried and calm, and he joined them, twisting and turning to match their direction as they lazily tried to shake him off their trail. Eventually, he let them go and found himself at the north end of the bay. His shoulders felt tired from the unaccustomed swim, so he headed to shore, took off his gear, and strolled back down the beach to Little Maho.

As he walked, he kept his eyes out for sea glass, those little shards of beautiful pollution that the gods of the sea turn into sandblasted jewels. He found a few beauties, pieces of green and brown and clear, even some rare blue. He collected them for Kat, an offering for the kindness she'd shown him.

There are places on this earth where the gods linger, grant blessings, and leave traces of magic. Maho was one such place. The meeting with the manta was proof of that. The Eden-like beauty of the seascape below the waterline was another. And the sparkle of the sun off the sand and the sea foam and the bits of broken glass—even the seaweed tossed up in complicated fractal knots—spoke of the wonders of creation.

James met Kat for lunch at the pavilion, and she suggested a nap afterward, as she was feeling tired after giving three massages. They found a spot under a thicket of trees that lined the beach, spread out a blanket, and lay down next to each other. He wasn't surprised at how tired he felt, but only at how she seemed to match his energy level. But then, she'd been working hard all morning and perhaps hadn't slept so well the previous night with him in her bed. She snuggled up to him with her head on his arm, and they drifted off. They woke up in the midafternoon, their bodies entangled like lovers. They got up and headed back to her tent. Inside, James reached into his pocket and pulled out the pieces of sea glass.

"Oh, they're beautiful!" she exclaimed.

One piece was about the size of a quarter, and if you had a little imagination, you could make out the shape of a lopsided heart. It was a lovely emerald-green color.

"It's perfect!" she said and kissed him. He kissed her back.

Kat pulled gently away. "I'll put them on my altar as an offering to Ganesha, Remover of Obstacles."

"Who?"

"This guy."

She arranged the pieces around a small statue that looked like a chubby, seated man with the head of an elephant. He sat on a wooden box at the end of the tent, away from the door. The box was draped with a colorful scarf, and there were also a few seashells, some candle stubs, a small brass bell that might have been from Tibet or Nepal, some beads, and dried flowers.

"He's a Hindu deity," Kat said in a low voice. "And if you pray to him, he can help you with problems and tough times in your life,"

"Ha! I didn't know you're religious!" James teased.

"Well, can't hurt." She continued fussing with the altar, not looking at him. After a moment she stood back. "Hey, there's a project you can help me with."

She pulled a plastic box out from under her bed and opened it. Inside were dozens of bags of beads made from shell and wood and stone. She took the bags out of the box and arranged them neatly on her bed. They formed a rainbow of colors. James recognized some of the stones because as a college undergraduate his favorite course had been mineralogy and crystallography, a core requirement for his geology degree. He could see agate, amethyst, citrine, malachite, moonstone, shell, and many others.

"What's all this?"

"I'm making malas," Kat replied and touched the necklace she was wearing. "Malas are like Buddhist rosaries. You use them for chanting, praying, that sort of thing."

"Hmmm...Buddhist or Hindu...now I'm confused. Which are you?"

"Funny! Yoga people wear them, and I make them and sell them to the folks who come here. Plus, I love the idea of a fashion accessory with significance, not just beauty.

"How'd you get into making them?"

"I saw a friend's. It was beautiful! All stone and wood and metal beads—with a silk tassel. I asked where I could get one, and they were damn expensive! So, I learned how to make them. The yoga teachers and students who come here love them and pay well."

She demonstrated how she designed the malas, how she picked out the colors that went well together, and how certain stones had healing properties.

"When you make a mala, you have to consider more than how it looks, although that's important too. You have to think about how the stones go together energetically. What chakras are represented, and so forth."

James suppressed a reflexive impulse to scoff at such New Age nonsense. As a person who'd spent hours visualizing himself on a bed of healing rose quartz in hypnotherapy sessions, he was slower now to assert such scientific hubris.

Kat showed James her mala, the one she wore around her neck. It'd been blessed by a Hindu saint, and she treated it with reverence. There was yellow citrine and clear crystal and blue lapis lazuli. It featured a rose quartz pendant in the shape of a shield with a lapis bead held in the center by silver wire. She explained that the knots separating the individual beads had been hand-tied while the maker repeated a mantra of healing. Kat certainly looked vibrant and healthy compared to him, so perhaps it worked.

"That's really beautiful," he said. "I could even see myself wearing one if it wasn't a girl thing."

"It's not a girl thing, silly! Men wear them too. You should try it. You might become a little more enlightened. Like my guru."

She had a guru? He pictured a long-haired, skinny guy with glowing eyes and a lecherous smile who preyed upon gullible women. Was he feeling jealousy around Kat? Yep. It was his ancient weakness, rising up in his gut like yesterday's pepperoni pizza.

They picked out stones for a mala she was making for a customer, and she showed him how to tie the knots between the beads. It was painstaking work.

"As you tie each knot, you repeat a mantra," she instructed. "Or the name of a deity, or whatever energy you want to put into the necklace."

"So, if I was making a mala for someone special, I could repeat 'I love you' with every knot?" he joked.

She gave James an appraising look. "Or you could think of something you love about someone with each knot. There are 108 beads in a mala. If you can come up with 108 reasons to love someone, you probably do."

For several hours they sat there, quietly knotting beads onto the cords, she leaning into him with guidance and assistance, he trying to wrap his fingers and his mind around the process and the concept. At first he was clumsy, his big fingers fumbling the beads and losing the thread, but eventually he caught on to the rhythm of it. It was really cool to see the mala taking shape—the colors, the patterns created. And the silent chanting of a mantra was a real challenge. But James began thinking why not—as Kat suggested—really make each of these into a "fashion accessory with significance"? Not just in some esoteric, religious way, like chanting a mantra, but in visualizing someone you'd loved. Take the hours of knotting to meditate over what had worked and what hadn't. He'd joked about chanting "I love you" as each bead was knotted, but why not actually do that? Or chant "I forgive you"? Or "I release you"? Or whatever? Maybe it could be an amazing way to process a past heartbreak. Like his relationship with Willow.

As they were cleaning up for dinner, with two new malas almost completed after three hours of laborious effort, James brought up the subject. "So, you think I could design a mala, choose stones that somehow, I don't know, represent someone, my relationship with that person, and sort of tie up that energy in the knots of the mala, so I can move on?"

Kat looked at him and grinned. "You mean Willow? Do it! Exorcise that demon bitch! Or honor her memory or whatever. And you can keep her mala and take it out and stare at it when you feel lonely, or I can sell it for you to some unsuspecting yoga chick and then she can deal with her!"

They both laughed at the idea of a haunted necklace adorning the neck of some poor tourist, and James suddenly felt a twinge of deep, but strangely melancholy, affection for Kat. She was so funny and smart and sassy. She hesitated a moment, and then reached into the box and pulled out another bag and showed it to him. It was an unfinished mala. There was lapis lazuli and labradorite, gold filigreed beads, a sea-green translucent stone that might have been chalcedony, and citrine.

"This is a love mala I'm making."

"Wow, that's gorgeous!" he said. "Who's that for?"

"Someone special."

"Oh? Who's the lucky fellow?" His jealousy was burning again.

"Never you mind," she said and stuffed it back in the box out of sight. "Time for dinner."

She dragged him out of the tent and up to the pavilion for a sunset buffet. They sat with some rowdy visitors from England who regaled them with witty British conversation and humor. They shared several bottles of white wine and laughed and sang and generally partied pretty hard.

A bit tipsy by the end of the meal, James and Kat bid the Brits goodnight and wandered down to the beach with a blanket over their shoulders. It was deserted and peaceful. Out over the ocean, the light from the quarter moon was just enough to frost the rolling swells and breaking waves with silver sparkles.

Still buzzed from the wine and the laughter, they spread out the blanket, and Kat lay down with her head on James's shoulder. They relaxed into the easy comfort of the soft sand beneath them, the dark sky above, and the gentle rhythm of the waves. Not for the first time, James visualized Grandmother Ocean as a giant living creature, with the waves as her breath, breathing out when they crashed on the beach, and breathing in as the water rushed back to itself. Above them, a myriad of stars filled the night sky, undimmed by any light leaking from nearby cities, a billion tiny pinpricks in the black fabric of space and time, a clandestine peek into realms impossibly far away, where the gods and goddesses danced their celestial dance.

Beneath that sparkling panoply, Kat and James sank into the easy flow of their interests and fascinations, just like always. They talked about auras and halos, chakras and energy meridians, and how similar concepts appeared in the medicine and spirituality of almost every culture. They talked about the phases of the moon and its effect on tides and women's bodies. And when the subject turned to love, she rolled over toward him, and he could see her face, glowing, inches from his. There was that inner light again.

"OK, lover boy. Spill it. Tell me about Willow. Did you love her?"

James squirmed uncomfortably. "I don't know. I think so. I guess."

"*I think so? I guess?* That's your first clue! If it was love, you wouldn't guess!"

"Well, we had this thing. It was so weird. We were drawn to each other like with some…magnetic force. It was so strange."

"So you were attracted to each other…blah, blah…still waiting for the *love* part."

"She called me her *soul brother.*"

"Maybe you were. Still not love."

"But how do you explain the attraction? I mean, it was like magic!"

"Did she choose you or the other guy?!"

"Fuck you. You already know she chose Dan!"

"That's my point! Thank you! She chose *him.* You had *attraction.* Woo hoo! It was powerful, and *you,* you were sick and lonely and vulnerable. She's beautiful, a real goddess. I get it, but did she love you? Did she *choose* you? No!"

"Nope. She didn't." James rolled over onto his back and looked up at the stars. He couldn't bear her sharp gaze directly into his truth. She lay beside him, her stare burning his ear.

"Still hurts though," James admitted to the stars.

She snuggled up to him, put her arm over his chest, and draped her leg over his pelvis. She nuzzled his ear. He expected sympathy. But this was Kat. He should have known better.

"Suck it up, buttercup," she whispered gently, almost purring. "Poor baby! Whining over a failed relationship! Makes me want to *puuuuuke!*"

She exploded with an awful gagging noise in his ear, like a cat coughing up a fur ball, and James pretended to push her away. Then they laughed and rolled into each other's arms and fell silent, except for their close, heavy breathing. He could see her eyes glinting with reflected starlight, looking deeply into him, questioning, challenging, waiting. *Take the lead, buttercup.*

His body buzzed with hyperawareness of her closeness. Her lips were right there, waiting to be kissed. Warmth was radiating off her body, inviting him in. Her cheek was soft and tender and already resting on his arm.

He—couldn't. He pulled her face into his chest to avoid kissing her and instead hugged her, because—hell—he really *had* come to visit as a friend, and last time he'd been the shitty bad boy, giving nothing, taking whatever he could get, and this—this felt different. He no longer had that same desperation, that fear. Instead, he wanted to not spoil—this.

They retreated back to safe topics like God and Truth and the entropy of the universe. They discussed black holes and the golden ratio of Euclid and nautilus shells. She introduced James to the names of Hindu deities who would pop up later in his life with great importance, Rama and Sita, Durga and Lakshmi. They talked for hours, anything to avoid acknowledging the giant elephant that had just walked into the room, the one the gods had painted with huge symbols that represented male and female energy—and sexual union, and love.

As the evening wore on, more stars became visible, and the moon drifted lower on the horizon. At some point James looked into her eyes again and saw desire smoldering in their depths. The elephant smacked him with his trunk. *C'mon, buttercup!*

OK. He kissed her gently on the lips. She kissed back, and this time it was her caution that prevailed. They did not kiss again. The elephant settled down, content to let them contemplate the information they'd just exchanged with the touch of lip on lip, to let it marinate, simmer, grow, mature—to come to fruition if it would. No need to hurry. They were still friends. But now there was an electric current buzzing continuously between them, and the information crackling along those pathways had nothing to do with friendship.

~~ *A Rude Guest* ~~

Love
is a rude guest.
She never asks permission
to knock
upon your door.

She just shows up,
uninvited.
At awkward moments,
inconvenient.

And if you do not make her welcome,
she will linger,
misbehaving.

Upsetting the furniture.
Writing on the walls.
Stealing all your wine.

Until finally,
when she has driven you mad,
you say,
"I see you,"
and she settles down,
smiling.

~~ * ~~

Chapter Ten

~ * ~

Midnight Blue Glass

Their days at Maho began to fall into a rhythm. They'd sleep next to each other every night in her tent, their bodies rolled together in the easy comfort of familiarity. And then in the morning Kat would head off to work, and James would swim and make malas for her inventory. She gave him a book on crystals and chakras and energy healing, and he waded through it, sometimes laughing, sometimes shaking his head, and sometimes nodding. In the afternoons, they'd tire themselves out with snorkeling and sailing trips, and yoga and hikes up the surrounding hills, anything to burn off the sexual tension that was building up. Intuitively, they were recalibrating their relationship, building something that ran deeper than desire, something subtle, but tremendously powerful in its subtlety. So powerful it had the potential to outlast any bodily craving, outstrip desire, survive passion. They were building trust.

One morning while Kat was working, James spread out a blanket under the trees on the beach and began to make Willow's mala. His connection to Willow was still a mystery. Pure chemistry and—not much else. Sparkles of her memory haunted the back of his mind, and he wanted her—respectfully—gone.

James started playing with beads, laying them out on a white towel so that he could see their colors and how they complemented one another. Eventually he chose

Amazonite for her sky eyes
Silver for the sound of her laughter
Carnelian for the first chakra, blood, life vitality
Lapis lazuli for deep blue magic
Citrine for the second chakra, sexual energy
Rose quartz for healing

The knotting took three hours, and he really tried to stay focused, chanting, "Thank you. I release you. Goodbye." At first he felt self-conscious, almost embarrassed, but he stuck with it. Ultimately, he ended up with a beautiful mala that he wouldn't sell to anyone. No, he would keep it, to remember the magic, honor what they'd had with a crystallized memory of connection, like a poem written with stone beads and knotted cord. James showed it to Kat.

"Very nice! How do you feel?" she asked.

"I don't know. Maybe a bit lighter. Like I let go of something, or it let go of me."

"Cool. So maybe you cleared away some space."

"Maybe."

That night, they went into Cruz Bay with the English to hit a few bars. They rode in the back of Mr. Fred's taxi truck, lurching around corners and swaying up switchbacks. James had been at Maho for nine days and was feeling stronger and well-rested. Their destination was a bar called Shiny's, a neon-lit dive in the back streets of Cruz

Bay, a couple of blocks from the harbor. It had live reggae music, cheap drinks, and local color. The place was so relaxed that you paid the bartender two dollars, and she would give you a plastic cup with ice, a small can of pineapple juice, and an open bottle of Mount Gay Rum. You mixed your own drinks, as strong as you liked.

They found a table near the entrance, away from the stage, and settled in—Kat, James, the three English guys, and their two English girlfriends. One of their women had stayed back at Maho, feeling a bit tired. The English were party animals and were on their way to getting drunk.

Someone started dancing, and soon the bar was hopping: skinny local guys in dreadlocks and gold chains dancing with island hotties in tight shorts and T-shirts sporting bizarre logos like "Island Cherry" and "Maximum Fun." One local came over to their table and sat down in an empty chair, like he owned the place. He was a young guy, maybe thirty, with a gold front tooth, dreads, and a huge smile.

"Welcome to my island!" he said, and then he saw Kat.

"Kat, my island love!" he crooned as he got up and hugged her. "My white chocolate mama!"

Kat hugged him back enthusiastically—called him "My licorice stick!"—and sat in his lap with her arm around his shoulder. James watched out of the corner of his eye to see if there was cause to be unreasonably jealous. They talked closely, her face inches from his, and at some point, he looked over at James, then back at her, and smiled. A few moments later, she got off his lap and came and sat back down with James.

The young guy, smiling, came over to them. He bent down so he could be heard over the noise and looked James in the eye. "This woman, she is special. You take very good care of her."

He patted James on his shoulder, gave a big grin, then walked over to a group of his friends who were leaning against the wall, laughing and watching the dancing and occasionally making some comment to the ladies on the floor.

"Who was that?" James asked.

"Oh, that's Shiny."

Ah, so he did own the place after all.

"Friend of yours, I take it?" The green-eyed monster had James by the neck and was ruffling his feathers.

"Very much so," Kat replied with a grin. "One of my best customers. He loves a good massage."

She saw his look and laughed. "What's your problem? You've been off in the arms of Miss Indecisive for the past few months! Think I've been just sitting around waiting for you?"

James forced a laugh. "No problem. Just curious."

She leaned in and whispered in his ear. "He's just a really good friend. Helped me out of a jam once in here with a drunk guy." She leaned back, watched for his reaction, and then added, "He's also a really good lover."

"Hey, that's cool," he mumbled.

No, it wasn't. But in a way, it was, too. Seeing her be desired by other men not only made him jealous. It made him want her more. And it made him really question *why* he felt that way. Was it his innate competitive streak? Or was it the cancer, and the way it made him want to cling to anything and anyone that seemed bright, joyful, and alive? Maybe. Or maybe it was the elephant of the gods, crowding into the room, all painted up and his ears flared out wide and his trunk pointing at James, insisting. James pushed it all away from his mind and drank a huge gulp of his rum drink.

The evening settled into a nice mellow vibe until a bit later, when some Aussies came in from one of the sailboats. They were in a fighting mood. The crowd had thinned out by then, and it was just the very drunk English, Kat and James, and a few of Shiny's friends. Suddenly out of nowhere the Aussies were shouting and breaking bottles and throwing punches. The English were useless, but Shiny and his guys were holding their own. One large Aussie had picked up a bottle and was about to bring it down on Shiny's head when

James took him down, driving him to the ground with a perfect wraparound tackle. The Aussie landed on his back on the concrete floor, and the fight went out of him. Another guy grabbed Kat by the hair, a mistake he paid for, and then Kat was dragging James off and shouting that they had to go.

She waved at Shiny as they ran out the front door, a police siren wailing down the street. Shiny just grinned and waved back, and then turned just in time to dodge a wild punch from an Aussie.

They ran down to the harbor where Mr. Fred had his taxi. Kat was laughing, but James was breathing so hard from the adrenaline that he was hyperventilating, and his hands hurt. He wasn't usually a fighter and typically would do anything to avoid violence, but not when it came to a woman. Especially his woman. Was Kat his woman? Tonight, the question that they'd been avoiding charged back into his awareness like those Aussies into the bar. James told himself it was a stupid question. She could not be "his" if he was not "hers."

Mr. Fred heard their story with stolid eyes. White people behaving badly. He'd seen it all before, so many times. Even though it was late, he agreed to drive them back to Maho. As they were pulling out of the parking lot, the English staggered up, the women supporting the men, who were so drunk they could barely walk. The ride back in the lurching, swaying bed of the taxi truck would be fun.

Sure enough, once the taxi got rolling around those switchbacks, it was a pukefest as the Brits blew lunch over the side, and Mr. Fred called back through the open partition, "Hey mon! Don't be spilling your innards on my seats!"

Kat and James huddled as far away as they could from the catastrophe that was unfolding around them, trying not to laugh but failing miserably. Oh, the humanity!

Back at the resort, they thanked Mr. Fred with an extra-large tip and saw the Brits off to their tents, helped by security. After the taxi ride, they both needed some fresh air, so they headed to the beach with their blanket. Down at the beach, the gods were throwing a party, too. They'd brought clouds of ghostly phosphorescent algae into the shoreline, and the waves were bigger than usual, crashing with explosions of blue and silver sparkles, blue from the glowing algae, silver from the light of the moon on wave tops and cresting water.

Other than the gods, they had the beach to themselves. They spread out the blanket in their favorite spot and sat down to take in the show. Kat sat next to James, her knee pressed against his thigh. After so many nights of sleeping wrapped around each other, their body contact felt normal, natural, but tonight there was more electricity than usual flowing between her bare skin and his.

Out beyond the waves, blue streaks of algae glowed in drifts that roughly paralleled the shore. Occasionally a fish would jump, and a fresh spot of dark water would glow, ripples of blue fire expanding outward from the splash. Above them, the stars burned an especially bright gold and silver and—if James looked hard enough and squinted a little—ruby red and flame orange.

"You see those stars?" asked Kat after a while, looking up.

"Yes." James was no longer looking at the stars. He was looking at the contours of her face, flashing ebony and ivory in the moonlight.

"Those stars exist because of the Divine Feminine," she continued.

"What's that?" James's eyes slowly caressed her throat in that shadowed place beneath her moonlit jaw. He wanted to kiss her there.

"The Divine Feminine is the power of Shakti, the feminine power of the universe."

"I thought Shakti was a condiment. Some sort of Indian spice, like curry powder." James was thinking back to the Arapahoe Yoga Ashram retreat, where Parvati had used the word *shakti* to describe the great flavor of the food.

Kat turned her face toward his, caught him smiling at her from inches away. "Dude, you're still drunk. Focus." Kat took his face in her hands and kissed him on the lips. He tried to kiss her back, but she pushed him away with a laugh. "Now that I have your attention, listen up, Grasshopper. This is important."

She settled back on the blanket. "The universe is created by the gods. The god Shiva represents male energy, raw power, potential. That raw power, that male energy can do nothing because it has no form, no focus, no direction. His consort, the goddess Shakti, represents female energy. She takes Shiva's energy and gives it form, design, structure. Everything you see around us, all the beauty in the natural world, the stars, the ocean, the birds, and their songs, all have form because of Shakti, the Divine Feminine. It is their dance, their union, that creates and changes the universe, keeps it dynamic, growing."

"They say behind every great man is a great woman," teased James.

Kat punched him on the arm, hard.

"Ow!"

"This is the twenty-first century. Shakti walks *beside* Shiva, not behind him! Equal partners!"

James rubbed his arm. Partners. He and Kat. It could happen, if they only let it.

Kat leaned over and kissed James on the cheek. She then stood up, pulled off her clothes, and he could see her naked flesh glowing silver in the moonlight. She looked down at him, a tombstone angel in a midnight churchyard, then turned and ran down to the water. Blue and silver sparks splashed around her legs as she waded in. Shakti incarnate, shaping his life, giving it form and function and beauty, if he let her.

It was an invitation James couldn't ignore. He tore off his clothes and ran after her and caught her just as she reached the breaking waves. She turned her face up to his, and he kissed her. Her soft, familiar warmth ignited his cool skin, and he pulled her closer as the waves crashed over them. She brought his face down to her breasts, then leaned back as he picked her up bodily. She wrapped her legs around his waist, and they made love in the surf as the sparkling black and silver and blue waves surged past them again and again. Salt water filled their eyes and their ears and their mouths as they kissed, and they choked and swallowed, but still they made love, until one giant wave knocked James off his feet and pushed them toward the shore. Laughing, they helped each other out of the water onto the wet sand, and there they finished their lovemaking with an unspoken urgency, as if their time together was running out like the last grains of an hourglass. And after their passion had passed, they lay there naked, entwined as one with the sea and the sand and the night sky.

~~ *A Lover Who Burns* ~~

Bring me a lover who burns.
Bring me a lover
whose body is consumed with red fire,
whose touch sets a bonfire in my veins,
whose skin turns to burning silk under my fingers,
whose hair curtains my face like smoky incense.

Bring me a lover
whose mind sparks blue fire,
whose wonder is as infinite as the universe,
whose curiosity flashes like summer lightning
over a sea of grass.

Bring me a lover
whose heart blazes with green fire,
who refines my imperfect attentions
into gold,
in the furnace of her love.

Bring me a lover
whose soul radiates white fire,
whose spirit leads mine to dance hand in hand
with gods and goddesses whirling,
like galaxies, in the night sky.

Bring me a lover who burns.

~~ * ~~

Chapter Eleven

~ * ~

Citrine

Over the next few days, they made love every night before sleeping. They made love every morning before their swim. And when she came back to the tent after working, they often just lay in each other's arms—naked, talking, breathing, feeling the currents of electricity flow between them in a cloud of spinning love particles sparking off each other in the eternal dance of creation and annihilation.

This time around, they concentrated on loving each other mindfully. And as the tides of passion ebbed and flowed through their bodies, the pages of the past were ripped one by one from the book of their history and scattered in the wind. They let it all go—the complications, the hurts, the jealousies, the feelings of unworthiness. They forgave each other. And even as they became lovers, they remained friends, able to say anything to each other.

"Show me your poetry," Kat demanded one morning.

"Why?" asked James.

"Because this is a new thing for you. Just curious what it's all about."

James took out his laptop, and scrolled through a few poems for her.

"I thought poetry was supposed to rhyme," she said. "I mean, this stuff is OK, but where's the rhyme? You know, 'Roses are red, violets are blue, blah, blah, blah.'"

"Are you mocking me?"

"Yes! C'mon, Shakespeare, show me what you got!"

"You want me to write you a poem that rhymes?"

"Can you? I don't think you can!"

"Gimme an hour!"

James sat down with his laptop while Kat grinned and made faces at him and worked on a mala. After an hour, he had something:

~~ *A Love Beyond All Limits* ~~

Declare your heart an outlaw,
a bandit without sanity.
A blasphemer of propriety,
make love to my deepest vanity.

Become an arsonist of passion,
a priestess of carnal sin.
A highwayman of desire,
set fire to my skin.

Ravage my raw emotions,
and unearth my greatest treasure.
Become a thief of reason.
Dig for my deepest pleasure.

Promise me forever,
and make me taste your tears.
Help me feel your longing,
pour honey in my ears.

Pillage my very soul,
and I will love you always.
A love beyond all limits
past the ending of my days.

~~ * ~~

"This is for you," James said as he turned the laptop so she could read it. Kat smiled as she read, and as James watched her face for reaction, he saw tears well up in her eyes.

"Hey, are you all right?" he asked.

Kat just turned and buried her face in his chest. She sobbed, long, hard sobs, clinging to him.

"Hey, lover girl," he soothed. "I'm gonna be all right. I'm gonna beat this cancer. You'll see. I plan on staying on this planet for a long time."

Kat nodded, but continued sobbing, her face buried in his chest.

* ~ * ~ *

One afternoon, they sat near each other on the beach in the wet, cooler sand above the receding waves. James was staring out at the far horizon, at the hazy line where the sky touched the ocean. Something about gazing into infinity, with an actual point upon which to focus, seemed to draw the toxicity out of his body. It became a meditation. His breath slowed, as did his heart rate. He could feel years of stress flow out of his eyes and onto that vista, to be swallowed by the misty distance while his ears were caressed by the gentle rhythm of lapping waves. He could have sat there for hours.

"Hey, I'm done," Kat said. "What do you think?"

James looked over at what she was doing. They had collected bits of shiny emerald-green sea glass from broken beer bottles, and Kat had created a simple design in the sand that looked like this:

The symbol was glowing in the sun, the tiny shards of green glass standing out against the speckled background of black and tan and white sand. It seemed to resonate in some way with his mental state.

"Umm, that's beautiful," he said. "I've seen that symbol on T-shirts and such."

"It's the Sanskrit symbol for the word *om*." Kat looked at him funny. "Never heard of it?"

"Sure I have. I just don't read and write Sanskrit."

Apparently, the gods do. In later years, James would see that symbol again and again, and each time he would remember her sea glass *om* as it caught the afternoon light and glowed with an inner green fire. It burned into his mind, a mandala for meditation, a reminder of the peace and serenity that resides at the center of all creation. A gift of memory from Kat and a symbol for all that is right in this world.

His last night in Maho, they sat at the pavilion with a bottle of wine and watched the sun go down. A sailboat on the horizon made for a perfect postcard sunset, and they toasted each other.

"To my skinny, cancer-ridden best friend," she said. "May he rise above this temporary health challenge."

"To my best friend and lover, a woman who burns with a secret fire," James countered. They clicked glasses and drank.

"I wish I didn't have to go," James said. "My kids miss me, and I suppose so does my business partner."

Kat smiled. "Maybe I can come visit. I love your kids. They're both so smart and adorable!"

They spent most of that night face to face, whispering secrets in the dark and feeling the silken heat of each other's skin beneath the simple cotton covers of her bed. They talked of life and love, of poetry and promises. They kissed each other more than 108 times and woke up with the dawn, having slept reluctantly, unwilling to give any hours of their time to dreams.

At the airport, James looked at Kat in the morning sun, trying to memorize every curve of her face, every wisp of her hair. If anything, she seemed more beautiful than the day he'd arrived on St. Thomas and first saw the inner light glowing from her luminous self. That light was stronger now, but was her face a bit thinner? There were new lines and shadows around her eyes, but they'd been up most of the night. He probably looked a bit worn himself. In any event, she was gorgeous, and James would miss looking at her, locking eyes, and having her read his thoughts.

~~*

James flew home to Colorado, they spoke every day for a week, and she promised that she would look into plane tickets. Then one night, she gave him the bad news. She had to fly home to Kansas City, to see her sister, Mary Ellen, who had been diagnosed with terminal cancer and was failing. James was disappointed, but as someone who was fighting cancer himself, he understood the value of being surrounded by love and support.

Kat flew to Kansas City the next day, and when they spoke, she told him that she would be staying there for a few weeks to help care for her sister. They spoke for hours into the dark of night, just as if they were lying in the same bed. He went to sleep with a smile on his face, knowing that somewhere in the world his woman was thinking of him at the same time.

Several more days went by, and James came home from a run. He called Kat to see how she was doing with her caregiving. "Hey, sweetness. How's your sister?"

Kat sounded tired. "She's not doing very well. A lot of pain, can't sleep… ."

"Oh, baby girl, I'm sorry. I hope you're doing OK. You're a hero to be taking such good care of her."

"Well, we're family. That's what we do."

"Can I come see you? Maybe help out in some way? I really miss you!"

"I miss you too, lover. But no, it'd be better if you didn't come. This isn't really the right time. I need to focus on her."

James was disappointed, but he understood. Kat had such a good heart. She needed to do everything she could to help her sister, and he would just be a distraction.

For the next three weeks they talked almost every day. Sometimes she sounded good. Other times she was obviously exhausted from the twenty-four-hour care she was giving. In the meantime, he continued to work on himself. He was running regularly again—through the clear, cool Colorado mornings on the Bobolink Trail—with Rocco as pacesetter and coach. He was lifting weights and drinking protein smoothies, building muscle. And he was taking a few beginner yoga classes at a studio downtown. James attacked his alternative medicine sessions with renewed hope, and life was good. Well, not perfect, because he didn't get to see Kat at all, and he missed her.

The kids enjoyed his more positive outlook on life, too. His kids always knew pretty much which way the wind was blowing, and it affected them. They had fun outings to Pearl Street to see the jugglers and contortionists on the mall. They bought ice cream at Ben and Jerry's. They went to their favorite sushi restaurant, Sushi Zanmai, where the raucous guys behind the sushi bar would yell something that sounded like "*Ee-o Soi!*" in unison every time someone came into the restaurant, and the owner would come out and play "Happy Birthday" on his electric saxophone whenever someone had a birthday. Chris hated vegetables and fish and would eat only white rice and yakiniku beef, and Annie was already a vegetarian, so she would only eat veggie sushi, but it was their favorite restaurant. James ate everything, and lots of it, and was gaining weight. He was back up to 180 pounds and feeling good.

Then one night, he tried calling Kat before bed, as was their custom. No answer. He left a message, thinking she was probably busy with her sister, who seemed to be declining rapidly, expecting that she would call him back later. But he didn't hear back that night, or the next, or the next. Something bad had happened. James was sure of it. Maybe her sister had died, and she was deep in mourning or busy with arrangements. On the fourth night, he called again, and someone finally picked up.

"Hello?" said an unfamiliar female voice.

"Uh, hi, I'm trying to reach Kat Rogers. Did I misdial?"

There was silence on the other end of the line. Then the voice said, "Is this James Wilder?"

"Yes, this is James. Who's this?"

"I'm her sister, Mary Ellen."

James felt a shock go through his body. "Where's Kat?"

"James, I'm so sorry, but Kat passed away yesterday."

The room spun as galaxies shattered and exploded and came crashing down around him, skewering his soul with their splinters. "Whaaat?" he croaked, his voice barely audible.

"She passed away. She was very sick. You knew that, didn't you?" James went blind for a moment, as understanding flooded his brain with impossible data. Kat had been the sick sister, not Mary Ellen! Kat had gone home to be with her family, to die in their arms, not his. She had lied to him. *But why????*

"I'm so sorry, James. I thought you knew. She's been dealing with an aggressive blood cancer for months—was diagnosed six months ago. She'd been doing really well, down in the sunshine and the sea. We thought she was beating it. She looked so good, but then, suddenly, it just didn't work."

She went on with more details, but by then he'd gone deaf. Kat was gone. After an appropriate time listening without hearing, James thanked her and was about to hang up when she added, "She left you a letter. I mailed it to you yesterday."

After James hung up, he called Elizabeth and asked if he could bring the kids over to her house for the night. She said yes, and he calmly packed them up. They knew something was up and that it wasn't good.

"Daddy, are you OK?" asked Annie. "Did Kat's sister die?"

James bit his lip and shook his head, unable to speak. Chris and Annie exchanged glances. It was really bad, and they felt it.

James dropped them off at Elizabeth's house, went home, and closed the door. He stood in the middle of the living room, every muscle as tense as his balled fists, as the walls closed in on him, the pressure built inside his head, and the roof collapsed. Then he cursed the gods, those pricks who had fucked him, again.

"Why Kat, you motherfuckers, why?" he screamed, his knuckles as white as his face.

Rocco jumped off his bed, looking at James with alarm. Cursing the gods wasn't enough, so James started to break stuff. He smashed a lamp, picked it up and threw it down on his coffee table. Rocco scrambled away, barking with alarm. He grabbed a vase full of yellow flowers and hurled it at the fireplace. It exploded in a starburst of water and ceramic shards and flower petals. Rocco raced around the room, growling and barking wildly at whatever it was that was attacking. James grabbed a picture off the wall and flung it across the room, where it buried itself in the drywall. Rocco yelped and ran upstairs to hide.

"Fuuuuuck yooooooooou!" he shouted, his eyeballs popping out of his head. He picked up the next nearest thing at hand, a book off the coffee table, a star guide to the constellations, and was about to rip the pages out of it when he saw one of the yellow flowers at his feet, still perfect, dripping from the water that had flown everywhere. And suddenly he heard Kat's soft voice in his ear, as if in echo from a place long ago, "Suck it up, buttercup!"

James stopped in his tracks and saw her face in his memory, smiling, heard her whisper in her most suggestive voice in his ear, "Weakness doesn't get you between my legs, lover boy."

He dropped the book, sagged slowly to his knees, and sobbed as the depth of his loss drove a stake through his heart. Rocco found James there and crawled up to him, whimpering and whining. James cradled Rocco's trembling body as he rocked back and forth, and Rocco alternately licked the salty tears off James's face and howled.

The next day James flew out to her funeral in Kansas City. Her sister, Mary Ellen, looked like a younger version of Kat, dressed in black. They hugged, and he laid a wreath of yellow flowers on her grave. Then he came home to a misty, unusually cold Colorado.

Waiting for him was Kat's letter. It was inside a plain white envelope addressed by someone else's hand. With it was a small package wrapped in brown paper, addressed to him in her own beautiful writing. He sat on the couch, took a deep breath, and opened the letter first.

Dear James,

Don't you hate it when a letter starts that way? Never a good thing. Oh well. If you are reading this, then you know that I'm gone. It's hard for me to write that, because I guess I haven't come to grips yet with my own mortality. Sort of like knowing that the picture that everyone will see at my funeral has already been taken. Sorry, I ramble.

Lover boy, I miss you terribly, and I'm sorry

I lied to you. But I know who you are, how hard you would take this, and I guess I didn't want to cause you pain until there was no alternative. Or maybe I just chickened out. And somehow, telling you I was sick would seem like I was trying to compete with you for who was the sickest, who had the worst cancer, or whatever. See, I'm way off track again, and I'm getting tired.

Sweetheart, I'm going to die. You won't see me till it's over. I know you'll be in pain. But please know that I'm thinking of you, right now, as I write this. And I promise I'll always haunt you somehow, maybe in your dreams, maybe in your nightmares, haha! Who knows? Just remember that I loved you, I love you, and will always love you 108 ways, and maybe we'll meet again, somewhere. You're an amazing, interesting, complicated man, and I'm grateful for the times we spent together. And as for getting over me, I know you will. So suck it up, buttercup. But please miss me a little, anyway.

All my love,
Kat

James opened the package next, barely able to see through his tears. Inside was a simple, small box wrapped in the dried leaf of some tropical plant. It was tied with raffia. He unwrapped and opened the box. He felt, more than saw, the smooth beads of a mala inside. He took it out. There was lapis lazuli and gold filigree. There was sea-green chalcedony and gray labradorite with blue sparkles. There was yellow citrine. There was a knot between each bead, tied by a woman who had thought of a unique way she loved him with each knot. And there was a single red gem, a ruby maybe, a secret bead at the back of the necklace that no one would ever see, hidden by hair or collar, but that would always be there to remind him that she loved him every time he looked at it.

The sun did not show its face, and it rained for three days, as the gods finally broke their silence and mixed their tears with his.

Chapter Twelve

~ * ~

Sunstone

That winter James took his kids down to Maho Bay, and they stayed at the eco-resort where Kat and he had spent those glorious days. They didn't stay in the same tent. That had been assigned to the new massage therapist who arrived to replace Kat shortly after she left for home.

The kids loved Maho Bay, the beautiful beach at Little Maho, the fish and the reefs, the ice creams in the afternoons at the snack bar, and the lizards that wrestled in the tree branches and sometimes fell with a loud plop onto the wooden walkways in front of them. Over the years, they would return during spring break or Christmas. It became their favorite place to go.

For James, St. John would always be more than special. It was here that Grandmother Ocean had sent him the manta ray as a messenger of goodwill. It was here that Kat had given him several more pieces of life's puzzle, along with her mind, her heart, and her body. It was here that he had entered the water on that first time back with his kids and said his usual prayer of thanksgiving to Grandmother Ocean while he released a wreath of yellow flowers to float on the waters, a memorial and an offering to the spirit of Kat.

Annie and Chris were with James when he placed the flowers on the water. They knew it was important to him, and he wanted them to understand that it was OK to mourn the passing of a loved one. As they waded back out of the water, Annie turned her tearstained face up to his and said, "Daddy, I never told you this, but I liked Kat more than all of your other girlfriends. She was pretty cool. And you were always the happiest with her."

James picked up his little girl and buried his face in her shoulder, his tears mingling with hers. *Thank god for my kids,* he breathed.

That afternoon, he spread out a blanket on the beach where Kat and he had lain many nights discussing the stars. The kids ran off to frolic in the water, and he put down a white towel and began making her mala. He'd wandered through shops in Boulder seeking just the right beads, and finally he'd found them.

Blue sea glass for the pale waters of the Caribbean
Moonstone for her inner light
Green sea glass for the fourth chakra, the heart chakra
Midnight-blue glass for magic phosphorescence
Citrine for yellow buttercups and second chakra energy
Sunstone glass for beach sand and sunshine

Every one of these beads glowed with inner light, and that to him captured the essence of Kat. As James knotted the beads onto the cord, he thought of 108 ways that he loved her, missed her, and was grateful to her, and he watered each knot with his tears.

James would return often to Maho Bay over the years, to place a wreath of yellow flowers in her memory and to lie on the beach at night searching for her face among the stars. Kat was transcendent, a friend who'd brought him wisdom and humor, tenderness and passion. All values he hoped without hope to find again someday, in another lover. And she was right. James would eventually get over her. And he would always miss her, a little.

~~ *Remember This* ~~

Someday our sun will die,
and all our stars will fade.
Remember this, and love anyway.

Someday our moon will fall from the sky,
and sink into an ocean of darkness,
and the sparkle of joy that we see
gazing into each other's eyes,
will dim with our dying vision.
Remember this, and love anyway.

Someday the songs we have sung
will disappear into echoes,
the poems we have written
will scatter on the wind,
the love we have made
will wash away from this earth
like flowers petals in a spring rain.
Remember this, and love anyway.

In the eternal dance of lovers,
of Shiva and Shakti,
shifting between creation and destruction,
form dissolves into formlessness,

all that is solid becomes liquid,
all that is liquid becomes air,
all that is air becomes empty space,
and empty space
becomes the slumber of gods.
Remember this, and love anyway.

~~ * ~~

The Third Mala

A Mirror Image, but Don't Be Fooled

~~ **This Exploration of Beauty** ~~

"I'm swearing off love,"
I vowed to the darkness.
"I can't stand the heartache,
and misery,
and pain of great loss."

So I rose from my bed,
and departed the dreamscape,
seeking answers to questions
that needed solving
before morning.

And at the edge of a seashore
I found Hafiz singing
an intricate melody that perfumed the moon,
and kissed it goodnight
as it sank past infinity
at the edge of the world.

And as stars emerged into brightness
to light wave tops and shoreline,
I settled beside him
and took in the breathing
of waves on the sand.

"I'm lost," I admitted.
"Can't find solace in slumber.
Love's puzzle just plagues me.
Keeps me riddled with doubt."

Hafiz only laughed
and pressed a shell to my ear,
and as I listened, I heard
voices scattered, like driftwood,
over beaches of centuries.

"You think that your head
gets to choose what you feel?
Your heart is your empress,
and love's no democracy.

Be grateful that hearts
rule like mystics and gypsies,
follow feelings and urges,
their motives a mystery.

For love is the magic
that changes music to rubies,
weaves silver through poems,
and sets fire to dreams.

Your job in this life
is to feel your humanity,
and so become close
to your maker's divinity.

That's why this affliction,
this exploration of beauty,
this so-human condition
you call love, is divine."

Out over the ocean,
the clouds drifted in starlight,
and my heart slowed its beating
to rhyme with the waves.

～ * ～

Chapter Thirteen

~ * ~

Red Coral

After Kat passed away, James wanted to turn his skin inside out so that he couldn't feel anything. He wanted to contract into a little ball, with as little surface area touching the world as possible. He went to work, because he had to, and he avoided his few friends, because he couldn't think of anything to say to any of them. They'd call and leave messages, and he didn't call back. He was only able to open a crack when Annie and Chris were with him, and sometimes he sat in their rooms after the bedtime story until they fell asleep, and then he'd weep silently, the tiny opening in his heart allowing just enough pain to leak out so that he didn't explode.

When the kids were with Elizabeth, he tried everything he could to stay numb. He watched TV and old movies, anything to kill the hours between waking and sleeping. Rocco was his only comfort, and he would stare at James with that pure, worried look that only a dog can give.

James quit reading poetry. Didn't want the opening that deep poetry would bring. He quit writing poetry. He quit his healing sessions with Theresa and the acupuncturist and Mary Two Bears. He quit it all because it was all about looking inward—feeling his feelings, touching his spirit—and all that had turned to pain.

Coincident with his loss of faith, his blood tests went bad, and the line he'd been holding against the cancer began to fail. His oncologist was very concerned and urged him to consider some radical new conventional treatments. There'd been advances made with both surgery and radiation, and he'd found a program that specialized in prostate cancer. The program boasted an 85 percent success rate and a very low incidence of impotence and incontinence as side effects. James parked the kids with Elizabeth, who was very sympathetic. "Honey, you need to do this," she said, using language that had been banished from their relationship. But she knew him so well and was alarmed by how pale and gaunt he looked, how hopeless and lifeless his eyes had become. James went in for treatment. The whole process took about ten weeks, with the first week being surgery to implant pellets of radioactive iodine in his prostate, followed by three weeks of recovery, then seven weeks of daily blasts of radiation.

At first, when he was lying there being irradiated, he could feel the X-rays passing through his body. He was amazed. He'd had plenty of X-rays before but never felt anything. Yet this time, if he really paid attention, he felt them like a gentle wind blowing through his tissues. And then, after a few treatments, he felt nothing. Why? What possible reason could there be for him to feel the X-rays and then not feel them? He knew he wasn't imagining it—he could close his eyes and tell exactly where the machine was pointing, so his scientifically trained, rational mind had to accept that it was fact.

James wished he could talk to Kat. He imagined the conversation. He would say, "Hey lover girl, there's this really weird thing going on. I can actually feel the X-rays going through me!"

And she would say, "That's because you're in tune with your spiritual body, bro. It's pure energy; it feels the X-rays."

And he would say, "But how is that possible? I've had X-rays before but never felt them."

Kat would look at him with sympathy, as if pitying his slowness, and say, "Dude, remember when you were meditating, and those three jewels smacked you right between your eyes? That's your sixth chakra, what the Hindus call your third eye. You got an upgrade to your wiring."

"Um, OK, so why did it go away? Why don't I feel them anymore?"

"Well, the X-rays are basically carpet bombing your spiritual body with highly energetic nuclear particles, shredding it."

At least that's what he imagined Kat would have said, along with teasing him about his scientific hesitation to believe her. But maybe the gods did hate radiation. If so, no wonder, then, that they went silent, and he settled into an existence that became grayer and grayer.

For a year, the radiation left him more fatigued than ever. It filled his core like a huge pool of black, stagnant sewer water. Some days he could barely get out of bed, and even walking seemed a chore. The worst was having to pee, however. Every time James went to the bathroom, he knew what was coming. A sharp burning in his urethra as his urine came into contact with places where radiation had burned tissue. And ejaculation was out of the question. James found himself sleeping at odd hours of the day and lying awake in the dead of night as he slowly recovered from the disease and the treatment.

At the same time, the economy went into the Great Recession of 2008-2009, and demand for new housing in Boulder dried up. Wilder and Klein laid off half their workforce, and there was less for James to do. Even so, his work schedule remained flexible, and sometimes he'd be at the office when no one else was around, surrounded by ghostly cubicles and darkness. Eliu gave James plenty of space, given what he was dealing with, and James somehow pulled his own weight.

Theresa stopped by his house one day, when James was outside, looking at his dying grass, and wondering if it was worth it to even cut its scrubby tufts.

"James, I've come to say goodbye," she said.

"Where are you going?" he asked.

"Home to El Salvador. With this economy, things are bad there, too, and I have my children and grandchildren to think of."

"You can't bring them here?"

"No, immigration is so hard," she replied, her face showing a sadness he'd never seen. "I have to go there, help if I can."

"I'm going to miss you! Your sessions have meant so much to me."

Theresa smiled, patted his cheek. "You're going to be fine, James. I see it. Just keep writing poetry." She gave him a hug, and he never saw her again, but over the years, as he read about the disintegration of her once-beautiful little country, he'd imagine her with her family, and hoped she was OK.

In those challenging days, James focused on his own family, too. He went to Chris's soccer games and Annie's theater productions, and Rocco got him out of the house to walk the Bobolink. And even his relationship with Elizabeth improved. Some weekends she sent home-baked bread and salads with the kids when they came over for their time with him.

And time passed.

One Saturday morning he was doing some overdue dusting of his bookshelves, and his favorite book of Sufi poetry caught his eye. Poems by Rumi and Hafiz, and many others. James opened it for the first time in months, and the beauty on the pages sent waves of longing through him. He could feel his chest cracking open as grief and loneliness and despair oozed out like lava flowing down the side of a Hawaiian volcano. Salty tears singed his cheeks, and he wondered how many more of his days and nights would be spent alone. James needed a shift, a new attitude, new friends, and new energy in his life.

That afternoon, he wandered downtown to The Yoga Studio and took his first yoga class since Kat passed away, taught by a guy whose torso was covered with tattoos. James was wearing an old pair of running shorts and a cotton T-shirt, and he rolled out his rented mat at the back of the room. There were about thirty other students in the class, mostly young and female with a sprinkling of middle-aged women and men. The class participants started in a seated, cross-legged position on their mats as Steven, the teacher, said a few words about mindfulness. Then, just as James's knees were starting to scream, the dharma talk ended, and everyone began to move to Steven's cues and instruction.

"Move like you're flowing through honey," he urged, "slowly and mindfully."

The class lasted an hour, and by the end James felt as if all the channels in his body had opened up and his blood was circulating out to his farthest extremities in a slow, unimpeded current. For the first time in a long time, James found peace, so he started going to several classes a week. Yoga gradually became a lifeline, a connection to a world of kind people and positive vibes.

His yoga teachers spoke often of the serenity that meditating could bring, and James decided to give it another try. He and Annie went downtown to a store that sold Tibetan art, brass singing bowls, and religious items, and remembering Kat's makeshift altar, he picked out a small statue of Ganesha, Remover of Obstacles, carved from hibiscus wood. Back home, they put Ganesha on a little Chinese table under the west-facing window in his bedroom. James added Kat's mala and some flowers, and Annie contributed a few of her favorite seashells.

"Daddy, these will help you remember Kat," she said, and hugged him. James began a practice of meditating in front of his little altar for twenty minutes every morning.

And some more time passed.

One good thing about the passage of time is that things can

change, even when you're not paying attention. James had woken up every morning for seven years, each time remembering, "Oh, shit! I have cancer." One forgets while sleeping, so every morning it was like getting the bad news all over again. But after several years of good blood tests, James finally started to believe in a future. It was the summer of 2012, four years after the death of Kat. Business had improved, and Wilder and Klein Custom Builders were back to full strength, building new houses and remodeling old ones.

James hired an architect to design all the structural remodeling projects his house needed, and Wilder and Klein carried out the work. They replaced his roof, installed skylights over the master bedroom and bathroom, covered the exterior of the house with tan stucco, and added a screened-in, covered porch facing west. It was unusually hot that summer, the hottest on record, and Annie and Chris brought coolers of iced drinks out to the workers, who were all Latino and who smiled and said *"gracias!"* at the gesture. Even though they were technically his employees, James was amazed at how hard the guys worked, toiling under the hot sun, tough, focused, efficient. The kitchen and bathrooms still needed to be done, but that would have to wait for another day.

During his weekends, he personally tore out the dying grass in the front yard and put in a Zen garden with interesting rocks and a wide, gravel pathway. He found a small stone Japanese *hoto*, or "jewel stupa," in an antique store, and he strategically placed it so that it looked different from various angles around the garden. He planted some low, mounding evergreen shrubs and clumps of spiky grass, and he planted seven trees, the surest sign of optimism. It felt good to be outside, sweating, digging through the hard earth with a pick, and then, when it was soft, kneeling and mixing in rich, organic matter with his hands. People passing by began to stop outside his house to admire the garden and the clean, modern vibe of his property.

His forty-fourth birthday came that summer, a reminder that his days were spilling through his fingers like dry sand. Annie had blossomed into a beautiful young woman just finding her path at sixteen and Chris was a budding athlete at twelve. For his birthday, James took the kids camping, high up in the mountains above Boulder, to an area just below the tree line where there was a lake. They pitched a tent, laid out their sleeping bags, and made a fire in the fire ring. That night, as they sat around the campfire, laughing and telling ghost stories and roasting marshmallows, James felt a sense of peace and completion that had escaped him for years. And after the kids turned in, he remained sitting outside, watching the night sky. Taking in what Kat had called the Divine Feminine. It was all there in the sparkle of the stars and the cool, peaceful sighing of the pines and his two beautiful, loving kids asleep in their bags. It was there in the slow, steady flow of life in his veins and the graceful goodness that enfolded him at that moment. Everything he could see and hear and feel, it was all the goddess Shakti, bringing beauty and order and grace to the Universe. Life was good again, with color and vitality and a strong, positive flow.

On the wall of his bedroom, James had a poster-sized photo of himself taken during the Boulder Peak Triathlon ten years earlier, when he'd first moved to Colorado. The photographer had caught him careening around a corner on his bike, standing on his pedals, his mouth open and leaning forward like he was sprinting for the finish line. The number 224 was clearly visible on his racing bib and on his helmet, and it was written in magic marker on his arms. He'd actually been training to do the Boulder Peak for a second time two years later when a random blood test turned up the cancer.

Now, seven years after that diagnosis, James decided to sign up for the Boulder Peak for a third time, to prove to himself that he was back. He started running, hit the gym for weights and swimming, and cycled for hours up the hills around Boulder. Between the yoga and his training regimen, James felt more fully in his body than ever. One glorious morning, when he and Rocco were three miles into a run on the Bobolink, he knew he was finally back. Gliding down the path in the summer sun, the soft breeze kissing his naked chest, his heart was beating smoothly, and his breathing was rhythmic. It was no longer a struggle. It was liberation, an open-eyed, moving meditation, and his life force flowed joyfully through his veins.

Two days before the race, James went into town to pick up his race packet. The sun was shining, and it was a crystal clear September afternoon. James showed his ID, selected his official race shirt, and walked out to the car. Absentmindedly, he opened the big manila envelope with the race materials and slid out his bib. It was number 224!

Coincidence? Perhaps. There were about two thousand bib numbers issued, so the chance that it happened randomly had the same odds as a two-thousand-year flood hitting Boulder that summer. But given how much the gods loved to fuck with him, James knew they were sending a message. They didn't want him to think they'd forgotten him. No sir, they were back. And magic was coming his way.

On the morning of the race, James arrived at the Boulder Reservoir just as dawn was breaking and checked in. He parked his bike on the rack in the transition area, laid out his gear, and went for body marking. When he got back, the spot next to him had been filled. Number 225 was a tall, athletic woman with short-cropped, blonde hair.

James immediately thought she might be a former Olympic swimmer or a volleyball player, which was quite possible given Boulder's status as a mecca for world-class athletes. She had a tanned and healthy face with high cheekbones and open blue eyes that seemed to look out to far horizons. Obviously, someone who spent most of her time outdoors. She had surgical scars on her right knee, probably an old ACL or some such athletic injury, and her left elbow and upper leg had fresh reddish streaks of "road rash" where she'd clearly lost skin against pavement. Like him, she had her number scrawled on her shoulders, and her age, "42," printed on her left calf.

"Nice morning for a race," James said as he smiled at her.

"Yeah, it's gonna be perfect," she replied.

Face to face, she was only a couple of inches shorter than him and, like him, she was dressed in a racing singlet and shorts. Suddenly, he had the distinct impression of looking into a mirror and seeing a female version of himself.

James nodded at her recent wounds. "What happened?" he asked.

She looked down and chuckled dismissively. "Training ride last Tuesday, up Sunshine Canyon. Some asshole in a pickup tried to run me off the road."

"Looks like he succeeded."

"Nah. I slid out on purpose to avoid him."

"No shit?" James knew what she was talking about. Rednecks in pickup trucks didn't mix well with spandex-clad cyclists riding expensive bikes. He'd been lucky. Only shouted curses, gunned engines, and other threats. No one had blatantly tried to kill him yet.

As two thousand other triathletes settled in around them, James and the blonde athlete compared running shoes, admired each other's bikes, and agreed on how much they were looking forward to the beer after the race. The triathlon was scheduled to go off in waves based upon sex and age group. She was in an earlier wave, so when her turn came, James walked down to the beach with her, wished her luck, and watched her disappear into the maelstrom of flailing arms and legs at the gun. There was something incredibly attractive about her: her appearance; her body language; the vibe she gave off of someone who never backed down from a challenge. Yeah. He grinned, and hoped he'd see her at the finish.

When his wave was called, he claimed a spot at the front edge of the mob. As a strong swimmer, he wanted to get out ahead and swim in clean, not choppy, water. He cruised through the one-mile, open-water swim, hammered the twenty-seven-mile bike ride, and held on to stagger home in the six-mile run. Total elapsed time, three hours and four minutes. Not bad. The boy was back! Blissfully tired and exhilarated, James wandered up to the beer tent and stood in line for his beer.

"Hey, 224, how'd it go?"

He turned, and it was her, looking sweaty and radiant.

"Awesome, 225, awesome," he replied. "Three hours, four minutes. You?"

"Call me Charlie." She held out her hand. "Choked a bit on the run," she continued. "Did three hours, three minutes, and 47 seconds." And then she smiled a smile that said, "Kicked your ass, Chump!"

"Damn! Knew I shouldn't have stopped for that second banana!" James grinned back, impressed. James and Charlie drank their beers and lingered, chatting about life. Her real name was Charlotte, but she'd trimmed off the frills like she'd trimmed off her hair because the name Charlotte struck her as too complicated, too formal, like a fussy old aunt who always buttoned her blouse up to her throat. Charlie was the equal of any man when it came to doing the stuff that her men liked: rafting, cycling, running, triathlons, rock climbing, hiking. And she did it all, not as the cute, weak girlfriend, but as the equal partner, and often leader of the expedition. James had never met anyone like her.

They made their way back to the transition area, and as they packed up their gear, joking and chatting, James learned that she was recently divorced and headed to something the following Wednesday night called the Rebounders Seminar. This was a seminar designed for people recovering from a breakup, a divorce, or some other loss. James decided on the spur of the moment to go, knowing he could use some help with relationships, and besides, Charlie....

Chapter Fourteen

~ * ~

Carnelian

The first night of the Rebounders Seminar was orientation and getting to know one another. And the rules. The first rule was that there would be no dating between participants until the program was over. When Charlie walked into that first meeting, many of the guys vowed to break that rule. James waved at her, but she was surrounded by people and seemed to be enjoying herself, so he chatted with a few of the other participants. It was apparent that a lot of folks were really struggling.

There was Deirdre, a young woman in her thirties who clutched a photo album to her chest and obsessed over her perfect wedding, wondering how it had all gone so wrong. And Giuseppe, a pudgy, balding little guy who couldn't stop weeping at the slightest provocation. There was Doris, a sixty-year-old wife of a preacher who'd been married for forty-two years and was dumped for a parishioner. And Ed, a software engineer who, well, for all James could tell, bored his wife into leaving. What they all had in common was fresh personal devastation.

That first night was all about introductions and helping people adjust to the fact that they would be talking about their losses, fears, anger, and loneliness. Debra, the facilitator, assured them that by the end of the ten-week program everyone would feel like a new person and that the journey would be worth it. The seminar would meet weekly, usually at someone's house. The classes would take place in the evenings and always include a potluck dinner.

To get things started, James volunteered his home for week number two. He cleaned the place up, the kids were with Elizabeth, and he was ready for twenty-four guests. For the potluck, James provided the "divorce chicken." A friend of his had described "divorce chicken" like this:

"Divorce chicken is a roasted chicken that costs about nine bucks and tastes vaguely like it was cooked by someone who gave a shit, like your mom or your wife before she left your sorry ass. And if you were broke or just being careful, you could get two or three meals out of one, unless you were depressed and eating to appease your loneliness, in which case you ate the whole thing."

There'd been plenty of nights when James ate the whole thing, as well as a pint of Ben and Jerry's. Tonight, as his contribution, he'd bought three.

James piled a healthy heaping of coleslaw, potato salad, and chicken onto his plate and went to sit on the screened-in porch. Even though it was early September, the evenings were still warm enough to eat outside. The porch was popular, but he got lucky and found a spot next to Charlie anyway.

"Yo. Good chicken," she said, a conversation starter that only a Rebounder could appreciate.

"Thanks. Slaved for hours." James smiled his biggest fake smile.

"Sure you did. And I love the plastic boxes you served it in. The ones that say Original Roasted Chicken. $8.99."

"Yeah. Nothing but class. That's me." Rocco had followed James out from the kitchen, and now his face was relaxed into a toothy grin of ecstasy as Charlie scratched him behind the ears. She looked up at James and smiled, and he noticed that her lips were natural, no lipstick, maybe just a hint of lip gloss.

"By the way, I love your house. All the color on the walls!"

"Thanks. Not finished yet. Still have the upstairs—"

"And the fossils and minerals. What's up with that?"

James took a swig of his beer. "My undergrad degree. Geology. I've always loved science, the natural world."

"Me too!" she said. "I took a lot of geology courses right here at CU. My degree's in English, but I loved science."

"So, you've been in Colorado for a while?" he asked. "Where're you from originally?"

"Back East, but I always wanted to live in the mountains. Boulder's perfect!"

They fell silent as they both concentrated on eating, and then James waded back in. "What do you do for a living?" he asked.

"I've got an MBA and work for a local private equity firm."

"Yeah? I got an MBA, too. Spent ten years in the Big Apple, a different life, really. But since we moved back to Colorado, I've been in residential construction."

"That seems like a big shift." She took a sip of her beer.

"Long story. I worked on a trading desk, even did a year in London. In a way, it was great, but not really my thing. And we were struggling, with the hours and the stress and the expense—"

Charlie just nodded sympathetically.

"Anyway, we were having problems, so we moved out here to Colorado. We got divorced, I found a job with a builder, and the rest is history. What about you?"

"Fell in love with a Frenchman. Senior year in college. I figured there was a better chance at an international job with an MBA."

"Did you go? To France?"

"Nah. Turns out I wasn't invited." She fell silent.

"Huh," was all James said.

"I saw the bikes in the front yard," Charlie brightened up. "Tell me about your family. How many kids?"

"Two, a girl and a boy. Annie and Chris." James grinned, the automatic, involuntary grin of the proud parent.

"Hah! Me too! Lauren and Toby." She grinned back. "Dude, we sure have a lot in common. I wonder what else we share?"

"I don't know. Try me." A warm glow was spreading through his chest. Charlie felt so comfortable, in a best-friend, cool-girl, sexy tomboy sort of way.

"What's your sign?" she asked. "I'm a Gemini with Virgo rising."

"I'm a Gemini, too. Have no idea what my rising sign is."

"I'll bet you're a Scorpio rising, you have that vibe." She smiled again and locked her eyes on his, an open challenge of frank, confident sensuality. And James suddenly realized what it was about her smile that transformed her face. She smiled like she was opening a present on Christmas morning and didn't know what it was, but was sure that it would be something good. That look of expectation drew him in, made him want to see what was going to be unwrapped, too.

They moved on to other topics, but the hook had been set, and she was already reeling him in. She was intriguing and familiar and fun, and they started hanging out, meeting for bike rides and hikes and coffees. Over the next few weeks, they discovered more ways that they were the same. James had a scar on his left shoulder blade from an injury. She showed him hers. James had been married for ten years. So had she. It was like looking in a mirror that the gods held up in front of his face. She had the female version of most of his characteristics, and in a weird, almost narcissistic way, he relished it. A woman just like him! Someone he could understand, get along with, maybe even love. There was only one problem. She really *was* just like him.

One Saturday, they met for a hike up at the Shadow Canyon Trailhead, at the foot of the Flatirons, where a hard, thick layer of red sandstone called the Fountain Formation tilts up dramatically, sometimes almost vertically, as if the mountains had pushed up through a brittle pie crust.

It was a very warm day for October, with high, thin clouds that gave little shade. There was a slight breeze underneath the pines. Charlie wore a pink tank top and running shorts, and she greeted him with a smile.

"Hey, sport," she said as she hugged him. Her body felt firm and toned with just enough softness. James got lost in her magnetism and held her a bit too long, so she gently extracted herself. They headed up the trail, with Charlie leading the way. Soon, they were climbing steep stairs that rose through pines up the backside of the Flatirons. They hiked steadily, breaking every now and then to drink water and chat. At some point, James told her about his love for the Caribbean, the turquoise waters, the reefs, the fish.

"Mmmm," Charlie said, laughing easily. "I love the ocean more than anything. Sailing and snorkeling and scuba." She looked at him over her shoulder. "Who knows? Maybe we'll both live in the islands someday."

Once again, she was back to mirroring him. It was like shared secret knowledge, an inside joke.

"Yeah," he played along. "We could be neighbors, have little grass shacks on the beach, with two hammocks under the palm trees."

"Or maybe just one," she said casually.

There she was again, with that not-so-subtle challenge. OK, time to ask the obvious question.

"So, what's up with you on the relationship front? Are you seeing anyone now?"

She kept hiking, not looking at him as she replied. "Sort of. Not really. There's a guy Back East in Connecticut. Same town where I grew up. I try to get back there every six to eight weeks to visit family, and sometimes we hang out."

Of course. James felt his heart drop. "Oh, that's cool," he replied, trying to sound upbeat. "But long distance relationships…they can be tough."

"I guess." She kept hiking. "I'm not in one."

"Would you ever move back there?" James pushed, his jealousy demanding more from her.

"No, I love Colorado."

"Well then, maybe your guy can move out here." It was more of a question than a statement.

"Why would he do that? He's got a great life back there. Owns a boatyard and restores old wooden sailing ships. It's beautiful, right on the bay."

"But what about you?"

"What about me? He sees me when he wants." Her response had a defensive tone to it.

"Does he ever come out here?" James pressed.

"Nope." She continued hiking.

"Hmmm, must be tough!"

"No, it's not," she countered smoothly, maneuvering around a fallen log. "It's fine and works for me, too. He's just a guy. He doesn't own me."

"So, he doesn't care if you date someone here?"

Charlie stopped hiking, stood still for a moment, then turned around and faced him. This time, her mouth smiled, but her eyes didn't. "Look, James, I just got out of a long marriage. I'm enjoying my freedom. I do what I want. I date who I want. Him, someone else. It doesn't matter."

They resumed hiking but didn't speak of relationships anymore. The message was clear. Back off the questions.

Over the next couple of weeks, they met to hike, do training rides on road bikes, and run on the many trails around Boulder. And as the days passed, James found himself imagining a future together. They obviously had chemistry, liked each other as people, and shared the same interests. Those three elements seemed to him to be the critical components for a successful relationship. Then she missed week four of the Rebounders Seminar. Debra announced that she was out of town, and James immediately knew where, although Charlie hadn't told him she was traveling.

Chapter Fifteen

~ * ~

Citrine

The fifth night of the Rebounders Seminar was Anger Night, and the idea was to write a letter to your ex and say all the stuff you needed to say, no matter how bitter or painful. You would never actually send it to your ex, but you were encouraged to read the letter aloud to the group if you wanted to. You could curse, scream, cry, whatever it took, since the idea was to exorcize the anger, cast it out of your body.

The participants broke into smaller groups of five or six, in separate rooms so that everyone would have a chance to speak. Giuseppe, the little balding guy, was in James's group, and he was particularly eloquent. Between howls, he ranted at his ex who had apparently left him for his cousin. By the end of his monologue, he was literally foaming at the mouth. Deirdre, the devastated bridezilla, concentrated on feelings about her wedding and all the effort that had gone into it, including the perfect dress and the perfect flowers. She described how her asshole ex had ruined it by later running off with one of the bridesmaids, a roommate of hers from college. James wasn't really mad at anyone except the gods, and somehow this didn't seem the forum for excoriating them. He chose to remain silent.

Charlie was in another group, and James met her afterward when everyone was saying goodbye.

"Hey, stranger. Welcome back."

She just smiled weakly.

"How'd it go?" he asked. She looked at him blankly. "The anger session. Did you rip anyone a new one?"

"No," she replied in an uncharacteristically subdued voice. "I had no right to be angry at anyone."

"Really? Why not?"

"Because I destroyed our marriage. It was my fault." She spoke in a low voice, her face averted.

"Oh. Well, I didn't say anything either. My ex died," he said, trying to help. "Hard to be mad at her for that."

Charlie looked up at him, and there was a tear in her eye that she hurriedly wiped away. "Oh gosh, I'm sorry."

"Hey, it was a while ago. And we weren't married or anything."

"So not your wife," she said, brightening.

"Nah. Not Elizabeth. Sheesh. That anger's been dead and buried for a long time. I've no desire to dig it up."

"Well, next week is Grief Night, and maybe you'll have something then."

The next week he did. James agonized over what he could say about Kat. Grief night was famous among Rebounders alumni. It was the most emotional of the sessions. Even those who hated their exes were encouraged to acknowledge the sadness they felt around the ending of their relationship. James would have to open the crack in his heart, let some of the pain out. He wasn't sure he knew how, or how to control it if he did.

During the week, Charlie asked to meet him for coffee but canceled at the last minute. James wondered what that was about but never found out. They ran five miles together the next day, but she only apologized without explanation.

Grief Night was back at James's house since he was one of the few seminar participants who had a place that could hold twenty-four people. Many of the others were living in tiny apartments, either for economic reasons or because they were still in temporary quarters in the aftermath of their divorce.

James decided to let his poetry speak for him. Charlie was in his group this time, and she sat next to him on the couch when they read their grief letters aloud. James read this poem:

~~ *Just Passing Thoughts* ~~

A cherry tree blooms in the morning sun,
and then its petals fall
like pink snow to the earth.
And that is beauty.

A birdsong is born
in the joy of flight
above a grassy meadow,
and then is blown away
by the passing breeze.
And that is beauty.

A raindrop starts as a wispy cloud
high up in the sky,
spends its youth as a dewdrop
on a blade of grass,
reaches adulthood as a sparkle
in a rushing brook,

and disappears into the vastness
of the deepest sea.
And that is beauty.

We are the cherry blossom,
the birdsong,
the raindrop.
We are all just passing thoughts
in the meditations of God.
And that is beauty.

~~ * ~~

He read the poem in a low voice, and partway through, he felt the grip that he kept on the crack in his heart start to slip, and the pain began to leak out. He had to stop and take a breath, and as he did so, he felt Charlie's hand slide up his back to that place between the shoulder blades where people instinctively rub you, right behind your heart, to comfort you. He could feel the warmth of her hand penetrating his shirt, could feel her empathy pouring in. He didn't know if she was helping him hold back tears or was helping the crack to widen, but somehow, he stumbled through the rest of the poem, even though his voice betrayed him and got lost in his throat.

By the end, everyone else in the room was crying, too. But it was that kind of night. Everyone cried in sympathy with one another. They cried for Charlie as she admitted her shame in ending her marriage by having an affair. They cried for Deirdre as she lamented the useless photographs of the happy bridal party, taken by the expensive New York photographer who'd been flown out special. They even cried for Ed, the boring software engineer, who was left with nothing but his spreadsheets and calculations when his wife dumped him for a salsa teacher. At the end of the evening, there were many hugs all around as everyone felt closer to one another and lighter in spirit, a surprising catharsis that James had thought he was too numb to experience.

Later that week, he left work early and met Charlie at the Bobolink Trailhead for a mountain bike ride. They rode south to Marshall Mesa, about four miles away, on dirt paths that ran next to South Boulder Creek. At Marshall Mesa, they climbed up over the hill to the flats and followed the trail to where it crossed the highway and then opened up into the foothills of the Rockies. Soon the path became more technical, with exposed rocks and potholes. Charlie was a very experienced rider, and she led the way. James had bought a new mountain bike, ostensibly because his old one was a rusty old relic but in reality because he needed every technological advantage to keep up with her. Like anything she did, she was balls to the wall, flat out, as if she had a date with tomorrow and couldn't wait to get there.

It was a good ride, about thirty miles in three hours, and they stopped at the halfway point and sat on a boulder looking out over the valley below. The season was teetering between summer and winter, and the leaves were golden on the aspens and cottonwoods and willows and just starting to fall. Occasional gusts of wind kicked up clouds of gold and swirled them past in drafts that felt both warm and cold. Charlie leaned against James, her head on his shoulder, and he put his arm around her. God, she felt so good! He wanted to turn her toward him, kiss her top lip right where it taunted him with its upward tilt.

"I like you, James," she said, and rested her hand on his leg.

"I like you, too, Charlie," he replied.

"Four more weeks of Rebounders."

"Yep," he answered, and they said no more, the promise in the subtext saying it all.

During the rest of the ride, his thigh burned where she'd touched him, as if her hand had branded his flesh like a cave painting, glowing red ochre against white skin. Maybe if he looked, he'd also see prancing bison chased by stick figures waving spears.

They finished with a downhill race through Doudy Draw, skirting boulders and dodging trees and roaring around corners. James trailed her by a bike length, then put on a burst of intense effort and somehow pulled even at a wider patch, where he managed to pass her. She cursed fluently and caught him at the finish, and laughing and joking, they cruised back to the car on blacktop. The sun was already behind the hill, and it was getting chilly. They got off the bikes and his legs felt well juiced, his butt sore from the seat. James stretched his back muscles to free up the tight places while Charlie pulled on a purple sweatshirt. He watched her fluff out her hair. She was a shapeshifter, toying with his desires. She'd kick his ass on a ride one minute and make him want to tear her clothes off the next.

"Dinner?" he asked as they loaded the bikes onto the rack.

"Sorry, I've got plans," she said. "But I'd love a raincheck."

She smiled at him with those dazzling white teeth, and somehow her saying no seemed like a yes.

He dropped her off at her house and went home. Oh yeah, he had the kids that night anyway and had forgotten, his brain scrambled from her smile and the hand that had branded his thigh, claiming it for her own. "Keep it together, James," he said aloud as he showered.

James didn't feel like cooking, so he took Annie and Chris downtown to stroll among the tourists on the Pearl Street pedestrian mall. The sun was just disappearing behind the mountains, and the streetlights were coming on, and that made everything look warmer, like an old-time painting of a village square. They stopped to watch one of their favorite street performers, a Jamaican man with graying dreadlocks, wedge himself into a tiny Plexiglas cube. He folded his arms and legs at impossible angles and somehow managed to climb into the tiny box to the cheers of the crowd.

James gave Annie a couple of dollars to drop into his hat, and they wandered on until they came to Hapa Sushi. They sat on the outside patio, the perfect place to watch the people strolling by, jackets pulled tight, arms interlocked. It was getting colder. An occasional gust of wind swirled the leaves, but the restaurant fired up a pair of large patio heaters, so everyone remained warm and toasty.

About the time James was finishing his sushi, Charlie came walking down the mall with a tall guy named Vlad that he recognized from the class. She was snuggled on his arm, her gaze warm and inviting up to his face, and they sure looked like a couple on a date. So much for the first rule of Rebounders. Vlad avoided his gaze, and Charlie just played it cool. James nodded as they passed, but inside he felt shocked and betrayed. What the hell???

Back home, after sending the kids to bed, he settled on the couch with a glass of red wine and a movie. He tried to watch the movie but kept seeing Charlie over and over, wrapped up with Vlad. Eventually, exhausted from the ride and the long day, he fell asleep on the couch, and then migrated to his bedroom and finished out the night.

At the next Rebounders meeting, James was in a small group with Charlie, Deirdre, Ed, and Vlad. He was still put off by having seen Charlie on her date, and now she was sitting next to Vlad, laughing and chatting. The exercise for the evening was one in which everyone had to talk about something that had sabotaged their relationships in the past.

Deirdre started out. "I was very clingy," she said. "Anything he did, I was right there, like a barnacle on a rock."

She made a gesture that looked like a cat pouncing on a mouse. "I smothered him. I was too much." She then went into details about her wedding, how she'd planned for it ever since she was a little girl, and how her obsession had poisoned their relationship. James felt sorry for her and sorrier for her ex.

Ed was next. "I analyzed everything. I had to know the outcomes, the probabilities. I sucked the life out of everything we did before we did it." There was more, but it was too depressing to listen to.

James started to nod, his thoughts buzzing like bees around Charlie, remembering her touch, and her promise, "Four more weeks." The bees droned on, making him sleepy.

And then it was Vlad's turn. Vlad admitted that he had an unfortunate nickname among his friends, "Vlad the Impaler," because his penis was so large that he couldn't keep a girlfriend. He said it almost as if he was bragging and admitted that he loved breaking in a new woman, loved their expressions of astonishment at his Eighth Wonder of the World. Everyone in the room woke up as he spoke, and James looked at Charlie, jealousy burning like a hot coal in his chest. She was smiling at Vlad as if the secret he was sharing was her secret too.

Yep, he thought. *She knows. Fuck!* His stomach boiled with a toxic mix of disappointment, jealousy, anger, and resignation. After class, as the whole group mingled and chatted, Charlie hung out with Vlad, laughing and joking as if James wasn't even in the room. Clearly, James had misread whatever connection they'd had.

Over the next couple of weeks, he did his best to push her out of his mind. He didn't call her to ride bikes or go out for a drink, and he avoided her at Rebounders. She phoned twice and left messages, but he never called back. Instead, he poured his energy into finishing the fireplace in his living room. Whoever had originally built the house had scrimped on materials in the oddest ways, and the crappy fake stone that constituted the fireplace surround had bothered him since he'd moved in. Six months previously, he'd demolished the cheap, poorly made mantle, and then in the manner of do-it-yourself projects, the fireplace had just sat like that. Now, armed with a wet tile saw, James replaced the fake stone with red travertine marble. He fashioned a new mantle out of a reclaimed cherry plank that had been scavenged from of some hundred-year-old ruin down in Denver, and he finished it with a deep red stain. And another little corner of his home was transformed into something beautiful.

He also spent more time with his family. Annie had become a tall, slender young woman who attracted too much attention from the boys, especially the older ones. She still had the face and the world-view of a young girl, though, and James worried about the dangers that lurked out there in the cold, cruel world of teen romances. Since he'd never attended a coed high school, her first prom was his first prom, and he vowed to screen her suitors with a keen eye and a sharp sword. Luckily for Annie, Elizabeth took over the majority of the fuss and bother over the dress, the shoes, and the boy. James and Elizabeth had settled into a cautious truce over the years, and with the passage of time and the remarriage of Elizabeth to a doctor with a lucrative private practice, their relationship had found new ground as mostly cooperative coparents. Prom week came, and James proudly took pictures as Annie wobbled out of Elizabeth's house on unfamiliar high heels, towering over her nervous, twitchy, fuzzy-haired date.

"Have fun, munchkin!" he called as she stepped into the limo where a dozen other kids waited.

"Daaaad!" she groaned, her eyes rolling. James chuckled to himself. He and Chris had a fun night planned, watching old movies and eating pizza. After the limo pulled away, James said goodnight to Elizabeth and her husband, and he and Chris headed home to Rocco.

Charlie receded out of his immediate awareness, but even so, sometimes he'd wake up in the middle of the night, in that hour when negative thoughts expand into the dark emptiness and fears multiply. He'd lie there, unmoving, staring at the ceiling, thinking, wondering, feeling. One night, he'd fallen asleep with the skylights unshaded, and when he woke up several hours later, he could see the moon and the stars wheeling above him. His memory drifted back to Maho Bay, to the sandy beach and Grandmother Ocean breathing in and out, and to the blanket spread out under the stars. He lay there for a while watching the clouds drift past the moon as words rubbed together in his mind and verses formed. And then he got out of bed and poured his loneliness onto the page.

~~ *That Golden River* ~~

Last night in a dreamscape,
I wandered a lonely shore,
seeking comfort in the memory
of you.

And as I walked that deserted beach,
I heard
in the rhythm of waves washing smooth pebbles,
your familiar sigh of breath,
whispering secrets,
scattered lines of poetry
from other times and places,
a love lost,
a soul ripped asunder.

I turned my gaze
to the half-moon that glowed,
a giant, tilted bowl
pouring a river of gold
from the far edge of night
across wave tops to my feet.

I stepped into that river,
followed wispy tendrils of your scent,
faint echoes of your voice, your laughter,
always ahead,
always just out of reach.

Above me, in the night sky,
diaphanous clouds,
drifting scarves of cotton

caressed the moon's curves,
and I felt again the silken heat
of your skin against mine.

And just as my heart reached for you,
to the places where touch
still burned in my memory,
I woke,
to the bright light of morning,
to renewed loss, and yet,
another day closer
to holding you again
at the far end
of that golden river.

~~ * ~~

Chapter Sixteen

~ * ~

Gold Cord and Tassel

Finally, the last weekend of Rebounders arrived, and the plan was to load everyone into a bus and drive into the mountains for an overnight campout. At midnight of that Saturday, the class would officially be over, together with all restrictions on dating. Several potential couples were already talking about that campout as if it would be their first date, and, of course, he knew about Charlie and Vlad. James had zero expectations of anyone and showed up at the rendezvous with his backpack, tent, sleeping bag, sleeping pad, and some food to share. Also, a bottle of red wine and a six-pack of beer, a bit of anesthesia to help him get through what would probably be his last evening in proximity to Charlie.

It was a beautiful autumn morning, brisk and sunny with a chance of snow flurries in the overnight forecast. Everyone loaded up into the bus and headed for the mountains. Vlad was there, seated in the back with Charlie, Deirdre sat next to Giuseppe, and Ed was sitting with Doris. James sat by himself, doodling on a small notepad, trying to get some ideas down for a poem. It wasn't going well. His mood had swung back to bleakness the previous week at Rebounders when he couldn't avoid seeing Charlie and Vlad, hanging out and laughing. Why couldn't that have been him? And now, his mood was exacerbated by the joviality in the back of the bus. He looked back down at his notepad. What he had so far was a work in progress, but maybe he could massage it into something decent.

~~ *Love Is A Prisoner* ~~

At the end of a passage,
filled with dust and despair,
behind doors of burnt copper,
and a lock of dark steel,
there's a cell haunted by shrouds,
where air doesn't stir
and light is a stranger.
In that place frozen in time,
the darkest vault of my heart,
Love is a prisoner,
fed scraps of failed hopes
and crumbs fallen
from dreams.

~~ * ~~

James stared at the page for a while, seeing only Charlie's face. *James,* he thought. *You're such a fucking drama queen! You need to just stop this!* He put his head against the window and closed his eyes. He must have drifted off because suddenly he woke to someone sitting next to him, her leg warm against his, and her head resting on his shoulder. It was Charlie. Was she asleep? Her hand rested lightly on his thigh. In her lap was James's notepad with his poem. As he sat there, hyperaware of her presence, her scent so close to his face, she sat up.

"Hey, stranger, how've you been?" she asked, yawning and stretching, smiling at him, massaging his thigh with her hand.

"I'm good," he replied, not sure what else to say.

"Haven't seen you much lately," she continued. "You haven't called me to ride or returned my calls."

"Yeah, well…" James shrugged.

"Hmmm." She picked up the notepad and read the poem silently. "You wrote this? It seems awfully sad. You're pretty good with words, though."

"Ah, just something I've been working on. Not getting what I want. Kinda lame."

"I don't think it's lame," she said. "'Love is a prisoner. Fed scraps of hopes and crumbs fallen from dreams—'"

She paused. "That's how I feel. Kind of dead inside."

"Really? I thought you and Vlad—"

She looked at him, as if searching his face for clues. "What do you mean? Vlad's just a friend. I like men. I'm not in love or anything."

"That's cool. Whatever." James didn't know what to say.

She squeezed his thigh. "Hey, Rebounders ends tonight! You ready to party?"

James smiled with humor he didn't feel. "Sure."

He couldn't connect with her. Too much damage, maybe, or too much potential for disappointment. It didn't matter. He wasn't buying. He was firmly back in the gray zone. Sensing his disaffection, she gave a shrug and got up.

"OK, see you later around the bonfire."

James forced a smile and nodded, and she left to wade back into the more party-minded group at the back of the bus. The beer was already flowing, and there was laughter and light.

James turned back to his poem. "…the darkest vault of my heart…where air does not stir, and light is a stranger." Yep. That's how he felt. Dead inside, she'd said. That too.

~~*

The campsite was a level spot under some ancient pines. The ground had been swept bare of loose rocks and had a nice layer of forest duff and detritus. There was a permanent fire ring laid out in the middle, wide open to the sky with plenty of clearance from the trees. A stream ran past one edge of the campsite, and the burble of running water lent a calming soundtrack to the evening. Everyone helped out and piled up wood for a large bonfire for a "Burning Away" ceremony that would mark the end of the class.

James pitched his tent apart from the rest in a quiet spot tucked between some spruces. The duff and pine needles there were thick and made a soft mat under the floor of the tent. He laid out his sleeping pad and his bag, stashed his backpack, and went out to the fire ring.

Dinner was a potluck of hot dogs, beans, stew, and a few other dishes people had brought. The beer and wine were flowing, the fire was crackling, and people were eating and drinking and socializing.

James picked a spot at the edge of the group and sat on a log close enough to the fire to get some heat, but not so close that he felt seared. His interaction with Charlie had left him feeling hollow, uninspired for social banter. He cracked open a beer, but his morose reflection lasted only briefly, because Debra was calling everyone together for the Burning Away ceremony. They were to take turns, step up to the fire, and toss into the flames whatever they wanted to leave behind, to clear space for their new lives. That could be their letters from Grief Night and Anger Night or whatever they wanted.

James felt a kiss on the back of his neck, and turned to see Charlie smiling down at him.

"Hey you," she said.

"Hey."

"You ready to throw your Grief and Anger letters into the fire?"

James shook his head. "Nah, I got nothing. Never wrote an Anger letter, and my Grief letter was a poem, a good one. Not burning that."

"I have an idea." Charlie smiled at him. "What about your other poem? The one you wrote on the bus?"

"What about it?"

"Do you like it?"

"Not particularly."

"So let's burn that! She grabbed him by the shoulders. "Burn it for both of us! You *and* me. All that crap about locking up love in our hearts. Burn that shit! It's perfect!" She hauled him to his feet.

"Wait, what?" Was she mirroring him again? Did she really feel as empty as he did? What about Vlad?

"James is going first!" Charlie announced, and dragged him up to the front of the line. The crowd cheered, and James could think of nothing else to do, so he took his notepad out of his pocket and ripped out the poem.

"OK," he mumbled. "I'm uh … leaving behind sadness over failed and lost loves. Not carrying that forward with me. Looking ahead to better things."

He babbled a bit more, making no sense, until Charlie grabbed him and kissed him hard on the mouth to make him shut up. She released him, and the crowd cheered. James hesitated, then crumpled his poem into a ball and tossed it into the fire. The crowd cheered some more, several people hugged him, and James moved to the back of the crowd.

Charlie went next. "I'm giving up shame" was all she said.

She tossed her Anger and Grief letters into the fire but added one other thing, a wadded-up piece of cloth that she threw into the middle of the flames. When she turned toward James, the firelight glinted briefly off tears that stained her cheeks. She pushed her way through the crowd and buried her face in his chest. James wrapped his arms around her and held her until the sobs subsided.

Meanwhile, Ed got up to the front. He yelled some stuff about calculations and predicting the future, about letting go of control. Then he picked up a huge suitcase, opened it up, and pulled out charts and graphs and folders and notebooks and hurled it all into the fire to a huge roar. He dove into the crowd for more hugs than he'd probably ever had in his life.

Deirdre went next, and inspired by Ed, she yelled about letting go of perfectionism, control over everything, and how she wanted spontaneity in her life. She followed that up by throwing her letters into the fire, hurled her precious wedding albums in, and finally, shrieking and in the moment, pulled off her sweater and shirt and tore off her bra, which she hurled into the fire. Topless, she danced around the fire to shouts and screams of delight.

It went downhill from there. Vlad got up and tossed his letters, followed by his pants and underpants, and joined Deirdre in dancing around the fire, her topless, him bottomless, and soon others were joining in. Rebounders was over, and people were free to do what they wanted.

Charlie dragged James away from the fire. Once out in the shadows, she framed his face with her hands and kissed him, deeply, slowly. As usual, she was leading, and he was struggling to catch up. What the hell? She had him spinning between despair and delight. He wanted to tear her clothes off, feel her long arms and legs wrapped around his own. She was so strong and yet so feminine with her athlete-warrior body, incredibly sexy and physical, and he wanted to feel her strength matched against his strength, her desire against his. She could be his perfect partner, if she chose, but what were the chances of that? While all these thoughts raced through James's mind, Charlie was opening the buttons of his shirt.

"Let's go to my tent," she whispered, her lips caressing his ear.

"No, let's go to mine," said James. His body was responding to her, and his mind's hesitation was being trampled in the rush. All right. If he was going to do this, he was going to take the lead. And if it worked out, great. But for tonight, he would just let things play out.

He pulled her to his little hideaway and opened the tent flap. She crawled in, and he followed, turning to zip up the entrance. By the time he turned back around, she'd taken off her top and was opening her jeans. He took her face in his hands and kissed her forcefully. She tasted of red wine and desire, and James felt any remaining hesitation stripped away with his shirt.

He pushed her back onto his sleeping bag and pulled her jeans off her body. She wasn't wearing any panties. He grinned and let her unbuckle his pants. Yes, maybe she was just what he needed, at least for this night.

Chapter Seventeen

~ * ~

Double Carnelian

The next morning, James woke up with Charlie sleeping peacefully by his side. Dawn-breaking sunlight dappled the roof of the tent, and he carefully opened the flap to let in some fresh air. Charlie's breathing was soft and rhythmic, and he studied her face as she slept. Her skin glowed with captured sunlight, from trips down rivers, up rock faces, across wave-tossed waters. Seasons of laughter and cares had etched tiny lines around her eyes, and there were a few gray hairs at her temples, silver frosting on a crown of gold. A tiny scar on her forehead, a birthmark on her neck. Little imperfections that punctuated her fresh-faced beauty and made her interesting.

The previous night had been everything he could have imagined. She was strong, sexy, and adventurous. She knew how to lead and how to follow, too. And for him, he couldn't believe that he'd gone almost four years without sex, ever since Kat had passed away. The sex had been great, but the connection had been even better. She felt like she belonged with him. Familiar, comfortable, and yet, and yet…. There were danger signals. Emotional static, conflicting agendas, triggers for his jealousy. Vlad and that guy Back East. Where was she with them? James doubted they'd magically fade away just because she'd slept with him. He wanted something more than physical love, something like he'd had with Kat. Could that ever truly happen with Charlie?

Charlie stirred and reached for him, her hand warm and soft as it caressed his face. "Good morning," she breathed as she rolled over and pressed her naked breasts and belly against his.

"Mmmm, good morning," James whispered, and nuzzled her face and neck. Her sleepy, soft warmth was intoxicating.

"It's so nice to wake up to you," she sighed.

"Yeah, I could get used to it."

"You might have to."

Again, there was that challenge, delivered with a smile and a suggestion. She hooked her leg over his hip and pulled him gently down on top of her. Maybe there was a kernel of magic that could develop if they just gave it a chance. Maybe she'd choose him and drop the other guys. Or maybe the gods had sent Charlie to James like a midterm exam, to see if he'd learned anything yet.

Later that morning, they emerged to a camp just waking up. A fire was going, and people were making coffee over camp stoves and stirring up bowls of pancake batter. There was a touch of frost in the morning air, and snow glinted off the distant mountaintops. The tang of wood smoke made him hungry, and James was dying for some water.

"I'm going to change clothes," said Charlie as she kissed him on the cheek and turned toward her tent.

"Hey, how about a real kiss," James replied as he turned her back around and kissed her on the mouth.

She laughed through the kiss and held his face in her hands. "OK, boss." She kissed him again, slowly, then walked off to her tent, looking back over her shoulder and smiling. James saw Vlad emerge from a tent with Deirdre, who looked a bit the worse for wear, her hair a tangled mess and a dazed expression on her face.

Ed was sitting with Doris, and they sipped coffee from a couple of ceramic mugs. Giuseppe had made a new friend, and they were laughing as they ate scrambled eggs from camp plates. Debra, the mistress of ceremonies, was taking pictures of the smiling faces, so different from that first night of the Rebounders class, when many appeared broken and sad.

After breakfast, there was a hike to the top of a nearby hill, and the group seemed light and happy. Charlie drifted away to talk with some of the women, and James hiked for the most part alone, lost in reflection. They spoke a few more times that day and on the trip home, always with a crowd of others around, so they never had the chance to process what had transpired. As they left the bus, they promised to connect later that week. James went home feeling strangely unsatisfied and uncertain of what they were to each other.

The next day, at the yoga studio, he was sitting out front, putting on his shoes after class when a young woman came up to him.

"Hi. My name's Julie. You and I are gonna work together. Here's my card." James took her card and looked at it. It read, "Julie Fox, psychic." Despite her unconventional approach, Julie looked pretty normal: thirty-something, athletic, with a pleasant, intelligent face and white-blonde hair. Like all the other women in the studio, Julie was dressed in yoga clothes and barefoot. She had a pleasant smile and a brisk, businesslike manner.

"Um, why are we working together?" James asked. "Why do I need a psychic?"

"Because you have questions."

"But how do I know you have answers?"

"OK, ask me a question. Let's see if I do." She smiled again, but her face told him to hurry up, that she had a busy morning to get to.

"Right here?"

"Sure!"

James studied her face, looking for a reason to believe her. "OK, if you're a psychic, tell me something you couldn't possibly know just by googling me," he said after a pause.

She smiled. "You write. In a red book." She spoke without hesitation or uncertainty, as if she were describing a painting on a wall.

James shrugged, but inwardly he was impressed. "Lots of people write," he said, "and lots of people have red books. Diaries, notebooks, day planners—"

"Your book has a flower in it." Her words stunned him. How did she know that?

"OK, you got me," he grinned sheepishly.

Julie got up to leave. "Tomorrow I have a slot at 3:30 p.m. Thirty minutes, fifty bucks. Bring cash. My address is on the card. See you." She grabbed her yoga mat and headed out the door.

The next day, he arrived at the address on the card. It was a small, nondescript tract home in North Boulder. She gave him a hug and had him sit down on an ordinary couch in an ordinary home office. No turban, no crystal ball, no gypsy scarf. Just a brisk, businesslike manner and a digital recorder so he could play back her revelations as often as he liked. She spent the first ten minutes of their session describing what was going on in his life. Things that had him openmouthed with amazement. Specific things that couldn't be deduced from just his appearance. Like his poetry.

"James, I see you writing about love. About the trials and tribulations of relationships. That's your great lesson in this life."

"How do you do this?" he asked. "How do you know things?"

"I just see them. Sometimes it's really clear, something specific, like I saw you and knew we'd be working together. Sometimes, it's cloudy, and I only see potential, and that's triggered by a client's questions. I see answers, or potential answers. Actually, most of the time it's like that." She smiled. "So, ask me some questions."

James took a deep breath. Yes, he had questions. Many of them. "OK, well, I've met this woman named Charlie. She's really cool and seems kinda perfect for me. It's the weirdest thing. She's like my mirror image. We share so many interests, so many aspects of our lives."

"Yes, you do," Julie confirmed. "In many ways, energetically as well as materially. You match very well, but it's also confusing, because your mirror image is not the same as you. It's a reflection, a reversal. So, don't be fooled."

"But couldn't we be great partners?"

"I do see her marching in step with you, yes, but she's exactly one step behind, and not where you are in life, not yet anyway. She's suffered a loss, and like you did, she's dealing with it by hedging her bets emotionally."

"Do you mean other men?"

"Yes, she's not letting herself get too involved with anyone right now, even though she really wants to eventually. Maybe that could be a problem?"

"What should I do?"

"Your karma and hers are intertwined right now, but I can't see for how long. Let her go through her process. She may come around to your point of view, or not. If she does, it would be a good match. But she might choose something else."

"Hmmm, and then what?"

"You'll have many alternatives, James. You're evolving into greater alignment with your purpose in this life. We all come into each life with a lesson or lessons to learn. Your lessons are around love. And of course, since she's your reflection, hers are too. Charlie may be a stepping stone to something greater. I can't tell. But you haven't decided that you're all in with her, either. And that's OK. People come into our lives to teach us something, not necessarily to stay with us forever. And as you grow into yourself, you become more attractive. I see more people coming toward you. You will have more to choose from."

James called Charlie later that week, and she came over. It was a chilly night, and he'd built a fire in the fireplace. She arrived at the door, her blue eyes gleaming in the firelight as she took off her silver-colored down jacket and pulled off her cowboy boots. She smiled her Christmas-morning smile of expectation, and instantly he was eager to unwrap whatever gift she was bringing. As it turned out, it was some special massage oil she'd bought at a boutique down on Pearl Street. It looked like a bar of soap, but it was supposed to melt when rubbed on the skin and develop a healing bouquet of herbs and wildflowers.

"We've got this lovely fire going," she said as she kissed him. "Why don't you lie down in front of it, and I'll try out this stuff on your back?"

"Only if you let me rub you next," he replied.

"I'm counting on it. You didn't think this was a freebie, did you?" She kissed him again, her mouth open and her tongue flicking his front teeth playfully.

James had come to terms with Julie's advice about Charlie. Let it happen, let it unfold in its own time. Vlad and "Back East guy" had been locked up in a remote corner of his mind, out of sight. He spread out a bedsheet on the carpet in front of the fire, and they rubbed oil into each other's skin. Soon, they were both naked, covered with oil and using their whole bodies to massage each other. Their entire beings focused on the senses, the feeling of skin sliding past skin, the smell of floral oils tempered by smoke, the taste of wine tannins and alcohol and salt in their mouths. Curiously, the sensations created by their slow writhing were enough. Neither wanted it to end, so they drew it out, made it last far into the evening, until the wine bottle was empty and the fire burned down to coals. By then, James had pulled a blanket off the sofa. They were still feeling chilled, so he led her upstairs to his bedroom, where they finished the night under the skylights that pierced the ceiling. They fell asleep in the wash of silver beams of moonlight, and the next morning after she left, he wrote another poem, this one written in the broadest part of the day, when sunshine washes away despairing thoughts and optimism has a chance. Was he starting to fall in love with her? Or could it be that the comfort and ease that he felt with her was more about potential than reality? He sighed and wished that life was less complicated. Oh well. The poem at least was simple, a perfect flowering branch pruned from the tangled bush that was their relationship.

~~ *The Full Moon* ~~

The full moon
crept into my bedroom last night
and found you
in my heart.

She washed you
with silver light
and pearls,
and left me with your kiss
at dawn.

~~ * ~~

Chapter Eighteen

~ * ~

Double Citrine

A few weeks went by. Charlie and James got together frequently, to run trails and ride bikes, to drink happy-hour wine downtown at The Med, and to soak in her hot tub under the stars. Inevitably, they would end up in her bed or his, exploring the many ways two people can give each other physical pleasure. And in bed, she was just like she was on a race course or hiking or on her bike—going flat out, full speed ahead. She was insatiable, the most sexual woman he'd ever been with. But it wasn't just the sex. Her face would light up with that magnetic smile when she saw him. Her voice was like a song that could either soothe him with sensuality or stimulate him with excitement. James forgot about the other guys. He didn't ask, and she didn't tell. He kept his blinders on and tried to sell himself as the perfect guy for her. Surely if he could meet all her needs, the other guys would naturally fall away. Julie had said he would have alternatives. He didn't want any. He just wanted Charlie.

One night they were in her hot tub, enjoying the stars rising behind the mountains. The air was cold, and they kept their bodies immersed. She was facing away from him, and she half floated, half sat in his lap, her head resting on his shoulder and her butt brushing his knees. Her hair tickled his neck, and she turned her head and nibbled his ear, kissing him with her warm breath.

"So," she whispered in her sexiest voice. "Do you have any fantasies?"

"Hmmm, what do you mean?" James asked.

"Any secret desires you'd like to act out with me?"

Damn she was hot! He felt tingles all over. He thought about it and didn't have anything specific in mind at the time, but he liked the spirit of it.

"Well, there's that thing with the rubber snakes and the trapeze."

She laughed, turned over to face him, and kissed him on the mouth. "Mmmm, rubber snakes...my favorite," she whispered. She rubbed up against him, breathing heavily into his ear. "Tomorrow, nine p.m. Come over. Bring massage oil."

"Yeah?" James kissed her back, slowly. "What do you have in mind?"

"I have a friend..." She nibbled his lips, her breasts brushing his chest under water. "A little fantasy of mine..."

James's heart did a flip-flop in his chest. A *ménage à trois*? Isn't that on every guy's bucket list? He'd never done that! It would be crazy, outside the box, certainly outside his comfort zone, but rolling around naked with two women at once? Pure sex without any requirement for emotional involvement? The other woman would be an enhancement, like the massage oil, or one of Charlie's sex toys. How could that be bad? The idea got them both excited, and they made love right there in the hot tub, under the stars and the midnight sky.

The next day would be something new, something exotic. James thanked the gods for sending him this sexy, uninhibited playmate. He didn't know what sort of future they had together, but the present was interesting and fun.

The next evening James got himself ready like a kid before prom night. He shaved even though he'd shaved that morning. He used a bit of cologne, just a spray into the air that he walked his bare chest into. He put on a clean pair of jeans and a soft silk shirt. He wore boots and a brown leather jacket with a sheepskin collar. He picked out a nice bottle of red wine, a full-bodied cabernet. At the last minute, he also grabbed a bottle of champagne. James had no idea what the protocol was for a *ménage à trois*, but wine usually helps any event. A thought crossed his mind. *How many times had she done this before?* This was new to him but maybe old hat to her. And what would her friend look like? Would she be tall or short, skinny or fat? Would she be another sex goddess like Charlie, or would she be a plain-Jane friend she was trying to help out? A million crazy questions swirled around in his head. He had a severe case of butterflies, and he hoped it didn't show.

Right at nine o'clock, James knocked on her door. He could hear music from inside, some sort of muffled Middle Eastern beat throbbing through the walls. He was so nervous, his hands shook as he held the bottles. Charlie opened the door, and she was wearing a Japanese kimono bathrobe with scarlet designs on it. She looked flushed and sweaty, and her hair was awry, as if she'd already started.

"Come on in, we were just getting warmed up," she said, her voice thick with sensuality. She took his jacket, dropped it on the couch, and led him to the bedroom. The music was coming from inside.

She led the way in, kissing him. The room was dimly lit with two candles by the bed, and the smell of sex was heavy in the air. Clearly, they'd been going at it for a while. James couldn't see the other woman, just her vague shape under a thick jumble of sheets, blankets, and pillows. Huh. For the first time it occurred to him that maybe *he* was the accessory, not the other woman! Suddenly, he felt off-balance, and unsure of just how he fit in the picture. Charlie took the bottles from his hands and set them down on the bedside table. The music throbbed, a low vibration that dripped through his body like chocolate syrup down ice cream. Charlie nibbled his ear as she unbuttoned his shirt.

"You smell nice," she whispered, caressing his chest. Her robe was open, and James reflexively dove in. He ran his hands over her sweaty torso and breasts. He kissed her, and she kissed back, slowly, sensuously.

He felt another pair of hands reaching around him from behind and starting to unbuckle his belt. Whoever was behind him was kneeling on the bed and breathing on his neck. Something was off. James disentangled from Charlie and reached down to the hands on his belt. They were very large. He pried them loose and turned around to see who was back there. It was Vlad!

"What the fuck?" James jerked his body away from both of them. Vlad was naked on the bed, and from the looks of things, ready for another go with whomever he could grab. And it was clear that he fully deserved his nickname. James was in no mood to be impaled. He stumbled away from both of them, moving toward the door.

"What the fuck, Charlie! What the hell is this?"

"My fantasy, James. What did you think?" She advanced toward him, reaching for him, but whatever magic James had ever projected onto her was gone, and all he wanted to do was get the hell out of there. Vlad was sitting back on the bed, laughing at him, his face a mask of Dionysian lust and debauchery.

James burst out of the room, grabbed his jacket, and ran out the door. The cold night air cleansed the smell of sex and lust from his nostrils but couldn't erase the scene from his mind. He jumped into his car and drove home, where he poured himself a shot of tequila with shaking hands and downed it. Then he collapsed, laughing hysterically.

What the hell! What had ever possessed him to assume that Charlie's fantasy would be a *ménage à trois* with two women and one man? Clearly, in retrospect, James should have realized that was more his fantasy, not hers. And Vlad had never gone away. She'd probably been banging him as often as she'd been banging James, and perfection for her would have been for both of them to bang her at the same time. James had let his ego get in the way and somehow assumed that everything would be his own projection. The gods howled with laughter, and for once James laughed along with them. They'd sent him Charlie as a midterm, and he'd flunked miserably.

Charlie called him the next day, and they agreed to meet the following week at the Teahouse downtown. James needed some time to process what had happened and to calm down.

On the appointed day, he arrived early and found a spot in the corner where they could talk privately. She walked in, looking as lovely and collected as ever. She sat down across from him, a wry smile on her face.

"Are you OK?" she asked.

"I'm fine," James replied, even though he was still shaking internally.

"Let's talk about what happened."

"I'd rather not. I just need to apologize. I thought that we had something we could build on…like a real relationship."

"And you thought that introducing another woman into that would be OK, but not another man."

James laughed. "Yeah. Stupid, huh? I mean, somehow, I figured— I mean, I wondered if you were…"

"If I were what?"

"If you were…bisexual." There it was. It just slipped out. Charlie just looked at him a moment, as if weighing the consequences of whatever she would say next.

"I am. Or I was. That's why my marriage broke up."

"What? You really were a lesbian?"

"I don't know, James, I tried it. With a friend. She fell in love with me, and I was kind of flattered, and curious. It was wonderful, but it cost me. My man, whom I loved, and my family. And I don't need that confusion in my life anymore. I like women, but I *love* men."

"I'm sorry. You didn't really need to tell me about it."

"I guess I wanted you to know." Charlie leaned back and turned on her smile. "Now let's talk about us. I like you, James. I really do. And I'm sorry if I surprised you with what my idea of a *ménage* would be. But I'm a single woman, and I'll do whatever I want, with whomever I want, whenever I want. And if that's OK, we can date."

It was as if the gods were playing back to him a recording from his own past, from when he'd been the playboy with three girlfriends at once. Those same words had passed his lips, and he knew exactly what she meant, how she felt about him, and how this relationship was going to end.

James looked at her, at how magnetic she was. How she was like his reflection, his mirror image. They had so much in common! James wanted her all for himself. Except that was not what she was offering. She was offering a sliver of her world. Two, maybe three, days a week. Two, maybe three, nights a week—when she would be locked in sweaty embrace, skin to skin, with James. The other nights, it would be some other guy. Vlad the Impaler. The dude Back East. And whomever else she wanted to bring into her spinning wheel of love, with her as the hub. James was being offered the position of spoke, one of many. And like so many of the women he'd dated when he was the hub, he no longer wanted to play. It would be like dating an obsolete version of himself. The gods had held up a mirror and asked, "Do you like it?" James didn't. He'd been like her, still was like her in many ways, but perhaps he'd grown a bit, learned something. Maybe he *was* a step ahead, like Julie said. What James really wanted from a partner was what he'd experienced briefly with Kat—a true connection, not just sensory stimulation and ego gratification. He had to pass. James stood up, gave her a kiss goodbye, and left a few bills for the waitress.

James saw Charlie from time to time, riding road bikes to Lyons or at a triathlon. They'd smile and wave at each other, and then she'd turn back to whatever guy or guys she was with, and that would be it. She was his mirror image, so similar, but different too—his reflection. And definitely a step out of synch. She still needed to process what he'd processed. Maybe he fell in love with her because she felt so comfortable, so familiar, like a female version of himself. Or maybe because she seemed like a prize for making it back from the two most devastating events of his life, his cancer and the death of Kat.

For Charlie's mala, James chose the colors of fire.

Red coral for the first chakra, the return of life force
Carnelian for the second chakra, and intense sexuality
Citrine for the third chakra, and the self-will to come back
Gold cord and tassel for recovery and reward
Double carnelian because she was his mirror image, a reversal
Double citrine because she was his reflection

His meditations, while knotting the beads, were more about gratitude that she'd come into his life to help him climb out of his hole, and relief that it was over. When James finished, he had a gorgeous mala that he could look at, remember the good, laugh at the ridiculous (oh Vlad!), and taste again the sublime.

As for James, he knew that his way lay ahead. He was eager to find out what Julie had meant when she said he would have alternatives. He resolved to keep trying to evolve into a better version of himself, to be the best James Wilder he could be. Or, as the wise Julie had once said, "You need to become the kind of guy that the kind of woman you want would choose." He still had a lot of work to do.

The Fourth Mala

Blue Girl

~~ *The Art of Loving Slowly* ~~

"Please love me,"
she said,
"just very slowly."
A softly whispered plea,
a plan.

"Please serve me Love
in a wine glass.
A tender bouquet,
a sip,
a memory to be savored.

Let's explore
the drawn-out moments,
a stroll through kairos time,
faces close,
in quiet conversation.

Let's dance,
but a slow dance,
move gently to the music,
the music of slow fire.

Let's speak in poems,
measure words,
and rhythm,
and many layered meanings.

Let's linger over details,
build dramatic tension,
the sensory unwrapping
of a precious gift.

We can only do this once,
so let's become experts
in the art of loving
slowly."

~~ * ~~

Chapter Nineteen

~ * ~

Amazonite

Anahata chakra, the heart chakra. The green chakra, glowing like sea emeralds. That was the color of the mala she laid on his mat. "A gift," she said. But that was not the gift. That was just an invitation to the dance.

Three months earlier, James had seen her sitting behind the front desk at The Yoga Studio. She had an olive complexion, dark curly hair, big hoop earrings, and a red and gold Indian scarf that made her look like a gypsy. She was holding the scarf in front of her face like a veil, and all he could see were her pale blue eyes. She was laughing and joking about something, and somehow, she glanced at him when he walked out of the locker room, still flushed and sweaty from a hot yoga class. It was a *coup de foudre*, a lightning bolt, and this time, James was nimble enough to catch it with his eyes and not let it smash through his heart. But he noticed her, enough so that he went home and looked her up on the roster of yoga teachers.

Her name was Saraswati Stowe, and she was a senior teacher who'd recently joined The Yoga Studio. James had never met her or taken her class, but he'd heard of her reputation. She'd been teaching for over twenty years, had owned her own studios, and was a featured presenter at many yoga festivals. She was a disciple of Amanda Roberts, one of the great yoga teachers in the States, and like Amanda, very much the feminine warrior-poet in her teachings. Also, she was going to lead the yoga teacher training he'd signed up for.

Well, this will be interesting, he thought.

That first night of the training, they sat in a circle lit by candles. The four teachers were all ethereal yoga goddesses in their thirties who looked as if they'd stepped out of the pages of a yoga magazine. There were sixteen other students, twelve female and four male, and all appeared to be very young. As a forty-seven-year-old man with graying hair, James felt a bit like someone's dad who'd wandered into the wrong room.

Saraswati ran the meeting and asked everyone to call her Sara. She told them that her father had been a Mormon missionary who'd met and married her mother in Jaipur, India. He was a professor of religion but died when she was twelve. Her mother was from the Brahmin caste in India. Her family didn't approve of the marriage, so Sara's mom and dad moved to the States. They named her Saraswati, after the Hindu goddess of knowledge, and now Sara was obsessed with learning about her Indian roots. And that had brought her to the study of yoga.

Her mother and father must have been very attractive people, because the mix of their DNA gave her pronounced Eurasian features and beautiful, dark olive skin that offset her striking blue eyes. And somewhere in her family tree there was size, because she was built differently than the other yoga teachers. While they seemed like delicate refugees from ballet class, with slim hips, long legs, and flat chests, Sara was taller, with full breasts, well-muscled limbs, and a curvy ass. She dressed with an exuberant, bohemian sense of style and adorned herself with Indian scarves, jangly jewelry, and eclectic hats. Her most distinguishing characteristic, though, was a long scar that started on her right cheek near the corner of her mouth and ran in a straight line up to her temple and into her hair. It gave her an exotic, dangerous beauty.

After telling about herself, she asked everybody to introduce themselves. Their names, why they were there, one important thing about their lives. Melinda was there to deal with anxiety issues. Rebecca was there to heal an eating disorder. Jane was recently separated from her husband and looked like a deer in the headlights. Luke had just returned from backpacking around the world and wanted to work for social change. A few actually desired a career in teaching yoga, but they were the exception rather than the rule.

James said he was there as part of a fitness goal and to get more grounded. That was enough. Besides, what could he say to these young kids that would be relevant? He didn't get away with it, though. Sara spoke up and asked him to describe one interesting thing that would define who he was.

"Um, I write poetry," he admitted to the circle. James was grateful it was dark in there because for some reason he suddenly felt embarrassed. Sara didn't let him hide though.

"What kind of poetry?"

"Poetry—about love." His face was burning. "Like the Sufis. Rumi and Hafiz. I mean, they inspire me—"

Sara arched her eyebrows and moved on, and James tried not to pay attention to the curious glances that the younger ones were casting his way. Already his age made him the oddball. He could only imagine what they were thinking.

The course ran for ten weeks and met every Saturday and Sunday. Each day would start with two hours of yoga, then two hours of lecture on anatomy, the history of yoga, Hindu mythology and cosmology, and how to structure a class. The afternoon usually included a workshop on poses, followed by more yoga practice, then more lecture. By Sunday evening of each weekend, James had done as much as four hours of vigorous yoga a day, and he'd crash early and sleep like the dead.

Weekdays weren't much easier. James attended at least one, and sometimes two, regular studio classes daily and studied for at least two hours before going to bed. Inevitably, he would dream dreams steeped in the stories of Hindu gods and goddesses like Rama and Sita, Durga and Kali, and Shiva and Shakti. Physically, he developed more strength, flexibility, and muscle definition than he'd ever had before. He stood straighter, slept better, and looked younger. His face relaxed, and he smiled more. Yoga really was the fountain of youth.

James also found that he didn't feel so out of place anymore, being older than everyone else. Yoga teacher training evened things out, and he began to see the younger students as simply fellow travelers on the strange and dusty road of life. His more extensive experience meant only that he'd been wandering a bit longer than they.

Sara led most of the classes. She talked about teaching yoga as poetry in motion and backed it up by reading her favorite poems before every practice. She spoke confidently of mantras and magic, beauty and rhythm, and James fell in love with her lessons, her stories, her humor, and her intelligence. She was larger than life, Shakti incarnate, a magnificent manifestation of the Divine Feminine.

James tried his best to not fall in love with her; he really did. He'd been down that rabbit hole too many times before, and besides, he knew there was no way they were ever going to connect, except as student and teacher. He couldn't help himself, though. He started to fantasize about what it would be like to just hang out, discussing yoga, the Hindu deities, and poetry. She clearly had a connection to the gods, and that drew him toward her like a moth to a flame. In the end, it was poetry that broke him. It happened about three weeks into the course at her private yoga studio. She wanted to meet one-on-one with each student, and he was the last.

Her studio was on the second story of a building downtown, and James arrived early, and she arrived late. He was hanging out on the street, watching the cars go by and enjoying the sun. She handed him a paper cup of hot chai tea, unlocked the door to the stairwell, and led the way upstairs.

The studio confirmed much about who he thought she was. The walls were painted a peaceful, rose-tinged beige, the floor was made of smooth oak planks, and there was a bank of windows that opened westward with an unobstructed view of the mountains. Under the windows, a statue of Ganesha stood on a low altar that was draped with a saffron-colored scarf and decorated with candles, brass bells, crystals, and malas. Around the rest of the room she'd placed many more statues of deities—James recognized Shiva, Kali, Nataraja, and others. A floor-to-ceiling bookcase along one wall was filled with books on everything from yoga and Hindu writings to poetry, psychology, and mythology. Original art covered the rest of the horizontal surfaces except for one place where mirrors stretched from floor to ceiling.

They sat on a couple of cushions near the altar to Ganesha, and she locked her eyes on James. "I've taught ten thousand hours of teacher trainings," she said. "Every class is different, and in every class, I get to meet interesting people. You kind of stick out. You're obviously more mature than the rest of the students, you've got a very strong practice, and you seem pretty serious. Maybe a bit too serious…too intense."

"Thanks, I guess. I've often been accused of being a bit high-strung, that I need to lighten up."

"Yoga is all about the breath and learning to get out of your head. Intensity comes from the head. Get into your heart. Find peace. Yoga is supposed to help you reduce stress, not add to it."

James tried to chuckle, but it came out as forced.

"So, tell me about you," she continued, shifting her legs and settling in on her meditation cushion. She sipped her tea and looked at him over the edge of the paper cup.

"Um, what do you want to know?"

"How'd you get into yoga? Why teacher training? And why now?"

"A girlfriend introduced me to it. Years ago. I tried it out a bit, but it never really stuck. I was more of an endurance athlete, doing triathlons. You know, stuff like that. Then I began to get worn down and came back to yoga as a form of cross-training and stress relief. I got hooked, developed an interest in Hindu mythology and deities…and here I am."

It went on like that for a couple of minutes—her asking him about his life, James giving answers, and her probing deeper. No answer fully satisfied her. Always she wanted a little more. Finally, she set her tea down on the floor, leaned forward, and cupped her chin in her hand. Her gaze intensified, and her eyes bored into him.

"You write Sufi mystic poetry." She said it like a statement, not a question. "My mother's from the Punjab, and she loves the Sufi poets. She raised me to love them, too, especially the insight and the humor. Can I hear some of yours?"

"Well, I'm certainly *not* a Sufi," James said with a laugh. "But, you know, Rumi and Hafiz, their poetry really resonates with me, and when I write, I feel like their style creeps in, maybe a little bit. As for my stuff being mystic, well, I'm not even sure what that means." He shrugged his shoulders.

"Real mystics never call themselves mystics. And besides, labels mean different things to different people. Who cares, as long as *we* know what we mean? I have my own definition of mystic. Let's hear something, and I'll tell you if I think you're my type of mystic or not." She smiled and took another sip of her tea.

James fumbled in his backpack and pulled out his book of poetry. His mother's scrapbook, with a red, leather-bound cover embossed like crocodile skin, and clear plastic sleeves for pages that held about thirty poems and one little painting of a flower.

"I wrote this one yesterday. It came to me at the end of class, while lying in *shavasana*." *Shavasana* was the last pose of a yoga class, in which the students lay on their backs, fully relaxed and meditating, with their eyes closed and the palms of their hands facing up.

~~ *God's Greatest Gift* ~~

God's greatest gift
is imperfection.
Only the most skilled artists
build flaws
into their favorite work.

Like the crack in a fired pot,
filled with gold
and turquoise,
to show where the true beauty lies.
Proof
that God loves you the most.

Cherish your flaws!
God does.

~~ * ~~

When James finished reading, she sat silent for a moment, as if tasting a sip of an unfamiliar but expensive wine. "You wrote that? In *shavasana?*"

"Yeah. When we were talking in class, you know, about valuing our own imperfections, I remembered seeing a picture of a shattered Japanese rice bowl that'd been repaired with molten gold. The beautiful pattern of cracks was accentuated…highlighted…and to the Japanese, the bowl was rendered more beautiful and more valuable than before. Special, unique. A metaphor for life. They call that technique Kintsugi."

Sara looked down, not speaking, her hand subconsciously touching the scar that ran down the side of her face, a leak of unexpected vulnerability beneath her larger-than-life persona. As soon as she did that, James cringed. What the hell? What had possessed him to read that particular poem?

After a moment, she sat up a little taller and looked him in the eyes. "Thank you for that. That's really beautiful. Really."

His expression must have revealed his embarrassment because she reached over and touched his hand. "Hey, it's OK," she said. "That poem's beautiful. And true. Not everyone sees that."

She smiled as if he'd discovered a secret she'd never shared with anyone.

"I write my own poetry, too," she continued. "But never had the courage to read it in public."

"You? Too scared? How's that possible?"

"My first husband...yes, I've been married and divorced twice, since any mistake worth making is worth repeating. Well, he used to tell me it was crap...that I was making a fool of myself."

James shrugged and grinned at her. "Sometimes, you just gotta say, 'What the fuck.' Look at me. I'm forty-seven, taking a yoga teacher training with twenty-year-olds. What the fuck! I write poetry about love. What the fuck! Am I making a fool of myself? Who cares? And would it matter if someone thought I was? Fuck, no!"

She relaxed a bit, her eyes smiling at him. "One of my favorite lines! 'Sometimes you just gotta say, What the fuck!' *Risky Business*, Tom Cruise!"

"That's right! Are you a movie buff?"

"Absolutely!"

That set the stage for the rest of the hour. James revealed that he hoped to be a full-time writer someday. Sara disclosed that despite her mother's Hindu roots, her family hated her career choice of teaching yoga. He shared that he was divorced and a father of two, and she admitted that in the wake of her two failed marriages, she'd decided to avoid relationships altogether. He told her about surviving cancer, and she described the challenges of life as a celebrity on the yoga festival circuit. Their hour together flew by, and by the end of it, they'd bonded, as if in exposing their little failures and insecurities they'd built an unexpected bridge of trust.

As they were leaving her space and she was locking up the door, Sara turned to him and said, "James, the path of mysticism is hard. Mystics see things and hear things and feel things in ways that others don't. By any measure, they are certifiably crazy. I applaud it, but I don't recommend it." And then she smiled, her eyes unguarded.

James met her eyes, and for the first time saw how pale their blue was, like the midsummer sky veiled by thin wisps of clouds. "I'll try to remember that," he heard himself say, as if from far away.

Years later, James found this poem in a slim volume of her published poetry that he picked up in a used bookstore. He didn't know if she wrote it before or after their meeting. Only that it fit her perfectly.

~~ *The Mystic's Call* ~~

A mystic sees all the world
as beauty,
and that love and despair
are indivisible,
and infinite.

A mystic hears a deeper melody,
writes words as liquid objects,
paints portraits with silken love-strokes,
and builds poetry
like temples.

A mystic tastes music
as a flowing river of honey
that carries her orchid heart
over rapids
and waterfalls
of agony and ecstasy.

A mystic wrestles feelings
like untamed living creatures,
like blooming wildflowers,
like vines
entwined as lovers.

A mystic worships the goddess moon,
a white lotus
breaking the surface of night,
softening darkness,
easing the harsh burning
of life's sun.

The mystic's call
cannot be ignored.
That which is known
cannot be unknown,
unfelt,
unheard.

Like the sacred sound
of OM,
the fiery scar of mysticism
cannot be unburnt
from the heart.

~~ Saraswati Stowe ~~

Chapter Twenty

~ * ~

Labradorite

His conversation with Sara stayed with him all that evening and floated at the top of his consciousness when he woke the next morning. James already admired her knowledge and her inspiring presence, but the vulnerability he'd glimpsed made her even more interesting. It was like seeing a third dimension inflate a two-dimensional work of art. If she'd been a portrait before, now she was a sculpture, to be examined and admired from all directions. James decided to text her to thank her.

> *Hey, I really enjoyed hanging out with you yesterday.*

Surprisingly, she texted back immediately.

Wow. I was JUST picking up my phone
to text you the same thing!!!

> *LOL. Great minds think alike.*
> *How are you?*

Inspired. I've been on fire since
our time together. Last night I wrote
for two hours in my journal. Today I
got up early, ran, wrote poetry.
Thank you!

James stared at the screen. Really? Inspired? On fire? What was she trying to say?

> *Thank me? LOL. Thank YOU for*
> *taking the time to get to know each of*
> *us students.*

I always do that.
Never know who you'll uncover.
A potential protégé, a future
great teacher, a marvelous poet.

> *Haha! Yeah, let me know if you meet*
> *any marvelous poets!*

Maybe in you I met all three.

Huh. James didn't know what to say, so he didn't respond. He fed Rocco, let him out into the backyard to do his business, and finished cutting up some fruit for his granola. After a few minutes, his phone buzzed again.

Two hearts that speak the same
language are like two wings on
the same bird. - Hafiz

The words stared up at him, written in stark black and white on the tiny screen. No sound. No face to scan for context. Just words. Why did she choose that quote? Was this just an idealistic sentiment, or was there a message here? In any event, he had to respond in kind. He scrambled around the house looking for his book of Rumi poetry. He couldn't find it. Damn! He grabbed his own book of poetry, flipped through it, and found something that might work.

> *For love is the magic*
> *That changes music to rubies*
> *Weaves silver through poems,*
> *And sets fire to dreams.*

Wow, never heard that one.
Who wrote it?

> *I did. It's from a longer poem,*
> *"This Exploration of Beauty."*

Love it! James, I feel like we're
kindred spirits! Can we send each
other poetry every day? You've
sparked something in me.

Send each other poetry every day? Was this more than just a game between two word-loving people? Was she saying that she wanted to share her deepest feelings? Because that's what poetry was, deep feelings encoded in the music of words. James felt an ancient glow spring up in his chest. Sparks indeed. He texted her back.

Consider me sparked as well.
Can't wait to do it again.

You're a special soul.
I feel so lucky that our paths
have crossed.

Maybe it was more than luck.

Call it fate then. Don't forget.
Send me a poem tonight.

James wandered around all that day in a fog, the Greek chorus of gods chattering as they debated the possibilities. He was infatuated, enthralled, mesmerized by a magical woman, but this time it was different. He didn't fantasize about her body or kissing her. No, he basked in her spirituality, her powerful presence, her knowledge. She'd chosen *him* to exchange poetry, share ideas, feelings and inspiration, and he began, for the first time, to visualize her as more than his teacher, their heads together, whispering secrets in words no one else would understand.

After that, they texted each other every night, and sometimes in the morning as well, sharing poetry from Hafiz, Rumi, Kahlil Gibran, and others. Often, he'd send her his own poems, too, for her approval and acknowledgment. Their conversations lasted for hours, delving into spirituality and the meaning of life, and they even ventured into discussions about whether Great Love was really possible or only a fiction of the arts. A love that could make time stand still, transcend space, and survive war and famine and death.

During the day, James attended as many of her studio classes as his work schedule would allow. He usually took a spot in the second or third row, not so close as to crowd her, but close enough that she was in his line of sight. Sometimes she would meet his eye and smile, as if sharing a secret. Each class began with a greeting, followed by a poem, which she read aloud from her journal. Often, it was a poem she'd sent to James or he'd sent to her the night before, and he would grin with pleasure at his insider's knowledge.

James brought her little gifts. A flower, a new journal, a card with a poem. He wanted to share anything he thought was beautiful because *she* would understand. As his work schedule allowed, he became her gofer, running small errands and solving her problems. If she needed a flat fixed, he drove her. If she needed her lease renewed, he looked it over. In the weekend teacher training classes, James strove to be her most dedicated student.

Nevertheless, she kept her physical distance, as if daylight reminded her of the protocols of the teacher/student relationship and she needed to rebuild the boundary that crumbled every night under the onslaught of their texting. She refused to speak by phone and they were never alone together, which James found frustrating, but it was what she was offering, and he accepted it gladly.

Seven weeks into the course Sarah led the students through a vigorous, two-hour class that focused on backbends and heart-opening sequences. From simple to complex. From upward dog to full wheel, and everything in between. And in the aftermath of so much opening, Sara had all of them take out their journals.

"To finish today, you're going to do a very important exercise. One that will illuminate your lives as students of yoga—indeed, as citizens of this planet—and how you bring forth your light in community. Today, you're going to figure out your *sva-dharma*, your life's purpose. Your *raison d'être*. Why you were born, and what gift you bring to the world. So, for the first step, open your journal and write down everything that you think you are, everything you think you value, and who you want to be. Everything that defines you, your hopes, loves, dreams, desires. Make it as detailed as you like. And then I'll tell you about the second step."

The room bustled with activity as students got out their journals and pens, and it then gradually stilled as everyone bent over his or her work. James wrote a page that described his love of the outdoors and the natural sciences, the sea and the mountains, and the night sky and his garden. He expressed his gratitude for his children and said he hoped to have a family again someday, with a wife and a loving home. He detailed his plans to become a writer and how writing poetry made time stand still. He wrote it all down and looked at his page. There it all was, his life if life were perfect.

After thirty minutes, Sara spoke again. "Now, look at what you've written, and boil it down to the essence. One, maybe two paragraphs."

Everyone went back to work. James picked out his most important sentences, tried to consolidate them into compact, well-written thoughts. After another half hour of editing and re-writing, he felt pretty good about his two paragraphs.

"And now, boil it down to three sentences," Sara said to a chorus of groans. She was smiling. Heads went back down, and pens scratched again at the pages. Another fifteen minutes went by.

"OK, now look at what you've got," Sara said. "I'm sure it's wonderful, but we want the essence of the essence. Look for one word, the most important one, and add a few modifiers and perhaps a verb. Boil it down to one sentence. And then we will read them aloud."

More groans, and fifteen minutes later, when James completed the exercise, he had six words. His *sva-dharma*, his *raison d'être:*

To seek, create, and enjoy beauty.

Six simple words, as powerful as a motto engraved on a coat of arms. Maybe written in French, under crossed writing quills and a heart.

Chercher, créer, et apprécier la beauté.

He could have used the word love instead of beauty, but beauty encompassed love as much as love encompassed beauty. When it was his turn, he read his six words to the class, and Sara was smiling, her expression not one of surprise, but of acknowledgment, as if she'd already known what he was going to say. And James marveled at the elegance of the exercise as he realized the brilliance of it and the freedom and direction it gave him.

* ~ * ~ *

Six days before the final exam, Sara texted him just as he was wrapping up a day at work.

> *Oh Mystic Poet, I'm going to*
> *Stephen's class tonight.*
> *Practice with me?*

James stared at the text. They could practice yoga together, side by side, not as teacher and student, but as—what?

> *I'm there. Save me a spot!*

> *Done. Glass of bubbles after?*

James felt his pulse quicken. Was the boundary crumbling now? Was this a breakthrough? He took a deep breath.

> *Of course!*

It was dark when James arrived at The Yoga Studio. He changed hurriedly and went into the classroom. It was crowded, but Sara was already there, her mat laid out in the front row next to the teacher's. She'd saved the spot on the other side of her by putting down her yoga towel. When James walked in, she smiled and moved her towel aside. Blushing, James thanked her and unrolled his mat. He felt like all eyes were on them because he was a student and she was a teacher, and her gesture could be noticed and remarked upon by many in the small, tight community. He started to loosen up. She was like an exotic, predatory cat next to him, stretching, reaching, bending her powerful, exquisitely feminine body with style and grace.

Once the class started and they were moving in synch to the cues of the teacher, it was heaven. James was intensely aware of her presence so close to him in the packed room, and he tried to mirror her fluidity and balance. The class was rigorous, and by the end he was drenched in sweat, and his yoga towel was soaked. She glowed a bit from the exertion but otherwise looked as fresh as ever.

At the end of class, as they lay face up in *shavasana*, side by side, James felt the electricity in his fingers reaching out to hers, inches away. He fantasized that she would slide her fingers over and touch his, but it never happened.

After showering and dressing, they met outside the yoga studio and walked down the mall to Riff's, a quiet Pearl Street restaurant with low lighting, exposed brick walls, and dark wood. They slid into an intimate, isolated booth in the back corner, facing each other. They scanned the wine list, and she picked out a bottle of pink champagne for James to order. When the wine came, she raised her glass in a toast.

"To mystics," she said. Her smile was completely relaxed, unguarded. James felt like he was finally face-to-face with Sara the woman, not Sara the teacher.

"I really liked practicing next to you," he replied, smiling.

"Really? Why?" She sipped her champagne and regarded him over the rim of the glass. Around them, the other diners were lost in their candlelit intimacy, two-dimensional silhouettes cast on their shroud of privacy in the corner booth.

"So many reasons...I loved watching you move...crazy

beautiful—"

A shadow flitted across her face, so briefly James almost didn't catch it. Then she smiled and looked down at her glass as if studying the bubbles. "James…I'm just a girl."

Just a girl? By any definition she wasn't "just a girl."

"A crazy-beautiful girl."

"You're sweet." She mouthed a kiss, her perfect lips pursed as she blew it toward him, and then she laughed.

They sat in silence that wasn't exactly awkward, but still cried out for a confession. James bit his lip. Practicing next to her had felt like foreplay, a prelude to something more intimate and physical. Just days before, such thoughts had seemed like forbidden religious art, hidden behind lock and key for fear it would upset the ecumenical balance of his mind.

"Can I confess something?" he asked.

"Something bad?" She arched her eyebrows at him.

"Maybe. I've started having impure thoughts about someone in the class."

"Really?" She laughed again, easily, like a cat stretching languorously. "James, romances happen all the time between students in yoga teacher trainings. It's totally natural, with so much time together, so much vulnerability."

"She's really beautiful, but I don't know how she feels."

"Well, perhaps you should let it just be. Let it marinate, until the training is over," she said gently. "Let yourself return to the real world, and then see if the feelings are still there."

She didn't ask who the woman was, and that was as far as James took it. Their conversation wandered away from the minefield of yoga class attractions and into safer territory, the realm of ideas. They finished the bottle of wine, and she said she had to get home to bed. James paid the tab, escorted her to a taxi, and received a hug goodnight. That was it.

As he drove home, his mind spun with possibilities. She had to have known where he was going with his little confession, hadn't she? And yet, she didn't shut him down totally, either. Yes, she was his teacher, and there were strict protocols that had to be observed in such a relationship, but she was so much more than that, too. She was his muse, his inspiration, his image of perfection in a partner. Wise, strong, someone who could teach him so much! She brought strengths to the table that offset his weaknesses, and he was sure what he could offer her was equally advantageous. By the time James was pulling into his garage, hope had made love to optimism and birthed a fantastical future together. Her voice was whispering a poem inside his head, and he had to get to his writing desk and capture it. He opened another bottle of wine, poured himself a glass, and sat down at his laptop. By midnight, he'd written The Avatar.

~~ *The Avatar* ~~

Hafiz and I
were sitting in a cafe,
sipping tea,
watching the sun descend in fiery splendor
over the shadowed mountain,
and he told me about the Avatar.

"She's a woman of perfection,
a human incarnation,
a living goddess,
the peak of God's creation.
But you won't find her hanging around
this tea shop.

She lives far to the south,
across the desert of desperation,
past the sea of sorrow.

They say no man has ever seen her face,
only her eyes,
peeking over her veil.

And yet, her beauty sends men to madness,
rushing out to slay dragons,
conquer kingdoms,
prove their worthiness,
when all she wants
is a lover.
But not just any lover.

A lover who burns,
whose heart
enfolds all the world
in the fire of his compassion.

She wants a poet whose words
light a flame
in every heart that hears them.
A man who says things that few can say,
but all can understand.

She wants a warrior
to take his place beside her,
a pillar of strength,
a partner in truth,
to navigate life's labyrinth
together.

A suitor who kneels,
not to beg, but to invite.

A champion whose arms are strong,

yet gentle,
whose embrace gives her space,
to stretch and grow,
to reach her full potential.

An artist who seeks beauty,
not as something to possess,
but as something to worship,
with reverence and awe.

She wants a philosopher
who can gaze up at the heavens
and name the stars
that shine on her face, also.

She will suffer no man to come to her
who cannot look into her heart
and find the place there
reserved for an equal,
not a master of that
which cannot be commanded.

She waits for her love,
not with hope,
but with faith that he will come."

Hafiz drained his cup,
lost in contemplation of such a wonder.
Then he turned to me,
his knowing smile broad.
"So, why are you still sitting here?" he asked.

~~ * ~~

That night, James fell asleep quickly, and wild images and

sensations swirled through his dreams. He didn't usually remember his dreams, but that night there was magic flowing through his awareness, and he dreamed that he was sleeping on a bed of soft pearls, all rolling and slipping and shining their pearlescent light into his eyes and heart and brain.

The next morning, his phone buzzed just as he was getting out of bed. It was a text from Sara.

> *A bottle shared is like prose. Add*
> *bubbles, and you have poetry. – Sara*

James laughed and texted her back.

> *Good morning Beautiful! You're up*
> *early*

> *I ran for thirty minutes, made breakfast,*
> *meditated. And wrote that little aphorism,*
> *inspired by last night Do you like it?*

> *I do! Very appropriate! Did you sleep*
> *well?*

> *Like a baby. I always do when I*
> *practice in the evening. You?*

> *Like someone cast a magic spell.*

> *LOL! OK, your turn. Where's my poem???*
> *I want a JW original! Off the cuff.*

> *Hmmm. Gimme a sec.*

James set down his phone and picked up a pen. He thought for a minute, then scribbled a few words on a pad of paper that lay close at hand. With a grin, he grabbed his phone and typed.

> *You and I are twins*
> *in thought and manner.*
> *Yet, different in all*
> *the ways that matter*
> *to man and woman.*
> *Perhaps we should rub away*
> *our differences,*
> *round off our edges,*
> *and become as one? ~~ JW*

OMG! That is too funny! Pretty
suggestive though

I don't know. I think it could work

James didn't hear back from her, and the minutes ticked by. Ouch! Perhaps he'd been too direct, maybe spooked her? He paced around the room, waiting, then gave it up and went to take a shower. A half hour went by, and the phone beeped.

I'm teaching at 10:30 this morning.
You coming?

James checked his schedule of meetings. Yep, he was free from 10:00 a.m. on. Plenty of time to get over to the yoga studio.

Wouldn't miss it!

As usual, Sara's class was packed. James found a spot in the second row, laid down his mat, and waited for class to begin. She walked in with her journal and malas and scarf and settled onto her mat at the front of the room. The class waited with respectful silence.

"Good morning, yogis," she began. "One of the things I love about this community is that we have so many wonderful and accomplished people in the room. Look around you. Among your fellow yogis are doctors, scientists, world-class athletes, and poets. We are truly blessed in this community. And this morning, I want to read a wonderful poem, not from Rumi or Hafiz, but written by one of you, someone in this room."

James started, surprised. She'd said nothing about this. Was she really going to read one of his?

"So please settle in a comfortable, seated position," she continued. There was a rustle in the room as forty people grew silent. His heart was pounding. "This is called 'The Gods Looked Down on Us.' I'll keep the writer anonymous."

~~ *The Gods Looked Down on Us* ~~

The gods looked down on us
and said,
"You are our favorite children,
so why so sad?
Have we not given you
the sunlight
and the moonlight
for your love games?

We created you
to fill our ears with laughter,
to fill our hearts with longing,
to fill our souls
with the sweet music of your sighs.

Your job

is to love one another.
Get to work."

Sara read his poem with grace and sincerity, conviction and reverence, no different from when she read the great Sufi mystics. As she read, James lowered his eyes and tried to suppress a grin. A young woman on the mat next to him saw his reaction, smiled, and mouthed the question, "It's you?" He shrugged his shoulders, but his smile slipped out. He felt exposed at the core level, and the muscles in his back cramped and spasmed as he listened, and yet it was exhilarating, too. Out of the corner of his eye, he strained to see the reactions of the other students.

The woman next to him smiled and mouthed the words "Really great!" James just nodded and kept grinning.

"That's going to be the theme of this class," said Sara, finishing and rising to her feet. "Love is work, the work we were put on this earth for. Not always easy, not always fun. It's messy and complicated and hard. But it keeps the gods amused."

The students laughed.

"Today's lesson is that your job is to love each other," she continued. "Everything else flows from this. Today, we flow from love."

Throughout the entire class, James flowed effortlessly from pose to pose, fueled by adrenaline. At the end, several people approached Sara for a copy of the poem. One was a visiting yoga teacher from Massachusetts. Sara pointed all of them in James's direction, so he was no longer incognito.

Later, back in his office, James texted Sara.

> *That was incredible! Thank you!*
> *Never had someone read my poetry*
> *in public before.*

Honored to be the first!

Won't be the last, I'm sure.

Wow, it was a rush!

*You light shines brightly, Dear Poet.
Hey, crazy idea --- come to India with
me! I'm leading a retreat there in
December. You can be my assistant!*

Your assistant??? Could I do that?

*Why not? I need an assistant.
You'd be perfect.*

Sara and he, together in India? That would be his fantasy blossoming into fulfillment.

*What are the dates? Gotta sort out
my kids.*

*I'll send you an email with the info.
It'll be great. Students coming from
all over. I want to experience India
with those who'd see the poetry in it.
Please? It would be fun!*

James stared at the tiny screen as the more cautious gods shouted warnings that echoed down the empty corridor of his mind labeled Rational Thoughts. Wait a sec! What's this really about? Maybe she was just in yoga teacher selling mode. Yoga retreats were expensive, and if he signed up for the retreat, he'd be shelling out thousands of dollars—to her. Then he remembered her smile as she looked at him over the wineglass, her face unguarded, open, and alive, her shoulder-length curls brushing against her shoulders. She'd chosen him again! First, exchanging poetry, and now, India. He slammed the door on the corridor of Rational Thoughts and ran around the corner to Hopes and Dreams. There, the door to a future with her was cracked open. He smiled. Sometimes, you have to walk through that door to find out what's on the other side. Sometimes, you just gotta say, "What the fuck!"

> *Always wanted to go to India. Count me in!*

> *Wonderful! I'm off to some big meetings. Text me later?*

> *Of course!*

Work that afternoon was a dull shuffle of documents. Building permits, accounts payable, marketing plans. And while he processed them, all he could think about was Sara. And India! What would that be like? Mercifully, the workday finally ended.

Back home, James prepared a grilled steak with mushrooms and a big salad. Annie was living in a freshman dorm up at the University of Colorado, so dinner would be for just Chris and himself. Miraculously, with the onset of puberty and a voracious appetite, Chris had grown out of his hatred for all vegetables and had come to love salads with lots of avocado and tomato. He'd even invented his own tasty dressing, a balsamic vinaigrette with a touch of mustard. Already he was almost as tall as his sister and sprouting like a weed.

After dinner, James helped Chris with a geology project for high school. They set it up on the dining room table, where Chris spread out a big map of the rock outcrops around Boulder and a shoebox filled with samples collected on his last field trip.

"Dad, I just don't get this stratigraphy stuff."

"It's simple, Chris. Stratigraphy is just the layers of rocks and sediments, like a cake. The oldest ones on the bottom, younger ones on top."

"I know that, geez! But these rocks that get all twisted and fractured. How do I know which formation these samples come from?"

Just then, James's phone buzzed.

*Oh James --- I need some
inspiration. Got any?*

James smiled. Something must be up. This was early for Sara to text. "Hey listen," he said to Chris. "I gotta take this. So while I do that, look at the rock samples, figure out what they are, first. Sedimentary, igneous, metamorphic. And then we can sit down and find where they fit on the map."

"Daaad," Chris whined.

"Just give me a minute. You can do this." James left Chris pouting over his homework and went to sit in the kitchen. He texted Sara.

Where are you?

*At my studio. Designing a
program for a festival.*

*It's pretty late. Why are you still
working?*

*Huge deadline. But I feel --- blah.
My fire has gone out. I'm stuck.
But I don't want to bother you.
You're probably with your family.*

James felt a pang of guilt, but it faded quickly.

Nah. Not busy. What do you need?

I don't know. Something. I'm procrastinating.
Poem from you?
A real one, from your book.

"Dad!" Chris yelled from the living room. "This red rock we got from the Flatirons. Is that a sandstone?"

"Yeah," James yelled back. "Also called a composite. Lots of cobbles and pebbles from an ancient streambed."

"Are you going to be a while?" Chris sounded annoyed.

"Just a few more minutes."

"Man, tell her you're busy!"

"Hush!"

James focused back in on the tiny screen in his hand, at her last words in black and white. Was Sara giving him permission to say what had almost boiled over in him at the restaurant the night before? He could send her "The Avatar," but no, it was too long for a text. And besides, what he wanted to say had to be said directly, with clarity and as few words as possible. She'd opened the door by inviting him to India. Was he reading the signals right? Dare he risk it? Right now? He drew a deep breath.

OK. I was saving this.
Warning! It's strong medicine.

I need strong medicine.
Heal me, my mystic poet LOL!

I wrote this for you...

James typed out his poem, one that had come to him in the first moments of waking a few days before.

I want to drink your heart

Like the finest wine.
But first, you must pour it
Into the cup of your outstretched
hands,
And raise it to my lips. ~ JW

After James pressed *send*, his heart pounded audibly in his ears. He took a series of long slow breaths to calm down. The card was laid and played. How would she respond? Like a tiger, prodded with a stick poked between the bars of its cage, would she react with a purr or a snarl? Rejection was a distinct possibility. The seconds ticked by and his chest ached with adrenaline. He wandered back into the living room, helped Chris match up a few of his samples with the map. Finally, his phone buzzed. He took it back into the kitchen.

James, that's beautiful!
You wrote that for me?
You have me simultaneously speechless
and wanting to say a lot.

> *Well, you asked for help restarting*
> *your fire. I can only share what*
> *burns inside me.*

You do know I don't want to
be in a relationship right now?
That I CAN'T be in relationship
right now!!!

> *No, I remember you said you were*
> *single*

James, I have to learn to be with

myself. Be celibate. Go inwards.
Learn to love ME. Like a spiritual practice.
Besides, I'm a terrible failure at relationships.
Nothing but pain.

Sarah had told him that she'd been alone since her last divorce, but she'd never said why. James waited for more, but nothing came over the tiny screen. He finally typed in a message.

But what about love?

What about it?

Rumi says "Gamble everything for love." Consider this me, placing my wager.

Silence. A couple of more minutes ticked by without a response. James went back into the living room to check on Chris's progress. Chris was on his phone texting friends. His rock samples lay scattered on the table, the project unfinished.

"Hey, get off the phone!" James ordered. "Finish your homework."

"What about you?" Chris replied with teenage petulance. "You're on the phone with *your* girlfriend."

"She's not my girlfriend, and I'm not in school."

"Oh no? Coulda fooled me." The insolence in his voice didn't disguise the truth of what he was saying.

James' phone buzzed again, and he went back into the kitchen for privacy.

Are you saying you love me? You hardly know me! What could possibly make you think I'd be worth it?

Seriously? How can you even ask???

*Your worth is immeasurable to
the right man. Me! And besides,
we speak the same language! The
language of mystics! You've said it
yourself.*

James was typing frantically, his lofty, impossible words pouring out through his fingers onto that tiny screen, words that didn't say, couldn't say, exactly what he wanted to say. Argh! Why had he even broached the subject? Why had he been so *stupid?* A declaration of love *by text?* Really? Face-to-face, James would have been able to convey so much more with tone of voice, facial expressions, body language. He would have been able to read her eyes, gauge reaction, judge inflection. But texting stripped their conversation of every nuance and expression just when those subtleties were needed the most. Shit. He was in too deep now.

*What about the poetry you send me,
and I send you?
Are you saying that it meant
nothing?*

*Sufi poetry about love can be
interpreted two ways. As love for
the carnal and love for the divine.
These days I prefer the divine.*

*Hey, don't discount the carnal! LOL
Besides, we both want Great Love!
Love that inspires poetry! You've
said so yourself.*

I do, but I ask myself - how could

I even know what Great Love is?
Poetically, it's all so easy.
In real life not so much.

James tried to think of a rebuttal, but she was right. This stilted conversation via text was proof of that.

Anyway, I gotta go. Gotta get
something written down for this
stupid project.

James mentally kicked himself. What had he expected? For her to declare her love for him and abandon her spiritual practice or whatever it was, right then, over a few texts? He was a fool. But he could still make it worse.

I hope I don't end up regretting
sharing that poem with you, playing
that card.

She responded immediately.

Please please please don't regret
playing that card! It's there, and I'm
well aware that I may have encouraged
its play, and I need to ask myself why.

Those last words on the screen echoed in his consciousness and he deflated even further. "*I need to ask myself why?*" Clearly, she was chastising herself for leading him on. He typed a response that was as dull as he felt.

I gotta get back to some stuff. Good

luck with your project!

Thanks! Sleep well tonight.

James scrolled back through their conversation, hoping to find something, *anything*, of redemptive value in what he had blurted out in their conversation. His mood plummeted into the depths as the reality of their relationship sunk in. He helped Chris finish his homework and then took Rocco out for a walk on the Bobolink Trail.

The late sun of midsummer had just sunk over the mountains to the west, and overhead the moon was almost full. Rocco sniffed the evening air, no doubt filled with the crisscrossing scents of creatures creeping off to bed or coming out to prowl. As they walked through fields of tall grass and skirted prairie wetlands, the crickets and frogs started their serenade. The sky grew dark. Somewhere nearby, an owl hooted, and across the fields a coyote yipped. Rocco stiffened, looking in the direction of the coyote. James wondered if the coyote spoke in a language Rocco could understand. Or was his message just an interesting noise? A slight breeze picked up, blowing in cooler air from the mountains as clouds sailed past the moon. After about an hour, they turned around and came back to the trailhead. At the end, their way was lit only by moonlight and fireflies, and his agitation was as dimmed as the moon shadows on the path.

That night, James dreamed that he had to get from one side of school campus to another. The bell for class was sounding, and he ran down twisting corridors and up stairs, down sidewalks, and across lawns to get to his classroom, but he kept finding himself headed in the wrong direction and never approaching his destination. He woke in the morning still dreaming that dream, and he recognized it because it was a recurring dream, one that had haunted him his entire life.

Chapter Twenty-One

~ * ~

Rutilated Quartz

It was Saturday, testing and graduation day for the yoga teacher training course. James arrived at the studio a little before 9:00 a.m. He laid his mat down on the vinyl floor along with his usual provisions—water, snacks, towel, notebook. It would be a long day, with continuous yoga until 4:00 p.m. The students would take turns teaching and being graded by the instructors.

People were still milling about, chatting, and comparing notes when Sara arrived, trailed by her assistant. She smiled at James and handed him a paper cup of tea.

"Blueberry oolong. One of my favorites," she said.

James tried to hide his surprise. He smiled back and thanked her, the picture of a perfect student thanking his teacher, but inside he fought an impulse to drag her out of the studio, to some place where they could talk. Alone. Face-to-face. So many important words had been exchanged via the thin thread of texts, as unfulfilling as a teaser to a movie, and he needed to know what was real and what was projection.

Sara proceeded up to the front of the room, greeting the other students and teachers along the way. James pushed her out of his mind and turned back to some gentle stretching.

The room quieted down, and Sara clarified the rules of the exam. There would be four groups, each teaching as teams for an hour. James's group had chosen him to teach the peak, or hardest pose, and then take the class through warm down, into final *shavasana* and the guided meditation at the end. They were to be the last group to go, so that meant he would have all day to think about it.

The morning flew by as the first two groups taught their classes. They had their hiccups, one person forgetting the sequence and another losing her voice to nerves, but for the most part it went well. The bar was set high. James felt exhilarated yet calm, like he was right where he was supposed to be.

When lunchtime came, he sat cross-legged on his mat and ate alone as everyone else went outside into the sunshine to chat, laugh, and share food. He wasn't really hungry but forced himself to eat anyway. Afterward, James sat silently with his eyes closed, trying to clear his head and meditate. He'd just managed to drift into that silent place of only breath when he felt a soft hand on his shoulder. He opened his eyes and saw Sara looking down at him.

"How're you doing?" she asked.

"Good. I'm good," James replied, and forced a smile, surprised to see her.

"This is for you, a gift, a thank-you for my beautiful poem," she said, and laid a mala of small emerald-green stone beads at the top of his mat. "I want you to wear it today. It was blessed by my teacher."

James picked up the mala and studied it. Green, the color of love energy in the Hindu tradition.

"*Anahata*, the heart chakra…" she continued. "Your poem… no one has ever said anything…or written anything to me…so… beautiful."

"Thank you," he said as his eyes met hers, and for a moment he imagined that there was something more, hidden deep in those pools of blue. Then her walls came back up, and she smiled and moved away toward the front of the room. James watched her go and felt both close to her and impossibly far away.

His teaching went well. Maybe it was because of Sara's mala, which bathed his heart chakra with its emerald-green *anahata* light even through his shirt. When his turn came, James stood confidently at the front of the room and workshopped the peak pose, which was Side Crow, appropriate for a level one class. He had twenty people twisting sideways and balancing their knees on their right elbow as they teetered above their mats. Most made it into the pose, a few for the first time. James then led them through a wind-down sequence and into the final relaxation pose of *shavasana*. After a guided meditation in *shavasana*, he brought them up to a seated position. In closing, James recited an invocation he made up on the spot, borrowing from the poem he'd written to Sara.

"…and as you go forth into the world, to shine your light as yoga teachers, cup your hands in front of your heart, and let your heart pour into that cup your best intentions, your learning, and your compassion. And then offer it up to your students with humility, to be drunk like the finest wine."

Afterward, James would remember and cringe at how corny it was, but at the time, his words were heartfelt and very much in keeping with what everyone had been moving toward the entire day and, indeed, the entire course. When he finished, the room was silent. James had spoken his invocation with closed eyes. He opened them and looked around to gauge the reaction. Sara was staring at him with an almost theatrical expression of amazement on her face, her hands over her heart. Out in the classroom, people were smiling and nodding, and one classmate broke the silence by saying aloud, "What just happened?" Everyone, teachers and students and guests alike, started clapping and cheering—for his group, for themselves, and ultimately because the course had come to an end.

After class, everyone went out to Shine, a local restaurant and bar favored by the yoga crowd. The drinks were flowing; everyone was dancing, drinking, and eating beetroot hummus. The tribe was celebrating. James danced with a number of the students but kept looking around for Sara. She was nowhere to be seen. He was exhausted, both physically and emotionally. It'd been a big day. He wondered where she was and why she hadn't joined her students in the celebration. After about an hour, he excused himself and headed home.

Rocco greeted him at the door with his happy dance, and they went out for a short walk on the Bobolink. They strolled through the late evening, and the stress of the day drifted away on the soft breeze that sighed through the cottonwoods. Between leafy treetops, James could see the moon hanging just over the mountains. Venus, the evening star, was aligned nearby, and other stars were just beginning to glimmer in the background as the sky grew darker. Rocco tracked tiny footprints and interesting smells, zigzagging back and forth across the path, his nose to the ground. They walked for half an hour before returning home.

Back at home, James collapsed into a hot bath with Epsom salts. It was getting late, and he thought he might hear from Sara. He didn't. And he was frustrated. It was as if she'd erected a huge fortress around her heart, one with walls inside walls. After he'd find his way past one wall, another appeared. He thought of sending her a poem, per their nightly vow, but nothing he could think of seemed appropriate. He slept poorly that night and tossed and turned. He often felt aches and pains in his hips and shoulders after so much yoga, but this night, he was especially sore. James woke the next morning to his phone beeping. It was a text from Sara.

I'm not sure what to do.

> *About what?*

About you.

> *Yeah? What do you mean?*

*You want so much more than
I can give right now. I've been
down that road. I don't trust
myself. I don't trust love.*

> *Sara, the past is the past. The present
> is what we will make of it.*

*The past casts a long shadow
over me. And you act as if we
were already having an affair.*

> *Well, we've done it all except for the
> sex part…*

*Please! That's not funny! I consider
celibacy a spiritual practice. Intimacy
just muddies the waters. Destroys clarity.
These days, I desperately need clarity.*

> *Clarity is good. But if we only
> interact via text, then clarity about
> us is the last thing we get.*

LOL were you ever a lawyer?

*Teacher training is over! You and
me, can't we move past the teacher/
student thing?*

James, I need time.

Time for what?

*Time to find out if I'm going
to stay with this spiritual practice or not.
Can you give me time? Can you give
me space?*

I'm more interested in the affair…

*Lol. You and me --- who are we
to each other? Do we really even know?*

*Exactly my point! We need to spend
time together, face to face.*

*There are reasons I've dedicated
myself to celibacy, and I can't
just abandon that over --- attraction*

*So you admit you're attracted to
me?!*

*Of course I'm attracted to you!
Attraction is easy. Love is hard.
Relationships are hard. You want
a relationship. I could tell the
moment I met you.*

Ouch! Am I that transparent?

*Your poetry says it all. You're a hopeless
romantic. You have impossible ideals
and unattainable desires. You're
doomed to be disappointed by anyone
who loves you, and I'm not sure that I want
that person to be me.*

I doubt you'd disappoint me.

*You have no idea what I'm
like in a relationship. I'm a handful.
Willful, selfish, spoiled. Complex.
Hard to love. I've failed at love
too many times.*

The texts were coming fast and furious, like she'd turned on a tap. James watched the words appear on his phone, and wished he could see her face, read her eyes and hear her voice as she said them. This scrolling line of letters, without facial expression, body language, and tone of voice, bereft of nuance and context, was, at best, a lobotomized approximation of a conversation, squeezed through a lifeless bottleneck. He sighed.

*I want to experience India with someone
who'll see the poetry in the people,
the temples, the history! The deep, deep
holiness of it all. I want you to come with
me! You would love it!*

*But what about your space? Will you
need space from me in India?*

I don't know, James. I only know
I need my space now.

James felt whipsawed by the push-pull. She was attracted to him? She needed her space? Did she mean any of this, or was this just a word game for her? Were they taking one step forward, or two steps back? It was exhausting.

Can you give me what I need? So I can,
maybe, give you what you want?

Could he? James felt caught in a familiar trap. What was the matter with him? Willow and Charlie, both happy to entangle with him, both unwilling to commit because of various reasons. Why was he betting that this time would be different? Hadn't he learned anything? And this affair with Sara was worse. It was an affair of the mind only, like two word-loving people locked in separate cells of a dungeon, tapping out a conversation on the rock walls. And even though she'd admitted attraction, she didn't seem to value it highly. She saw it as a trap, a temptation away from greater things. At least that's what she said. What feelings did she really have? And why was he jumping in again? James shook his head. His mind took over for his heart and started calculating the odds of disappointment. They were high. Could he just keep saying "*What the fuck?*" no matter what obstacles she threw in his way? He sighed. Why did he even bother asking himself the question, when he already knew the answer?

Yes. Yes. Yes. Yes. Yes. Yes. Yes.
How many ways can I say yes to
you?

I guess we will see ---

*You need to know I have a terrible
history of falling in love with
unavailable women. I had SWORN
never again!!!*

She answered right back.

*Can you love me, but love me slowly?
I'm highly imperfect.*

*I don't care about imperfections.
Love is all about loving the imperfect*

*Then you'll have a lot to work
with LOL. You must promise me
that no matter what, NO MATTER
WHAT, I won't lose you.*

I can promise that.

Promises easily made, hard to keep. But at least they were finally
on the same page, edging their way onto opposite ends of a narrow,
crystalline bridge of fragile glass made of fancy words and lofty ideals, spanning a chasm of predictable disappointment.

Chapter Twenty-Two

~ * ~

Moonstone

A week later, James got a call at midnight. It was Sara, sobbing her words. "James, I'm having a bad night." She went silent for a moment, but James could hear the strain in her breathing as she sobbed silently.

"Hey, I'm so sorry. What's going on?" James spoke as calmly as he could. Something big must have happened. She never called him.

"My dreams. They're horrible! I thought they'd gone away for good. But tonight—" She broke away with a long series of sobs.

"Hey," he soothed. "How can I help? What do you need from me?"

"Come over? Please? I don't want to be alone."

She let James into her apartment. Her curly hair was awry, and her face was streaked and puffy from crying. She was wearing a long gray cashmere bathrobe that barely covered her ample curves, and a pair of fuzzy slippers. He wrapped her in his arms and hugged her and kissed the top of her head, and she sobbed anew into his chest. He just held her until she finished, and then she pulled away and led him to her couch. She had a fire lit in her fireplace.

Her home was a tiny one-bedroom apartment in a house on Maxwell Avenue, an expensive district up against the foothills. Her decor matched that of her studio space, with the walls crammed with original art, bookcases, and statues of Hindu deities. It had a warm, eclectic feel to it, a familiarity, as if she and James and Rumi and Hafiz could hang out there and drink wine and read poetry and explore the big questions.

She sat facing James on the couch, one leg tucked under her and the other resting on the floor. She had a mug of tea resting on the coffee table. "Want some?" she asked. He shook his head.

"Tell me what's going on," he said. He'd never seen her like this, so uncontrolled.

Sara took a sip of her tea and composed herself. "I've been feeling stirred up lately, like I can't find my footing. During the day it's OK, but at night—"

"What happens? Can't sleep? Or bad dreams?"

"Sometimes it's one, sometimes the other. It just wears me down."

"And what are the dreams about?"

"The past. Sometimes about…my family. Things that have… happened."

James noticed a framed formal family portrait of her family on the coffee table.

"May I?" James asked. She nodded, and he picked it up. The colors of the picture were faded and the costumes dated, as if from the 1980s. Sara might have been twelve years old, her hair cut with bangs across her forehead in an awkward pageboy. She was wearing a party dress, standing in front of her parents, her father's hands on her shoulders. He was tall and blond, a good-looking man in his forties.

Her mom stood next to him, an exotic, dark-skinned beauty in a sari. Her two older brothers flanked the parents, handsome young men who shared Sara's Eurasian features. There was also a dog.

"Beautiful family," James said.

"That was right before my father died…and I got this," she touched her scar. "It was a terrible accident. A drunk driver crashed into us. That's the last picture of us all together." Tears welled up in her eyes again.

"I'm so sorry," he whispered in her hair as he held her. She shook with a few more sobs, then pulled away, composing herself.

"That was a long time ago. But it's always left me with a need to understand *why?* Why are we here? What's our purpose? What's the value of even one day of human life? How can it be taken away so easily? I guess that's what drew me to the study of yoga. The big questions."

"Those keep me awake sometimes, too."

Sara fell silent, as if she'd run out of things to say. She turned toward him and buried her face in his chest.

"I'm tired," she sighed. "Stay here with me? Hold me close? Just to sleep?"

"Really?" he asked, surprised. "You want me to stay?"

"Just to sleep. Promise?"

James nodded.

She stood up and led him to her bedroom. It was a small room, almost like a closet, with only one window. James would have felt claustrophobic, but the continuation of the decor from the living room made it warm and inviting. Her king bed took up most of the room, and she pulled back the bedspread and scattered the dozen or so colorful pillows that covered it. She looked at him silently as if assessing him one last time, then took off her bathrobe, revealing a baggy white T-shirt and lacy panties. She climbed into the bed.

James kept his briefs on and climbed in next to her. She turned her back to him, and he spooned her with one arm around her waist, the other pillowing her head. She sighed and shifted her buttocks up against his pelvis and relaxed into the comfort of full body contact. Her body was very firm under the soft feminine padding that made her so perfect. His fingertips buzzed with energy where they touched her belly. His mind and body were awash with scarcely contained excitement, and it was impossibly erotic to be holding her. She had to have noticed his arousal, but her breathing slowed and her body spasmed briefly with electric jerks of her muscles releasing as she fell asleep. James remained wide awake, his lips against the back of her neck, breathing in her perfume. She used an exotic combination of scents that had him guessing. Cinnamon, jasmine, ylang-ylang? He lay there, intensely aware of the slow, steady pulse of life cradled in his arms. He felt her heartbeat against his chest and listened to the flow of her breath. Awake, she was powerful and commanding and his teacher. Asleep, she was vulnerable and soft and precious.

A thousand questions swirled around in his head as the parliament of gods debated anew, shouting back and forth, the leaders calling for order and the back benchers raising crazy demands. Was he in love? Or was he in love with the *idea* of love with such an exotic, amazing, accomplished woman, someone who could teach him so much? Their potential together seemed deep, mysterious, and filled with intriguing possibilities. But what did she feel? Clearly, she needed something from him; otherwise, why was he in her bed?

The arguments went back and forth, and fistfights broke out over what it all meant, but in the end there was never any doubt about what James was going to do. He was going to stay close, give her whatever she needed. She was vulnerable and had reached out to him, and he was determined to honor her wishes. He buried his face in her neck and her hair, took a deep breath, and fell asleep.

While he slept, he dreamed, and in his dream Sara came to him, her dream-self eager and willing to meet his deepest desires with her own. She was completely naked, sitting on top of him. She was Shakti incarnate, a magnificent manifestation of the Divine Feminine, with twelve arms and flawless golden-brown skin. Her round breasts had large, erect nipples, and she started riding him, slowly, taking what she needed, almost sobbing in her desire, and then faster and faster until she came, a release that had her straining against his pelvis as she gasped in the agony of orgasm.

James started to wake up and knew he was dreaming, but it felt so real, and he fought to stay in his dream. He kissed the dream Sara, his face almost merging with hers, and knew it was his turn to take what he needed from her. James wanted to see her and feel her and love her from every angle. Her magnificent body was a temple of the flesh, and with every part of his physical self he worshipped her. The dream Sara was strong and teased him, urging him on, then pulling away, but he was stronger, and they wrestled, tumbling across a bed of soft, green grass until she cried out in the throes of another climax. His own body felt like it was ready to explode with desire. It swelled and swelled and….

James woke lying on his back. It was just after dawn, and light was spilling into the room. Sara had rolled over toward him. Her arm encircled his chest, and her left leg was thrown over his pelvis. She had her head on his shoulder and her breasts pressed against his side. She still wore her T-shirt and panties, and he still had on his briefs. So, it had been just a dream after all.

James became intensely aware of her warm femininity, especially where the soft flesh of the inside of her thigh lay across his pelvis, and this time, his arousal must have awakened her, because she stirred, rubbed her pelvis up against him and murmured something in his ear. She brushed his lips with hers, briefly, and then opened her eyes. Fully awake, she sat up in shock, and clutched the sheet to her chest.

"Oh my god, James! What happened? Did we—"

James looked up at her, her hair disheveled, her eyes wide with panic. "Hey, no, we didn't," he said soothingly. "At least I don't think so." He smiled and tried to keep it light.

She backed away from him and clutched the sheet tighter. "Are you sure? My dream…it seemed so real! I felt us—felt you—"

James reached for her. "I'm pretty sure it was a dream, but it was good! Let's make it real."

Sara seemed to relax just a bit. She wrapped the sheet a bit more tightly around her body, creating space between them. "No. We can't. Not yet. I'm…I'm not ready for that."

"In my dreams you were."

"In my dreams, too. But this isn't a dream. This is real. And I think…you should leave before…before we ruin everything."

"Sara—"

"No, James."

He sighed. "OK. I'll go." He got up and started to dress. "But let me know if you change your mind—"

While he pulled on his pants and buttoned his shirt, she stayed seated on the bed, wrapped away from temptation by the tangles of the sheet. She blew him a kiss as he departed.

Chapter Twenty-Three

~ * ~

Green Jade

That morning, back at his own place, James was on fire. His passionate union with Sara in the dreamscape had felt sacred, holy, as if their mutual desire had been decreed by the gods themselves. And she'd dreamed what he'd dreamed, too! He paced around his house as words swirled, coalesced into sentences, and formed into verses. He ran to his desk, had to get the words down before the magic faded. She was his muse and had already inspired a renaissance flowering of poetry that was quickly filling his red poetry book. Within an hour, he had captured his feelings in another addition, one inspired by her favorite poem by Rumi, "Like This."

*~~ **Yes** ~~*

If you ask me,
does the sun rise every morning
into the blueness of the sky?
I would gaze into your sky eyes,
and in my drowning,
murmur,

"Yes."

If you stare up at the heavens
and wonder,
do the jeweled galaxies wheel and orbit,
spelling out your name?
I would point to the brightest,
and say,

"Yes, right there!"

If you wonder,
where does poetry come from?
Cup your hands
in front of my heart
and then raise them to your lips,
drink deep,

and know.

If fear shortens your breath,
and you must find shelter
through dark days and darker nights,
just enter the space
between my arms

and chest,

and exhale.

If you are sinking into longing,
and despair of finding Great Love,
look up,
see the crescent moon,
and know that its radiance

shines on my face also.

If you wander into danger
and take wrong turn after wrong turn,
and discover your compass broken,
don't despair, find my eyes,
look deep

and see True North.

How did Rumi love Shams?
"Like This."

How do I love you?
"Like This."

But if you must count how many ways
I can say yes to you,
count all the grains
of sand on the beach,
and number all the waves,
and it will not be enough.

~~ * ~~

The next day, James printed the poem out onto a sheet of the cream-colored card stock framed with gold filigree, wrapped it in expensive Japanese block print paper, and gave it to her before her yoga class. She was seated behind the front desk of the yoga studio, checking students in, and she took a moment to come out front and hug him. For the next several weeks, they continued in limbo. In her public classes, she would often smile at him, read a poem from her journal, then as all the students were getting into whatever the first pose was, she would lay her book down in front of his mat, open to the page with the poem. That gesture drew a few curious looks from the other students, but he didn't care. And occasionally, when James was lying in *shavasana*, she would come over, place her hand on his chest, right over his heart, as some beautiful piece of music played. In those moments, James imagined he could feel her love pouring into his heart. But she never said the words "I love you."

One day, she asked if she could swing by his house in the evening to see it for the first time. James ran around like a crazy man, picking up clothes off the bedroom floor and putting away the piles of paper and old mail that had accumulated on the dining room table and kitchen countertops. James was a clean person, but with the addition of a couple of teens and a dog, he had a home that looked lived in.

By the time she arrived, James had the house in good order, some nice music going in the background, and a bottle of her favorite pink champagne chilled in the fridge. She walked in looking gorgeous and exotic, unwrapped her scarf, and took off her fringed moccasin-style boots. She looked around and smiled.

"Nice! And I love your garden out front! Just the sort of place a mystic would have."

James kissed her and gave her the tour. She admired the colors on the walls and the artwork and furniture from China and Japan and India that he'd started to collect. She laughed delightedly at the monkey chandelier that he'd found in an antique store.

"Hanuman! Of course you'd have Hanuman here."

Hanuman was the monkey-headed god of the Hindu pantheon, the god who kept forgetting how powerful he was and who was in service to Rama, the king of the gods. James had heard the analogy before, from Willow, but this was Sara. She saw the world through the kaleidoscopic lens of the Hindu myths, and he was sure there were many layers to what she'd just said that escaped him.

She touched some of his mineral specimens and lingered over a beautiful, fist-sized chunk of rock that was dark like coal, heavy like silver ore, and glowed with a rainbow of iridescent colors ranging from blues and greens to gold and pink.

"Wow! What's this? A chunk of mystery space rock? A piece of Mount Olympus?"

James laughed, picked it up, and showed it to her. "That's bornite, or peacock ore. One of my favorites."

"I love peacocks. Very important to us Indians."

He handed it to her. "Take it; it's yours."

She looked at him, those blue eyes widened in delighted shock. "I can't! It's too beautiful!"

"Yes you can. It chose you. It's yours. An exotic peacock stone for an exotic princess."

She laughed and kissed him on the cheek. "Wow, you are the silver-tongued poet!"

They sat on the couch and toasted each other with delicate flutes of pink champagne. They chatted lightly, and she looked around the room, relaxed and easy. Suddenly, she put her champagne flute down on the coffee table and leaned forward, her face in her hands, as if she had a headache.

"What's the matter?" James asked.

She sat silently, not answering. Her body shook as if she was having a chill.

"Hey, you OK? What's wrong?"

She slowly sat up and looked him in the eyes, her face clouded with something. Was it fear?

"I just had the most powerful vision. I looked around this room and saw all of my stuff here. My furniture, my art. As if I lived here—"

James smiled at her. That didn't sound so bad. "Yeah? Well, your style and mine go pretty well together."

She didn't return his smile. She looked like Scrooge after seeing a vision of Christmas Future. "I've gotta go," she said, and abruptly stood up from the couch.

"Hey, you sure you're OK?"

"Yes, yes, just need to go. I need to go home. Right now."

She gave him a peck on the cheek and practically ran out the door. James sat back down on the couch and looked at the almost-full bottle of pink champagne. What had she seen in a future with him that looked so horrible?

James booked an appointment the next day with Julie, and she shared some insights into Sara's behavior.

"Sara has a whirlwind of feelings surrounding her right now. Unfinished business, both from recent history and her childhood. Maybe even karma from another life. You represent safety and security on the one hand. On the other, you represent a threat to the only world she has ever known, and that is the adrenaline rush of insecurity in relationships with unsafe men. By unsafe, I mean men who are almost sure to abandon her, just like her father did when he passed away. People get addicted to their trauma."

"So is that why she ran away?"

"I'm getting that that is correct, up to a point. She saw a stable future with you, represented by seeing her furniture in your house, and that scared her. She isn't ready for that."

"Is that because she doesn't love me?"

"Let's look at this another way. Do you love her?"

"Of course! She's perfect. Intense, powerful, a genius at yoga. She could teach me so much! She sees beauty in words and feelings and ideas—we connect through poetry! Calls us *mystics*. I'm sure she doesn't mean that in the traditional sense, but I like the *idea* of it."

"You have a very strong connection for sure," Julie added gently. "And it's powerful to find someone who sees and feels the world the way you do. But again, is that the same as love? Love is inexplicable, random. Love often makes no sense."

James thought back on his inexplicable connection to Willow. That had certainly been random.

"She's asked you for patience. Love is all about giving, not getting. Give her what she wants, and let her come to you, or not," Julie continued. "I feel very strongly that there's a powerful lesson here for both of you, a lesson that's still unfolding, and maybe you've come together to teach each other."

That night, Sara sent James an email of one of her poems, one she'd never read in her public classes.

Dearest Poet,

I wrote this many years ago. In a different life, really. One of my first poems. Showed it to hubby number one, and he laughed at me. I've never shown it to anyone else.

xoxo
Sara

~~ *Blue Girl* ~~

I am just
A little girl
My body small
My shoulders slight
A child,
In a blue, dark world,
An anxious place.
Dim, a backdrop of
Almost despair.
Almost devoid

Of hope, of light.

I am alert,
Curious
But watchful,
My only defense
The ability
To see it first,
To know it's coming.

My golden eyes
Leak light
From my enormous soul,
My God seed,
My guarded secret,
The only spark of color
In this blue existence.

These child eyes look
Straight into your heart.
Who are you?
What do you bring?
Does your world have color?
Sunshine?
A light to match my soul?

Can you see me?
Deep, deep inside,
Past my golden eyes?
Inside my heart
I hold the sun!
If you can see that,
Maybe,

You can help
This God spark,
This blue girl
Open, transform,
Blaze forth
And reveal her golden light,
And goddess-flood
This dim blue world
With color.

~~ Saraswati Stowe ~~

James read the poem three times. It was stark, powerful, mysterious. Its raw emotion spoken with childlike honesty humbled him. He felt honored that she'd trusted him with this sharing, that somehow buried in those words was a clue as to who she was, even though he had no idea what it all meant. He texted her to let her know he'd received it.

Hey, amazing poem. Very complex

Don't know if it's as good as
James Wilder, but it's what I wrote
Hard to share --- please like it!

I do! I do! Thank you for sharing it
with me!

Hey, can you come over?
We need to talk.

James didn't need to be asked twice. On the drive over, he tried to imagine what was waiting for him. Would she be wearing her cashmere robe? Would they end up in her bed again? Would they finally consummate their attraction for each other, turn his dreams into reality?

Sara met him at the door, fully dressed. She wore a smile, but it was one of formal greeting, not desire. She gestured to the couch, and he sat, looking up at her, questions at the tip of his tongue. She held up a hand.

"I have to say a few things, James, and I want you to listen before you speak."

"OK." This was not going the way he'd hoped.

"I think you're wonderful," Sara continued, "and I don't want to screw this up. So, I need you to give me some space."

"Space for what?" James interrupted.

"James, I asked you to listen!" She sat down next to him on the couch and took his hand into hers. "You're a wonderful man, and I might be in love with you. Sometimes I think I am, and sometimes I think I'm not. But I've made a decision. I know myself well enough to know I need time! I'm disoriented. Don't know what I'm doing! I can't have a full-time partner now. I'm still trying to consider my spiritual practice. And I need to think about me and what I need. Where I want my life to go."

"What does that *mean?*"

Sara looked down at her hands and took a deep breath, as if collecting her strength for what she had to say next. She exhaled, then looked up at him again.

"That means that I might start dating again, but I don't want to go straight into a committed relationship with anybody. Certainly not with you. I care too much about you."

"What? You mean you want to get involved with someone, just not me?" James stared at her, not believing what she was saying. She regarded him for a moment, as if carefully choosing her next words.

"Essentially, yes. James, you're too much for me right now. Too intense. I need a light touch. Some laughter. Some…frivolity."

"I can be frivolous!"

"No, no you can't. That's not you. You're a serious man. A Lover with a capital L. Someone who desperately wants a partner, and I… don't. Not right now."

"But Sara, what am I supposed to do? I'm in love with you!"

"I know! I know you are! And that's the problem. I'm not in love with you. Not the same way. Not yet. You are so much further down the road to certainty than me."

And there it was. The truth, hard and cold and real. James let go of her hand and stood up. There was no reason to hear any more.

"Please, James, just give me until India. Let me recalibrate myself. Give me space and time, and a good memory to carry with me until India. And then, if we are still meant to be together, we can be."

"You still want me to come to India with you?"

"Yes, it will be wonderful! Seeing India with you! That's *our* place, where we can be together. I know it! I feel it! But that's four months away! Until then, I need to be free, to explore, to be single. Make mistakes! I'm a mess, and I want to be in a committed relationship again from a position of strength, if that's in the cards."

"Sara!" He was pleading.

"Not right now! Right now, I need to be single."

And there it was, the tone of finality in her voice. The lover from the dreamscape that haunted his imagination was gone, perhaps forever. The imperious teacher was back, as was the distance between teacher and student. James turned toward the door. It felt like the end.

As he was leaving, she added, "I still want to send poetry every night, if you are willing? I don't want to lose you."

James nodded absently, still in shock, and drove home. Rocco was waiting for him at the door, and he got down on his knees and wrestled him a bit and scratched him behind the ears.

"You still love me, don't you boy?" Rocco just wriggled and said something in dog talk that translated roughly as "You bet!"

"Want unconditional love?" James asked the walls. "Get a dog! Fuck!"

Rocco had been with him for ten years and had outlasted every woman he'd dated. He didn't need to recalibrate himself, ever. He just wanted to be James's best pal, no questions asked. James took him out for a long walk.

His heart felt like a tin can crushed by the boot of unforgiving karma. India! Four months away. And what would that four months be like? Purgatory, with no promise of redemption. Could he hang in there with her while she went through whatever she had to go through as a "single woman"? Would he be able to rise above his jealousy, his Achilles heel, to allow her the freedom to explore so that they could potentially be a couple afterwards? It was a mess, and James had trouble twisting her words into anything that sounded like a promising future together.

That night he didn't send Sara a poem, and she didn't send him one, either, but he wrote this one, wrote it down without a single modification, as if it were dictated by the gods.

~~ *Until India* ~~

India,
enchanting, entrancing, unknown,
like the heart of a lover
only just unveiled.
A candle seen through shadows,
a melody heard through water,
a whisper in the wind.

Until India,
the moon will emerge
four times, a sacred number,
from darkness into fullness,

a white lotus breaking night's surface.
Once to erase your past.
Once to light your present.
Once to cut my heart.
Once to rekindle hope.

Until India,
I drown again,
and again and again
in the memory of your sky eyes.
And as I fall
into those deep wells of soul,
will I see fear or love?
Recognition,
or regret?

Until India,
you remain a cipher,
a gypsy woman, a myth,
as you fly untethered,
a feather on the breeze,
horizon undetermined,
landing where you will.

Until India,
when we meet again.
to test old agreements,
take an inventory of losses,
and see
if your heart
still remembers mine.
Until India...

~~ * ~~

Chapter Twenty-Four

~ * ~

Carnelian

The next four months weren't purgatory; they were hell. James tried to keep going to Sara's classes, but everything had changed. She no longer put her journal down in front of him after reading her poetry. She always found other men to bend over, touch, "adjust," and he found himself swimming in jealous bile that poisoned his thoughts.

One day, he waited to talk to her after class, to see if she would go to tea, and watched her dash out of the yoga studio to catch up to some guy from the class. She pushed right past James with just a cool smile and didn't even look back after she caught up with the other man. James's heart burned with anger and embarrassment, and he felt kicked in the stomach. He began to hear rumors from fellow yoga students that she was going a bit crazy, taking this guy or that guy home.

The evening conversations via text were a thing of the distant past, and her plea to exchange poetry every night seemed as forgotten as her words "I never want to lose you." She started reading aloud her own poems instead of Rumi in class, and James was happy about that. She'd found the courage to share them publicly, and he gave himself a little credit for helping her to get to that place. Her poetry was always about her pain and her loves, and it was always beautiful. She had a unique voice, and the poems filled him with even more longing and regret and loneliness, because from what they described he could tell that they were about someone else, not him. He was crushed. Poetry, their secret language, had been drained of its magic, and the message was that their connection was over. James was back in a familiar place, on the outside looking in.

He confronted her one day, when she didn't manage to elude him. "Hey, why're you never available? Not even to chat? And what's with these other guys?"

Her response was quick. "James we're not in a relationship! I'm being single. Doing what I want. Until India, remember?" She looked at him with anger in her eyes and walked away.

James started to become obsessed, wondering who she was with, what she was doing. He would drive past her apartment, looking to see if the lights were on and wondering if she was alone. At one point, driving down the street and looking up at her dark window, he literally smacked himself in the head and said aloud, "James, you stupid shit! What are you doing?"

James even became jealous of her interactions with women, sure that everyone was having sex with her, not just guys. She'd begun hanging out with one young girl who'd recently appeared, and they seemed inseparable, dressing alike, walking arm in arm, leaning in and talking in an intimate fashion. Rumors swirled, and he heard them. Everyone who was close to her was the enemy, the competition. James was losing his mind.

He tried to keep his head up and concentrate on work and his family, the other important parts of his life. Chris was playing for the varsity soccer team at Boulder High, and James volunteered as a coaching assistant. Annie was a freshman at the University of Colorado, and she let James take her and three roommates out for dinner from time to time. But even the kids knew he was out of sorts.

"Dad, what's with you?" Chris asked one night at dinner. "You're so grumpy these days!" James had prepared a dinner of salad with grilled salmon, and Annie was visiting even though her dorm was only fifteen minutes away.

"I think he's in love," said Annie. "Must be. Just like Suzie, my roommate. Can't live with her right now." James had laughed it off, but it was eye-opening that his mood was so openly broadcast out into the world. His poetry was taking a dark turn as well, with gloomy verses about lost love and heartache. Ever since he'd met Sara, he'd been on fire with the volume and quality of the poetry he was writing, but she was also further away than ever from becoming what he really wanted, which was a partner.

He still went to her classes, although not as religiously. It hurt too much to see her interactions with everyone else. And he still did favors for her as a friend, even helped her move when her lease ran out. She was always polite but kept him at arm's length. Some of his friends said she was just using him, but he clung to the faint hope that they could navigate these waters until India, when all distractions would be burned away and they could resume their pure, mystic connection.

Things finally came to a head in November, six weeks out from India, when she asked him to drive her to a weekend yoga conference up in the mountains where she would be a featured presenter. James jumped at the chance, thinking that they'd have time to sit together, alone in the car, and talk things out. That maybe she would finally see what she was doing to him and that they could get back to where they'd been.

He took that Friday off from work and showed up at her new

apartment, ready to drive her to her conference. James even booked a hotel room and bought himself a ticket to the conference because she said she had no comps to give away. She came down from her apartment, but she was not alone. She had her mysterious, young female friend with her. Sara introduced her as Bonnie, and she and Sara piled into the back of his car. For an hour and a half, James sat alone in the front seat, almost as if he was the hired chauffeur, and for the entirety of the trip they laughed and giggled and cuddled in the back. He felt completely ignored.

He tried to be friendly, to engage Bonnie in conversation, but her answers were monosyllabic, and she clearly viewed him with disdain and suspicion. Sara seemed just fine with how she treated James, and her complicity hurt worse than anything the young brat could say or do.

By the time they pulled into the mountain resort where the conference was being held, James was livid. Sara had ignored him the whole way except to give an occasional direction. He'd been used, sent a message. It was so clear that he meant nothing to her anymore, and he wondered if he ever had. What the fuck!

He dropped them off and then turned around and headed home. Five minutes after he left, he got a text from Sara.

Hey, where'd you go?

James ignored the text, he was so angry. He just kept driving, and a few more texts came in.

Hello? Are you still here?
Dinner is at six. Will you join us?

James dropped his phone onto the passenger seat and refused to look at it anymore until he got home, right as the sun came out from behind the clouds and warmed the cold breezes that were kicking up the November leaves. He parked the car in the garage, unpacked his bag, and ignored his beeping phone. James needed to burn off his anger, so he started pulling on cold-weather cycling gear for a road bike ride. Finally, his phone rang. He picked it up and saw it was Sara. There were also twelve new text messages, all from her. He left the phone on his bed, unanswered, and headed out for his ride.

The weather was turning colder, and the sunlight was thin and weak in the midafternoon. Nevertheless, he churned out twenty miles on a loop from his house up along the Front Range toward Lyons, riding the shoulder of the busy highway. The cars and trucks roaring by set up strong sideways drafts that buffeted him, but he didn't care. He was in the mood to hammer the pedals and even growled as he pounded up the rolling hills.

James was furious, but he'd realized a long time before that anger directed outward is really anger redirected from the self. Here he was, a picture of ridiculousness, a middle-aged man who'd fallen in love with his yoga teacher! What a cliché! Could he be any more pathetic? Any more ordinary? Any more mediocre? Where was the magic in his current situation? The gods had clearly sent another curveball his way, and he'd swung and whiffed. They'd also gone remarkably silent.

When he got home, it was just getting dark, and a bank of gray clouds over the mountains threatened a cold rain overnight. His legs were nicely juiced, but his guts still boiled with a toxic mix of anger, embarrassment, disgust, and frustration. Stirred up and still needing something to calm himself, James poured a shot of tequila. It burned as it went down his throat and exploded like a bomb in the hard knot twisting his stomach. Ah, at least he felt that. He carried the bottle to the coffee table and poured another shot.

"Fuck me!" James cursed aloud and downed the second shot. This time, it didn't feel so good. His words, hurled at the air, seemed empty and ridiculous, a child's tantrum. He stared at the bottle, hating it, hating himself, hating everything. When would he ever grow up? What was it about unavailable women that drew him in like a moth to a flame? Why was it so hard to find a woman who was fun and intellectually stimulating, and, most importantly, cared enough for him that she actually *chose* him? Not the other guy or the potential to be with other guys, but just him? Willow and Charlie and Sara—there was a pattern there.

You need to know I have a terrible history of falling
in love with unavailable women.

His text to Sara had foreshadowed this mess. He'd already *known* it was foolish, but he'd jumped in anyway. When the gods want you to learn a lesson, and you stubbornly refuse to do so, they will bring it back again and again until you do. Time means nothing to them. One life or ten lifetimes to learn a lesson—it's all the same.

James succumbed to despair and the tequila bottle and fell asleep, having not read Sara's texts or listened to her voice message. The next morning, the sound of someone insistently ringing his doorbell and Rocco barking woke him. It took a moment to figure out why he was still on the couch and why the tequila bottle was almost empty. When he opened the door, Sara was standing there.

"Why'd you run off? Why didn't you answer me when I texted?" Her voice trembled with barely suppressed emotion.

James's head hurt, and his stomach lurched. "Come on in," he said, and stepped aside. Rocco sniffed her and gave her a greeting lick on her face when she bent down to him.

Sarah walked into the living room, and James followed her. They sat on the couch, he in his rumpled clothes from the night before and she still wearing her down jacket.

"Nice," she said, looking at the bottle and the strewn decorative pillows. "Someone have a pity party here last night?"

Anger boiled up inside him, and James said nothing, just glared at her. He was done. She saw his expression and recoiled.

"James, I'm so sorry. I've been such a bitch to you. I feel like I've lost my mind and can't seem to do anything right. I know I've been a terrible friend, and I'm barely hanging on as a teacher. I'm not sure I can fake it anymore!"

She started to cry. James didn't care. The toxic mix of hangover and resentment seethed in his guts.

"So what do you want from me? Aside from free taxi rides and such."

"Ouch! That was mean. Is that what we're doing now?" Sara composed herself. "I want your patience! I *need* your patience! If you really love me, let me catch up to you! You're so much more certain than I am. I thought we had a deal, that I would be free until India."

"Yeah, well, you are free, just like we all are, always. But I'm not immune to how you treat me, and what you do with others."

"Did you even listen to my message? Read my texts?"

"No."

"So you didn't hear that I've made a decision? That I've had enough of the crazy world of dating, about how I wanted to…try to be with you?"

Those were the words he'd been waiting for, but they didn't register. The fire of his anger had taken hold in all the resentments that had piled up over the past three months, and the conflagration consumed everything in its path.

"And what about your little friend, Bonnie?"

Sara laughed a bit nervously, leaned toward him and touched him on the knee, as if seeking forgiveness.

"Sorry, she would have had her own room. Three would have been a crowd for what I had planned."

"Why would that be a problem?" The words just came out. "You seemed awfully cuddly with her. Who is she, anyway, your lover?"

Sara jerked back as if he'd slapped her. She stared at him, stunned, then slowly got up to leave, her face changing from pleading to disgust.

"No, you pig! She's my daughter! She just came to visit me last month! I've told *no one! Nobody knows*, because I had to give her up for adoption when I was very young. She was…an accident. The result of my stepfather. He—"

Her voice trailed off in her throat and her skin grew pale. Her eyes flashed from anger to despair to emptiness. She turned for the door. James felt the blood drain from his brain as an intense realization hit him in the gut. Oh my god! *Blue Girl!* It was all right there in front of him, the answer to why she was who she was. Why her dreams about her family haunted her. Why connection and intimacy were so difficult, and why she tried so hard to control access. In his anger and jealousy and frustration, he'd flailed away blindly and smashed her in her most wounded place. And the ugliness inside him had spurted out in the vilest way possible.

"Sara, I had no idea! I'm so sorry!"

James tried to grab her arm, spin her back around, but she just pulled away, shaking. She wouldn't listen to his begging, wouldn't look at him, and just marched down his front steps, never looking back.

James stood there on the front steps and watched her go. His muse. His inspiration for so much of his best poetry. His Avatar… gone. And with her, whatever lofty aspirations he had created for himself. They rained down in pieces from the heights where he'd placed them. Mystic poet…yoga teacher…friend…lover…*basic decent human being*. All broken shards of crystalline illusion that could never be put back together again. Not with her. Maybe not even with himself.

Later, Julie would tell him that it wasn't all his fault. "Remember, Sara had her own part in the destruction of trust that happened between you. And you couldn't have known about the deep traumas from her past."

"No, I was awful."

"Well, it wasn't your finest hour. But let's look at this another way. Maybe one lesson here is that the things you loved about Sara, you could have had as teacher-student, or even as friends," she said. "It didn't have to be romantic. Sometimes the strongest relationship one can have with the opposite sex isn't sexual. You were drawn to her teaching, her command of yoga, her poetic interpretation of the whole vibe around yoga. And she was drawn to your intellect, your maturity, and your gifts as a poet. Perhaps the confusion was around how you defined the nature of your connection."

His head heard Julie, but deep down inside his rebellious heart, James truly believed that he'd had a chance, narrow though it was, at a Great Love with Sara. She'd asked him to love her slowly, but in his selfishness, he'd cared only about his own need for reassurance. She'd asked for space, as much to save him from the fallout of her process as to give her the opportunity to come to him with grace and clarity. In his jealousy, he couldn't even do that.

Intensity comes from the head. Get into your heart.
Find peace.

Sara's words echoed back to him, their truth burning a lesson into his consciousness that should have already been there. Fear inhabits the head, warps perception, and gives rise to hate, mistrust, and jealousy. Love inhabits the heart and gives rise to empathy, compassion, and trust. James finally heard her, too late.

James didn't go to India with Sara. The magic between them was broken. She left The Yoga Studio and within a year became some lucky guy's wife. That guy was lucky because he came to her when she was finally ready. Her new husband happily supported her, freed her from the requirement to make a living, and eventually she took up writing full-time. Her daughter moved in with them, became a part of the family for a while. James knew all that because the yoga community in Boulder is tight, and everyone knows what everyone else is up to. He didn't know exactly what others heard about her and him and the circumstances of their falling out. But his yoga buddies would occasionally console him, assure him that he was still OK in their eyes.

In later years, James would sometimes see her books in bookstores when he was on tour, slim volumes of elegant poetry and poignant memoirs. Always deep, always soulful. And he'd think about what might have been if he'd had more patience. The universe doesn't just demand patience. It makes you learn it, relentlessly, unconditionally, completely, like a law of physics.

As for the gods, James was pretty sure he'd failed their latest test. Had he lost their trust as well? Would they ever send him another chance at redemption, at a relationship worthy of poetry? A Great Love? Only time would tell.

~~ *The End of Magic* ~~

When the golden light flickered and faded
from my love's eyes,
I could feel it coming.
It was the end
of magic.

Now,
Where once bloomed love's garden,
a dust devil whirls,
kicks up torn scraps of poems
and broken synchronicities,
and scatters them forever
'cross a dried-out hardpan,
an ancient seabed,

strewn with strange fossils,
and dark dreams.

Maybe someday,
treasure seekers will come here,
panning riverbeds,
mining rock,
seeking rare gemstones
prized by lovers and artists,
mystics and poets,
for their color,
their dazzle,
their fiery vibration.
Rubies of Great Love
still faintly in echo.

But for now, 'cross the hardpan
the dust devil whirls,
churns pages to fragments,
sandblasts words into letters.
Grinds up meaning,
blows away relevance.
The death of connection
once mystic,
now desolate.
An old story, forgotten.
A Great Love, relegated,
like Ozymandias,
to obscurity
and dust.

~~ * ~~

The Fifth Mala

To 1,001 Nights of Bad Poetry, Good Wine,
and Lantern Light!

~ *An Annoying Drunk* ~

I keep running into
my old buddy Hafiz
at love temperance meetings.

I go there to swear off the stuff,
and he always finds me.
Like that annoying drunk
at the wedding,
he corners me, his breath
boozy with the wonder of Love.

I try to shrug him away,
but he's good!
Been doing this a long time,
seven hundred years!

I give him a thousand reasons
to never let love
darken my heart again,
and he opens me.

With quick wit, and glib tongue
my pants are off
before I even know what's happened.
Seduced once again
by that master salesman
of Great Love.

I swear, next time
will be different.
Next time my heart gets broken,
I'll just drink myself silly
instead of reading
his damn poetry.

~~ * ~~

Chapter Twenty-Five

~ * ~

Obsidian

Winter solstice, late December. The end of the cycle of longer nights and shorter days. The time when the tilt of the planet away from the sun reverses, and it begins to lean in again, as if the sun were its lover and whatever lover's quarrel caused their separation was fading. A perfect time to burn away old habits, old ideas, old quarrels, and welcome in the new.

She was hidden behind a screen as James started his personal practice in the yoga studio high up on the top floor of Soulfire Hotel and Retreat Center. The studio had no walls, only a roof, and it was open to the sounds and smells and liquid light of late afternoon Bali. He had no idea that he wasn't alone. He moved through a standing sequence, sweat dripping off his jet-lagged body in the thick, heated air. The farmers were burning rice straw a few fields away, and tendrils of acrid smoke brushed his nasal passages from time to time. James discarded his sweat-soaked shirt and continued into a forward fold. His hamstrings were tight from the thirty-three hours of travel across fourteen time zones, from Boulder to Ubud, Bali. *Chaturanga.* Up dog. Down dog. Roll forward to plank. Repeat.

She made no sound, and he did his practice alone for forty minutes, from simple to complex, from easy to hard, opening hips and shoulder joints, stretching calf muscles and burning abs. Across the fields came the evening calls to prayer from the local mosque, and his only answers were long breaths in and long breaths out as he moved mindfully, as if swimming through molasses.

When James finally left the open-air studio, she came out from behind the screen. Nabila, woman of exotic beauty, the hauntress of dreams yet undreamed. As yet unknown, like an unexplored continent on an old map, bearing just the notation "Here be Dragons."

James felt a presence behind him and turned on the stairs to look back up in the deepening gloom, but he saw nothing. As he departed, she smiled a smile he never saw, dazzling white teeth glowing in a shadowed face. Later, she would tell him that she'd watched him, chosen him to fulfill a promise. She was his Persian princess, his courtesan of lantern light. He just didn't know it yet.

Soulfire sits back from the road, down an asphalt path that winds through groves of fast-growing crocodile trees. Words written in white pebbles whisper a powerful incantation as you pass over them and approach the entrance.

Inhale.   *Exhale.*   *Breathe.*

A little stream runs next to the path, and you can usually see young boys, grown men, and even sometimes women bathing naked in the water. The water doesn't look very clean, but in a steamy climate like Bali, its refreshing coolness provides a welcome respite from the heat.

Soulfire itself rises up from the side of the hill, built on a terrace borrowed from a thousand years of growing rice. Banana groves, coconut palms, orchids, and birds of paradise dominate the lush foliage that wraps the grounds in an intimate jungle hug. At the entrance, a large seated Buddha in lotus meditation solidifies the message of the white pebbles.

Inhale.   *Exhale.*   *Breathe.*

James came to Bali shattered by recrimination and self-doubt. He didn't know what he valued anymore, or what his place was. He mourned the loss of his illusions about himself, about his worth as a person, a lover, a friend, and a poet. He needed stillness. He needed yoga. He needed healing.

Walking up the path to Soulfire, dragging his suitcase behind him, it started with those magical words.

Inhale. Exhale. Breathe.

Follow the path.
Follow the twisting tendrils of smoke.
Make offerings.
Ask forgiveness.

Sit with silence.
Move with mindfulness.
Feel your feelings.
Let them go.

Start afresh.
Be.

The intimate hotel had only twelve rooms, each of them exquisite and wonderful. The manager had shown James to the Dragonfly Room, a healing womb that featured a wonderful canopied bed, an attached bathroom, and a balcony that looked into the jungle. His first order of business had been to flush away the stress and fatigue of travel with yoga. And now, the late afternoon session had opened up the floodgates of sweat on his body.

James walked down the steps from the darkening studio and retreated to his room. A tall glass carafe of water stood handy on a side table, and he drained two large tumblers. The shower was cool, the water flowing from an overhead rain fixture as if he were standing under a jungle waterfall. He washed away the thirty-three hours of plane rides and fourteen time zones and four airport terminals. He washed away toxins of loss and despair from deep in his body. He washed away sadness and loneliness and let familiar numbness flow in to replace pain with the absence of pain.

James put on his favorite short-sleeved Tommy Bahama shirt and a pair of shorts and strolled barefoot down the open wooden staircase to the main floor of Soulfire. He walked past low settees of green upholstery and orange pillows and down to the open-air kitchen. Agung, the manager, bowed and smiled.

"*Om Swastiastu,*" he said. "That means hello in Balinese."

James stumbled through a repetition of the phrase several times as Agung patiently helped him with pronunciation.

Agung's stature didn't come from his height or tiny frame, but from his large smile and warm, friendly eyes. James towered over him, but their physical difference seemed immediately irrelevant. Agung was of average height for the staff, who all gave the same impression of kind, gentle, helpful spirits.

"Would you care for dinner?" he asked, gesturing to the dining area next to the pool.

"Thanks, I'll start with a beer," James replied.

Agung smiled and led him to the dining area, which overlooked the infinity pool and, beyond that, rice fields and banana groves and coconut palms.

"In Bali, everything happens outside," he said. "As you can see, here are roofs and floors, but common areas are open. It's like this at my compound, too."

James sat at a table by himself. There were eight other tables, mostly empty, but it was early yet, and Agung told him that many of the other guests coming for the retreat were arriving later that evening, from Australia, Europe, and Asia. One table at the far edge of the dining space had a "reserved" sign on it.

Agung brought James a beer, and he settled in to look around. The dining area had a perfect view of the sunset, and the scattered clouds above the palm trees were lit, as if catching the light of a hot fire from beyond the horizon. Bands of dark blues, oranges, and pinks stretched across the sky behind the black silhouettes of the palm trees, and bats fluttering overhead signaled the emergence of the earliest evening stars.

James sipped his beer, thinking how nice it was to be alone, without demands or concerns or other voices asking for something. He had only his own breath, his own thoughts, his own demons for company.

Bali was his escape, a million miles from Boulder, away from family and friends and the ghostly harem of female spirits that haunted his memories and stalked his dreams. He needed a break from feminine energy. He needed to go inward, look at himself. Not focus outwards. Not grasp at promises and temptations.

Originally, James was supposed to be in India, finally connecting with the woman who'd been his greatest teacher and muse, but that plan had crashed and burned on the front steps of his house in a conflagration of harsh words. James was without his kids for Christmas anyway, so he'd searched the internet and found this yoga retreat in Bali. The teacher was someone he'd never met, and that was fine, as James would be able to start fresh without any lingering residue on his reputation.

"What can we bring you for dinner?" The server was a friendly, middle-aged woman with a smile.

James noticed the menu she offered but didn't look at it. "Please, just bring me something good. You choose." He smiled back at her, not wanting to make decisions.

She understood, just smiled and nodded, and took away the menu. James sat quietly, trying not to think. He watched the bats overhead, fluttering like leaves in a silent storm, chasing insects. He watched the colors of the sky darken as the sun sank farther beyond the horizon. He watched two farmers in straw coolie hats cross the far rice field, heading for a hidden path that would carry them homeward. From somewhere beyond the banana groves came the sound of dogs barking, a car engine starting, and strange, mumbled religious chanting broadcast on loudspeakers from a hidden temple. And all around him were the pervasive noises of little jungle creatures singing, croaking, chirping, and rustling. He soaked in the ambient bath of nature's music. It reminded him of crickets in summertime Colorado or tree frogs in the Caribbean.

The server brought him a salad with grilled fish, some fried rice with an egg, and a little side dish of *sambal*, a spicy Indonesian condiment made with coconut oils and chili peppers. The food was fresh and flavorful and spicy. James ate slowly, savoring each bite like a time-out from life.

He was almost finished, and the server was pouring another beer when a group of people came into the dining area. One woman and four men. The woman appeared to be someone rich and important; the four men seemed to be bodyguards and servants. They did not look Balinese. She might have been a rich Arab or Indian. Two of her men wore turbans and were armed with police-style pistols and webbing. The other two looked like professional assistants, perhaps secretaries or advisers or some such. The woman might have been in her late thirties or early forties, with shoulder-length black hair and a pretty, modern face that wouldn't look out of place in an upscale restaurant in London or Paris or Karachi. She was smartly dressed in a tailored white skirt, a white sleeveless top, and gold jewelry. She sat by herself at the reserved table. The two bodyguards took up standing positions at the edge of the dining area, and the two assistants sat at the next table.

James sat quietly observing while she gave orders to the men, orders to the server, and then sat back in her chair, facing him across the room. After a while, her eyes met his and he raised his glass with a nod. She nodded back and then looked away. James made a point of not staring at her since he didn't want to be rude and also didn't particularly care for any conversation.

About the time her food arrived, James finished his second beer and got up to go sit on the deck overlooking the pool. The pool was lit with low lights, and there were a few tiki torches burning at the edge of the deck. He walked over to the darkest part of the deck and sat down, hanging his feet over the side and facing the jungle. It was a drop of about eight feet to the rice fields below. Out at the edge of the deck the ambient sounds of jungle life were louder and the lights were all behind him. He sat there for a good half hour, just taking in the evening, trying his best not to think about anything. After a while, he heard a noise behind him as someone walked up to where he was sitting.

"Mind if I join you?" It was a male voice, and James turned and looked up. The new arrival was a very tall man with dreadlocks, wearing shorts and a T-shirt. He was carrying a couple of bottles of beer.

"Sure," James said. The guy sat down in the dark next to him and handed over one of the beers.

"I'm Trevor," he said with an open smile. "You've found my favorite spot to sit in the evening. Love to listen to the jungle."

He stuck out his hand, and James shook it.

"I'm James. *Om Swastiastu*," James said, which caused Trevor to chuckle.

"*Om Swastiastu*," he replied. "You picked that up fast."

He had a deep voice, and James could tell that he was an American.

"So this is your place?" James asked.

"Yeah. I built it as a sanctuary, a place to come to between tours. I'm a musician." Trevor was being modest. James knew who Trevor was and that he regularly performed to packed venues around the globe. James had felt extremely lucky to score a spot in the retreat at the last minute.

"And you've turned this place into a little boutique hotel, let people come invade your space?" James laughed. "You're a better man than me."

"I don't see it that way," Trevor said, also with a laugh. "I do it for the love." He clinked beer bottles with James.

"I get it," responded James. "This place has a great vibe. I love the yoga studio. Very peaceful. Relaxing."

"Yeah, that's my favorite part of the hotel."

"It's awesome. I was up there before dinner. Had to wash away the flight. Do some detox."

"That's what I do after traveling," Trevor said. "Did you meet Nabila? She was up there this evening."

"Who's Nabila?"

"She's that lady over at that table, with the bodyguards. Nabila Khan. Very nice, very rich. She's here for the yoga retreat. Kind of a surprise, last minute, but we found her and her people some space."

"Nah, I didn't see her. Pretty sure I was alone."

"Huh." Trevor went silent for a moment, then touched James on the shoulder and got to his feet.

"Hey, it was nice to meet you. Enjoy the evening. I'll see you at breakfast."

He left James alone to soak in the jungle sounds for a few more minutes. The night sky was very bright, and the moon was just coming up, three-quarters full. James could faintly see his moon shadow on the rice field below.

Nabila. The name was like cinnamon and honey on his tongue. He immediately banished that thought. He sat there for a few more minutes, then went to his room. The bed looked inviting, with soft cotton sheets and a white cotton canopy hanging down on all sides. Perfect for a romantic night with someone special. For a change, James was happy to be alone.

He climbed into bed, his body suddenly very drained, and fell deeply asleep. He woke in the middle of the night and heard a woman softly weeping. It was pitch dark, and the door to the balcony was open to the night air. The sound was coming from out there, but James could tell she was not on the balcony. Perhaps she was in the next room, and had her window open, too. He lay there, covered by just the sheet, listening to her soft weeping. It continued for maybe ten minutes, and then he must have fallen asleep because the next thing he knew, light was streaming in from the open doors to the balcony, and the air was already getting hotter.

James got out of bed, feeling refreshed. He pulled on some shorts and walked out onto the balcony. The warm heat of the sun embraced his naked chest as he stepped into the sunshine. Out in the fields, the farmers were already at work in the cooler part of the day, harvesting with hand scythes. They were covered from head to toe in blue and white clothes and wore straw hats against the sun. A tiny irrigation ditch ran along the edge of the rice field below him, and a swarm of brown ducks, dozens of them, came paddling into view. They were all quacking and splashing and pushing each other, as if in some morning rush hour.

In the distance James could see the roofs of temples and shrines rising between the coconut palms, strange umbrellas of black thatch stacked five and seven and even nine high, like shish kebabs of black mushrooms. From everywhere came the muted cacophony of life stirring, roosters crowing, motor scooters buzzing, dogs barking.

James looked around at the hotel itself. The grounds of Soulfire were very well maintained, with exotic blooming plants and lush foliage everywhere. Here on his balcony, a dozen pots of orchids fringed the railing, and as he stood there, a crystalline-winged dragonfly flew down and landed on a leaf, mere inches from his face. James studied it, and the dragonfly studied James, its bulbous green eyes turning this way and that, as if asking if James's loss of faith was truly fatal.

"Hey, little guy," James whispered. The dragonfly said nothing, just pumped its wings once. James smiled. Here he was, in one of the most beautiful, magical places on earth, eyeball to eyeball with an exquisite tiny creature that couldn't have been created by the most skilled jeweler on the planet, and he was depressed? In doubt about magic? No, everything that was wrong in his world was inside his own mind. The world itself was just fine. Sara had said that he was too serious. Too intense. So much so that he'd forced her to choose somebody else, *anybody else rather than him*, to reacclimate to the world of relationships. She'd wanted frivolity and lightness. He'd offered intensity and overthinking. No more. *No more!*

James thanked the little messenger, went back inside, washed up, and headed toward the dining area. This time it was full, and he took a spot at the last table, a community table for a dozen people. He nodded to a young couple who were already eating. They were Barks and Stephanie, two Americans living in Paris who had flown in for the retreat. Stephanie was a wholesaler of chocolate and came to Bali from time to time for its fledgling chocolate business. Barks was her husband, along for the ride. They chatted a bit, then excused themselves and left.

James had just been served breakfast when Nabila Khan arrived, surveyed the room, and sat down in the only available spot, across the table from him. Her two bodyguards stationed themselves at the edge of the room, their eyes scanning James for threats. She looked fresh and lovely in a yoga top, yoga pants, and her hair in a short ponytail.

"Good morning," he said with what he hoped was a

nonthreatening smile. She returned her greeting with a polite smile of her own.

"Your friends look like they want to pat me down for weapons." James nodded at the guards. "Perhaps they should come sit with us."

Nabila's smile changed to an expression of distaste. "I hate that they follow me everywhere! No, they are not welcome at our table!"

James's stint in London as an investment banker came in handy, as he placed her British-tinged accent as more Cambridge than curry shop.

"They seem very keen to protect you," he parroted back in her accent. *Frivolity!*

"You're an American, aren't you?" she said, her steady gaze seeing right through him.

"Yep. And let me guess. You're a princess from a fabulous Middle Eastern kingdom."

"Actually, I am, and any wise bloke who makes me unhappy—" She made a slitting gesture with her hand across her throat.

James leaned back in his chair with an expression of mock surprise. "A thousand pardons, Your Majesty! Please forgive my rudeness. This poor commoner suffers from a horrible combination of bad judgment and a loose tongue." *Lightness!*

Nabila smiled. "I'll forgive you this once, but only if you promise that it will happen again." She extended her hand. "I am Nabila, Nabila Khan."

James took her hand gently, and instead of shaking it, he bowed over it. "Wilder. James Wilder. At your service, ma'am."

She giggled and took her hand back. "So you're a long way from home, James Wilder. Here for the yoga retreat?"

"Yes, I am. And you, Princess Nabila? Are you also a long way from home?"

"I suppose. Although my family does have a compound on this island. I live in London."

"And does your family have a compound there as well?"

"My husband, or rather, my ex-husband, spends much of his time there. We have several houses. We also have homes in Qatar and Paris and Rawalpindi, Pakistan. I seem to live out of suitcases in hotels. I'm not sure where my home is anymore."

Nabila seemed to turn sad, and just at that moment, the server came to take her order. James took advantage of that time to study her. Her roots were clearly from the Indian subcontinent. Her profile showed the long, strong nose of Indian aristocracy. Her large, dark eyes were beautifully set, like two black pearls above cheekbones that could have been inherited from the concubine of a Mughal emperor. Her lips were soft and full and dark reddish brown, and her flawless skin had the color of strong café au lait. Tiny wrinkles at the corners of her eyes betrayed the fact that although she looked to be in her thirties, she might really be in her forties. Thick gold earrings hugged her earlobes and spoke of expensive Bond Street jewelers. She wore no rings or bracelets, only a simple gold chain that dangled a perfect pearl in the notch at the base of her throat.

The server left with her order, and Nabila turned back to him. "So tell me, James Wilder. Are you really a spy? With a name like that, you should be. MI6. Double O Eight or some such."

"Actually, I'm a poet. A very bad one."

"Really? You write bad poetry? And tell people that?"

"No, I write good poetry. The poems aren't bad; the poet is."

Nabila wriggled in her chair with exaggerated excitement. Her eyes sparkled with humor and delight. "Ooh, I detect a story behind your words! A sad tale, no doubt, of betrayal, lost love, and revenge."

"You got two out of three right. Still waiting on the revenge—"

"You feel like you deserve it?"

"Absolutely. I'm hiding here in Bali to avoid it. Maybe they won't find me."

By "they," James was referring to the gods, which was ridiculous, because if the gods don't officially make their home in Bali, they certainly spend a lot of time there on vacation. In Bali, gods are everywhere you look. In gardens and temples and parks. On street corners, beside doorways, on bridges and sidewalks. In the middle of fields and forests, on riverbanks and mountains. The people of Bali value the ubiquity of the gods in their lives and treat them with respect. Every day—at sunrise, noon, and sunset—they make offerings. They create their offerings out of palm fronds and flowers and food and spices. They decorate them with smoking sticks of incense and small metal coins minted for the sole purpose of offering tribute. As a result of their devotions, the Balinese are content, calm, and grounded in an awareness of their own place in the universe.

As James and Nabila sat at their table, bantering back and forth, a young woman came out of the kitchen bearing a large tray of offerings. They watched her place one at each side of the room, always with a respectful gesture and a bow.

Nabila nodded in the direction of the young girl. "I was speaking to the manager, Agung, about this yesterday evening, when she was doing the same thing. There are forty-nine places on the grounds where they offer to the gods and spirits, forty-nine! Amazing devotion!"

"Sounds like a full-time job."

"So, Mister James Wilder, famous bad poet secret agent, you will have to read me some of your poetry. I will be the judge as to whether the poet or the poetry is bad."

"Ah, Mrs. Khan—"

"Call me Nabila, please, and I am no longer a Mrs."

"Or maybe I should call you Princess."

"I'm not technically a princess."

"I find that hard to believe. You seem like a princess, complete with palace guards. Shouldn't they be carrying large scimitars and wearing pointed slippers with turned up toes?"

"Guarding princesses these days requires more modern weaponry and footwear. Never know when they might have to chase down a bad secret agent or bad poet."

"I stand warned."

They chatted a bit more over her meal of fresh fruit, eggs, and coffee. She was lively, bright, and very confident, and she laughed easily but also carefully, as if laughter were a commodity that had seen scarcity in her otherwise opulent lifestyle. James wondered what sorrows had tempered her natural spirit. What friction in her life had rubbed the sheen off her joy and trust and optimism.

She finished her coffee and looked at him with an appraising gaze. "So maybe this evening, after dinner, you can read me some of your poetry?"

"If you insist."

"I do. See you at yoga."

With that, she rose from the table and, trailing her guards, left the dining area. Trevor, the owner, watched her leave and smiled at James. It was almost time to report up to the top floor yoga studio for class.

James got up from his chair, stretched, and felt the tightness in his back and hamstrings. He needed to drink more water, do more yoga. And now this Nabila. What was that about? He was taking a vacation from women! And yet, "frivolity and lightness" had washed her up onto his beach, right when he'd just settled into his beach chair, his thoughts emptying, toes in the surf and an umbrella drink in his hand. It was like a call from the home office. "James, Her Majesty's government needs you. Drop what you're doing and report for duty!"

Bad poet or secret agent, either way, his destiny seemed to be tied, at least for the moment, to that of a beautiful, mysterious divorcée from London-Qatar-Paris-Rawalpindi.

Chapter Twenty-Six

~ * ~

Sunstone

Yoga class was about to start in the open-air studio at the top floor of Soulfire. The morning sun was already blasting the rice fields to the east, and a patch of direct sunlight spilled onto the edge of the smooth wooden floor that faced that direction. At the south end of the room there was a statue of Ganesha, apparently a favorite of yogis everywhere. Ganesha was carved out of white stone and wore a garland of orange marigolds.

All of the other students picked spots in the shade, but still feeling the need for deep heating after the frigid winter of Colorado, James took the spot in the sunshine. Nabila was on the far side of the room. Her entourage was nowhere to be seen, but then he noticed the screen at the back of the studio, and he figured they were there. They practiced for almost two hours. Rachel, the yoga teacher, put the class through a series of *namaskars*, or salutations, and James ended up feeling pretty well worked.

After class, everyone headed to the pool to cool off. There were drinks waiting poolside. Fresh fruit smoothies, mango lassies made with cool yogurt, and even beers for those who wanted to nap in the afternoon. James lolled in the deep end under the shadow of the palm trees, treading water and chatting with a couple of young women from Switzerland. There were a few guys, but most of the participants were female. So much for his vacation from feminine energy.

Nabila swam by herself on the other side of the pool. She wore a one-piece swimsuit with modest tailoring. James wondered if she was religious, if she was a practicing Hindu or Muslim. With a name like Khan, probably Muslim, but that might have been her ex-husband's name. She looked over at James and saw him studying her. She dipped her head under the water, smoothed back her hair, and swam over to him with easy strokes. Clearly, she was at home in the water.

"Bad Poet, why are you staring at me?" she asked with a wet smile. "Plotting evil?"

"Actually, I was wondering how you spell your name. In Arabic or Urdu or whatever you write with."

"I'll show you," she said and dipped her finger in the water. She drew this symbol on the dry concrete at the edge of the pool.

نبيلة

"Na-bi-la," she sounded out as she drew each curve. "In Arabic."

"That's really beautiful. Like it belongs on the wall of a temple or something. Or maybe a tattoo."

"Now there's a sign of true love. My name, tattooed on a body part. How romantic!"

"That would depend on which body part," James said with his most innocent smile.

"You *are* a bad poet, aren't you?" she laughed.

"Very bad, the worst."

"Don't forget our date tonight. You promised to read me some."

"So, it's a date now? Will you bring your bodyguards, so they can search me?"

"If it comes to that, I can do that myself." She gazed at him with the confident eyes of a woman used to commanding. And getting what she wanted. "Actually," she continued. "I plan to, how you say, ditch them, and you're going to help me do it."

She placed the palm of her hand on his chest, over his heart, and, if there hadn't been twenty other people in the water around him, James thought she might have kissed him, taken the kiss whether he was willing or not.

James defused the situation by placing his hand on top of her head and pushing her gently but firmly under the water. She fought him but not with much force, because under the water she was a fish and dove down between his legs and tugged at his swim trunks in passing. If they hadn't been well secured, she would have pulled them off, right in front of everyone. She escaped to the far edge of the pool, surfaced, and smiled at him, her eyes promising further retribution later. James smiled back, but inwardly he was in turmoil. He'd come to Bali to re-calibrate, to heal. And yet, here she was, a beautiful, interesting, intriguing, alluring deviation from his vow to take a vacation from feminine energy. A part of him already speculated that they would become lovers, and another part kicked himself for falling into a familiar prostration at the altar of Shakti, the Divine Feminine in embodied form. James had much to repent, and yet here he was, an unrepentant worshipper, again.

"Then you shouldn't have come to a yoga retreat infested with women, you hypocrite!" whispered the gods.

James took a taxi into town for lunch, to get away and clear his head. He found a nice open-air cafe inhabited by Western tourists, and he had a tasty chicken sandwich and a mango smoothie. The bill was cheap by Boulder standards, but he resolved to get more adventuresome and try a place that catered more to local tastes next time.

The afternoon was devoted to napping, writing poetry, another dip in the pool, and getting ready for dinner. Dinner was a family-style affair in the dining area, with all the tables set up in a long, continuous row. James grabbed a seat toward the middle, with a great view of the sunset. His dinner companions for the evening turned out to be Sophie from the UK and Cecile from Switzerland. Both were younger women in their thirties. Sophie, with short dark hair and a round face, had that friendly look of someone who spent a lot of time chatting in pubs. Cecile was the exact opposite—pale skin, long reddish hair that curled to the verge of frizziness, and a shy demeanor accented by thick glasses. They were best friends already but had just met on this retreat.

Dinner was a mix of dishes with fresh ingredients, many of them organic. There was grilled fish and chicken, salads, rice, and fruit. Everything was produced in the open-air kitchen that bordered the dining area, so the cooks and servers seemed like part of the family. When dinner had wound down to the desserts, Trevor got up from the table and grabbed his guitar, an old favorite that had a scratched and well-worn surface with a hole where his pick had worn through the wood. He sang reggae-tinged songs of one love and brotherhood, many of which James had heard on the radio, in bars, and in commercials.

After dinner James drifted with the crowd out to the deck and chose a seat next to a tiki torch. Nabila appeared next to him, looking fresh and lovely in another white sundress. She'd let her hair down so that it brushed her shoulders, and she was wearing a thick gold chain around her neck. She was carrying two drinks and handed James one.

"This is to loosen your tongue, Bad Poet. I'm ready to hear your poetry."

He took a sip of his drink. It was a gin and tonic. "Good evening to you, too," he said. "You're in a good mood. Where are your guards?"

"They're here," she replied. "Sometimes they're more effective working from the shadows."

"Hmmm, why doesn't that make me feel safer?"

"Why should it make you feel safer, Bad Poet? They're here to protect me, perhaps from you. There wouldn't be much deterrence if they made criminals feel safe."

"Good point."

"So where is your poetry? Time to find out if the poet or the poetry is bad."

"In my room."

"Hmmm, that might get a bit crowded in there with the two of us and my invisible bodyguards. They'd probably have to hide under the bed. Why don't you go get it and meet me up in the yoga studio? It will be quiet up there."

"Will do."

James smiled at her and drained his glass. Nabila seemed in a playful mood. This was going to be interesting. He went to his room and took his book of poetry from his bag.

She met him at the top of the stairs to the yoga studio. "Follow me," she said, and took his hand in hers. Her hand felt warm and soft, and a familiar electricity vibrated between their palms. She led him across the wooden floor to a corner where the thatched roof extended out over the rooftop. The extension covered a small deck just large enough to accommodate a daybed with a canopy. It had a flat, mattress-like cushion, and white cotton curtains hung down from above, offering a romantic privacy. Several colored cushions were scattered on the platform, and a lantern burned on a side table next to a bowl of fruit and a carafe of some colored liquid, probably wine.

"What's this?" James asked. "Are we acting out *One Thousand and One Arabian Nights*?"

Nabila laughed, a rich laugh that seemed to pour out tension and fatigue from her spirit and replace it with amusement and delight. "Yes, only you are the concubine Scheherazade, not me." She climbed up onto the platform and patted the spot beside her. "Come, Bad Poet. Read me your works. If I like them, I might spare your life."

James laughed and took a seat next to her, and she leaned up against him, her hand resting on his bare thigh as if they were already lovers. He opened his book, and she gasped at the pages etched in gold filigree.

"Nicely done! If the content is half as good as the presentation—"

"These are all love poems. What do you want to hear? Something upbeat or sad?"

"Read me your best poem! Impress me, Scheherazade."

"OK, I'll need a little wine first," he said.

She smiled and rose to her knees to fill two crystal goblets with red wine. In the lantern light, she was transported seven hundred years into the past, to the time and place of Rumi and Hafiz, and she looked every bit the Persian courtesan. With her regal nose and lips and chin, and a seductive curl of ebony hair escaping to frame one almond eye, her profile could have been copied from an ancient illuminated text. James half expected to see Arabic writing appear in fiery letters in the air around her and to hear ancient *ghazals* wailing of forbidden love.

She offered him the goblet and a toast. "To 1,001 nights of bad poetry, good wine, and lantern light!"

James raised his glass and met her eyes. There was laughter there, but also vulnerability, deep tenderness, and desire. And he read her this poem:

~~ *Such Beautiful Body Art* ~~

There's something about an ebbing moon
that calls for celebration.
So Hafiz and I

sat down in an open field,
under that moonlit sky
and drank in the chorus
of cricketsong
and fireflies
along with several bottles
of his finest love wine.

And before you know it,
Hafiz was up to his old tricks,
laughing stories,
singing poems,
the kind that only drunks
listen to.

And after a bottle or three,
we began to share
love histories,
laugh at love's sorrows,
opening our shirts,
and comparing love scars.

Hafiz showed his collection.
"This one right here,
this ugly, torn
patch of chest?
That's from the one
I married.
I had only a small heart then,
but the wound when she left,
was large."

"And this one over here?
Oh, she was a gem!
She gave me
a beautiful, twisted pattern,
a perfect image
of our time together!"

He showed me his scars,
I showed him mine,
we laughed till it hurt,
at our follies and fantasies.
And then Hafiz pointed
at a raw wound still gaping,
flickering dimly, leaking light
in the center of my chest.
"And that one?" he asked.

I pulled my shirt close.
With the light covered up,
the crickets faded to silence,
leaving only my whisper
to color night air.

"My heart, like that moon,
has to ebb into darkness
before it comes back,
and grows into fullness.
And when it emerges,
a slim, shining crescent,
a lunar new love,
only then
can today's lost beloved
be remembered with song."

Hafiz smiled, his eyes glowing.
"Looks like the scar, when it forms,
will be a real beauty!
Carved into your skin
in the shape of a feather.
Isn't love grand?
To give us
such beautiful body art?"

So we raised our bottles
and toasted the moon.
To love scars!
And drowned out the crickets
with song.

~~ * ~~

Chapter Twenty-Seven

~ * ~

Moonstone

Nabila sat silently after James read the poem. Her breath caught in her throat, and she looked at him with eyes that glittered wetly in the lantern light.

"Read it again," she finally managed, shifting her seat as if in doing so she could recapture her composure.

As James read it again her hand moved against his thigh, not in a sexual way, but as if her body were leaking emotional energy and she was trying to sooth herself with movement. When he was finished, she took a long shuddering breath and whispered his words to the night.

"My heart, like that moon, has to ebb into darkness—"

She lay back against the cushions, as if he was forgotten. James took a sip of wine, waiting for whatever came next. An outburst of tears? A request for another poem? Or maybe she would get up and leave. She did none of that. Instead, she just lay there, looking up into the darkness. And then she addressed him by his real name.

"You capture the bittersweet essence of heartbreak, James, and bring it forth to me to taste with my own tongue. It's as if Hafiz himself has whispered into your soul."

"Thanks. I've read only English translations of his poetry, never in Persian or Arabic. I suppose I have no idea, really, what his words sound like."

"And yet, his name appears in your writing."

"He's my favorite poet."

She lay silent for a moment, then sighed as if digesting a thought and letting it go. She rolled over and looked at him.

"You told me that you write very good poetry, and that seems to be true. You also told me that you're a very bad poet, so that must also be true. What did you do that was so bad?"

What could he say to her? Where should he start? He had much to atone for, and did he want to get into a confessional? Tell her of his shallowness? James decided to tell the truth, as simply and clearly as possible.

"I was unable to control my intensity and allowed it to destroy my chance at Great Love."

"Ah, Great Love," Nabila whispered. "A rare and beautiful concept. Only those with poetry in their hearts aspire to Great Love. The rest of us—" She smiled, a bit sadly. "I'm blessed to have what I have in this life." She said it with finality, as if she'd come to accept a life carved in stone, as fatal as breathing.

"And what do you have?" he asked, truly curious to know.

"I have three children, the blessings of my old age. I have immeasurable wealth. I have my health, and I have freedom, of a sort."

"And what do you not have, that you truly want?"

"Ah, Scheherazade, you dig too deeply! Be content that I've accepted your offering and spared your life this night! Tomorrow night, you might not be so fortunate."

"So, we're going to do this again?"

"That depends," she said, and crawled over to him and pushed him gently onto his back. She brought her face up close to his in the lantern light and looked deeply into his left eye, and then his right, as if she were seeking the hiding place of his soul. She shifted her gaze back and forth between the two, her dark eyes reflecting the lantern flame like two black pearls lit with an inner fire. Her mouth was parted, and her breathing soft, and suddenly James remembered a raven he'd once seen that had captured a pigeon and brought it down to the earth in front of him. Its claws pinned the pigeon to the ground as it looked its victim in the eyes, first turning its head one way, and then the other. Then slowly, as inevitable and implacable as that raven, she brought her mouth down upon his and kissed him deeply with a kiss that could have drawn his soul right out of his body. Unlike the pigeon, James kissed back, in pure pleasure, not pain, and gave his soul gladly to her searching tongue.

Hours later, they lay next to each other, content to feel the warm, soft contact of skin on skin. She'd made love calmly at first, then as her control slipped and her desires released, she'd become wilder, an untamed animal joyously freed from its kennel. He'd held her tightly in his arms as she went over the waterfall of ecstasy again and again. James had been with multiorgasmic women before, but none like her. It seemed as if she was insatiable, but finally she gasped and said, "Enough! I need to stop! I'll never make it through yoga class tomorrow!" And they laughed together at the absurdity of that statement.

The candle in the lantern also finally burned itself out, like the conflagration of their lovemaking, and they were surrounded by the night. Naked and uncovered in the warm air, he spooned her and nuzzled the back of her neck, drinking in her perfume mixed with the rich scent of her sweaty, sexually spent body.

"James, James, James," she whispered to the air as she stared out over starlit rice fields, her head resting on his arm. "Is there anything more magical than a night like this?"

James kissed her earlobe and pulled it between his lips. "You are the magic here, this night, my courtesan of lantern light." he said.

"My, you are the silver-tongued poet!" she laughed. "Perhaps I should have your name tattooed on my body. In Arabic."

"Which body part?" he asked, and she giggled again.

"Someplace that doesn't show, in very small script. Like the head of a pin."

"That's not much of a commitment to love."

"Is that what this is?" She sighed. "I thought you were on a *hajj* to find Great Love. A love greater than this."

There was no response James could make to that truth, so he stayed quiet.

"Sometimes, one never has the opportunity to find it," she continued.

"You were married—"

"Yes, I was. But marriage in my world has nothing to do with love. It has to do with families and business alliances and money."

"Really? What is your world?"

"You've seen the men with guns, my bodyguards?"

"Yes, wondered about them—"

"Well, they are there for several reasons. To protect me, and to protect the family name."

"Whose family? Yours or your ex-husband's?"

"They are one and the same. I am the mother of his children. I cannot ever truly leave."

"And he?"

"He's had a full life. Other wives. And mistresses. In the world of the rich and powerful, women are trophies, to be admired and possessed, either privately or publicly. And yet, I'm very lucky. He's truly loved me, in his own fashion."

She rolled over to face him. "I have no hope of Great Love, only stolen moments like this," she breathed into his ear, her longing for something more tinting every word with the color of despair.

She held James fiercely for a moment, as if she could imprint his body into the memory of her flesh, then sat up and began to collect her clothes.

"I have to go back to my room. Morning comes, and with it, my life as Nabila Khan."

"And tomorrow?"

Nabila looked at him and smiled a bittersweet smile. "Perhaps Scheherazade, you will survive another night. Wait five minutes after I've left before you go to your room."

She kissed James again and, fully dressed, left him there on the mattress under the curtains. She called out to her men as she approached the stairs. James didn't see or hear them, but he assumed they'd stood guard at the bottom of the stairs so they wouldn't be disturbed.

A few hours later, in the morning yoga class, they practiced next to each other. She moved with inexpert grace, as she was not a well-trained yogi. Nonetheless, she was beautiful in her efforts to master the poses. She looked at him, and he looked at her, dispassionate to the outside observer, but to each other, a secret shared. Afterward they joined the rest of the students in the pool and made a studied effort to not linger in each other's personal space, preferring to keep their new liaison private.

After lunch he retired to his room and sat on the balcony, watching two birds interacting in the branches of a tree. The female sat motionless on her branch while the male hopped around her, flapped its wings, and did whatever it could to get her attention. The message was obvious. That was him out there. He'd jumped at the first opportunity into an encounter with an interesting woman, even while trying to process the breakup from another. He'd totally abandoned any attempt to chill out and take a break from feminine energy.

Was he even capable of not engaging someone like Nabila? Did he have the necessary wiring, or was his on/off switch frozen into the on position? Maybe he was just addicted to the dance, constantly making the choice to engage because the addict always says yes to his drug. And if he was going to engage, could he at least do it differently? More lightness, less intensity? Had he learned anything from the debacle with Sara? James shook his head, embarrassed. He was better than that. He resolved to steer himself away from the tar pit of his thoughts. *Just feel. Don't overthink.*

Out over the rice paddies, plumes of smoke from burning straw drifted lazily from a distant field, adding a smoky tang to the afternoon air. Three farmers toiled in the hottest part of the day, their coolie hats providing shade as they threshed sheaves of rice onto large squares of cloth, an unchanged, tedious, meditative process repeated season after season, year after year, century after century. What did they think about as they spent their hours out in the hot sun? Did they think at all? As he watched them, he realized that he, too, needed something meditative, something repetitive to purge his mind of the shame and disappointment that still haunted him. He needed to make Sara's mala. Perhaps the exercise of knotting 108 beads and requesting forgiveness in a mantra would ease his heart, allow him to move on.

James remembered seeing a bead market down the road from Soulfire. They'd passed it on the way from the airport, and he'd noticed the sign because it featured a picture of a mala. He rented a scooter from Agung and managed to negotiate the crowded streets to the market. The afternoon heat was thick with humidity, and his daypack clung wetly to his soaked back. He rode with throngs of other riders, a swarming school of scooter fish, swimming and darting in perfect chaos, honking and swerving, speeding up and slowing down, never touching, always in invisible contact. For them, it was as natural as breathing. For James, it was something new, awkward, exciting, and challenging. He felt too large, perched on the cramped seat, his big gringo knees sticking out in wide angles as he folded himself onto a space designed for someone a foot shorter and sixty pounds lighter.

The bead market was like a scene out of an old Hollywood movie, a technicolor bazaar where he perused strands of green chalcedony and blue kyanite, different pinks of rose quartz and rhodochrosite, orange carnelian and yellow calcite, indigo lapis and gray labradorite. There were iridescent black shell beads that had depth, and white shell beads that glowed like pearls. There was cloudy moonstone and green malachite, ancient bronze filigree and precious beryl. James ended up buying enough beads for twenty malas, a sign that he didn't know what he wanted. But for the first time in months, he felt a glimmer of a sense that his feet were finally touching the right path.

Back in his room, he sat down and spread out the beads. He surveyed them, knowing that somewhere in that myriad of colors and swirls was the answer to his needs. He finally chose:

Labradorite for mystic connection
Amazonite for the pale blue of her eyes
Rutilated quartz for deep knowledge of Hindu mythology
Moonstone for the magic of exchanging poetry every night
Green jade for the anahata chakra, the heart chakra
Carnelian, for the second chakra, for creativity

James begged forgiveness with each knot. He mourned the loss of mystic connection. And resolved to be a better human being, to learn patience and lightness, and allow space. It took him more than three hours to knot the 108 beads onto a continuous necklace. In the end, he felt calmer, more grounded, somehow cleansed, and very thirsty. He also felt a yearning to be with Nabila again, to see her smile, feel her soft skin, taste her lips. The addict still needed his fix.

James arrived late to dinner, and Nabila was seated with Trevor and several others at a table. There were no free seats, so he took his plates out to the edge of the deck and ate his dinner alone. It was OK because he was a loner anyway, and the jungle noises and the three-quarter moon kept him company.

Later that evening James was sitting on the top stair of the yoga studio with his poetry book in hand when Nabila appeared, flanked by two bodyguards and one waiter carrying a bottle of wine.

"Ah, the faithful concubine Scheherazade waits for his mistress," laughed Nabila, and James wondered if she'd had a bit too much to drink.

"At your service," he replied, rising to his feet and bowing.

The evening was much like the previous one except that they started with the lovemaking as soon as they were left alone, both of them needing the other after a day of building wanting. They didn't even open the bottle of wine until they were spent and lying in each other's arms. As they lay there, James traced the trails of stretch marks on her belly, his fingers following the channels through her skin like braided streams in a high mountain valley.

"Tell me about your children," he whispered.

"Ah, my delights and my sorrows," she sighed. "Every mother has them, and they are sweeter than any love a man can give her. Kamal, he is the eldest. Has a head for business like his father. Already he does important things in the company. Saayed is so proud of him! Wants him to be the next president of the firm. Akbar, he is the middle son, the most passionate, the most poetic. He reminds me a little of you. All ideas and fire, and he loves the ladies. Kabir, he is the most difficult. Has taken a strong interest in religion. I worry that he is changing, becoming too rigid, too judgmental. Thinks more about the next life than this one."

"Maybe he'll grow out of it."

"I hope so. He was arrested in London three days ago for jihadi activity. I'm frantic with worry. He's so young! Only eighteen. Saayed is working to get him released, but even with his influence, it's difficult."

"Beware flags and the men who wave them—"

"Is that a quote from one of your poems?"

"Something I'm working on. The world's too full of people right now who lead the impressionable to disaster by waving banners of false patriotism and false spirituality."

"Bad Poet, it has ever been thus. Don't you read history?"

Chapter Twenty-Eight

~ * ~

Solid Gold

The next day at lunchtime, James took a ride to the countryside. It was Balinese rush hour, when school kids changed shifts. The younger ones go early, and the older ones take their place in the early afternoon. They all ride scooters, sometimes two or three at a time, brothers and sisters, neighbors and buddies and classmates, their ages indicated by the different colors of their uniforms. James marveled at ten-year-olds negotiating traffic, dodging vans and trucks and other scooters, but somehow everything seemed to flow pretty well.

The roads grew less crowded as he ventured farther from Ubud. He motored through villages, past terraced rice fields, and crossed rivers and streams overhung with trailing vines and palm fronds. The air grew cooler as he went higher, closer to the volcanic mountain that dominated northern Bali. James stopped at a roadside *warung,* a restaurant for locals, and by means of hand gestures and smiles, ended up eating an incredible meal of rice with chicken, vegetables, and spicy *sambal*, washed down with a bottle of *Bintang*, the local beer that reminded him of the lighter Japanese beers. Feeling well refreshed, he headed back to Soulfire for a much-needed nap. These late-night trysts were fun but were taking their toll on him physically.

While James slept, someone slipped an envelope under his door. It was addressed to James Wilder in a careful, masculine hand. He opened the envelope, and inside was a business card from a Mr. Kahlil Abrami of Fortress Security, Qatar. There was also a hand-written note that said,

Mr. Wilder,

My employer, Mr. Saayed Khan of London, Bahrain, Qatar, and Rawalpindi, requests that you have an interview with me personally, given your association with Mrs. Nabila Khan. In the interests of discretion, please meet me at the front gate of this hotel at 3pm.

Thank you for your assistance in this matter,

Kahlil Abrami
Senior Investigator

What the hell was this? James got out his laptop and googled Saayed Khan, London. Up came 200,000-plus hits, but the first page was all about Khan Industries PLC. As he scrolled through headlines, he began to get a hint of how big this "matter" might turn out to be. Per *Forbes* magazine, Mr. Khan was on the list of the top one hundred richest men in the world, with a net worth estimated at over $20 billion. Industrial concerns included heavy industry, shipbuilding, defense, real estate, and banking, with operations worldwide but centered in the Middle East and Europe. Another page described him as a native of Pakistan, now a citizen of many countries. Still another, dated two years before, characterized an eightieth birthday bash in London as "the event of the social season." Philanthropist, patron of the arts, bon vivant, and pillar of his community. And old. Digging a bit deeper, he found a story from some obscure magazine asking if he was indeed a devout Muslim, given his lifestyle choices. James sat back on his bed, looking up at the canopy.

"Nabila," he asked aloud to the air. "What have I gotten myself into?" It was clear that there was no way to avoid a meeting with Mr. Khan's representative, so James took a shower to clear his head, put on his best clean clothes, and headed for the gate at 3:00 p.m.

Mr. Abrami was waiting for him next to the meditating Buddha. He was about fifty, average height, with short curly hair graying at the temples, and a face that could have been at home behind the counter of a falafel stand or pizza place. He smiled as James approached, but only with his mouth. His eyes were purely professional, assessing him with a practiced probing gaze that indicated he was no vendor of Mediterranean fast food.

He shook James's hand with a polite but iron grip and walked him down the path to a waiting car. As they walked, they exchanged pleasantries about the weather in Bali and how beautiful the countryside was. There was a driver, an Indian man who looked like a former soldier with military mustaches and dark sunglasses. He held the car door open and James and Mr. Abrami climbed into the back seat. James knew better than to ask where they were going. The only card he held in this game was how he comported himself. He took long, even breaths and did his best to look unconcerned and calm.

They drove through Ubud, up narrow streets overhung with dangling vines and clogged with scooters, past temples crawling with monkeys and tourists, and finally pulled up at an old whitewashed colonial-era building that housed a restaurant called Indus. James let out a restrained sigh of relief. Apparently, they weren't taking him to a distant rice paddy to be planted with next year's crops. Not yet, anyway.

They walked through the front door into a gallery that was hung with beautiful original art, then down some stairs into the dining room. Mr. Abrami spoke with the maître d', who showed them to a table on the terrace. When James stepped out onto that terrace, he was stunned by the view that looked over a very deep gorge cut so sharply below them that the bottom was hidden from sight. In the distance, across treetops and rooftops, was a volcano. James had never been to a more beautiful spot for a come-to-Jesus talk with a hired killer.

They sat at a table alongside the railing. Mr. Abrami ordered some appetizers and sparkling water. James ordered a beer, determined to enjoy his last day on earth, if that's what this was. Once the food arrived, the small talk was over. Mr. Abrami pulled his iPhone out of his pocket.

"Mr. Wilder, my firm has done a bit of a background check on you. May I?"

He indicated the phone in his hand. James shrugged, trying to look unconcerned.

"Confidential report on Mr. James Cornelius Wilder, fresh this morning. Once upon a time, an investment banker in New York. Now a partner at a construction firm in Boulder, Colorado. Resides at 1757 Grizzly Lane with his daughter, Annie, son, Chris, and dog, Rocco. Lovely family, don't you think?"

He turned the phone so James could see the picture, and it was something James had posted on Facebook a couple of months before.

"That's very impressive, but all of that info is publicly available."

"Of course it is. However, in this case we dug a bit deeper. Mr. Wilder apparently banks at Chase, account number 2127073525, approximately $16,235.16 as of this morning. That's not very... interesting, is it? What else have we got?"

He scrolled through the report. "Hmmm, here we go. Cancer

patient. And yet, a September 15 blood test reads negative for cancer markers. Considered fit and healthy."

He looked at James and smiled. "Congratulations! My uncle died of prostate cancer. It's an unpleasant way to die."

He went back to the report. "Mr. Wilder's personal life. He's most recently romantically linked to a yoga teacher named Saraswati Stowe." He looked up at James. "Ah, well, no need to dredge up failed loves. You seem to have had several. Unless you want me to continue?"

"No."

He put down the iPhone and fixed his steely gaze on James. "Do you know what comprehensive security is, Mr. Wilder? Of course you don't. Why would you, or anyone, for that matter? Let me explain. When you see me, when you see Mrs. Khan's bodyguards, you see the tip of the iceberg. The vast majority of the security surrounding the Khan family is unseen, like that part of the iceberg beneath the surface. And I assure you, it is comprehensive."

Mr. Abrami took a bite from a skewer of shrimp kebabs. He took a sip from his sparkling water, then looked at him again with those steely eyes.

"I want you to think of the Khan family like a human body. Mr. Khan is the brain, Mrs. Khan is the heart. Consider me part of the immune system. My job is to protect the body, keep it healthy, identify threats, and if necessary, eliminate them."

"I understood that the Khans are now divorced. Am I wrong?"

"I do not comment on their personal lives. I just make sure that the interests of the family are protected at all times."

"So, what do you want from me?"

"You seem to have gotten very close to Mrs. Khan very quickly. I want to know why. That is not usual for her, by the way, so you must have made quite an impression on her."

"She likes poetry. I'm a poet."

"Really? And have you published anything? My report doesn't

say anything about it."

"No. I plan to, someday, if I survive this conversation."

Mr. Abrami smiled a humorless smile. He leaned back in his chair and made his final point.

"Please understand, Mr. Wilder. Be very careful with what you do. Mr. Khan cares very much for Nabila…as do I. She is a remarkable woman. Do not trifle with her. Spend time with her, and when she is…finished with you, move on, and don't look back. Don't think that you can take anything that is not yours."

So that's what this was about! Apparently, it was OK that James was sleeping with her, but he was being warned not to get too attached.

"One more thing," Mr. Abrami continued. "Please do not let Mrs. Khan know we've had this discussion. She is a wonderful woman, but willful, and not very cooperative when it comes to protecting her best interests. Her cooperation is, of course, optional. Yours—" He paused for effect. "…not so much."

Chapter Twenty-Nine

~ * ~

Glass Fired Beads

M r. Abrami dropped James off at the side of the road where the pathway to Soulfire began. James retraced his steps to the front gate that he'd taken three days earlier, but now the words *inhale, exhale, breathe* held a different meaning as he passed over them. He tried his best to shake off the residue, the implied intimidation, of the extraordinary meeting he'd just had. Evening was just around the corner, and the sky was turning pink over the palm trees.

Out on the deck, people were gathering for cocktails, and James joined them. He needed a stiff drink, so he ordered a double scotch on the rocks. He was chatting to Sophie when Nabila came up. She smiled and indicated with her facial expressions that she needed to talk. James excused himself from Sophie and led Nabila over to the edge of the deck, where they could have some privacy.

"I came to your room this afternoon, and you were gone," she said. "The front desk told me that you went into town."

"I did."

"They said you were meeting someone."

"Yes."

A cloud came over Nabila's face.

"May I ask who?"

"I could tell you, but then they'd kill me."

"James, don't joke with me!"

"I'm not. He was very serious. I believe him."

"Damn it! You see? How they interfere? Try to control me?"

"Why can't you break away? You *are* divorced, aren't you?"

"You don't understand. In my world it is not so simple."

"So tell me about your world. Help me understand."

Her face crumpled under the emotion, and James could see she was fighting tears. He wanted to take her in his arms and hold her, but he couldn't do that in front of the crowd.

"Nabila—"

"Come to my room in five minutes," she said, her eyes begging. She composed herself and turned to walk away through the knots of people laughing, chatting, and drinking, isolated in her own little bubble of pain. James watched her go, then went up to the bar and asked for a bottle of white wine. The selection was limited, and while he was speaking with the bartender, Trevor came up beside him.

"Hey, how's it going, man?"

"Pretty good, Trevor."

"And Nabila? You guys doing OK?"

"Sure. Sure we are."

Undoubtedly Trevor already knew about James and Nabila and their liaisons on the top floor of the hotel because Nabila's security staff had to coordinate with his.

"What do you need, James?" Trevor asked, grinning.

"Just trying to get a bottle of white wine, to go."

"No worries. Not sure what I have, but I'll have some sent to your room."

A thought occurred to James. If he was going to be hemmed in and controlled by Mr. Abrami, then James would play things his way.

"Tell you what. Send your guys out for some very expensive champagne, the best, and send that to Nabila's room. You can charge it to Nabila. And send along some dinner too."

"You got it, bro." Trevor replied. James thanked him and went upstairs to Nabila's room.

Nabila opened the door wearing red silk lingerie under a white linen robe. She'd been crying and came straight into his arms.

"James, I'm so sorry that I've gotten you involved. My life is a mess!"

James turned her face up to his, kissed her on the lips. Her makeup was running under her eyes, and she tried to wipe away her tears. He captured her hand and held it while he kissed the wetness off her cheeks. He took off her robe and pressed her body up against his, felt her warmth through the smoothness of the lingerie.

"Let's get into bed, and you can tell me about it."

James pulled his sweaty shirt off over his head while she unbuckled his belt. Nabila got down on her knees and slid his pants down to the floor, then gently brought her hands back up the inside of his legs. She caressed him carefully, stoking his growing fire, then looked up at him, smiling shyly, before she put him in her mouth. His day had been challenging, demanding the greatest level of self-control, and yet within seconds he felt every shred of that control slip away. Clearly, even though Nabila had been in a cloistered marriage for all of her adult life, she'd either been taught or had intuited exactly how to use her lips and her tongue to maximum effect.

Later in the bed, James returned the favor, and she cried out repeatedly as he used his own mouth to bring her to orgasm again and again. Finally, they lay quietly in each other's arms. After a few minutes, a knock came at the door. The timing was such that James wondered if the knocker had come earlier, heard the considerable racket from inside, and prudently withdrawn until a more appropriate time to make a delivery. James got up, threw on some shorts, and opened the door. One of the staff was there with a big grin on his face, a tray of food, and an ice bucket with a bottle of Dom Pérignon. James thanked him and brought everything to the bed.

"What's all this?" Nabila asked.

"The dinner you just paid for," he said, opening the champagne and pouring two glasses. "Never had Dom before, but then again, it's not every day that you get to sleep with a beautiful, insanely rich woman right after being threatened with death by her staff. Wasn't even on my bucket list, but in retrospect, maybe it should have been."

James raised his glass to her. "Cheers!"

She raised hers back. They ate and drank. Then, a bit tipsy, they cuddled while sitting up against the headboard. She rested her head against his shoulder, and he stroked her hair.

"This man who interrogated you, do I know him?" she asked.

"I don't know. Fortress Security, a Mr. Abrami. Average height, cold eyes. Said he'd be very upset if I told you about him." James sat up a little taller and turned her to face him. "OK, Nabila. Tell me the truth. Are you divorced, or are you still married?"

Nabila started to cry again, but James just shook her gently by the shoulders.

"Hey, listen! There's no wrong answer here. I just need to know what's going on. So we can figure out what to do."

"Do? There's nothing we can do! I'm married, and yet, I'm divorced."

"What does that even mean?"

"My husband, Saayed, is eighty-two years old. Has health problems, can't—" She paused and looked down at the bed, the writhing in her voice echoing the agony in her body language. Then she continued, suffering over the words like they were the admission of some terrible guilt. "He's a kind man, a great man, and…he loves me.

I gave him his heirs. He is…grateful. So, he agreed to temporarily divorce me. Three times…once for each son I bore him…any more than that, and I would be really divorced." Tears continued to fall.

James sat stunned as glimmers of understanding, fractions of implications, and the calculus of consequence whirred in his head, and a thousand pathways to the future spun out before him like the yellow brick road, only with the haunted forest on all sides.

"So, if he divorces you temporarily, that means—"

"That I…go back to him." Nabila looked up at James, her eyes gleaming wetly. "And he accepts me back, and…that's it; we are married once more."

"That's the most…remarkable…thing I've ever heard."

"I've never told this to anyone, James!" Nabila was pleading with her whole body, her eyes frantic through the tears. "You must keep it a secret! It could be really big trouble for us if the outside world found out."

"How does he divorce you? Isn't that a pretty big deal for a guy who owns half the Middle East? How's it legal?"

"We don't get legally divorced. It's an agreement between him and me. He opens the golden cage and lets the bird fly free, for a few weeks, and then, I return."

"So, you're really married."

"According to our imam, we're not. Saayed says, 'I divorce you,' and we're divorced in the eyes of God and in our own eyes. The legal system doesn't have to get involved."

"You've done this before?"

"Twice. The other two times were a disaster. You are my third… and last…marriage holiday." Emotions warred across her face and glinted in her wet eyes. Shame. Defiance. Hopelessness. Hope.

"And do you love him?" James asked, searching her eyes for truth.

"Of course I love him. I'm a good wife!" Now her face read of indignation and a determination to believe her own words. James found himself wondering if she had the same definition of love as he did and then immediately discarded that thought. He knew there was no universal definition of love.

"Wow. What do others say? Your relatives, your social friends, the press?"

Nabila just looked at him incredulously, then laughed through her tears. "When you are Saayed Khan, nobody speaks ill of you. His contemporaries all have personal lives that are far more compromised than his. If his...accommodations for a young wife are... unorthodox, then they are not really the concern of anyone else. As long as she is discreet, and does not embarrass him, her privileges of freedom would not be curtailed. At least, that is his promise to me."

"And your promise to him is to always return."

"Yes."

"So I am—?"

"My opportunity to taste freedom," she replied, wiping her eyes. She kissed him slowly, her lips wet and salty with her tears. "To choose. To feel what I feel, and act on it. To take a risk, to let my heart be foolish! Have you any idea how rare that is? For someone like me?"

"I get it, but what about us? I mean, here we are, and it's not just you; it's me, too."

"I know, James. And I'm sorry. But you will always be a rare, wonderful part of me, for the rest of my life, no matter what you decide to do."

"So, what does that give us, Nabila? Four days? And then you're gone forever?"

"Yes, but we have each other now! We can still live a lifetime in these next few days." She was pleading, trying not to cry again, but her eyes leaked tears. "Love a lifetime! Make memories that even *you*, with all your worldly adventures, will remember on your deathbed. James, that's all I have. All I can offer. What else can we do?"

James looked at her, incredulous. "And after, we don't talk on the phone, we don't text, no email?"

She looked away and nodded.

"And I just go away. Forget about you?"

She nodded again, her shoulders slumped, her head bowed.

"But someday, you'll be a widow—"

Nabila shook her head. "No, James. Please. There is no future for us. Please accept that all we have is right now. I wish it were otherwise, but I cannot hope for an early death for my husband. I cannot even think that way."

James lay back on the bed with his eyes closed, taking long breaths. He felt as if he'd just sprinted up an alley, chasing after her as she drove off in a taxi to the future, a future that left him with nothing to show—again—for all his years of trying. Trying to understand love and sex and women. And yet, he was no victim. He wasn't even supposed to be here with her. He was supposed to be alone, reflecting on his shortcomings as a human being. The gods always have the last word.

Nabila lay down with him, her head on his shoulder, her tear-streaked, worried face scanning his for reaction, her trembling hand resting over his heart. "James?"

"Hey, it's OK. Just give me a moment." He looked up at the ceiling, as if wisdom were somehow hidden up there, maybe in the cracks in the plaster. His mind was spinning, shifting from pure despair to trying to think his way through, like always. Julie had said he didn't like to commit to loving someone unless he knew what was going to happen. Well, with Nabila, the calculus had changed, and he knew exactly what was going to happen, and when.

And why was love even a question? They certainly had attraction and physical chemistry. She was beautiful, sexy, and from what little he knew of her, a good person. But how deep did his feelings go? And what about her? Did she actually care about him, James Wilder, or was he just a romantic escape from the gilded cage, a fantasy she could conveniently place in her scrapbook of memories, safely sequestered from any interference with her real life?

He remembered his last conversation with Julie, a few days before he got on the plane to Bali. "You've been hurt so much that your head is always going to try to convince you that nothing's worth it," Julie had said. ""That avoiding pain is more important than taking a chance at love." But that's not the way a heart works. Your heart is like Arjuna from the Bhagavad Gita. Acting for the action's sake, unattached to outcomes. Your head is attached to outcomes, but not your heart. Your heart can't think. It can only feel."

His heart. He already felt something for Nabila. Was it just affection? For her smiles and her lovely accent and her charming Persian princess persona? Or was it love, young and just budding out on the thorny branch of his life history with women? She'd certainly gotten under his skin. "Na-bi-la" was already etched like a tattoo— somewhere. And what could he do now, faced with this impossible dilemma? It seemed he had only two choices. He could wrap his heart in protective armor and push her and her expiration date away. Or he could peel away even more armor, love her as completely as time would allow, and take from the experience whatever lesson the gods were offering.

"*Gamble everything for love,*" the gods whispered.

"*Act for the action's sake,*" they cajoled.

"*Get out of your head and into your heart,*" they commanded.

He kissed her eyelids closed. He caressed her cheeks and the puffy, wet places with his lips. He kissed her nose, that perfect aquiline symbol of her regal ancestry, and he kissed the tiny, downy hairs that dusted her cheeks and upper lip. He tried to memorize every line and curve of her face, knowing that the privilege of caressing her features was already burning away like a votive candle, offered with a prayer to the gods. Na-bi-la! He felt a lurch of despair descend upon him like a black cloud, but he pushed it away and took a deep breath. He exhaled slowly and felt a terrible weight leave him, one that he didn't even know he carried. The weight of expectation. And from the uncrowded space granted to him by lightness, he began to see the silver lining in that black cloud of circumstance. With no expectation of tomorrow, Nabila and he were free to be completely present, completely real with each other. There was no future to safeguard or build toward, no history to explain or understand. They were two blank slates, writing only the present moment in ink that disappeared as soon as it dried, as doomed as the dinosaurs with the asteroid of future promises hurtling toward them. And from somewhere in his own not-too-distant past, he heard a voice whisper, "Sometimes, you just gotta say, 'What the fuck!'"

"OK, Mrs. Khan," James said with a sigh. "If we're going to pack a lifetime of memories into four days, we'd better get started!"

Nabila threw her arms around him, smiling through her tears. "Thank you, James. I know I have no right to ask you to love me. I'm a mess."

"I'm no bargain either, my dear. But we're all we've got!" He breathed in her warmth and her scent as they clung to each other, their embrace a shelter that, just for a moment, offered comfort and respite from the passage of time and karma. Two refugees from inexorable fate.

"You know, James," Nabila whispered. "I think you and Saayed would be great friends if he ever met you. He's a deep thinker, a lover of poetry. Very progressive for his time and culture. That was my first thought when I met you. That he would approve."

Downstairs, there was a dance party going on. James could hear the revelers shouting and dancing as the party cranked up.

"Let's get out of here," he said, and got out of bed.

"And go where?" Nabila asked.

"I don't know. Someplace where no one knows us; no one follows us."

"How will we go? What should we bring?"

"We go on a scooter, and we bring the clothes on our backs. And money. Anything we need, we can buy."

"That's crazy!"

"Yes, it is. You wanted this, remember?"

They snuck out of Soulfire undiscovered, the dance party going on poolside providing just enough chaos to cover their escape. James went out first and took the scooter past the front gate. Nabila came afterward, wearing local clothes and a cheap headscarf. Neither carried bags.

She jumped on the back of the scooter, and they roared away into the darkness, direction unknown. Actually, roared is not the word for any speed on that scooter. It topped out at about sixty kilometers per hour, and James was still a bit unfamiliar and cautious in his driving. Nevertheless, Nabila clung to him with her arms wrapped around his chest as they rode, squealing in excitement and terror as they zoomed blindly around corners and down hills.

It was a beautiful night. The moon was almost full, and the streets were quiet except for the barking of dogs as they motored by. They settled into a smooth rhythm of swooping curves and passed gradually out of the more densely developed environs of Ubud. Out in the countryside they rode past terraced rice fields and through groves of banyans and bananas. Through tiny hamlets and villages still stirring with life. Here and there, strings of colored lights festooned a tree or bush or shack, perhaps marking the presence of a local *warung*. They were climbing steadily, as all roads in this region of Bali trended either toward the volcanic mountains or away from them, dictated by the deep gorges carved by the rivers that drained their slopes. After about an hour, they came to a sign for "Nataraja Guest House" and pulled into a well-lit parking lot.

The Nataraja was perched on a hillside with moonlit views of the valley and rice fields below. It had a thatched Balinese roof, lush landscaping, and statues of various deities guarding the entrance. James and Nabila went inside and were greeted by a tall Danish man and his Balinese wife, who were just getting ready to close. They led them to their best room, which featured a canopy bed, a separate bathroom, and Moorish-looking lanterns as lamps. It was perfect.

James and Nabila thanked them and closed the door. They looked at each other, a bit incredulous that they'd pulled it off.

"Well, now we've done it," James said. "Mr. Abrami will have my balls on a platter."

They both laughed and fell into each other's arms and onto the bed. They kissed slowly and started to help each other disrobe.

"Shower first," said Nabila. "I feel all hot and sweaty."

"Mmmm, I like my women dirty," James breathed into her ear as she struggled to free herself.

"And I like my men clean." She laughed as she pushed him away.

They used their whole bodies to wash each other, the soap and water foaming as they lathered luxuriously under the falling water. Afterward, they resumed their writhing in bed, their skins lubricated by some massage oil they had found in a small bottle on the bedside table. The hosts of the Nataraja would get an extra star in TripAdvisor for that.

They slept wrapped in each other's arms, sleeping deeply and fully as they both felt, for the first time, the release of expectations, fears, doubts, and anxieties about the future. They knew exactly how long they had together, and that freedom from complications kept them centered in the present moment. And the present moment was her skin and his skin, her breath and his breath, her lips and his lips, their connected bodies pulsing with life and a growing sense of oneness. With nothing outside their immediate awareness that needed attention, they disappeared into each other. And maybe, that was the point.

The next morning, James woke to roosters crowing from all directions, heralding the sunrise, and Nabila's face looking down at him. She was propped up on one elbow and smiled when he opened his eyes.

"Mmmm, in my dream you were a rooster," he said, and pulled her over onto himself for a kiss. Her body felt soft and warm. And familiar. James was getting used to her face, her smile, her eyes. Her smell and taste and sound. How her body fit into his and his into hers. There is so much to know about a person before you can say you know her. So many facets to explore, learn, imprint into the muscle memory of your movements and thoughts. So many emotions to decode, categorize, and respond to. So much to fall in love with. And then, James remembered. He buried the impending heartache under a smothering of kisses, to be dealt with at the appropriate time.

That day they rode the scooter west, following a narrow road up over steep mountains edged by terraces of ancient rice fields and down into valleys where the road was overhung with damp vines and dripping palm fronds. They dodged street dogs and gaggles of children and oncoming trucks. They ghosted through rainstorms and hazy sunlight and village after village. They stopped at small *warungs* for snacks and water and to use the bathroom. And midway through the afternoon, they pulled up to a tiny roadside stand that was selling fresh coconut water.

The vendor was probably a farmer, wiry and dark-skinned from the sun and sporting a well-worn Manchester United T-shirt and a pair of shorts that might have once been white. It must have been his day off because he was lounging on a raised daybed under a thatched roof of sorts with his slim, beautiful wife and two small children, a boy and a girl. Like their parents, the children were slightly built and short, and they had very beautiful features. There were a few chickens pecking at the earth and a dog sleeping in the shade under the bed. Beyond the flat area that had been borrowed from a rice paddy, the mountainside dropped away to a breathtaking view of a deep valley and steep green mountainsides across the way.

They bought two green coconuts that the farmer expertly opened with his machete. He shaved away one end of the thick, fleshy covering and created a small hole for a straw. With a flourish, he presented them to James and Nabila, and they drank. The coconut water was cool and refreshing, a welcome respite from the heat and humidity of the day. James gave him 50,000 rupiah, about three bucks and triple the price a local would have paid.

"You like coconut?" the farmer asked with a heavy accent.

Nabila smiled at him. "Yes, we like it very much."

The farmer smiled back with what seemed like genuine happiness. "Where you from?" he asked.

Nabila answered him. "We're from England."

"Ah, very nice English. How long you stay Bali?"

Nabila and James looked at each other.

"A week," James replied.

"Have you seen waterfall?" the farmer asked.

"No, we have not."

"You must see waterfall. Come."

He was very insistent. He gestured excitedly for them to follow and took a few steps toward the rice fields. There was a little pathway along the edge of the paddy that led to a line of trees a few meters away.

"I don't know. Dare we go?" asked Nabila. "He has that long knife!"

The farmer was carrying his machete and using it to point down the path. "Come! See waterfall. Very private. Very romantic! Come!" He saw their reluctance and noticed their stares at his machete. "It's OK! No criminal! No criminal!"

He placed the machete on the grassy earth with a broad smile and gestured for them to follow him. James looked at Nabila, and she shrugged, so they did. The farmer led them down the path that went through a grove of bananas and some kind of palms, and then the terrain started to slope sharply downward into a ravine. From terraced rice paddies, it became steep and wild. They crossed a tiny stream, ducked under low branches, and skirted clumps of dark bamboo. In the distance James could hear the sound of rushing water. It was hot and humid, and the thought of a refreshing mountain waterfall seemed more inviting every moment.

After a few more minutes of steep steps down the hillside, the ground leveled off to reveal a gentle stream winding along the path, and they followed it to a curtain of flowering bushes and large elephant leaves that shielded the mountainside. The roaring of water could be heard behind it, and a cool mist of water wetted James's face. The farmer pulled aside some large leaves and invited them to step through. They did, and inside the natural curtain was the most perfect jungle pool, with a waterfall pouring over a lip twenty feet above them. The water fell in a continuous sheet past hanging banyan roots and flowering plants into a pool so clear that they could see every pebble, every grain of sand on the bottom.

"You like? Very romantic! You have private! I go back up," said the farmer with much gesticulation and many smiles. He put his hands together in front of his heart in the Balinese gesture that means everything from hello to thank you, and with many more smiles and bows, he left them alone.

"Well, we're still alive," James said, arching his eyebrows as if in disbelief.

"No criminal! No criminal!" replied Nabila and laughed.

They looked at each other, and with one mind, started stripping off their sticky, sweaty clothes. The water was fresh and clean, cool from its travels from raincloud to jungle leaf to forest floor to stream bed, and finally via waterfall to their pool. At first it felt icy cold to their fevered skin, but as their body temperatures normalized, it was wonderful and refreshing. The pool was about chest deep in the deepest part, and James met Nabila there, skin to skin, and felt the heat of her body against his, tempered by the coolness of the water everywhere else.

"He could be watching," Nabila said, her arms around his neck, her belly and breasts against his.

"He could be selling tickets," James replied, and they both laughed.

They didn't care. They were invulnerable to watching villagers or farmers with machetes. They had escaped the comprehensive security of Khan Industries. They had promised each other *now*, and *now* is where they were, alone, in a private romantic pool under a jungle waterfall, their lips tasting the coolness and the heat, the sweetness of coconut and the sweat of skin, and most of all the freedom from *yesterday* and *tomorrow*.

Chapter Thirty

~ * ~

Citrine

For the next two days they cruised the mountains of Bali, staying in little inns by the side of the road at night and exploring the villages and temples and jungle by day. They fell in love with the scooter which moved slowly enough for them to see what they passed, and which could be easily parked wherever they came upon some new wonder to admire. They took selfies in front of vistas of rice fields and temples, with groups of kids, and by waterfalls. It seemed that every guy selling coconut water had a secret waterfall that he wanted them to see. "No criminal! No criminal!" became their running joke.

They bought cheap T-shirts for James and batik dresses for Nabila. They ate in *warungs* and drank Bintang Beer. They reveled in the moment, the freedom, the spontaneity of life lived without destination or plan. Time stood still for them while it marched on for everyone else. And yet, in the end, time always wins.

For their last days together, they wanted something special. James had read about the snorkeling at Pemuteran, the best in Bali. Paradise for him always included coral and reef fishes. The good news is that on an island, you can eventually find your way to wherever you're trying to get to. By the evening of their third day on the run, they pulled into a resort on the beach and rented a private, gated villa with their own pool, surrounded by blooming shrubs and coconut palms and bamboo. Inside, the villa featured a spacious suite complete with flowers arranged on the bed in the shape of a heart, and a bottle of passable champagne in a bucket. They toasted each other with the champagne, and then fell asleep in each other's arms.

The next day they rose early and had breakfast at the restaurant on the beach. Red melon and orange papaya, purple dragon fruit and yellow mango, all dripping with a sweetness impossible to find except in the tropics. Scrambled eggs and white rice and strong Balinese coffee. Throughout the entire meal they held hands, fed each other, and their bare feet touched under the table.

Afterward, James took Nabila on a snorkeling trip to an island off the coast that was part of a marine reserve and unspoiled. Their guide was a one-armed, sun-wizened man with crooked teeth and a snaggle-toothed grin, and as he piloted the colorful wooden boat out to the reefs, he chattered away in broken English, asking questions about America and London. They anchored out on the reef, and James held Nabila's hand as they swam past coral heads and sea fans, through schools of brightly colored fish and along steep walls of rock. It was her first time snorkeling, but she was at home in the water.

"James, this is so beautiful!" she exclaimed when they climbed back aboard the boat.

He kissed her, and thought how wonderful their lives together could be, if only fate were to allow it. He pushed that idea from his mind, because all it did was borrow pain from an impending, certain future.

After a picnic lunch on the island, they motored back to the resort. Back in their gated villa, they took a dip in their swimming pool. Their privacy was complete with the gate and the shrubs and bamboo surrounding the pool, and Nabila took off her suit and tossed it on the deck. Naked, she swam over to him and helped him pull off his shorts. James kissed her, and they made slow, sensuous love, each of them aware that this was perhaps their last time together. Afterwards, they retired to the bed indoors to laze away the rest of the day, wrapped in the cool cotton sheets. Dinner was room service, since neither wanted to dress. They were down to their last hours and wanted to spend them looking into each other's eyes.

Despite their best efforts to stay awake, they fell asleep in the depths of the night. The sun rose the next morning as it always does, and the crowing of roosters heralded the end of their honeymoon together, followed by a banging at the door. James sat up to the sound of helicopter blades carving the air somewhere outside their window. He looked out and saw a red helicopter perched on the sand fifty yards away, its rotors spinning. Nabila sat up, devastation on her face.

"Oh, James!" she cried, and flung her arms around him.

He held her while she shook with sobs, then composed herself and sat up. The banging on the door didn't stop, so James got out of bed, pulled on some clothes, and opened it. Mr. Abrami stood there, a grim smile on his face.

"Good morning, Mr. Wilder. I trust you slept well?"

James said nothing, surprised but not surprised to see him standing there.

"It's time for breakfast. In Denpasar." Denpasar was a good four hours away by scooter, so Mr. Abrami must have meant by helicopter. Nabila was already getting dressed, and they were out of there within ten minutes, no coffee, no shower. James tried to protest, but Mr. Abrami just repeated "in Denpasar, in Denpasar" to everything he said. James had counted on having Nabila to himself for at least a few more hours while they rode back to Ubud on the scooter, but the efficient Mr. Abrami had other ideas.

James and Nabila sat in the back of the four-seater helicopter, Nabila clinging to him but obedient to Mr. Abrami, James forced to go along because what else was he going to do? Mr. Abrami sat in the front seat next to the pilot, and once everyone was strapped in, gave them their privacy.

They wore headsets to block out the noise of the rotors, but it also meant they couldn't talk to each other. Nabila just looked stricken and mouthed the words "I'm sorry, James" and "I love you" before smothering him with kisses. Then she leaned her head against his shoulder, the ear cup of the headset digging into his muscle.

James looked out the window at the landscape whizzing by below. The jagged volcanic mountains looked like a landscape painted onto a Japanese screen, heavily draped with jungle foliage and shrouded in places by clouds, with gold and black temple roofs and brown rivers peeking through the trees.

The flight took about twenty minutes. They landed at a private helipad inside a sprawling compound on the outskirts of the city. The bird was returned to her gilded cage.

James was ushered to a luxurious guest room with an invitation to breakfast in thirty minutes. Under a long shower of cool, flowing water, he took inventory of his feelings and fought back onrushing janissaries of desperation and despair. He tried to wrap his arms protectively around his nascent love for Nabila, but he felt like he'd awakened in the middle of his recurring dream, struggling to get to class on the other side of campus and getting turned around and lost in hallways and wrong buildings.

When he stepped out of the shower, James found a set of new clothes laid out on the bed. There was a pair of loose white cotton trousers, a white cotton shirt with an open collar, an embroidered sash for a belt, and a finely embroidered vest that looked like it came from India or Pakistan. Everything fit perfectly, as if it had been tailored for him. He forced a grin and tried to prop up his sagging spirits. Whatever happened next, he would be going through it in style.

A butler in formal Balinese dress came to usher him to breakfast. They passed through rooms filled with beautiful artwork and furniture from all over Asia and the Middle East. They walked on priceless carpets from Iran and Turkey and China. They traversed gardens of flowers unmatched by anything he'd ever seen, even in Bali. They reached their destination in a private garden where a simple table was set under an elaborate Balinese roof. There was only one person sitting at the table. He was old, with a gray beard, a humble white turban, and dressed all in white cotton like James. The guide bowed to the gentleman and left.

"Mr. Wilder, I presume," were the first words out of the old man's mouth, and they were delivered in a cultured, Indian-flavored accent that exuded a sense of calm and command.

James nodded respectfully and took the proffered seat at his right hand.

"I am Saayed Khan," he continued. "And you have been making love to my wife."

His eyes were filled with merriment, as if they were discussing the most amusing yet sophisticated joke in the world.

"Apparently I have," James replied. "She told me she was divorced."

"Not an important detail, I assure you. She's a lovely woman, isn't she?"

"Very beautiful, inside and out."

"I have all the money in the world. I can buy any jewel, any piece of property. Any company. And yet, old age has given me the wisdom to value Nabila more than all that."

"In the short time I've known Nabila, I've come to believe that that is possible."

"She tells me you are a bad poet," Saayed Khan continued.

"She likes to call me that." James risked a smile.

"And yet, she has shared your poetry with me. May I call you James? I've heard so much about you that you seem more like a son or a nephew than a stranger to me."

"Please, call me James, if you wish."

"Yes, James it is. I assure you, James, that, as poets go, you are not bad."

Saayed's smile broadened, and his eyes crinkled at the small joke. He reached over to a side table and picked up James's book of poetry, the red scrapbook with a cover like tanned crocodile hide, the sleeves holding his poems printed on card stock edged with gold filigree. Saayed Khan flipped through the pages, stopping to admire one and shaking his head as if in wonder. He looked up at James.

"I hope you don't mind that I borrowed this. It seemed only fair, since you borrowed my wife."

"I can hardly complain. The exchange is far from even."

Saayed Khan smiled, his eyes glowing. "I've reached an age and infirmity where for me, the physical act of love happens only in my mind and my heart. Your poetry—" He didn't finish, just bent over the book and read a passage aloud.

"Bring me a lover who burns.
Bring me a lover
whose body is consumed with red fire,
whose touch sets a bonfire in my veins,
whose skin turns to burning silk under my fingers,
whose hair curtains my face like smoky incense."

He looked up from the page. "Your poetry makes me remember—"
James said nothing, only nodded.

"Do you know, James, I've learned that there are many types of love. Perhaps seven billion types, one for each person on the planet."

"That might be an underestimate."

"So true! You see? Nabila said we think alike, you and I." His smile broadened, and James returned the smile cautiously.

Saayed continued. "So yes, seven billion people, and each person can love many different ways, even with the same person. I myself have loved many women before Nabila, each in her own way. And Mr. Abrami assures me that you have too."

"Perhaps not as many as you."

Saayed waved his hand dismissively. "But you loved each of them differently, yes?"

"In my experience, love between two people is always unique."

"Indeed it is! You call love a shapeshifter in one of your poems. Infinite in its manifestations. How else could one man write so poetically about love unless he had the experience of seeing love from many angles?"

"Well, every relationship I've ever had has ended in failure. It does give you a certain perspective."

"Ah, the paradox of love! Is any opportunity to love another truly a failure? At least you and I have had the freedom to experience this paradox. We've experienced the highs and the lows, the excitement of new love several times in our lives, and terrible loss. My Nabila has not. She's been a good wife, a very good wife. And yet, I knew in recent years that she was not happy. I gave her everything money can buy, but money cannot buy everything. Another astounding paradox, isn't it? Especially to a man who has dedicated his life to the accumulation of wealth."

James said nothing, and Saayed continued.

"She married me when she was seventeen, an arranged marriage, as is our custom. I was forty years her senior, already older than her father. I'd lost my first wife and son in a terrible accident, and I needed an heir. She was a beautiful young woman of good standing, and her father was a very traditional man from our community, a doctor in London. Initially he was reluctant, but I made him a very good bride price. And she has benefitted, I think, from her life with me. I was a good husband to her for many years, gave her three children, Allah be praised!"

Saayed paused, and seemed to reflect on the past before continuing. "But now, in truth, I'm more like a grandfather or an uncle. I can hold her, but not love her. I sensed her wanting, her desire for more. And as you know, Nabila is…special when it comes to love. She needs so much…and she deserves to know passion, the highs and lows, just as you and I have. When I was a younger man, closer to your age, I would have been consumed by jealousy and anger at the thought of any man—" His eyes flared for a moment; then the calm returned. "Age has taught me that jealousy has nothing to do with love. You must love with an open hand, not a closed fist. That is one type of love that comes only after many years and much living."

Saayed's eyes looked off again into his own world. Reliving the past? Visiting the unknowable future? He sat as if in a trance, this time for long enough that James wondered if he'd had a stroke or a fit of some sort. But he came out of it and shook his head, as if clearing the cobwebs of otherworldly visions.

"As I said, she seems almost like a favorite daughter to me now. But she's not; she's my wife. I've done what I can to bend the rules for her. She's had her three marriage vacations, and she will have no more until I'm gone. And then, Allah willing, she will be free to experience passionate love again."

Saayed Khan leaned back in his chair, looking at James, his gaze once again firm and his voice steady. "I owe you a debt of gratitude, James, as does Nabila. You've treated her kindly and well, so she tells me. She understands, as I hope you do, that there can be no more contact between you after you say goodbye. I need your promise that you will honor her request, and mine."

He said it like a judge pronouncing a final sentence, not making a request. James had expected these words, and yet they still cut his heart in two.

James considered his alternatives. He had none. Mr. Khan was a man of immense resources and could squash him like a bug if he wished. And Nabila, she'd already told him days ago that he had to disappear from her life. She'd made her choice, an adult one, from her own free will. So there was nothing to fight.

"I promise," James conceded. "You're a lucky man. She loves you very much. She told me so."

Saayed Khan's eyes grew misty at that. "Thank you," he said. "I know you want her, and I know she wants you. Ah, the agony of lovers! Is there anything more sweet, more heartbreaking, than unrequited love? Our final gift, yours and mine, to her."

"That's an odd way to think of this."

"Is it? Love is the banality of real life, distilled into poetry."

"I should write a poem about that."

"You should. Keep writing poetry. You have something there. Perhaps someday the name James Wilder will be more well-known than Saayed Khan, and I will be able to say, 'I had breakfast with that young poet.'"

They did have breakfast. The conversation changed to Saayed Khan telling stories of how he built his business empire, and James pretending to listen while his thoughts were on Nabila and whether he would see her before the helicopter or private car swept him out of her life like yesterday's offering to the gods.

In Bali, they sacrifice to the gods every day, three times a day, with countless little handmade baskets of flowers, spices, food, and incense offered with love. And then the next day they sweep them up like fallen leaves, as transitory as the flower petals from which they were made, and do it all over again, fresh and new and sincere. And they do it without fail, without thinking that they are ever done or that they have wasted their effort or time making the offerings.

Maybe that was what Nabila's and James's brief affair was about. A brief blooming of beauty, a sacrifice, offered to the gods. A reminder that everything is temporary and that the only moment that matters is the present one, and that when it is gone, in the next present moment we must make the offering of love again.

Nabila came down to the garden just as they finished breakfast. She was barefoot, wearing loose, white cotton pants, a short scarlet top, and gold ornaments and flowers in her hair. James said goodbye to Saayed Khan, and she led James to a secluded daybed in the corner of the garden where she sat with him and poured him a crystal glass of wine. James drank in her image, memorizing every detail, every fleck of color in her dark eyes, the shape of her lips and her magnificent cheekbones. Somehow, he already knew Mr. Abrami had wiped all pictures of Nabila, all their joyful selfies from his iPhone and his iCloud. Comprehensive security indeed.

Nabila asked James to read her a poem, one last one. He opened his book and read the page where it fell open.

~~ *Infinite Love* ~~

There is only one way
to prove
my infinite love.

Kiss me again,
and again and again.

Keep trying to empty
the well of my love.

You will see that
no matter how often you drink,
there will always be more,
thirsty for your lips.

~~ * ~~

After James finished, she kissed him and held him tightly, and then took off one of her golden ankle bracelets and gave it to him.

"For Scheherazade," she whispered, her raven-black eyes washed with tears.

* ~ * ~ *

Out at the limousine, Mr. Abrami handed James his suitcase. "It's all there," he said. James believed him, having experienced his omnipotence and efficiency firsthand. As the Indian driver drove to the airport, Mr. Abrami and James chatted about the weather and the beauty of the countryside. They discussed the challenges of travel through multiple time zones. But they never talked about James and Nabila's escape from Soulfire. Mr. Abrami seemed unconcerned about their shenanigans, and his calm attitude deepened James's suspicion that they'd never really escaped at all, that his "comprehensive security" had known where they were and what they were doing at all times. Certainly, when their time was up, he'd found them easily enough.

When James checked in for his flight, he found that his seat had been upgraded all the way to Denver. He was flying first class, and the airlines must have been further alerted to his VIP status because he'd never experienced a more solicitous series of flight attendants and ground personnel whisking him through security and check-ins and boarding.

Back in Boulder the months passed slowly, and James often googled Nabila and Saayed Khan to see if there were any developments in their lives. Soon after he left Bali, he read that Kabir Khan, their youngest son, was cleared of all charges related to jihadi activity. Otherwise, details about them were scanty.

James found himself unable to move on. His heart ached with loneliness in the empty place where he felt

"a raw wound still gaping,
Flickering dimly, leaking light,
In the center of my chest."

James missed her more than he expected—Nabila, hauntress of his dreams, his Persian princess, his courtesan of lantern light. Their transitory love had been an offering to the gods, proof that all that ever mattered was the present moment, and yet, he couldn't leave her in the past. In other circumstances she might well have been the Great Love of his life, what he once thought Sara could have been if only he'd had patience. Or Kat, if Kat hadn't been taken by the gods to her own place in their heavens. Finally, James tried making Nabila's mala. He chose

Obsidian for raven black eyes
Sunstone for immeasurable wealth
Moonstone for Bali nights
Solid gold for Scheherazade's ankle bracelet
Glass fired beads for lantern light
Citrine for the second and third chakras

As he knotted each bead, James whispered, "I love you, I release you, I thank you," knowing that she had chosen her path freely, and he had to find serenity, acceptance, and gratitude with her choice. When he was done, he had a beautiful mala that represented her and their brief time together, but she still haunted his dreams. It seemed he would need to do something more radical to finally find peace.

One morning, James woke with a smile on his face, remembering their little joke. He went down to the local tattoo parlor and had her name tattooed on a body part. Na-bi-la.

نبيلة

Which body part? He was a bad poet, but not that bad. James had it tattooed on his ankle, a reminder of the golden ankle bracelet she gave Scheherazade. Isn't love grand, to give us such beautiful body art?

About four months later, James published his first book of love poetry. He called it *Hafiz and I: Faint Echoes of an Ancient Heart*. The first printing of fifteen thousand copies sold out almost immediately, with a single large order for ten thousand copies coming from Qatar. That order put him briefly on several bestseller lists. Na-bi-la.

> —I love you
> —I release you!
> —I thank you.
>
> Find serenity, acceptance and gratitude for the choice to move forward with open heart.

The Sixth Mala

The Fool, Bedazzled by Beauty, Traveling Light

*~ **Until Now** ~*

One day, I heard your voice,
a whisper on the wind,
the holy breath of secrets,
but I never answered,
until now.

Today, the music of your laugh
brings back memories of dreams
and chases silence
from my heart.

I painted a portrait of your face
a thousand times
upon the canvas of my mind,
but like a candle hidden in shadows,
I could only see your eyes,
watching, above the veil.

Today, your smile banishes
winter from my soul
and melts
my deepest feelings.

I've had many lovers
while I waited for you,
and always, it was your essence
lingering on my lips
long after their heat had faded.

Somehow, you were always here,
the memory of your skin
embedded in my flesh,
golden threads
sewn into a silken robe.

~~ * ~~

Chapter Thirty-One

~ * ~

Pink Beryl

Right after getting divorced, in that chaotic, collapsing time before his diagnosis with cancer, James visited his friends Joe and Sarah out in Oregon. They were modern hippies living the dream in a yurt on forty forested acres, with a stream to bathe in and an outhouse for plumbing. Joe would get up in the morning with Gustavo, their dog, and Rufus, their cat, and while Sarah made the coffee, he would sit out front on a log and pound on an African drum and sing as the sun came up over the trees. A burly man with a black beard and a large belly, Joe looked like a large gnome howling at the sky.

Sarah was into tarot cards. She had a plain, pale face and long, curly, red hair, usually pulled back in a bun, and she wore prairie dresses. At least that's what James called them because she looked as if she'd just stepped out of a covered wagon in the 1850s. She sat James down while he was there and read his fortune.

James quickly forgot what she said about his future, as at that time he wasn't a big believer in the irrational sciences, but he always remembered the first card she turned over. It was The Fool. James had her pull his cards a couple of more times, and he even tried it himself. It didn't matter if they pulled one card or three or five or seven—The Fool always came up. James had tried it from time to time since, and usually, but not always, The Fool came up.

What did it mean? A dozen different soothsayers could have a dozen different interpretations, but to James it was confirmation of his place in the deck. He wasn't the King or the Knight, or even the Six of Cups. He was The Fool, touched with a rare brand of madness. It gave him an explanation and an excuse for why he had so much difficulty understanding and relating to the other cards in the deck, the other people. In any event, when the gods flip over your card repeatedly as The Fool, you'd better take notice.

It happened again, a week before his fiftieth birthday, on Southwest Airlines flight 1563 into San Diego. James was sitting in the third row, on the aisle, and in the middle seat was a young woman with short dreadlocks, beads around her neck, and the faint whiff of weed emanating from her clothes. She was from Nederland, Colorado, a tiny mountain town a few miles west of Boulder. She had the optimism of someone who'd been badly disappointed in her first try at life, but given a second chance, had found something that really resonated and had embraced it fully. For her, that meant a life on the road, blowing to and fro on the wings of her parents' frequent flier miles. She was headed to San Diego to meet some friends for a road trip down into Mexico.

"Pick one," she said, holding out a well-worn and shuffled deck of tarot cards. It was the Rider-Waite tarot deck, and James knew it well. It was the same deck Sarah had used in Oregon. He smiled and picked one, knowing what it was before she turned it over. The Fool. Yep, that was him.

Turns out the girl was new to tarot. She had a well-thumbed guide and read from it. "The Fool, his face gazing skyward, seems unaware that he stands at the edge of a cliff, with only the barking of a little dog to warn him of his peril. Bedazzled by beauty, traveling light, all his worldly possessions hanging from a stick over his shoulder, The Fool is so filled with visions and wonder and excitement that he could easily fall to his death with a single misstep. Will he come to his senses and take another route, or will he plunge blindly ahead in pursuit of his dreams? While the card's value is zero, it is also the card of infinite possibilities, of starting over from the beginning, a wild card that can go in any direction." The irrational sciences. This was the first of three such messages James would get in the next twenty-four hours. Magic was afoot.

Coming into San Diego, James always felt like the plane was going to land on someone's rooftop. You can see the palm trees whizzing by, just below the plane. You can see the busy city streets. And just a few blocks over, the Pacific Ocean coming up fast. Somehow, the tiny airport materializes at the last minute, and the jet touches down inside one of the most beautiful cities in the States.

San Diego was one of his favorite places, and when the opportunity came up to be a presenter at the annual Yoga Monthly Magazine conference, James accepted the invite. He would be reading poetry from his book, *Hafiz and I: Faint Echoes of an Ancient Heart*. He'd never presented at the conference before, but he'd started doing readings over the previous twelve months from coast to coast, in bookstores, at writing conferences, and at yoga festivals.

There were two hour-long time slots to fill over a three-day weekend with readings and book signings, and otherwise he had a free pass to any class he wanted. There would also be a booth in the vendor's village selling his books, as well as cards and calendars featuring his poetry. His initial presentation was scheduled for mid-morning. But first, James had to check in and grab some breakfast. The flight had left Denver very early, and all he'd eaten was a yogurt from the airport Starbucks.

The Hotel Del Coronado sits right on the beach, a giant landmark with white walls and red, turreted roofs. Tourists flocked from all over to pay ridiculous prices for hamburgers and tacos at their seaside restaurant. James dropped his bag in the room and headed across the street to Cilantro's for some local chain-style Mexican food. The sun was burning off the morning fog that the locals called "June Gloom," and the air was pleasantly moist after the dryness of Boulder and the airplane.

He jammed down two breakfast tacos, then headed back to the hotel to meet Elaine, his liaison and contact with the organizers of the conference. Tall, blonde, and a yogi, she was waiting in the vendor village, where all the booths were set up in a large ballroom. Elaine was about thirty-five years old. She gave James a hug.

"Mr. Wilder, so glad to meet you!" she said. "Your 10:00 a.m. reading and book signing starts in half an hour. Can I show you to your conference room?"

"Sure, let's go," replied James. "Everything make it OK? The booth looks great!"

Elaine smiled. "Yep, we've got several boxes of books in the room and can come back here for more if we need to."

She gathered up a clipboard and her phone and led him down the hall. The conference room was a basic rectangle with two windows and space for about forty listeners on folding metal chairs. His chair would be on a raised dais at the end of the room. There was a microphone on a stand, fluorescent lighting overhead, and a statue of Nataraja. Elaine had warmed it all up by putting a small oriental carpet under his chair and draping a marigold-colored scarf around the statue.

James took his seat and looked around. If all the chairs were filled, that would be a great turnout for a poetry reading, but that was the beauty of a conference—a large, captive audience, staying on-site for three days, everyone needing to fill out their time slots with activities because nobody could do yoga all day long, every day.

They needed an occasional break—hence the panels of speakers, the yoga village filled with goodies for sale, the music and dance concerts, and James.

Elaine left him to settle in before the crowd arrived, and in the sudden stillness of the empty room, James took a few long, deep breaths to calm himself. As he did so, he reflected on how he'd come to this place in his life. The women he'd loved and lost, the long, empty periods wandering the canyons of loneliness. Reading poetry would be like a time machine, the verses transporting him back to those moments of creative inspiration when his heart had overflowed with passion or imploded with despair, and words had poured out onto the page. Sometimes at a book signing his voice would crack as he read, choked by the emotion of memory. He found it embarrassing, but his audiences didn't seem to mind.

This morning, the reading was no different. The thirty or so people who came seemed to enjoy the work, and he signed seventeen books. Afterward, he needed to wind down, so he headed to the beach. It had turned into a gorgeous day, sunny with no trace of the earlier fog.

James walked along the waterline, reveling in the feel of cool, wet sand between his toes. The ocean was dark, massive, and very cold, and the beach itself was broad, long, and lonely, with knots of tourists and locals scattered here and there. James preferred the warm, turquoise waters of the Caribbean, but the ocean anywhere was the home of the Grandmother. He whispered a prayer of gratitude to her as he waded ankle deep along the strand. Stilt-legged seabirds skittered ahead of him in goose-stepping platoons, their beaks stabbing like sabers at soggy seagull feathers and bits of dead crabs. Giant ribbons of kelp lay tangled on the wet sand, their rubbery stalks wrenched from the seafloor by an immense, unseen hand. And always, the cool onshore breeze carried the momentum of thousands of miles of unimpeded flow across the vast Pacific.

After his walk, James wandered back into the vendor village

at the hotel. There were booths selling yoga apparel, mats, books, and malas. There were booths selling vitamins and supplements and smoothies and essential oils. There were booths selling software and music for playlists and yoga retreats to exotic locales worldwide. And there were booths selling massage and reiki and acupuncture and chiropractic services. James stopped at a booth promoting some sort of vacation rentals, not because he was interested in renting anything, but because there were a couple of attractive women who smiled and invited him over.

"Hi," one of them said. "Are you James Wilder?"

She was very young, about thirty, with long brown hair and brown eyes. Her friend was older, quite a bit taller, built like Malibu Barbie, with wavy blonde hair, long legs, and large breasts. Both were wearing yoga pants and tops, the uniform preferred by most of the women in the conference.

James looked over his shoulder as if to see who they were talking to. "Who, me?" he asked, grinning.

"You are, aren't you?" The brown-eyed girl smiled, her eyes wrinkling up with delight. "I see your badge."

She was referring to the badge he wore around his neck. It was a pass that all participants carried. His was colored orange, not white, to show that he was a presenter, and it had his name in large letters across the front.

"I love your poetry!" she continued. "My fiancé and I are using one of your poems at our wedding next month!"

"That's great! Which one?"

"We picked 'Yes' because it describes us perfectly, how we feel about each other. We love it!"

"Thanks! Glad to hear it."

She rummaged around behind the table, digging through her daypack to pull out a copy of *Hafiz and I*. "Will you sign my book?"

"Sure." James took her book and noticed that it had been well-read. He loved that. A book that looked like someone had actually spent time with it, carried it around, spilled coffee or wine or tears on some of the pages, and bent back the corners of others to mark moments of inspiration, emotion, and enjoyment.

"What would you like me to say?"

"Um, how about to Carla and Danny, and then, oh gosh, I can't remember the words exactly, but that part where you say count all the waves and all the grains of sand on the beach…you know."

Of course he did. So James wrote:

To Carla and Danny,
Best wishes for your long and happy life together!

"But if you must know how many ways
I can say yes to you,
Count all the grains
Of sand on the beach,
And number all the waves,
And it will not be enough."
James Wilder

"That's perfect!" Carla said, and gave him a hug.

James felt satisfaction wash over his chest, a feeling that was becoming more familiar every time this happened, when a person connected with his words, and a transmission of emotion from his heart to theirs occurred. It was powerful feedback, almost as powerful as hearing "I love you" from someone.

"Hey, while you're here, why don't you take a pebble?" Malibu Barbie held out a bowl of small polished stones that had been engraved with single words and pictures. There were the usual suspects—*Love, Inspire, Devotion, Peace*—along with astrological signs and other symbols.

"Go on," said Carla. "Take one. For good luck."

"Sure. Why not?"

James reached in with his eyes closed and picked the first one his hand touched. He opened his eyes. It was a small brown pebble the size of a walnut, flattish and engraved with the shape of a scorpion.

"Huh. I wonder what that means?" he asked no one in particular.

"It's good luck!" said Carla. "So maybe that means you're going to meet someone who will sting you with love."

James laughed. *Me? Stung by love? That's not a prediction, that's a history.*

Malibu Barbie put down the bowl and picked up a paperback book with the title *Spirit Animals and Their Meaning*. She now read aloud from it, frowning.

"'...scorpions convey a spiritual message of isolation. Usually solitary creatures by nature, they interact with others only sporadically. When they do, they engage in intense relationships that never last, and soon find themselves in isolation again...' Hmmm. There's some stuff in here about death and rebirth...transformation...blah, blah, blah...oh, here's the good stuff: 'The scorpion is a strong individual who has the ability to inspire passion! The scorpion represents sexual needs and desires, obsession and intensity...' And more stuff about sex and desire and passion...hmmm!"

She looked at him over the top of the book, then continued reading. "Caution must be exercised when engaging with scorpions. The intensity will consume you and or the scorpion. Hence the sense that their deadly sting is fatal."

She put down the book and fixed James in her gaze. She had green eyes, with little brown flecks and yellowish glints of gold that reflected the suggestion of glitter in her eyeshadow. "Are you a Scorpio?"

He pried his attention away from her eyes and laughed. "Nah, I'm a Gemini. Someone once accused me of being a Scorpio rising, whatever that means."

"Interesting." Malibu Barbie looked thoughtful. "Yes, Gemini makes sense, for a writer. Maybe you *are* Scorpio rising—"

Carla jumped in. "Sorry, Angie's an astrologer," she said hurriedly, as if he might be offended by what Malibu Barbie was saying.

"I've got no idea what my rising sign is."

"Angie could do your chart!" Carla was trying to be helpful.

"Yeah, that's great," James said, feeling like it was time to move on.

"I'd do it for free, if you'd like. I'd like to do it." Angie was locked in again on him with those green eyes. James felt a familiar surge of energy from somewhere deep in his core, a place that had been mostly quiet since Nabila…a whirlpool stirring from deep slumber, beginning to spin, slowly moving waters that had lain still for too long.

James hadn't written anything new recently. No new poetry, no new prose. But that was his pattern. In love, he was in touch with creativity, with passion and despair, connection and loneliness, the two sides of the coin, heads and tails, light and dark. Not in love, life was gray, monotonous. No poetry.

He looked at the pebble again. Why a scorpion? What did it mean? Who was this woman Angie? And why was she here, now, in the role of keeper of wisdom, the translator of meaning? All this flashed through his head in a moment, and he had to answer.

"Sure, why not?" he replied.

"Great. What's your birthday? And where and when were you born? You can write that down for me in my book." Angie held out a journal with a blank page, and James wrote down the info she needed. "And don't forget your phone number," she added innocently. "So we can hook up for the reading."

"OK, I'm only in town for a couple of days."

"I'll be done this evening. I'll call you."

James smiled, thanked them for the pebble, and continued his perusal of the booths. Angie's words haunted him as he walked away. Perhaps he really was a scorpion in many ways, solitary, fatal to any potential for a relationship that came his way. And yet, he still considered himself a hopeless optimist. A believer in love and beauty and connection.

Chapter Thirty-Two

~ * ~

White Beryl

James was hungry again, so he went back over to Cilantro's for lunch, a burrito smothered with green chili this time. And guacamole. Afterward, he sat on the terrace of the hotel and let his food settle. It was moving on toward midafternoon, and the clouds slid along the horizon like ships coming into port.

After a while, he decided to take a yoga class. He looked in the program and saw that there was an Acroyoga class starting in a few minutes. Acroyoga is a type of partner yoga, usually a man and a smaller woman doing acrobatic movements with the woman up in the air riding the soles of the guy's feet as he lies on his back. He'd seen it before and was intrigued by the dance between male and female, between prop and performer.

James got up to leave and discovered that somehow he'd misplaced his orange badge. He had to go to the registration area and get a new one. The young guy behind the desk smiled apologetically.

"Sorry, Mr. Wilder. We're out of orange badges. I can give you a white badge. I'll put a note on it that says you're a presenter. I hope that's OK. You should still be able to get into everything. It'll be like a VIP badge that someone paid for."

"Sure, that's fine."

He'd be going incognito but didn't care. Being a celebrity was nice, but the novelty had already worn off. His new badge had his name in small letters and a hand-scrawled note on the back that said, "All Access—Presenter." He looked just like any other participant. James headed to his class, already a bit late.

The male presenter, an athletic young man in a tank top and board shorts, had just begun a demonstration. He was lying on his back on a mat with his legs up in the air. Balanced on the soles of his feet was a smaller woman. She was "flying" like superman, her pelvis supported by his feet, her arms swept back and her legs out straight. Then, like choreographed acrobats at a Cirque du Soleil show, they began to move, and all the while the guy described what they were doing. She folded up into an inversion where he kept her aloft with his feet on her thighs while her upper body hung upside down. He captured her shoulders with his hands, and she unfolded into a perfect vertical shoulder stand. They proceeded to move through a sequence of folds and rotations like human origami. Then finally she came back to earth, landing in an upright stance at the bottom of the mat and pulling her partner to his feet to a round of applause. The demonstration was impressive. James could see how so much trust and body awareness had to be built between the two partners. If only he had one.

The presenter asked everyone to break up into pairs, preferably one larger person as the prop and one smaller person as the flyer. It seemed like everyone had come with a partner or found one quickly except for James and a small, attractive, Hispanic-looking woman.

He looked at her across the room, and she looked back and smiled, a friendly, reserved, almost disappointed smile. He walked over to her.

"Looks like we're partners. I'm James."

"Hi. I'm Malena."

She held out her hand, and they shook formally, like a business introduction. Her voice was soft and musical, with a strong accent that might have been Mexican. Awkwardly, they stood there without speaking while the people around them chatted.

James took that moment to study her without staring. If she were a rose, she would be a bud, newly formed, her petals tightly wrapped around her core. Her hair was dark, almost black, and pulled back into a neat bun. Her face was pleasant but reserved, her expression studiously neutral. She had deep brown eyes that betrayed only intelligence, and creamy white skin devoid of blemish or mark. There were no lines on her face, only dimples in her cheeks when she smiled. From the structure of her strong nose and cheekbones, she could have passed for Middle Eastern or Italian or maybe even Indian. She had beautiful, perfect lips, and they were pressed together in concentration as she watched the people around her.

She was short, about five three, and dressed in purple yoga pants and a patterned white top. Her body was shapely and proportionate to her height. "Balanced" was a word that came unbidden to his mind. *Good thing she's small,* he thought. *I won't embarrass myself trying to lift her into the air.*

The class began with some exercises to get each partner familiar with touching the other and building trust. The first was just standing face to face, joining hands and then simultaneously leaning back, allowing the weight of one to keep the other from falling. Her hands fit well in his, not so tiny that they disappeared. However, the exercise itself didn't work so well for them. James was so much bigger, a foot taller and seventy pounds heavier, that she couldn't do much to keep him upright when he leaned back. The next few exercises were essentially more advanced versions of the first, where they had to share personal space and body contact and develop trust in the strength and attention of their partners.

Their first attempt at Acroyoga had James lying on his back and her launching into "superman" pose above while another couple spotted them on either side. James grinned at her, she finally cracked a real smile, and the awkwardness between them dissolved a bit. Eventually, they even tried an inversion, in which Malena hung upside down, her face inches away from his. He found himself wishing he'd brushed his teeth after lunch because he was working hard keeping her aloft and breathing into her face. Her eyes met his, and suddenly he knew she was thinking the same thing. Burrito breath. She laughed. Oh my god! James was so embarrassed. Finally, they did a pose where she sat up on top of his feet.

"OK!" continued the presenter. "Change partners!"

Malena smiled a pretty smile and went her way. James worked with two other women and a guy, and most of the time he was the base on the floor, but once got to fly also. It was fun but hard work. At the end of the class, he felt pretty tired.

The sun was about an hour from setting, so he decided to take another walk on the beach. Back in his room, James changed into some swim trunks and a T-shirt and went down to the shoreline. He walked along the water's edge, getting wet up to his knees when larger waves came in. The ocean was in a cold mood, rolling toward the shore in heavy, dark waves that rose up until they curled and broke and turned white, and then settled into dark again as they slid across sandy flats, sheets of gray glass pushing foam and bits of seaweed toward the high-water line to dissolve in stinging froth around his legs. There was a somber beauty to the bleakness, and it resonated with his loneliness.

James thought about his two readings, the tarot and the pebble. How did they go together? What were the gods trying to tell him? Was it a warning? "Beware! Danger ahead! Wake up, or your scorpion nature will kill whatever love is coming your way!" Maybe. But what love was coming his way? Angie? She was clearly interested, but the vibe, if there was one, was all about sex, not love. She called him just as the sun was setting. James saw the 310 area code.

"This is James."

"Hey, where are you?"

"I'm down the beach a ways. Just walking."

"Cool. I have your chart finished. It's very interesting."

"Cool." Mirroring her language.

"Meet you in the bar, or your room?"

This was it. His opportunity to play it straight. Or not.

"Hey, how about my room? Number 205. I'll be there in about thirty minutes."

"Sure. See you then."

James felt a jolt of adrenaline flow through his body. The die was cast. The walk back had him playing referee to all the voices that swirled within. Some were lashing him for his lechery. Others were softer, saying they were both adults here, and if something happened, then it was all good. Another voice asked if this was what he really wanted, empty physical connection to a woman. Still another shouted, "Yes! It's been too long." James found himself like Odysseus, unable or unwilling to steer away from the Scylla and Charybdis of Angie's eyes and body.

He arrived at his room and went inside. James had just enough time to change his shirt before the doorbell buzzed. He looked through the peephole, and there was Angie, with a bottle of wine in one hand and a bag over her shoulder. He let her in, and she handed him the bottle of wine. It was a white California chardonnay. She surveyed the room while he surveyed her. She was wearing jeans and an oxford shirt, open two buttons down the front and belted over the waist. She wasn't wearing a bra, only a gem hanging on a slender gold chain that drew his eyes to her cleavage. She had beautiful breasts. From somewhere, probably the spot between those breasts, came tendrils of perfume that went straight to the animal parts of his brain.

"Nice room. Never been in the rooms here before."

"Yeah, it's good," he said as he gestured toward the loveseat in front of the TV. James grabbed two drinking glasses from the bathroom, and they sat down, she with one leg tucked under herself and facing him. Open body language. The message was pretty clear.

"So, what did you find out?" he asked as he unscrewed the cap and poured the wine. "Any scorpions lurking in my chart?"

James handed her a glass and settled back on the cushions, reading her face. She looked back at him, assessing him as much as he assessed her, and she smiled, as if in agreement to a question he'd asked with his look.

"Cheers," she said, and they clinked glasses.

They both drank a sip, and then she set her glass down on the table and picked up her bag. She took out a leather-bound folder brimming with papers and drawings and opened it to his chart.

"Your chart. Very interesting," she said. "You're a Gemini, as you already know. Ruled by the planet Mercury. Very intelligent, good with words. Let's see. I'll just hit the highlights…you have your Mercury in Cancer, did you know that?"

Angie looked up at him, caught him studying her, and smiled a cryptic, Mona Lisa smile. James barely heard her through the miasma of scent and pheromones that curled toward him.

"Umm, nope. Did not know that. What does that mean?"

Angie turned back to the chart. "It means you communicate with words that carry strong feelings, like your poetry. You're quick to pick up emotions and moods in others. You're discerning and very curious. I'm getting that you love intellectual rapport, especially in matters of love. You can easily find yourself with more than one lover at a time." She looked up and smiled. "And you'd probably make a very good teacher, or even a cult leader, if you were bent that way."

"Really? Cult leader?"

Angie laughed. "I could see it." She turned back to the chart. "Your Venus is in Taurus. Interesting….That means that love for you centers on sensual, physical expressions. You are possessive and jealous...hmmm. You can feel threatened by fast-paced relationships, and yet your Gemini nature craves exactly that. That duality is a source of trouble for you because at your deepest core you desire predictability and dependability in your love relationships."

She paused and reached out to touch the bare skin below his neck where his shirt was open. He felt the burning of her fingertips in that unexpected place. "So complicated!" She smiled again, reeling him in with those eyes. Then she continued. "Venus in your second house...hmmm. You're attracted to quality. Hedonistic. You desire adoration, perhaps at the expense of gaining true love....Your chest and neck are your erogenous zones....You are very, very sensual, and stimulated most by touch and smell."

Of course. The women in his life who'd made the greatest impression had done so because of how good they smelled, the smoothness of their skin, and the energy in their touch.

"There's a bunch of other stuff. Not much about Scorpio, I'm afraid. So, I don't know what that scorpion pebble meant from an astrological sense. Maybe the scorpion really is your spirit animal, like that book said."

"Maybe," James replied, although he was more focused on the energy building between them, the sexual tension that had him wanting to reach out to her, follow that scent to those breasts.

"Except your Eighth House is in Scorpio. That indicates a desire for adventure and excitement. Beware though. I'm getting that too much adventure could put your life in danger at some point—"

She looked at him, followed his eyes to her cleavage, and smiled. She leaned back, brought her free hand up to her chest, and trailed her fingers slowly up and down the inside edge of her shirt, pinning his attention there. Her voice changed, got lower, sexier.

"Let's see, your Fifth House is the area of romance, self-expression. Your Fifth House is in Cancer. Hmmm...you will be in love often, up until the day you meet your one true beloved. You're a very affectionate lover, very physical, pay lots of attention to your partner, but also private and sensitive...."

"Seems like a lot of stuff about my love life." His voice was thick. His head was buzzing.

"Yes. There's plenty of other stuff, too, but do we care?" She put down her glass and leaned toward him, her gaze fixed on his lips.

"Not really."

James leaned forward toward her, mirroring her movements, his eyes tracing the outlines of her lips, which were the color of orangey pink roses just opening in the morning sun, half parted, and so, so close to his. He felt the warmth of her face, felt her breath like a gentle feather brushing his lips, heard it catch in her throat...and then he kissed her.

Chapter Thirty-Three

~ * ~

Pale Blue Beryl

They started on the love seat, kissing and leaning in to kiss some more. Her perfume mixed with the smell of her body filled his senses to overload. Her blouse came open, either by her hands or his, and her breasts, firm and heavy and full, found their way easily into his grasp. She ripped open his shirt and pushed him onto his back. She straddled his body, her blonde hair cascading around his face, and brought each breast up to his lips to be kissed, licked, and bitten gently. He reached down and found her belt buckle. Her belt didn't go through her pants loops; it was just tight around her waist and came off easily. Her pants had a single button and a zipper, and they were already open when his hands found them.

"Let's get to the bed," he whispered.

She stood up and led him by the hand, her touch warm and soft in his palm. In seconds they were naked and losing themselves in pure animal hunger, skin against skin.

Except something was wrong. His head was totally in the game, but his body was not.

"Mmmm, what's the matter?" she breathed into his ear, her body pressed against him, her hand reaching down between his legs. James twisted away, his heart racing.

"Just a sec."

She was hot and sexy and beautiful, and he was ready to go, except for a very uncooperative but vital part. What the hell? James took a deep breath, calmed himself down, and dove back in. They kissed and moaned and touched each other all over, and yet he was still as limp as a leaf of yesterday's lettuce, left out on the kitchen counter in midsummer.

Angie was pretty cool about it and did everything she could to resurrect the dead, but nothing worked. It was as if his brain was calling room service, "Please deliver one fresh boner to room 205," and his body was saying, "Sorry, that item is no longer on the menu."

After a while their heat passed, and James lay on his back, looking at the ceiling fan overhead that rotated lazily, clicking with each rotation. Angie lay with her head on his shoulder.

"Hey, no big deal," she said with a laugh, which meant that it really was a big deal. James couldn't look at her. She turned toward him, her breasts full against his side and her leg thrown over his pelvis.

"I really shouldn't even be doing this," she continued.

"Why not?" James asked, preoccupied with his own problems.

"I'm getting married next week."

"What?" He turned his head to see her grinning face, mocking him. He could also hear the gods collapsing in laughter somewhere behind him. Maybe in the bathroom.

"Really?"

"Yep. Getting hitched and moving to Michigan. I'm from back there."

"Huh," he grunted. "So all this was—"

"My own private bachelorette party. My fiancé comes into town day after tomorrow."

How about that for a curveball! For a second curveball! Nicely played, gods...two strikes perfectly thrown, catching the outside corner of the plate!

"OK. So maybe we can forget this ever happened?" James asked, half joking.

She punched him playfully in the ribs. "I'm not letting you off that easy! Let's get some sleep. We can try again in the morning."

"Sure. Why not?"

Angie lifted herself up onto one elbow. "After all, you're supposed to be the love poet."

"No, I'm the bad poet."

"What's that?"

"Just something someone used to call me."

"Sounds like a story there—"

"Read my memoirs."

"Will I be in them?"

"Depends," he said, and pulled her down for more kisses. At least his lips were still working.

The next morning James woke up to her breath tickling his cheek. She was deeply asleep, her face on the pillow inches from his, her body draped half over him. He felt pinned in place. He didn't want to move but really had to pee. James reached down and caressed her buttock. Slowly she opened her eyes and smiled.

"Hey," he said.

"Hey. Geez, what time is it?"

James looked at the clock next to his side of the bed. "Seven forty-seven."

"Shit! Gotta run." She jumped out of bed and rummaged around for her clothes.

"Where are you staying?"

"With Carla. She's cool. She'll cover for me."

"With whom?"

"Everyone. My mom. My sisters. Charlie, my fiancé. You ever been married?"

"Once. Long ago."

"I've been married twice. Third time's the charm!"

"And Charlie? Has he been married?"

"Never. He's a navy guy. Had a girl in every port, ya know? And now he's nearing retirement, gonna be forty-three with twenty years in. Ready to settle down."

"And you? Are you ready to settle down?"

Angie was just about finished dressing. She leaned down to the bed and gave James a kiss.

"We'll see. It's never taken before, but Charlie—" She shrugged and headed for the door. "Thanks. I had a nice evening. Maybe a raincheck on the sex?" She blew him a kiss and left.

Wow. That one came up like a squall on a sunny day at the lake. Blew furiously for a few hours, then miraculously, a sunny day again. But that failure to launch! James was actually glad they'd run out of time to try again. He didn't feel confident in his ability to perform.

He got up, took a shower, went down to the restaurant for coffee and breakfast, and then took another walk on the beach. It was cool and gray, the June Gloom hugging the wave tops and the ground, but he could see the sun trying to break through. A one-night stand! How long had it been since he'd done that? At least in recent years he'd tried to pretend that there was relationship potential with any-one he'd slept with. But he knew from the beginning that this was going to be just sex. Oh well. They were both adults. And his lack of—whatever you want to call it. What the hell? James shoved it out of his mind like a bad first date.

He got back in time for a higher-level yoga class with Kate Sperry, a popular teacher, in the large ballroom. There must have been two hundred people in the class. James rolled out his mat in the seventh row and took a few stretches to warm up. He saw Malena two mats over and waved. She waved back. He settled in on his knees as class started.

"Good morning, yogis!" Kate was a teacher in her midthirties, slender, with a huge mane of thick, curly hair the color of honey. She was famous for her challenging classes and social activism. "How many certified yoga teachers do we have in the room?"

James raised his hand with almost everyone else.

"Good! Wonderful! Today's class will be rigorous. Buckle up everyone."

The class was rough, but nothing he hadn't done before. The night's activities had left him jittery and stressed, and he really needed to work his body, find confidence again in his physicality. He flowed from pose to pose for almost two hours. By the end he was drenched in sweat.

As everyone filed out, James caught Malena looking at him. She smiled a warmer smile than the previous day's. She was wearing brightly colored yoga pants along with a purple top that exposed her shoulders and arms. He could see a tattoo of something pink on her right shoulder. He smiled back and nodded.

While he rolled up his mat, James peeked at her out of the corner of his eye, just curious to see what that tattoo was, and found himself watching a time-lapse movie of a bud opening up into a flower. Kneeling on her mat, she loosened the bun of her hair and shook it out. It fell in long satiny dark waves all the way to her waist like a shampoo commercial featuring a Tahitian princess. As her hair came down, Malena's energy changed. She looked younger, freer, as if whatever tempests had furled her petals were temporarily stilled. And fittingly, the tattoo on her shoulder was the most delicate rendition of a pink lotus, fully blossoming.

James stood up and slung his bag over his shoulder. He stopped by her mat as she was getting to her feet. "Hey, how's it going? Malena, right?"

She smiled. "I'm good," she replied in her strong accent. "And you, James?"

"Good, good. I'm good," James was almost stuttering, still shaken and off-kilter from the previous night and additionally disarmed by this woman who'd seemed so unthreatening only the day before.

"Having a good day?" he asked as they strolled toward the open door.

"Yes, it's nice to be here, not working."

"Where you going to now?"

"To eat some lunch, then class this afternoon. I think I take the slackline class on the beach; see what it's all about it." Her fractured grammar was adorable.

"Good idea. I always try to take classes that I can't get at the studio back home."

They walked together out to the terrace, their conversation still staggering around like an awkward newborn calf. The sun had once again burned off the fog, and it was a beautiful San Diego day. James wondered if she wanted to hang out. He wasn't trying to pick her up or anything. God no! She just seemed friendly and alone. What the heck.

"I'm going to grab some lunch and bring it out here on the terrace," he ventured. "Care to join me?"

"Sure. I have some lunch from home. I'll be out here."

They picked a spot at the edge of the grass where it met the sand from the beach and laid out their mats like a picnic blanket. He went into the little deli cafe and ordered a sandwich, some hummus and raw carrots, and two iced teas. He carried it all back out to the lawn and sat down next to Malena, facing the ocean. She'd brought some tacos in a glass container.

Malena shivered and wrapped her yoga towel around her shoulder. "It's cold here," she said, her teeth chattering.

The shore breeze had picked up, but to James it was a balmy summer day. "You think this is cold?" he asked. "Do you live in San Diego?"

"Imperial Beach, down the coast."

"Is that far?"

"Not far. Right next to the border, across from TJ."

"What's TJ?"

"Tee-hwa-na. Me-hi-ko." She sounded it out carefully.

"Oh, Tijuana. I've never been to Mexico."

She looked at him in surprise. "Really? I go there all the time."

"I heard it's dangerous. You can get robbed or whatever."

She laughed a laugh that wasn't pure laughter. There was a hint of defensiveness to it, and maybe some indignation.

"If you cross and drink like a crazy gringo, being stupid, sure you get rob, like any other place. That happen in San Diego, too. Where you from?" Her speech was a delicious salsa of wrong tenses and missing consonants, like the t's and d's at the ends of words.

"I'm from Boulder, Colorado. We have the mountains. No ocean, though. If we had the ocean, Boulder would be perfect."

"Boulder? Never hear of that. Are you born there?"

"Nope. Born here in California, in San Francisco."

"Do you teach yoga?"

"Sometimes. Why do you ask?"

"Because in class, you raise your hand. I will never think that you are a teacher."

"Oh really? What did you think?"

She laughed. "I think you're just a guy who comes to meet women. Not someone who actually knows about yoga."

James laughed too, but she'd struck a nerve. Ouch!

"And you?" he asked. "Are you a yoga teacher?"

"No, I would love to, but I canno afford teacher training, even if I love yoga. I have so many other priorities. My daughter, my rent, nursing school."

"Oh? But you come to these conferences. You must do a lot of yoga."

She laughed again, and this time her laughter was flavored with irony. "This is my treat. Once a year I come to see new techniques and to take classes with well-known teachers. Other days, I have to work. I have not much time."

"Yeah? What kind of work?"

"I'm a CNA, certified nursing assistant."

"Yeah? What do CNAs do?"

"I help cancer patients, in an oncology unit."

Cancer. The big C. The horrible long shadow of his past. Their conversation drifted to her job, about patients who needed her help with their most basic and personal human functions. She described what she did but left out the hard parts. Because of his own history with cancer, he knew enough to fill in the blanks. How patients took the news that they were terminal, and how they cried when they left the ward for the last time, to go home or to hospice to die. James had been lucky. He tried to not even think about cancer anymore. The demon that had haunted his awareness for seven years had been banished and replaced by other, lesser demons.

Malena spoke matter-of-factly, but her eyes belied the pain behind her words. Those deep, liquid pools of brown swam with a soft mix of compassion, soulfulness, and despair. And the rest of her face was a balance of God-given beauty and everyday humanity. Symmetrical cheekbones accentuated dimples that broke her face open when she smiled, and pure joy spilled out. And waves of shiny ebon hair with hints of deep red cascaded down the front of her right shoulder, hiding her breast and brushing her belly with soft curls. She'd been a tightly wrapped rosebud when he'd met her. Now that her petals had opened a bit, he was surprised and disarmed by the beauty revealed. He wondered what she would look like when the sun hit her full on and she blossomed into all her glory.

James shook himself out of his reverie. "So, what do you want to do with the rest of your day? I mean, other than the slackline class?"

"I want to go to the vendor village. To get a book, maybe met the author, get it sign-ed." She pronounced signed as if it had two syllables.

"Hmm. You read a lot?"

"Yes. Anything that can help with my English." She laughed, those dimples spreading wider. "My English is so bad!"

"No it's not! You speak very well!"

"No, it's bad. I know," she replied. "I used to work in hotels, back in Mexico. Vallarta, Mazatlán, TJ…there I thought I speak good, but not here anymore."

James found himself losing his capacity for witty banter. This woman had layers and layers of feminine soul, mellowed with a nuanced innocence that he couldn't quite put his finger on. Was it her personality? Her Latina upbringing?

"Are you married?" The words just spilled out, unbidden, premature. Somehow, she didn't seem to notice.

"No, I'm divorce. Just me and my daughter. She's in her first year in college." Malena said the last words proudly.

"I've got two kids. College also. Mine are twenty-one and eighteen. You look too young to have a college-age daughter!" It was true. She looked like she was in her midthirties.

"Well, thank you, but I marry very young," she said with a laugh. She got to her feet. "Sorry, I want to get that book," she continued.

"OK, can I come with you?" James asked cautiously. He didn't want to seem too eager, especially given her first impression of him.

"Sure." She smiled.

Her description of working in the oncology ward had found a disconcerting home in James's consciousness. Lots of people in the yoga world talk about compassion. "We're all connected, blah, blah, blah. Compassion for all living beings, blah, blah, blah." For Malena, compassion wasn't some lofty ideal worshipped for an hour in yoga class. It was her job, helping people with their most intimate struggles, the grossest manifestations of their humanity, cleaning up bodily fluids, changing diapers filled with shit and blood and mucus, and holding their hands while they cried through the terrifying destruction of their carefully nurtured self-images and descended into helplessness, pain, and despair. And all for close to minimum wage.

He found himself wanting to just be near this person who emanated goodness, who practiced more compassion in a single workweek than he had in his entire life. He didn't know it just from their conversation. He could feel it. He was like the dark moth of night attracted to the light. And the light lit a path that was unfamiliar, but that he knew he had to follow.

They cleaned up their food wrappers, rolled up their mats, and walked into the yoga village. James felt acutely aware of her presence, small and perfect, more attractive in every moment, her eyes lighting up at displays of clothing he was pretty sure she couldn't afford, at jewelry she would never have, and yoga vacations she would never experience. They wandered past the booths until they came to his.

"Here is where I want to buy the book," Malena said.

"Here?" James asked, completely taken by surprise.

"Yes. I love poetry. I want to come to his reading yesterday, but I didn't get here in time. I have to help my daughter with something for college."

The girl behind the counter recognized him and started to say something. He held up his hand, and she fell silent.

"Hmmm, so what book are you looking for?"

"I think he only has one. Hafiz and I."

"Let me get it for you. Please. It would be my honor." James picked up a copy from the stack and handed it to her.

Malena laughed and shook her head. "You don't need do that! I can pay it." She took out her wallet and started to count out bills. "I wish he will be here. I will love to have it signed."

She again pronounced signed as sign-ed. James had to tell her. "Malena, let me give you this book. And I will sign it."

Malena looked up from her wallet, her eyes confused, questioning. "You? Sign it?"

"Yes. I wrote it. I'm James…him…James Wilder. And I want you to have my book."

Malena took a step back. She looked stunned, and a little angry. "You? You're James Wilder? Why you didn't tell me?"

"Why does it matter? You didn't tell me your last name."

"It's Cortez. But you—"

James laughed. "Who were you expecting? Some guy in a turban, leaping off a white horse? No, it's just me."

Malena looked puzzled. She took a step back toward him, shortening the distance between them both figuratively and literally. "You are the James Wilder? I expect someone older, wiser."

James deflated a bit. "Well, that's nice. Here, let me sign that."

He took the book from her hands and opened it up. Inside he wrote:

To Malena

Love is the magic that changes music to rubies,
Weaves silver through poems and sets fire to dreams.

James Wilder

Malena took the book from him, looked at the inscription, then looked at him, her pretty face still recalibrating her expectations. James smiled and shrugged his shoulders. That seemed to break a dam. She smiled back.

"James, this is a big surprise. I did no expect to—" she searched for the right word, "know you."

"Well, now you do." He smiled back, and she gave him a shy hug. She quickly let go of him and blushed.

Just then, Angie walked up with Carla. "James, honey, there you are."

She walked right up to him and, in front of everyone, wrapped her arms around him and kissed him, full on the lips. She stayed pressed up against him while she whispered loud enough for everyone to hear. "Sorry I had to run out on you this morning. Hated to leave you." And she kissed him again, slowly and sensually.

Out of the corner of his eye, he saw Malena shrinking away, stunned. James pulled away from Angie, flashed a small, forced smile at her, and trotted after Malena, who was making a straight line for the door.

"Hey, wait up!" he said as he caught up with her.

"No, it's OK. You go be with your girlfriend. I gotta go," she said, walking furiously toward the exit.

"Please, I'd like to see you again. Malena, we're friends."

She stopped in her tracks and turned back to face him.

"Who? You and me? Or you and her?" Her eyes searched his, her chin quivering. Then she turned away and kept walking, out of his life.

James didn't see Malena that afternoon when he went to the slackline class, and he wondered if she was trying to avoid him. Then he smacked himself in the head and said aloud, "You idiot! Why is it always about you?" But it was. About the huge hole he had in his heart, the missing puzzle piece. And Malena.

That night the onshore breeze picked up, and through the open window of his room, James could hear the waves crashing on the beach. He dreamed vivid dreams all night, which was not unusual. But what was unusual was that he remembered the last one perfectly, even after he was fully awake, as if it were the memory of something real, only it couldn't have been, because Hafiz had Saayed Khan's face....

James was sitting on a beach, watching the changing colors of the sunset sky, and Hafiz/Saayed appeared, rising from the waves, water dripping like pearls from dreadlocks and beard.

"Good evening, young poet," he said, and he sat down beside James.

"Please go away. I'm not in the mood."

"That's because you're doing it wrong."

"Doing what wrong?"

"Make a better mala." Hafiz smiled at James, as if the meaning in his words was crystal clear.

"What the hell are you talking about?"

Hafiz rose to his feet, scooped up a handful of sand, and tossed it into the air in front of James. And as James watched, the grains of sand hung there in slow motion and grew into little round spheres, like beads, except that each bead was a moment in time, an event, an interaction with another person, an opportunity, and they all floated in the air before him, separate, unconnected, independent, before falling to the ground and turning back into sand.

"Make a better mala," Hafiz repeated, then turned and dove back into the waves.

Chapter Thirty-Four

~ * ~

Amethyst

Saayed Khan—how appropriate for Hafiz to morph into him, but "make a better mala"? James shook his head, as if clearing the vision from his awareness. He noticed that the message light on the phone was flashing. He called the front desk and was told that someone had left him a note in an envelope. He had no idea who that might be. Angie, to tell him goodbye? Elaine with an update on his speaking schedule? James yawned and climbed into the shower. He felt hung over, as if he'd drunk too many margaritas the night before, even though he'd had none.

On his way to breakfast he stopped by the front desk to pick up his note. It was addressed in a neat, feminine hand. James opened it up.

Dear James,

Sorry I leave in such a hurry. I apologize for my upset. I realize I have no reason to be angry. We are just friends.

Thank you for the book. I will always treasure it like a gift from you. Pardon my bad English! Here is your poem "The Art of Loving Slowly" in Spanish. Your poetry sounds wonderful in my language.

I am glad to know you.

Malena

~~ El Arte de Amar Lentamente ~~

"Amame por favor,"
ella dijo,
"solo que muy lentamente,
una plegaria susurrada,
un plan.

Por favor sírveme amor
en una copa de vino,
un suave aroma,
una probada,
una memoria saboreada.

Vamos a explorar
la imagen de un momento,
un paseo, en tiempo griego,
las caras de cerca,
una conversación bajita.

Bailemos,
pero una danza lenta,
gentilmente con la música,
la música de fuego lento.

Hablemos en poesía,
palabras medidas y rítmicas,
con muchos niveles de significados.

Repásemos sobre los detalles,
construyamos tensión dramática,
la sensación de desenvolver
un regalo precioso.

Podemos hacer esto
solamente una vez,
entonces,
volvámonos expertos
en el arte de amar lentamente."

There was no phone number, no return address. No way of getting in touch with Malena. It was a goodbye.

Shit! Not for the first time he found himself wondering what he'd done in a former life to deserve such bad love karma. Then he stopped himself and laughed bitterly. He stood at a perfectly logical place in space and time, filled with retribution for choices he'd made, pathways he'd taken. His marriage, when he worked himself to death, oblivious to the deep discontent of his wife. His year as a playboy, thrashing around for any sort of self-esteem, seeking validation in the shallow affections of random women. And then Willow, where he hurled himself headlong into the brick wall of someone else's relationship. Kat, dear Kat. James had no explanation for her loss, other than the gods needing him to learn *something*, but what it was, he still didn't know. Charlie, who could have been such a perfect partner if she hadn't reflected back to him his own flaws. Sara, that magnificent, talented, mystical, complex human being, beloved of the gods and needing something he couldn't give her, patience and healing. Nabila, his courtesan of lantern light, a test to see if he had the ability to love fully in the moment, with no attachment to outcomes. And now Malena? Strangely, she felt like a whisper of a promise, a glimpse of ease and rest and respect, a dive into compassion, an intriguing world of unfamiliar grace. A better choice. All from the space of a few hours together. But, like a whisper on the wind, she was gone.

James spent several months trying to track down Malena. There was no reason to believe she wanted to hear from him, but he had to try. What did he know about her? Her description: about five foot three, long dark hair to her waist, Mexican-born. In San Diego County, population 3.25 million, that didn't narrow things down very much. Her name, Malena Cortez. James googled her. There were twelve Malena Cortezes in Southern California on Facebook and other social media. None looked like her. She'd said she lived in Imperial Beach. Strangely, no one with that name came up there. James tried calling a couple of hospitals, asked if they had a Malena Cortez working there. No luck.

He went out for drinks with Eliu. They were celebrating a record month of business, and Eliu was in a good mood. He reminded James that he'd lived in Mexico for eight years, and he wanted to be helpful.

"You know, maybe her name isn't Malena Cortez," he offered.

"I'm pretty sure it is," James replied. "I wrote an inscription in her book."

"Yeah, but Malena isn't really a name. It's a nickname. She might be Maria Elena or something like that. Many Mexican girls have two first names. And they all work Maria in there somehow."

"Well that's confusing!"

"And Cortez might not be her real last name."

"What? You're kidding!"

"Yah. Quite often they will also have two last names, one from mom and one from dad. Could be Cortez Jimenez, or Sierra Cortez, or whatever."

"Maria Elena Sierra Cortez. Sounds like poetry."

"Dude! Not everything is poetry."

"This woman might be. She's amazing. Can't get her out of my mind. She was just so…authentic. And beautiful! You should see her. Her eyes…and with her hair down…and that lotus tattoo on her shoulder—"

"Oh, I know. Latina women. They are the hottest. No question. Reserved, quiet, then bam! They boil over on you. Sexiest women on the planet."

"I gotta find her."

"Good luck. You've got nothing to go on."

Eliu was right. Maria Something Cortez Maybe Something… short stature, long dark hair, beautiful. He'd just described half the women in Mexico. But there was that lotus tattoo.

James went back to searching the internet. He spent hours scanning Facebook pages of Marias, looking for her face. He found nothing. Eventually, he was forced to admit that he'd blown it. Again. And as a poet and a writer, he experienced that weird, almost out-of-body dichotomy of observing himself like a third party and at the same time plunging inward more deeply, fully exploring the emotion around his disappointment and painting its portrait with words.

~~ *Across A Dim Landscape* ~~

I see you,
briefly,
emerging from the fog of desire.
Your golden eyes

pierce my gaze,
then fade to dullness,
as you turn away,
spinning downstream
in a current I cannot follow.

Not me.
A few wrong notes
in the complex symphony
written by my heart
and the river flows back
between familiar banks
and carries you away.

The geography of music
in this alien blue world,
where the rules of physics
send musical notes whirling
in eccentric orbits,
leaves me disoriented,
unsure of up or down,
or where and how
to intersect that river again.

My flute and my harp
seemed perfect.
It was the bass counterpoints
that exposed me as amateur,
an unfortunate composer
of dissonance,
not desire.

What chance another eddy

will carry you past
where I stand on the banks?
What chance my next melody
will resonate
with your heart?

This blue world is dim,
hard to fathom
what is river
and what is banks.
I turn away and stare
across a dim landscape,
devoid of form,
bereft of direction,
no clue,
where and when, or if,
the next eddy
will carry you back to me.

~~ * ~~

Life returned to normal. Gray and lonely. James tried to date again, signed up for an internet dating service, but the gods intervened, and it was a total failure. Several times he found himself in bed with beautiful women, but somehow, he had no fire, no urge to merge. No joy in his johnson, no bone in his boner. He went to see his doctor. The doctor took blood tests. All normal.

"It could be your heart," he said. "Believe it or not, impotence can be an early warning sign of heart disease. It's all about blood flow."

He did an ultrasound of the carotid arteries in James's neck.

"These are an easy proxy for your coronary arteries. Usually if these are blocked, your heart's in bad shape."

His tests showed that James had the carotids of a

twenty-nine-year-old. "Hmm. That's because of all your years as an athlete. Nevertheless, while unlikely, I'm required to say it might still be your heart. However, I'm thinking it's more likely psychological. The male psyche is very delicate, in many ways more delicate than the female psyche. You need to be completely on board to be sexually aroused. I like to say that the most important sex organ we have as men is our mind."

That would have been news to a lot of women James knew, but the doctor was the one with the degree.

There was some more stuff. Bottom line, James didn't care, because either way, he was out of action. What the hell? He seemed to have come to a place where, every time he engaged physically with a woman, it would be in the back of his mind that failure to launch was a distinct possibility. And each time it happened, it increased the chance that the next time it would happen again. Delicate psyche indeed.

James met Julie, his psychic, for a reading.

"James, I don't get that it's physical. At least not completely. You did have a lot of radiation and scarring down in that general area from the cancer, but I think there's something else going on."

"What's that? Tell me, please, because this…this is no good!"

"I'm getting that your heart is fed up and no longer wants to mess around with casual lovers. Your heart really wants a partner."

"Yeah, that's always been true, but since when was that connected to…you know…my thing?"

"Sorry to spoil your fun, lover boy. Seems you've been rewired so that you can't have sex with just anyone anymore. You really have to be in love. You're being called to find someone. You aren't getting any younger! Time to stop yearning for love. Time to start learning *how* to love, completely, without reservation, meeting in the middle, engaging in the compromise that *is* a relationship. Your poetry, your writing, and your life will benefit."

"So, my heart?"

"I get that energetically your heart is particularly fragile right now. Be careful."

James wasn't sure he saw the heart-boner connection. And the doc's warning about his physical heart? It had been the engine that fueled him in triathlons and on long hikes and runs all the way back to his school days on the playing fields. His core, the center of his physicality, his identity as a large, athletic male. It was all he had. And then there was Hafiz and his weird admonition to "make a better mala." James filed it all away in the dusty pigeonhole of his mind marked "Don't Fuck with This." Maybe if he didn't think about it, it would all just go away.

* ~ * ~ *

That fall, James went back out to San Diego for a reading and a book signing at a bookstore downtown. It went poorly, only five people showed up, and he signed only three books. Feeling unusually tired and stressed, he ordered room service at his hotel and went to sleep early. The bed was hard and uncomfortable, and he made a mental note that next time he would stay somewhere else.

He woke up late in the night with a terrible pain in his back, right between the shoulder blades. "Goddamn hotel mattress!" James swore as he sat up. He must have slept funny. After a few minutes, he lay back down and managed to go back to sleep despite the apparent spasming of his back muscles.

A little while later, he woke up again, and the pain had spread and intensified, and it was relentless. It was strongest right between his shoulder blades, then very strong in his shoulders, and last but not least, in his chest. Something was definitely wrong. James rang the front desk, and the person on duty called a taxi that took him to the emergency room of a hospital that was only three miles away. It was the graveyard shift, dawn was just breaking in the east, and the nurse on duty sized him up as he staggered in the door. She pressed a buzzer, and another nurse appeared.

"Sir, please sit down. What are your symptoms?"

One nurse took notes while the other took his pulse. James described what was going on, gasping as the pain in his back took his breath away. A doctor appeared, looked at the notes, and asked a couple of questions. After a few answers he set down his clipboard.

"I'm pretty sure you're having a heart attack."

James looked at him as if he was nuts. "Can't be....I ran five miles yesterday! I just...slept funny, crappy hotel bed."

"Even so, we're gonna have to check you in and do a series of tests. Do you have any relatives or friends nearby?"

"No."

Tests confirmed the heart attack. They called in the cardiologist and wheeled James into surgery. When he woke up, the cardiologist was sitting next to him on the bed.

"Hi, I'm Doctor Gonzalez. You did have a heart attack, and I put in a stent. While all heart attacks are serious, yours was relatively minor. Since you've been an active athlete for so many years, you built up extra blood vessels that carried the load of the blocked artery. So not too much damage. You'll be back to running marathons in no time, if you wish."

James heard all this in a haze of dissipating anesthesia, and after the doctor left, he drifted in a semiconscious state as random thoughts and emotions meandered by like leaves in a passing current. Heart attack? How? The doc said marathons, but he did triathlons. Didn't that doc know anything? Make a better mala—beads of time and people and places floated by—Hafiz smiling. Shit! Another health crisis to deal with, and he was alone, again. Despair. Eventually, James fell back asleep, listening to the beeping of hospital monitors and distant murmurs of conversation.

His heart burned in his chest as if a coal had become lodged behind his sternum. James became aware of someone holding his hand. Her hand fit perfectly into his, and it was warm and soft. He felt her warmth spreading into his palm and up his arm to his heart, and the throbbing there eased. James struggled to open his eyes, and gradually the room came into focus.

It was Malena, looking at him, smiling, those liquid eyes filled with concern. She was wearing blue scrubs and had a badge hanging around her neck. Or was it just wishful thinking, and some other Latina nurse was holding his hand?

"James," she said with Malena's voice. "Can you hear me?"

James forced his eyes to focus. It was her! How? "Hey. What? Malena! How did you—" Every word was exhausting.

"I work here! I am in my unit, have to come to ER for a patient, and I see your name on the board. James Wilder! I had to check, and it is you! How are you feeling?"

James babbled some answer that got lost in a rambling tangle of words, and she hushed him. She sat with him for a few more minutes, then got up to go back to work. James released her hand reluctantly. She promised to stop by after her shift to see how he was doing. She smiled and left.

As James lay there, his thinking gradually cleared. A heart attack? What the fuck? James remembered something Julie had said.

"Your heart's an amazing organ. It pumps blood unbidden, sixty to eighty times per minute when you are healthy and resting, some multiple of that when you're exercising. Like your lungs, your heart keeps you alive, even when you feel uninspired and don't care. But your heart is also wired energetically to make you connect to others. Romantic attraction, yes, but also empathy. Love for your family or even an animal. Connection to a greater entity than just yourself. Your heart needs these connections in order to be healthy, just like it needs oxygen and blood flow. The cruelest punishment we can give another is not physical; it is to isolate that person from love, from connection to community, like solitary confinement. It kills their heart's source of nourishment. We become ill, crazy, and eventually die."

Julie's words had the ring of truth. Maybe his solitary, scorpion-like existence was killing him, would kill him eventually. He still had his kids, and he still had Rocco. But Rocco was old and wouldn't last much longer. His gray snout still poked James's hands to be petted. He still looked at James with those worried doggie eyes. He still walked with James on the Bobolink, even though they didn't run anymore, and they didn't go far. And the kids were both in college, and there was a natural distance between them and him as they went through the separation they needed in order to create their own lives.

Make a better mala.

The words from Hafiz reverberated in his mind as James lay there cracked open by the anesthesia. Fragile and raw, his pathetic self naked to the world, dragged out from beneath the disintegrating persona of James Wilder, love poet. A fraud. A sham. Body breaking down. A drive-by victim of his own intensity and inability to connect. Burning too hot, burning out too soon.

Intensity comes from the head. Get out of your head and into your heart. Find peace.

Sara's words echoed again in his consciousness, a lesson still to be learned at a cellular level. Intensity can be a good thing, can breed poetry when channeled through the heart. But when unfiltered, it breeds stress, impatience, overthinking, anger, frustration, separation, conflict, physical breakdown. James needed to find a way to get into stillness and stay there.

Chapter Thirty-Five

~ * ~

Red Coral

Later that afternoon James conference-called his kids.

"Geez, Dad!" said Chris. "Never thought you'd be one of those guys."

"Neither did I, Chris. Neither did I."

"But you're OK. Right, Daddy?" Annie's voice had risen to an octave above normal, and she seemed to have reverted back to a little girl in her anxiety over his health. James felt a surge of warmth as he listened to his kids' voices.

"Don't worry, sweetie. The doc says I'm OK. I can get back to running and everything within a few weeks. How's school?"

"Oh, you know, just trying to get through midterms." It was so good to hear their voices. James told them he'd be extending his stay in San Diego for at least a few days. He snoozed for the rest of the afternoon, and a little after 8:00 p.m., Malena came by his room. This time she had her coat and daypack with her. She sat by his bed in a chair for visitors.

"Hello, James. How you are feeling now?" She touched his cheek with her palm, as if she was checking his temperature.

"Much better, thanks," he said. He smiled at her, tried to look light and strong. She had one braid framing her forehead, and the rest of her hair was in a ponytail down her back. That hairstyle made her look very young, like a schoolgirl. Only the tiny wrinkles at the corners of her eyes that crinkled when she smiled betrayed her real age.

"What did the doctor say? Will they keep you for some time?"

"I have to lie still for two days so that the wound in my hip where they inserted the catheter can heal. They don't want it opening up."

"Do you have anyone checking on you?"

"Nope."

She smiled a different smile, this time of pleasure. "Well, I come by when I can. Make it sure you're OK."

"Thanks." His words seemed inadequate for what he wanted to say, but he had no opening for anything else.

"I tell the girls here you are a special patient." She smiled again and left.

That night James slept well, and the next day he lay in bed watching the news on TV. Seemed the world was going crazy, becoming unrecognizable. There was a new openness toward boorishness and hatred in the country. Politics had gone off the rails and landed in a deep mire of populism and racist rhetoric. Some asshole was screaming into the TV about immigrants and how they were flooding the country, bringing crime and drugs. Yeah, horrible people like Malena. James didn't want to hear it, so he turned it off after a few minutes and lay in his bed, staring at the ceiling, trying to empty his mind. The hours ticked slowly by, broken only by the cardiologist coming in for an update and various nursing checks. Malena visited briefly at lunchtime. She only got thirty minutes off in an eight-hour shift, and James felt honored that she chose to spend it with him. At the end of the day, she visited again.

"I'm being discharged tomorrow," he told her. "They're kicking me out, but they don't want me to fly for a few more days. Guess I'm going back to the hotel."

"That's nice. You like your hotel?"

"No, the bed's awful. I won't stay there next time I come. But I gotta go somewhere. Maybe back to the Del Coronado."

"That's so expensive! Too bad you know nobody here in San Diego."

"Yeah."

Malena sat silent for a moment, as if considering something. Then she spoke. "Maybe you come to stay in my place? I have two bedrooms. My daughter is at college. You could have her room. I can…take care of you there."

James was momentarily stunned by the unexpected nature of her suggestion. Why would she invite him, a relative stranger, into her home? He'd heard that generous hospitality was an important part of Mexican culture, but did Malena feel like she owed him anything?

"No, I couldn't do that! I'm sure your daughter doesn't want some random guy staying in her bedroom."

"She's read your poetry. She would no mind! She will like to have a famous person sleep in her bed. That's pretty cool." She laughed, her eyes teasing him.

"I'm not famous! Just a once-published poet. We're never famous."

"You are famous to me."

She said it like she meant it, and they talked a bit more, long enough for James to realize that her offer was serious. The next day he found himself pulling up to her place in her car. He was surprisingly weak from lying in bed for the better part of three days.

Malena's home was in a trailer park called San Lazaro Estates and located at the edge of the town of Imperial Beach. Her trailer was quite old but neat and clean. His room was tiny, with a single bed, faux wood paneling, and a cheap, plastic-framed sliding window for fresh air. The rest of the trailer was her small bedroom, a small living room with fresh flowers in a vase on the table, a tiny galley kitchen, and a closet-sized bathroom with shower and toilet. James noticed that in her bedroom, a crucifix hung, and next to it were two small icons, one of Saint Francis of Assisi and one of *La Virgin de Guadalupe*. Altogether, the trailer looked like it would blow away in anything over a middling breeze, but it had obviously been in its location for many years, so perhaps it was sturdier than it looked.

"I hope you don't mind. It's no fancy, but this is home. And the people who live here in San Lazaro, they're my family."

"No, it's wonderful!" replied James. "Thanks for rescuing me from that hotel."

It was a Sunday, and Malena had the day off, so once James got settled, they sat outside in lawn chairs on a tiny patio that Malena had created under a canvas awning. There were a few scrubby trees and some struggling palms in the common grounds between trailers, but otherwise the ground was pretty bare from drought and lots of foot traffic.

"How long have you lived here?" he asked.

"Not so long," she said. "Before divorce, I live with my husband in a nice place. We have a yard, two cars, and everything."

"Yeah? Was he American?"

"He was *pocho*, Mexican like me but born in America, so American citizen, yes."

"How'd you meet?"

"I was just a silly front-desk girl at a hotel in Puerto Vallarta. Very young. He was general manager. Very handsome! Good talker. I knew nothing of love." She paused for a moment, then added, "Perhaps I still don't know." She looked down at her hands, twisting her fingers in her lap.

"So, what happened?" James asked.

She shrugged. "He start drinking, going out, you know, party too much with friends. I know he party with women. Then he go for a week. Miss too much work. They fire him, and we loss the house, and no money. Some nights I just…cry."

"That's a shame."

"I try to get him to get help. He would no go. He disappear for a month; we divorce. Three years now."

Three years. A long time to be alone.

"Wow. Sorry to hear that. It must be tough."

"It was. It's better now, thanks to *mi familia* here."

They sat silently for a moment. James wondered what it must have been like, broke and alone with a daughter to care for in a country that was home but not *home*.

"And now? You seeing anyone these days?" As soon as he asked the question, James regretted it. A shadow dimmed her face like a cloud sailing in front of the sun. Clearly, he'd crossed a line into a difficult subject.

"Hey, I'm sorry," he hurried to say. "None of my business."

She looked down at her feet, wrestling with emotion. Finally, she turned her face toward him, and he could see despair in her eyes. "You believe in love. Your poems, they are about the same woman, or are there many?"

Now it was his turn to squirm. "Well, I've failed many times at love."

"Ah, so there are many, like that blondie at the conference."

"I didn't write any poetry about her."

"But you like her!"

"No, she was engaged. She's surely married now."

"What? But you and her—!"

His face, like his feelings, twisted into a hapless grin of embarrassment. She sat back, and her expression said it all.

"Ah, you are Johnny Casanova! Big lover of women."

James tried to shrug it off, but inside he felt a swirl of emotions. Embarrassment, shame, defiance against imagined judgment.

"I prefer to think of myself as an optimist" was the best he could come up with.

Their conversation moved on to other topics, away from the sudden minefield that was their love lives. The late afternoon San Diego sun was strong, but under the awning they were cooled by ocean breezes.

"I'm thirsty. Would you like to drink something?" she asked.

"Yes, please," he replied.

Malena disappeared back into the trailer, and his thoughts drifted back to their conversation. Clearly, relationships were a sensitive subject for her, and James was pretty sure he hadn't scored any points for being Johnny Casanova.

Malena reappeared with some guacamole, chips and salsa, and fresh-squeezed limeade to wash it down. It was the best guacamole he'd ever tasted.

"Wow! This is really good! Never had guac like this in a restaurant. What's your secret?"

"Serrano peppers and *mucho cilantro*," she replied, grinning.

As cocktail hour approached, her neighbors began to appear, returning from church or their jobs or family outings. They stopped by to say hello, greet James, and soon a table had been set up and food materialized as if by magic. There was Xiomara, an older Mexican woman who was probably in her late fifties but was bowed by decades of cleaning toilets and restaurants and bus stations. *"Encantada,"* said Xiomara, looking from him to Malena and smiling, her eyes crinkling with humor and kindness. Her little dog, Bella, and her granddaughter, Rosie, were with her. Rosie was an adorable four-year-old with big eyes whose mom was away working as a maid in the suburbs. She clutched an Elsa doll from *Frozen* and wore a neat pink T-shirt with Hello Kitty designs. Bella came up to him and sniffed his unfamiliar hand, then flung herself in a frenzy of excited tail-wagging at Malena, who picked her up and was rewarded with a face full of licks. Xiomara brought some wonderful *frijoles* spiced with *chorizo* and *jalapeño*.

There were Carmen and Guillermo, a handsome young *pocho* couple from next door who had a dog-grooming business and hope for a better future. Their trailer was the same size as Malena's, but they somehow found space for their two kids and Carmen's grandmother, Abuelita, a tiny, wizened woman with fearful eyes and no English. They brought *tacos al pastor*, with homemade corn tortillas, fried pork, and pineapple.

There were other neighbors who dropped by to say hello, shake hands with *el escritor*, and bring food and drink, and they all shared what they had, with no sense of lack or need for anything more. Everyone chatted in Spanish, sharing news and laughter and gossip. Since his Spanish skills amounted to a thin residue of the Spanish he'd picked up from the Latino construction workers at Wilder and Klein, James was pretty hopeless. He did catch a few words though. *Gringo* and *salsa* and *trabajo* and *policia*.

While James was taking it all in, a small, middle-aged, sun-leathered man in work-stained clothes appeared out of the shadows to speak to Malena. She gasped with surprise or maybe relief and hugged him, then pulled him off to the side, where they conversed in low tones that James couldn't hear. After much gesticulating and nodding, he hugged her again, held her hands in his as he said something with the sincerity of heartfelt gratitude, and retreated back into the shadows.

Malena came back to sit next to James, obviously stirred up emotionally—shifting in her seat and breathing in short gasps.

"Hey, everything OK?" he asked.

"It is now," she replied, collecting herself and exhaling deeply.

"Who was that?"

"He is Ramon. My friend."

"Does he live here?"

"He is part of *mi familia*. Has been here for many years. Cuts grass for rich gringos in Coronado. He had some trouble, but now he's OK." Malena settled in, and soon everything seemed back to normal. A little later, two of Malena's cousins who didn't live at San Lazaro also came by. Pamela and Berenice were about Malena's age and shared her short stature and long, dark hair. They could have been three sisters, the family resemblance was so strong.

"*Hola, chicas!*" Malena said as she gave each of them a kiss and a hug.

"*Hola, Malenita!*" They kissed and hugged back.

With them was a tall, dark-haired Latino man. He wore a white cowboy hat, a pressed, collared white shirt buttoned up to the neck, a bolo tie, and shiny black cowboy boots with silver toe caps. He stared at Malena and the cousins, then at James as if assessing where he fit into the puzzle. His eyes met James's, and he smiled, but only with his mouth, and then he turned away and walked over to a large cooler that had beer in it. The other men standing around it saw him coming and edged away. James watched him go, then looked at Malena. She was staring at the man, and her body language had changed. Her smile had lost its light. James touched her on the shoulder, and she jumped.

"Sorry. You OK?" he asked.

Malena shook her shoulders as if unconsciously ridding herself of an invisible weight and shrugged. "Sure. Why should I no be?"

James nodded over in the direction of the guy by the cooler who stood alone, looking over the crowd. "Who's that?" James asked.

"Juan, Pamela's husband."

"He doesn't seem too popular here."

"He works for *La Migra*." Malena said it with emphasis, like that explained everything.

"What's *La Migra*?"

"Immigration. ICE."

"He looks like someone important," James said.

Malena took a deep breath, as if preparing to say something difficult or important. "Well, Juan helps sometimes, when...*La Migra* takes someone away. He can do things, get them back—"

Just then Pamela and Berenice returned.

"What are you two talking about?" asked Pamela.

Malena held her tongue, leaving an awkward silence.

"Oh, Malena was just telling me about *La Migra*," James offered. Berenice started and shot a glance at Malena. Malena subtly shook her head.

Later, while Malena and Berenice helped Xiomara cook on the barbecue grill, James found himself alone with Pamela. Pamela's English was very smooth, as if she'd grown up in the United States. Turned out her mother had crossed the border when she was pregnant and had given birth to her child in San Diego, which made Pamela an American citizen. Pamela's family had stayed in Tijuana and she'd crossed the border every day to attend an American school along with thousands of her Mexican-American classmates. It was part of the everyday flow of the border, the give and take, the natural rhythm that flowed around an unnatural obstacle to ordinary life. James steered the conversation to her moody husband.

"So, tell me about Juan. Does he like his job?" he asked.

"Very much. It's an important job."

Juan stood by the beer cooler, looking like a prairie hawk perched on a fencepost, scanning the field for mice. His face was frozen in a mirthless smile. There was no one standing near him.

"He doesn't like to come here," Pamela continued. "He doesn't want to feel pressured to ruin anyone's day. He tells me things are changing, getting tougher. New bosses, new rules. It's getting harder for him to look the other way."

"No kidding? So, some of these people are here illegally?"

"Yes, many, even my cousin Bere," Pamela whispered to me. She pronounced it *Ber-ay*.

"Bere?"

"Berenice. We just call her Bere. Her visa finished. She could be deported. Poor Juan. He loves his job, but it's…complicated. Fights criminals, the drugs, and the gangs. But sometimes he deports regular people like Bere, too."

"But she's still here—"

"Yeah, Juan can do favors sometimes. Just today, he was able to get a man released. Someone from here that Malena knows. She asked Juan, and he found the guy, got him out. It's good to have someone important in the family."

James looked over at Malena, to where she was laughing and joking with Xiomara by the grill.

"Huh," he said as he took it all in.

Later, Malena and James sat under her awning, eating tacos and nachos and other goodies. Everything was so fresh and flavorful and spicy. Around them, kids ran and squealed and played games, and he was reminded of simpler times.

"Are all your neighbors from Mexico or Central America?" he asked Malena.

"Filipinos, too," she replied. "Maricar over there, she's Filipino. Many Filipinos in San Diego. They come with the navy. And Hector, he's from Dominican."

"And everyone gets along?"

"We're all the same, brothers and sisters, inside the skin." She pronounced skin as "skeen."

"Has everyone lived here a long time?"

"I am newest here. Only two years. I hope I can stay." Malena started to brighten. "Xiomara, she help when I first come. I was broken, no money. She even buys me food some days! And Hector, when I have no car, he gives me rides to work every day and pick me up at night. But now they say this place might get sold, to build condos. We see people in fancy cars coming to take pictures."

James could imagine that. The location, while not breathtaking, was flat and level and bordered on two sides by new residential developments that were displacing light industry. To the north, a used car lot was up for sale, too. The neighborhood was turning over, gentrifying, and driving out old businesses and low-income residents.

Just then Hector, who looked more African than Hispanic, started playing a drum and singing softly, a mellow, perhaps slightly sad ballad in Spanish. The song seemed well-known because several others joined in. Guillermo disappeared into his trailer next door and came back with a worn guitar. He strummed along with the singing, and as the crowd grew, the music became livelier and the rhythms faster, and the beer started flowing. Someone else brought a bottle of cheap tequila and cut limes, and the party took off. Soon the kids gathered back near the musicians, and they danced the way only little kids can dance, enthusiastically and to their own rhythm, more bouncing than choreography, stopping to look around and then starting again.

Malena and her two cousins got caught up in the infectious music and danced together, gyrating their hips to the *reggaeton* beat with the effortless sensuality of Latina blood steeped in salsa to just below the boiling point. They smiled and laughed and chattered in Spanish as they played off each other's moves, sometimes with their arms around each other. It was like watching Antonio Canova's sculpture of The Three Graces come to life and moving in ways that the sculptor could never have imagined.

Malena caught James gazing at her and came over to sit with him. "What you staring at, Johnny Casanova?"

"Just thinking, you have a face made for smiling."

Malena laughed, a lightness that had been missing since earlier in the evening. "I hear this always. My nickname when I was a little girl was Sabritas. Sabritas potato chips has a picture of a girl on the package with a big smile. That's me, Sabritas."

Malena. The girl whose smile could sell a billion potato chips.

They sat together and watched the other dancers in silence. Then she turned to him, her eyes filled with clouds and her lips pursed as though she were holding back something important. She briefly rested her hand on his shoulder, then got up to go chat with some of the other residents. Had she wanted to say something?

After Malena left him alone, James tried to center himself. He felt off-balance, even slightly dizzy, like a stranger in a strange land where the people, the music, the food and even the night sky were unfamiliar. Then again, he'd been feeling weird since the heart attack, and maybe he was just recalibrating to his new reality as a cardiac patient.

A bit later James noticed that Malena was missing, and he hadn't seen her for at least fifteen minutes. He was filled with a strange sense of disquiet and wandered slowly around the nearest trailers, looking for her. He was just coming back toward the patio near Malena's trailer when he saw the door open, and she stepped out, followed by Juan. James retreated into a shadow. Juan had her by her hand, and she was trying to shake him off. Juan pulled her back up against him, face to face. He said something in Spanish, loud enough for James to hear. Malena pushed him away without answering, and Juan released her. She strode away, and Juan stood there, staring after her.

James stepped out of the shadows. "What's up?" he asked, a question that was more than that.

Juan said nothing, just nodded and smiled slowly, his eyes locked on James. He walked away like a rooster on his home turf. James found Malena standing with a group of friends, and when he caught up with her, she wouldn't make eye contact.

"I'm very tire, and I work early tomorrow," she said in a low voice as she moved away, avoiding his touch. Back in the trailer, they said goodnight and retreated to their own bedrooms.

It had been an eventful day. James lay on his bed staring at the ceiling, and he could hear Malena in the tiny bathroom, taking a long shower. Waves of exhaustion swept through his body. Malena's neighbors had welcomed him without reservation, and yet he felt as out of place as Gulliver among the Lilliputians. These were the invisibles, the people he'd walked by on his way to important meetings and client dinners and business trips. Who worked off-hour shifts prepping food in restaurants, delivering newspapers, and sweeping the streets. Who cleaned offices and hotel rooms and bus stops, and did the dirty work in hospitals and clinics and assisted living centers. The working poor who often had to scrounge a living from multiple part-time jobs that offered no benefits, no health insurance, no pathway to advancement. Clearly, some were selling their labor for cash paid off the books. Like Ramon. And yet, somehow, here in San Lazaro, they'd created a vibrant, caring community, an oasis thriving in a weed patch of a financial desert. James had lived on the same cul-de-sac in a prosperous town for fifteen years and shared no such close interactions with any of his neighbors. If the roles were reversed, would he and his neighbors have welcomed one of these people with such open arms? It was purely a rhetorical question: he already knew the answer.

And Malena? She was obviously one of them. A hard-working, compassionate, gentle soul trading her labor for a precarious financial existence. And now the gods had brought her into his life, an exotic stranger bearing—what? Gifts? Lessons? Love? James slept fitfully that night, tossing and turning through vague, unsettling dreams that left only troubled feelings when he woke.

Malena was up before dawn, and he met her in the kitchen as she was brewing coffee. She was in her scrubs, and her hair was pulled back in a neat bun. She was a rosebud again, tightly wrapped against the harsh glare of the workaday world.

"Go back to sleep! It's early!" she said. She smiled, and his disquiet was pushed to the side.

"I will. Just wanted to wish you a good day at work and say thanks. For everything."

"You should rest. Read a book, or write one! Sorry, I have not cable TV. Too expensive."

James hugged her as she was leaving, and she hugged him back.

She looked up at him with those liquid eyes, and for a moment James thought she was going to ask for something, something intangible, like understanding, or patience, or forgiveness. The moment passed, and she flashed a brief, sad smile as if she knew he had glimpsed her world and already judged it. She left.

James sat at the little table and sipped his coffee. Maybe it was just the hangover from his troubled dreams of the night before, but his mind was uneasy and his spirit unsettled. San Lazaro might be the Garden of Eden to Malena, with her chosen family and safe little home, but he couldn't escape the feeling that something was slithering in the grass.

Later that day, when Malena came home from work, they drove down to Imperial Beach and walked along the sand. It was a spectacular September evening, a cool breeze blew from the ocean, and the sun was a few minutes from setting out over the far horizon. Malena wore blue jeans and a fleece over her blouse. Her long, gorgeous hair flowed down her back like a waterfall of cinnamon-flavored chocolate. She shivered in the cool air, and James put his arm around her. She tensed reflexively, then relaxed.

At times they waded into the water up to their ankles. Occasionally a wave would chase them up the beach, and Malena would squeal with laughter as they hustled away from the foaming water. Once, James had to lift her up above some froth that caught them unawares. Luckily, she was light as a feather; otherwise he could have popped his stitches. James felt a welcome tingle of energy flowing through his limbs every time their bodies connected, and she seemed to be getting used to him.

"I love the ocean," she said. "But this is cold! I miss the warm waters of home, Playa Estrellita."

"Where's that?"

"*Riviera Maya. El Caribe.* Very touristic in most places, but no in my town. My town is still small, hiding, friendly."

"Ah, the Caribbean. Best place in the world," James replied. "I hope to move down there someday. Live in a grass shack on the beach."

"By yourself? Sounds lonely."

"No, I would take my woman."

"Your woman? But you are Johnny Casanova! How you would be happy with just one woman?" For once, she smiled as she said it.

"If I find the right woman, it could happen," James said as they walked, his eyes on the sunset but his thoughts on her.

That evening, as they sat in lawn chairs out under the stars, she brought up the subject of love again. "You know why I first love your poetry? Because it bring me hope."

"I'm so glad to hear it."

"But now I know you better, I don't have so much hope."

"Why not?" Her comment nudged him out of the comfortable glow in which he'd been basking.

"Because if a famous love poet cannot find happiness in love, what can I find? I'm nobody! I've found nothing!"

"Malena, please don't think that my poetry makes me an expert on love. Far from it! I just write how I feel. Sometimes I'm sad; sometimes I'm happy. Mostly, I'm just grateful I can feel anything at all."

"If you could no write, what would you do to show a woman you love her?"

"Depends on the woman, I guess. I don't know. Sing her a song? Slay her a dragon?"

She laughed a bitter laugh. "Can you slay dragons, Johnny, or are you only good at words?"

"Dragons aren't real," he replied.

"In my world they are."

"What do you mean?"

She just shook her head and went silent.

Later that night, as he was heading to bed, she hugged him for a very long time, her face buried in his shoulder. Finally, she pulled back and gazed into his eyes, reading his question in their depths, then placed her hand over his mouth to preserve his silence. She turned and went into her bedroom, closing the door behind her.

James retired to his own bed and lay there, savoring the taste of her fingers on his lips. What had he gotten himself into? Malena was so beautiful and gentle and kind and yet, somehow, so...wounded. He didn't know very much about her, really. Did he want to dig deeper into whatever was going on in her life? And if he did, he'd have to think carefully about the consequences. Malena deserved much more than just his usual passion, neediness, and blind infatuation. Could he commit to following this path, wherever it led, whether to pleasure or pain, reward or punishment?

He'd proclaimed to the universe and all the gods that he was searching for a Great Love, a partner, his missing puzzle piece, and the tempest they'd whipped up in response had cast Malena onto his shore. She was like a beautiful shell he'd found at the waterline, half-buried in sand, and as James looked more closely, it was clear that he'd never seen anything like her before. Complex spirals, swirls of color, encrusted with jewels partly hidden by seaweed, a treasure not of this earth. What happens if you actually get what you want?

Chapter Thirty-Six

~ * ~

Purple Silk

While Malena was at work, James stayed busy. He went to the grocery store to pick up food for dinner, did a little reading, and engaged in some cautious yoga. Later in the afternoon James was hanging out on the patio when Ramon walked by. James nodded to him, and Ramon stopped to chat. He was dirty and dusty from a long day of yardwork, but his eyes crinkled with a smile anyway.

"Good afternoon, sor," he said in heavily accented English.

"Hi, Ramon. How was work today?"

"Very hot. Are you feeling better?" he asked.

"Oh yes, thanks. Malena is taking very good care of me."

Ramon took off his raggedy hat and frowned, shuffling his feet as if something he needed to say could only be expressed while moving.

"Malena, she is our…*angel*. She—" He twisted his hat in his hands as if he could wring the needed words out of the sweat and dust that stained it. The hat didn't relinquish any sounds.

"We love her," he finally said, and turned away toward his own trailer, leaving James with the distinct impression that those three words carried a much more detailed story encoded in their syllables.

When Malena came home, she seemed tired, but they headed to the beach again for a sunset walk. It was warmer that evening, but still cool enough for Malena to need a light sweater.

"I saw Ramon today," James said as a conversation starter.

Malena remained silent, but her expression briefly changed to guarded.

"He really seems to care for you," he continued. His words seemed to energize her.

"He's a good man. It's not fair!" she exclaimed.

"What's not fair?"

"That he fearing about *la Migra*. They…bother him. Juan—"

The sun chose that moment to slip beneath the horizon, and with no clouds in the sky to catch the red evening fire, the sunset was dull and uninspiring.

"What about Juan?" James asked.

"Juan—" She took a deep, almost shuddering breath. "Juan has promised—"

"Promised what?"

Malena shook her head. "Things. He has…power. I can't talk about it."

"Malena, let me help."

"Help? What you can do?" she said, her voice rising to almost desperation. "This is not just pretty words. This is not your world.… Keep away, please." There was bitterness at the end.

"Do you want me to leave? Go back to Colorado?"

"No! You…need to heal. Please stay. It's OK! It's OK!"

She grabbed his arm and clung to him, and her hand slipped into his. They walked along the water's edge in silence, high enough above the water line to avoid the wash of the waves. As the minutes ticked by and the sky grew darker, the residue of tension around their conversation dissipated. They returned home to her trailer and hung out on the patio chatting with random neighbors.

That night, when they headed to bed, she hugged James more closely than she had to date and kissed him, chastely, on the lips as if to seal their agreement to respect each other's boundaries. James went to sleep that night knowing that she wanted him near, but still well clear of some vaguely defined area of her life that remained in shadows.

The next morning, he was up early again to see Malena off to work. She had just finished making her lunch and was wrapping it up when her cell phone rang. She listened to the message for a moment, then hung up, and a shadow of exasperation crossed her face.

"What was that?" James asked.

"Work. They tell me I don't come in to work today. They don't need me." Her face flashed a hint of desperation before it settled into that controlled, neutral look he'd seen when he first met her at the conference. It was the impassive face, the mask she turned toward the world, her protection. She put her lunch back into the fridge.

"So, you get the day off? That's good, right?" he asked carefully.

"Well, not so good," she said. "Now I don't get eight hours money this week. That money pays my bills. Now, no money."

"What? They just tell you not to come in, and *not pay you?* That's crazy!"

Malena shrugged. "It happens once a month, sometimes twice. They call, tell me not to come in if not much work in the unit. Very... frustrate."

James did the math in his head. An eight-hour shift, fourteen dollars per hour...that was $112 off the top, gone from her paycheck—money to pay for gas, a week's groceries, a health insurance premium. What was Malena supposed to do with her suddenly available time? Scramble around and somehow find another job for the day? Really? How heartless! Clearly, her employers didn't give a damn about how they'd just screwed a financially vulnerable worker who'd committed her precious working hours to them. She was nothing more than a commodity, easily replaceable, to be cut when it suited the bottom line.

"It's OK," Malena said as she untied her bun and shook out her hair. "I will call Xiomara and let her know I help today."

James marveled at her resilience. He thought about the workers who did the jobs at Wilder and Klein. They were mostly subcontractors, not employees, and James wondered if they struggled with the same financial uncertainty that Malena lived with. Was he a part of this same system? He resolved to look into the issue when he got back to Boulder.

"Hey, how about if I pay you some rent for the time I'm here?" he asked softly. "I mean, I'd be paying for a hotel anyway if I wasn't here—"

"No!" Malena looked at him like she couldn't believe what he was saying. "You are my guest! This is no hotel!" She looked insulted and hurt.

"Hey, I'm sorry! I just feel so bad that they do this! I want to help."

"You can't help. Thank you, but this is not your world. This is the way it is." Her mask of neutrality was slipping, and her expression looked strained, as if the skin on her face struggled to hold back years of hardships that he'd never known, would never experience, and would never fully understand. James fell silent. Already he was paying for groceries and gas, but he resolved to find more ways to help ease the loss of her $112.

A bit later, while she was cooking up some eggs, a knock came at the door of the trailer. Malena smiled for the first time that morning. It was Xiomara, and she'd brought Rosie and her little dog, Bella, with her.

"Ah Rosita! said Malena. She said a few words in Spanish to the little girl who smiled and gave her a hug.

"Hi, Rosie," James said in his most friendly voice. Rosie just looked at him with her big brown eyes, her unblinking stare seeing all the way into his soul. Bella darted excitedly around the trailer, barking, while Xiomara and Malena conversed in Spanish. Finally, Xiomara hugged Malena and smiled at James.

"Thank you!" she said to him as she left. He watched her get into Ramon's truck, along with two other residents, and they drove away.

James looked at Malena. "So, we're babysitting?"

"Yes, of course! Xiomara and her daughter are working. We're family, even you today!"

"I feel honored."

"You should! Family is most important."

They spent the day doing errands, followed by a sun-drenched picnic lunch at the beach. Contrary to how the day had started, Malena seemed relaxed and at peace. Her magical smile was back, and James couldn't help but fall in love with the light that just spilled out of her. As they walked around town, Rosie held onto his fingers, and he was transported back in time to when his own little girl had walked hand in hand with him. It was awkward and wonderful, like a forgotten favorite song from his youth.

After lunch, they returned to San Lazaro. Rosie had fallen asleep, and James carried her in his arms with her head on his shoulder. She was as light and as precious as a bouquet of flowers, and he laid her down for a nap on Malena's bed. Malena sat with Rosie for a moment, caressing her hair as James stood in the doorway, quietly watching. He felt emotions that he hadn't felt in years. As Malena tiptoed out of the room, she made a quick bow and crossed herself in front of the crucifix and the icons, and then closed the door. They retreated out to the lawn chairs under the awning.

"Who's the saint in the icon?" James asked, even though he knew.

"Saint Francis of Assisi. My favorite saint."

"He's the saint of the animals, right?"

"That too, but first he was son of a rich man who give up all of his moneys to live among the poor people and serve them. I pray to him to help us here in San Lazaro." They sat outside on the patio, the door to the trailer open so Malena could hear if Rosie woke up.

At the end of the day, Xiomara stopped back by the trailer with Rosie's mom, Luisa, who'd returned from her job as a maid in the suburbs. Luisa was a plain, strong-looking woman with streaks of early gray at her temples. The circles under her eyes gave her face a look of persistent exhaustion, but her smile was genuine, especially when Rosie ran to her with Bella barking at her heels. James and Malena said goodbye, and Rosie turned back to give James a hug.

During the next few days, they fell into a rhythm where James worked remotely on Wilder and Klein business while Malena did her shifts at the hospital. Evenings consisted of walks on the beach, followed by dinner on the patio. His first night at San Lazaro, their chairs had been two feet apart, but every evening they'd moved a bit closer together. Eventually, they sat so close that their elbows or bare feet or fingers would sometimes touch. And, at night, when they were going to their separate rooms, she would kiss him goodnight, carefully, chastely, on the lips.

Finally, James had to go home, back to Colorado. Eliu had been patient, but James was needed in the office, so reluctantly he booked a flight. His penultimate night in San Diego, he and Malena sat outdoors, eating a dinner of tacos and salad at a long picnic table with many of her neighbors. The sun had just gone down, and the day's warmth lingered in the air. To the west, the sky above the horizon was fading from pale pink to deepening blue, and the earliest stars were coming out. They sat facing Pamela and Bere, and as they discussed family and work and life, Malena's bare foot brushed up against his and stayed there, the soft skin of her toes resting on the top of his bare foot. James responded by bringing his left hand down under the table. He found the back of her calf and let his fingers explore, slowly writing a poem of sensation on the flesh behind her knee. Both of them remained engaged in the discussion above the table, but the real conversation was going on below. At bedtime their goodnight kiss became particularly passionate, her breath coming in shuddering gasps, but like all the nights before, she broke it off.

"I canno do this," she exhaled.

"Why not?" His lips were exploring her neck while she tried to push him away.

"Please, please no. *No puedo. No*—" She extracted herself and retreated to her bedroom, closing the door. James went to his own bed and tossed there, awash with desire and questions.

His last night in San Lazaro Estates, they planned a little dinner, just the two of them. They were cooking an Asian dish, stir-fried veggies and shrimp on brown rice, and the trailer was filled with the sizzling aroma of garlic and ginger and toasted sesame oil. It was hot in her tiny kitchen, and they drank chilled white wine from mason jars. James was in a T-shirt and shorts, barefoot, and so was she, and they sweated with the effort to keep from touching each other. Even so, the electricity between them was sending white sparks of sexual energy every time they brushed elbows or bumped hips. Somehow, she kept getting in the way, until finally James dropped the cooking spatula, lifted her off her feet, and kissed her deeply. She responded by wrapping her legs around him and holding his face tenderly between her hands.

"James," she whispered in his ear as he carried her into her bedroom. "Don't ask questions. But this canno happen more than once."

"If I can't ask questions, then what can I do?" he whispered back.

"Write poetry," she sighed. And he did.

~~ *Holy Desire* ~~

My hands burn with holy desire.
Silk geometry,
sweet hillock to hip,
sparking fire.
My lips breathe softly
down your side.
A feather's touch,
a lucky wanderer,
a smooth glide
through tender valley,
to that most feminine curve
of all.

You sigh and turn,
a catalyst for change,
a seismic shift,
a trespass in that place of warmth.
An altered landscape,
uplifted hillocks,
deepened valleys,
explored from every angle,
the fecund mystery
of Woman.

~~ * ~~

The Seventh Mala

Make a Better Mala!

~~ The Opposite of Time ~~

"How long can love last?"
she whispered,
her breath
sweet honey on my neck.

"Love's a risky business.
How many years together
justify this giant roll of dice?"

I closed my eyes and drank deeply
of that precious moment.
How long indeed?

Great sages and scientists
all agree
that time is illusion.
Yesterday only memories,
tomorrow only dreams.

Great lovers and poets know
that time stops,
suspended,
in the presence of beauty.

So if time ceases to exist,
even in those moments
that we value most,
how can we measure time?

If we love so long
that one of us has to endure
the loss of the other,
that would be a blessing!
Proof
that love endures
and carries us
to that loving place
that all life leads to,
but not alone, not unloved.

How long can love last?
What span of illusory time
justifies this giant roll of dice?
To even ask the question
is to deny Love.

Love exists only in the Now.
Pure.
Unfettered.
Unmeasured.
Infinite.
By definition,
the opposite of time.

~~ * ~~

Chapter Thirty-Seven

~ * ~

Passion

Eliu had said it best. "Latina women. They are the hottest. No question. Reserved, quiet, then bam! They boil over on you. Sexiest women on the planet." That described Malena perfectly. A tightly wrapped bud that blossomed into a sensual, sexual, passionate flower. And something else. Her soft warmth against James's skin bathed his body and his heart with waves of heat and energy at just the right frequency, resonating like a perfectly tuned Tibetan singing bowl. Julie had said he needed to be in love to make love. Well, he must have been in love, because they made love, sensually, blissfully, completely. There was heat and passion, but more than that, there was connection and ease and grace.

When it was time to leave for the airport, James had to tear himself away from her. Not just because she was clinging to him but because he was clinging to her. Everything about her was like a second skin. A Siamese twin rejoined to him at the place they'd been cruelly cut apart at birth. They couldn't have been more different. James, large, male, pampered, and privileged. Malena, small, female, a survivor of tougher circumstance. They didn't share the same native language or culture. But all of that was irrelevant.

"I will miss you every day and every night," she whispered in his ear.

Life back in Boulder took on an additional element. Anticipation. She worked every second weekend at the hospital, so James flew out on the others to be with her. She had surrendered to their mutual desire, and as long as he asked no questions, it seemed that her admonition that "this cannot happen more than once" was forgotten. He was willing to go along with the situation, enjoying his new connection with a woman who seemed so good, so kind, so loving, that he felt he had found her, his missing puzzle piece.

Somehow, it seemed so easy. James would show up, they'd get reacquainted in her bedroom for a few hours, then emerge to immerse themselves in San Lazaro's *comunidad*. There would always be an impromptu evening gathering in the common space between the trailers. Malena would fire up her charcoal grill on her little patio, he would throw on chicken and steak and peppers and onions, and they'd start the party. Soon, her neighbors would come over and bring their lawn chairs and food offerings. Homemade tortillas, guacamole, salsa, beer, desserts. And after eating, everyone would get up and spontaneously dance to *bachata* and *reggaeton* music by Enrique Iglesias and Juan Luis Guerra and Gente de Zona. They'd shake their hips to Shakira. They'd drape their arms over each other's shoulders and lean back and sing to the lovesick melodies of the *mariachis*. And James would fake it, enthusiastically singing nonsense because he didn't know any of the words, and Malena would sometimes collapse laughing at him.

As James got stronger, he started doing yoga out on the parched grass next to Malena's trailer. She would join him when she came home from work, and he would teach her some advanced techniques. Eventually, neighbors asked what they were doing, and James invited them to join in. He made sure everyone had a yoga mat, and he'd give his cues in English, demonstrating the poses, while Malena would translate his words into Spanish. After a few weeks, the class had swelled to ten people. Guillermo and Carmen, Luisa when she was free, Hector. Even Ramon gave it a try. There were also some recent additions to San Lazaro, a young couple from El Salvador who'd arrived with a baby and nothing else. They'd been embraced by the community, with everyone donating spare clothes and furnishings and sharing food. And, as autumn approached, life at San Lazaro fell into an easy rhythm.

While back in Colorado, James worked on his own plans for the future. He brought in crews from Wilder and Klein to remodel the kitchen and update the bathrooms. He added a skylight to the walk-in closet off his bedroom and found a beautiful Chinese armoire to go in the dining room. His house was almost perfect, suffused with natural light from the skylights and color from the paint on the walls. His collection of artwork and mineral specimens completed his decor, and people who visited remarked at the beauty and serenity of his spaces. Out in his yard, the Zen garden was stunning with a miniature red maple and bonsaied evergreen shrubs. His home lacked only one thing, Malena, and he resolved to find a way to bring her to Colorado. But would she come?

One Friday she picked him up at the airport wearing sunglasses. When she removed them, James could see a large bruise around her eye and cheek.

"Hey, what the hell!" He grabbed her firmly by the shoulders. "What happened? Who did this?"

"Oh, nothing." She pushed his hands away and put her sunglasses back on. "A patient at the hospital got violence. They did that sometimes."

"Then maybe you shouldn't work there if it's so dangerous! We can find you something else."

"Leave my job? And do what?"

"It doesn't matter! Malena, I'll take care of you. Come live with me in Colorado! We can make it work."

"And *mi familia*? Xiomara and Luisa and Rosie? Ramon and Hector? And the others? What about them? I can't just leave! I have many things to take care of here! It's my…job. Someone got to do it. The ugly one no one else can do!" Her jaw was quivering.

"Malena, what do you mean? I don't understand."

"No, of course you don't! You never will!" Malena's face screwed up as she tried to force back tears. "Never mind. It's OK. Everything will be OK." She kept repeating those words like a mantra, as if repetition and hope would make it come true.

James wrapped her in a hug, wishing that his hug could shield her from whatever haunted her. It killed him, but he had to let it go for the moment. Her "family"? These were just her neighbors! But she was from a different culture, one steeped in obligation to family and community and friends. He was disappointed that she'd rejected his invitation to come with him to Colorado, but then he'd sprung it on her without warning, so maybe she needed time to get used to the idea.

That following Wednesday, back in Boulder, James booked a session with Julie. He knew some people would consider him crazy to spend money on a psychic, but Julie was much more than that. She was wise and the perfect sounding board for him.

"Malena is right," said Julie. "It's not your job to rescue her from anything."

"But that's crazy! I could bring her here to Colorado. She wouldn't have to worry about money—"

"Maybe this is about more than money. You mentioned her chosen family at San Lazaro. She feels she can't abandon them. Remember, this is about her karma, her choices. If you take that away from her, you isolate her, strip her of her identity as a member of that family. It would be like a divorce."

"I just have such a bad feeling about this—"

"I do, too. I sense that, in some way yet to be revealed, this is a huge test. For her, and for you. I can't see the future on this one. But it's big. Lots of moving parts. Lots of noise. Easy to miss the real lesson."

James left his meeting with Julie hugely dissatisfied. He needed answers, and she'd only confirmed his worst fears. It wasn't fair! Malena was such a good person and deserved a better life, one that he could give to her. And then he remembered what his boss on Wall Street had told him, back in the days when the last shreds of his idealism were being stripped from his soul. "Life isn't fair. You don't get what you deserve; you get what you take." James had rejected that cynical view, and every time he'd come up against the proof of its truth, he'd pushed it away, saying to himself, *"No, that CAN'T be right."* But this time, after seeing how hard the people of *la familia* worked, after seeing how they cared for and helped one another, after seeing how poorly Malena was compensated for her work and her compassion, he could no longer ignore that reality. Life was not fair. Period.

* ~ * ~ *

The word had gotten out that *el escritor* was *un poeta,* and the next time James visited Malena, he agreed to read something. Strangely, he was more nervous than he'd ever been before reading. What if these people didn't like his stuff? And how would they understand it when it was in English?

Malena solved the second problem by translating each line as he read. They started with the poem she'd already translated, "The Art of Loving Slowly." James read:

"Please love me,"
she said,
"just very slowly."
A softly whispered plea,
a plan.

And then Malena would read her part in Spanish:

"Ámame por favor,"
ella dijo,
"solo que muy lentamente,"
Una plegaria susurrada,
un plan.

As she read each line, James marveled at how beautiful the poetry sounded coming out of her mouth. Just as she had a face made for smiling, she had a voice made for poetry. In Spanish her words were soft, musical, and very, very sexy. They read about six poems, and afterward everyone clapped enthusiastically.

The crowd was milling about, and James was talking to Xiomara and Guillermo when Juan stepped out of the shadows and walked up to him. He was alone.

"James Wilder, poet," he said, smiling. Xiomara and Guillermo sidled away. "Very nice."

"Thanks. It's nice to be appreciated."

"Malena appreciates you, it seems." He said it clinically, but with a hint of something else.

"So it seems. Are you here with Pamela?"

"No. Just me. Working. Making the rounds."

"Working? Tonight?"

"Of course. I protect the integrity of these United States. Detain and deport criminals."

"And you need to do that here?"

"Maybe. Wherever there is illegal activity, that's where I need to be."

"Huh. It seems so safe here. Can't imagine that much is going on of a nefarious nature."

Juan smiled, but only with his mouth. "Nefarious. That's too big a word for these little people. Now *you*, you're a *big man*! With money, good clothes, a country club where you play golf with all your gringo friends while the little Mexican people cut the grass, make it all nice-nice."

He paused, brushed James's shoulders with his hands like he was straightening his lapels, his face inches from James's. "No, this is not your world, white boy. You don't belong here."

Just then Malena came up eagerly, then stopped when she saw them speaking. Her smile changed to studied neutrality.

"Juan," she said.

"Ah, Malena. I had no idea you have such a voice for poetry. I'm sad you never read me any."

She just looked at him as he smiled at her.

"I love poetry. Oh well, I must be going. You two were marvelous together! Perhaps we could get together sometime for a private reading," he said, but looking at only her.

"Goodnight, Juan. Say hello to Pamela for me," said Malena as she pulled James away.

"Are you OK?" James asked as they walked back to her trailer.

"Yes," she said too smoothly.

James stopped walking and grabbed her gently by both shoulders, turning her to face him.

"Malena?"

She avoided his gaze. "I'm tired. Let's go to bed."

That night when they made love, there was a desperation to her lovemaking, as if she could feel something precious slipping away. Afterward, she slept with her face buried in his shoulder and her arms around him. James lay awake most of the night, mentally tossing and turning even as he dared not move for fear of waking her. He kept coming back to the bruise on her face, seeing images of Juan. He had no proof that it'd been him, but something about Juan had bothered James from the beginning, some kind of shadow that flowed into the space around him. Juan had flashed his true colors, and they were the colors of a snake. A deadly, poisonous viper, unpredictable, slithering behind the scenes. Malena and Juan were tangled in some sort of dangerous dance, and James had to do something, but what? He was in Colorado most days, and anything could be going on back here in San Diego, and he'd never know. Why had Malena warned James away, and how far did his promise to not interfere extend? Argh! Exhausted, he finally fell into a shallow, troubled sleep and woke the next morning with her still in his arms—soft, vulnerable, precious.

Malena's room was tidy, bright, and a little bigger than his. She had a queen-sized bed with a flowered bedcover. On her nightstand was a cheap alarm clock, a small jewelry box, his book of poetry, and some small pictures of her daughter. James was sleeping in there now, but usually his attention was focused on her face, her incredibly soft and smooth skin, her perfect body. That morning, he noticed a brownish, walnut-sized pebble sitting on his book. It was just like his scorpion pebble. James picked it up. It was engraved with the word "BELIEVE."

"Where'd you get this?" he asked.

"At yoga conference, first day, before I meet you. I get it from that blondie you later—kiss. I visit her booth. She says 'take one,' so I did."

"Huh. What does it mean?"

Malena took a deep breath as if collecting all her courage to herself. "She says to not lose faith in what I hope for."

"Mmmm, and what's that?"

Malena smiled and kissed him on the lips, slowly and thoroughly. "I hope to meet my couple someday."

"Your couple? What's a couple?"

"My…partner! My love! I don't know how to say it!"

James laughed and pulled her up tightly. "Well, it worked. You met me.

"Are you my love?"

"I think so."

"I almost throw the stone away after I see you kiss that blondie!"

"What? You already liked me back then?"

"No! Yes, a little. You seem kind of man I like. Good-looking, do yoga. Not drunk. Then I find out you are Johnny Casanova! A pig, like all men."

She pushed him away, a grin on her face. James couldn't say anything. He *was* Johnny Casanova, back then. "I got a pebble too," he said almost as an afterthought.

"What yours say?"

"No words, just a picture of a scorpion."

"What that mean?"

"Well, Angie, I mean that woman, was an astrologer, and she thought that meant I was a Scorpio. But I'm not; I'm a Gemini. And then she read me some stuff about how maybe the scorpion was my spirit animal. That seemed to make some sense.

Malena lay quietly next to him, and he could feel her breath on his neck right below his ear. Then she whispered, so quietly he almost couldn't hear her. "But James, I am a Scorpio…."

* ~ * ~ *

Later that weekend, Malena was at the store buying groceries, and a knock came at the door of the trailer. James was in shorts and a T-shirt, sitting at the little table with his laptop, writing poetry. He opened the door, and there stood Mr. Abrami. Mr. Abrami looked pretty much the same—a bit tanner, perhaps, but still as lethal as a coiled spring.

"Mr. Wilder, so nice to see you again."

James stood there dumbfounded, vertigo roaring in his ears. He must have looked how he felt because Mr. Abrami offered his hand to step down out of the trailer, as if he didn't trust that James could make it unassisted.

"What? Why are you here?" James stuttered, thrown out of context by this ghost of the past.

"Mrs. Khan would like to see you," he replied, turning and gesturing to a long black limo parked on the street. The limo looked as out of place as a nuclear submarine at a sailboat marina, parked between a battered pickup and an aging Ford LTD with a shredded vinyl roof.

"Nabila?"

As James followed him barefooted across the sunbaked scrubby dirt to the curb, he tried to slow the beating of his heart. Mr. Abrami opened the back door of the limo and stepped aside. James ducked his head and crawled into the cool darkness of the back seat. As his eyes adjusted, he saw Nabila, dressed all in black that matched her eyes, looking at him. She had her hair pinned up in a formal do and was wearing a substantial but chic gold necklace.

"James," she breathed softly. "Please sit."

She didn't try to hug him, as if elegantly respectful of the time and distance that had grown between them. James sat in the seat facing her.

"How are you?" he asked, his mind whirring and his heart thumping so loud he was sure she could hear it.

"I am fine," she replied. "And newly widowed."

James guessed that was coming, but like seeing the whiplash snaking toward you before it lands, it didn't make the sting any less. Because he had come to admire the man that was Saayed Khan. He'd gradually realized what a lover he was, the sacrifice of his own ego he'd made to bring happiness to his beloved. James could never have done the same. Saayed Khan had become the face and voice of Hafiz when James wrote poetry.

"I'm sorry. He was…an inspiration to me. Are you OK?"

"I miss Saayed so much! After you left, we would read your poetry together. We found a new way to connect, to love each other. Through words and feelings. It opened us. Thank you, James."

She leaned forward and touched his arm, a touch he had craved for many months and never thought he would feel again. But now the quality of it was different, unfamiliar, as if the nerves in his skin had been recoded to recognize only one touch, one caress, and it was not hers.

James nodded to her and smiled and wondered if she could see the sadness in his smile in the dark limo. "So, what brings you here? To San Lazaro Estates?"

"I came to find you. To offer you…but now that I'm here, I can see…feel…that you would not accept what I would give."

She knew. Whether it was Mr. Abrami's comprehensive intelligence gathering or her own instincts, she knew he was no longer available.

"I had to see you for myself, even though I had little hope. Are you happy, James?"

Her eyes glittered wetly, a moisture James wanted to kiss away like he'd done in the past, but he couldn't.

"Yes, I'm happy."

Nabila took a deep breath and forced a smile.

"She is a very lucky woman."

"No, I'm a very lucky man."

They spoke some more, but the words that needed to be said had been said, and after a few more minutes, she kissed him and gave him his leave.

As James left, Mr. Abrami stopped him for a few words. "Be careful, Mr. Wilder. There's a storm coming." Mr. Abrami said it coolly, professionally, but there was concern in his eyes.

"What do you mean?"

"This trailer park is…in play, I think you say in America. My sources tell me that money out of Russia is…interested in a redevelopment of this land."

"Really? And why is that a problem?"

"The people who live here. Many have…less-than-perfect credentials. Documentation. And the weak are always easy pickings for the strong. Be careful."

"Thank you. But why are you sharing this with me?"

Mr. Abrami looked him right in the eyes, his gaze level and professional. "Mrs. Khan has asked me to…include you in our…comprehensive security. Not to monitor your activity, but to…protect you. Apparently, you still matter to her."

Surprisingly, Mr. Abrami smiled as he said those last words, not in a sneering or condescending way, and not even in a humorous way, but in a friendly way that let James see, for the first time, a hint of the humanity and compassion that hid behind his steely gaze. James thanked him, feeling an unexpected warmth toward this mysterious guardian, and walked back to the trailer, digesting the news.

The limo was the talk of the trailer park that evening. He told Malena about his conversation with Nabila, but not Mr. Abrami's last words.

"This woman, she was your girlfriend?"

"For a while, yes."

"She's very rich, yes?"

"Yes."

"You should go with her."

James took Malena in his arms and held her close, looking into her eyes. "I choose you. I wake up in the morning, a free man with a free will, and I choose you. Every single day."

And James did, with his full heart, mind, and body. She was his missing puzzle piece. That night, filled with the certainty of the choice he'd made that day, he wrote this poem.

~~ *Come to Me, Lover* ~~

You come to me, Lover,
while I sit in meditation,
writing poems to my love,
and you whisper in my ear,
"Oh, light of my life,
why do you choose me?"

I bury my face
in the fragrant skin of your neck,
and murmur,
"There is no choosing.
Choice implies
that I could take another,
and that I could never do."

You come to me, Lover,
when I am drinking wine
and ask me with your laughter,
"Does my love intoxicate you,
and inflame
your heart's desire?"

I kiss your ruby lips,
caress your cheek,
and look deep into your eyes.
"Your love overflows
the cup of my heart's longing,
drowns my thirsty soul
with passion,
and makes me drunk
with happiness."

You come to me, Lover,
in the middle of the night,
and press your breast on mine.
"Does my body please you, Love,
and comfort you
in your dreams?"

I pull you closer,
and drink your breath
from lips melting with our heat.
I feel the rhythm of your heart
beating against mine,
and whisper,
"Your skin is my skin,
your breath my breath,
your heart my heart,
and you and I are one."

You come to me, Lover,
at any time of day or night,
and ask me, why do I choose you?

I will always answer,
"We are twin suns dancing
in the bright blueness of day,
sister moons embracing
in the soft darkness of night,
two fires burning
in the heart of God,
drawn together by the radiance
of our Love."

~ * ~

Chapter Thirty-Eight

~ * ~

Love

It was a Friday night, a month later, and James had just flown in to San Diego for the weekend. Malena had helped him discard the long pants and office shirt, and they'd made luxuriously slow, sensuous love in her trailer, carefully reconnecting the missing parts of each other's bodies and souls. When they were finished and basking naked in her bed, James opened a special bottle of champagne he'd brought with him. He'd thought about Julie's words and had decided to act anyway. He wouldn't disempower Malena; he'd offer her a different choice.

"To us!" he said, raising his glass.

"*Por nosotros!*" she replied, laughing. "You have to speak Spanish if ever you meet my *familia* in Mexico."

"To *familia!*" he toasted again in his terrible accent, and they collapsed laughing into each other's arms. "Malena, I want to meet your family."

"OK, we can go visit."

"No, I mean I *really* want to meet them." James got out of the bed, grabbed his pants from the floor, and rummaged around in the pocket. He took out a small ring box decorated in dark blue and got down on his knee at the bedside. "Malena, will you marry me?"

Malena gasped in shocked amazement. She sat up straighter in bed, and the sheet fell away to her waist. Her hair, tangled from their lovemaking, cascaded around her shoulders and framed her creamy white breasts with curls of delicious cinnamon chocolate. Her face was like a painting of captured joy, of a moment that made so many other moments worthwhile.

"You would marry me?" she asked. "You would choose me?"

"I choose you, with all my heart and soul," James replied. "I want you to be my wife. You are my couple. My sun. I need you."

Malena started to cry tears of happiness as she reached for him. He intercepted her left hand and put the ring on it. She kissed him and whispered, "Yes! Yes! Yes, *mi amor!*" And they hugged, clinging to each other.

"Now I *have* to meet your family," James whispered. "Tell me about them."

"*Mi familia en Playa Estrellita.* It's just like my *familia* here, *mi familia de San Lazaro.* Some got homes and jobs, some good, some not so good. One brother, he's dentist. Another canno find work. Life is no so easy some places, just like here."

She fell silent, and he was acutely aware of the warm, silky softness of her breath against his neck.

"Let's go," she said suddenly, looking up at him. "Let's go now! To Playa Estrellita! Get away from here. We can swim every day. I'll take you to *cenotes*, big pools in the middle of the forest where the water is like crystal. And we would see birds and iguanas and maybe monkeys. And the sea! The waters are so clear, clear blue! We can eat *mariscos*, fishes grilled on open pits! You will love it!" She smiled, but above her smile there was a quick flash of urgency, almost desperation, in her eyes.

"*Mi amor*, it sounds like paradise! We can go there whenever you want." James felt himself letting go, like his entire body was exhaling, a long, cleansing sigh that released all his fears, doubts, worries, anything negative. He finally had his couple! His partner! She would be his *wife*; what a strange word to use after all these years of loneliness! And she'd come live with him in Colorado, and they'd also spend plenty of time down in Mexico with her family. She'd meet Annie and Chris, who already liked what they'd heard about her. Life would be complete.

His hand caressed the soft skin of her lower back and buttock. It was his favorite part of her body, the curves and the softness meeting so perfectly.

"I'll book some tickets; we'll fly down, meet your family—" James said.

"Yes, yes!" Malena got up on her knees and took his face in her hands, kissing him. "You will like it. In the evening we can walk to town, to *cenadurias!* Little places, where everybody comes to eat tacos, and it's no expensive, and everybody talk, talk! The *carne asada*, ahh! You don't get it here. Oh James, let's leave tomorrow! I—we can leave all this here—" It was as if popping the cork on his marriage proposal had also popped the cork that had held back her secret stresses and worries, and now they were flooding forth in an uncontrolled foam of words.

"Sure! Whatever you want." James held her close and kissed her, and she settled into his arms, her agitation gradually subsiding as he rocked her.

They finished the champagne, then got dressed and joined San Lazaro's *comunidad* in the weekend fiesta in the common space between the trailers, to share their news, show Malena's ring, and celebrate. Ramon and Hector, Guillermo and Carmen, and many others, smiling and happy. Life was not easy for some, but for the moment, all was well with *la familia de San Lazaro.* James and Malena partied with their friends late into the night and finally retreated to Malena's bed in the wee hours of the morning, blissfully exhausted from dancing and singing and all the good wishes from *la familia.*

They stayed in bed late, a lazy Saturday morning, and later sat out on the patio under the shabby awning, drinking coffee and accepting yet more congratulations from Malena's neighbors. It seemed everyone had heard the news. They huddled over James's laptop, checking flights, and booking tickets. Tickets to fly out to Colorado on Monday so Malena could meet Annie and Chris. Tickets to Playa Estrellita later in the month. And they even started to sketch out a long honeymoon, traveling the world. Malena had never been anywhere but Mexico and Southern California, and James wanted to take her everywhere. Malena was back to being Malena, strong, self-contained, turning a smiling face to the world, and her urgency of the night before had faded.

That evening, they were grilling up some chicken and vegetables, and the community was gathering. Tables were set and chairs arranged for an impromptu dinner. And then, from across the open space came the faint sound of a scream and a trailer door slamming. James looked up from his conversation as Xiomara pushed through the crowd to Malena. Her gray hair was wild, and her voice was cracking as a torrent of Spanish came pouring out so fast that Malena had to sit her down and take both of her hands into her own. In a low voice Malena asked Xiomara some questions. Xiomara replied with tears of anguish. Over the surrounding hubbub James caught only a few words, including *La Migra* and *policia,* but the most important one was "Rosie." Malena sat back, shock and disbelief etched across her face.

"Malena, what's happened?" James asked as calmly as he could, his hand on her shoulder.

"Xiomara's daughter, Luisa, has been arrested," she said, her own voice cracking. "*La Migra*. And Xiomara says Rosie was taken from Luisa." Malena's face flashed despair, her eyes widening into deep wells of vulnerability. Around them, the crowd was already reacting, people murmuring, parents instinctively gathering up their children and dispersing to their own homes.

"That's terrible!" said James. "What can we do?"

"I must talk to Juan," she replied. "That's the only way about it. He can help with these things." Malena's face changed as she put on her mask of control, her eyes narrowing to neutral, her lips pressed together in a half smile that showed no happiness or mirth. Her mask against a hostile world. Her invisibility.

"But isn't Juan the one who deports…illegal people?"

"Sometimes. But sometimes he can get someone back." Malena's tone was factual, devoid of emotion.

There it was. The serpent in the Garden of Eden. Holding out the apple of temptation. Malena received a call on her cell phone. She stepped away to take it, and after a few moments, she came back to him, fighting to keep her mask firmly in place.

"I need go out for a while."

"Where?" James asked.

"Juan says he will help—" Malena seemed out of breath, struggling with the words.

"OK, I'll take you," he started.

"No, Juan will come get me."

Just at that moment, a pickup truck flashed its lights in the parking lot, and James saw Juan get out and stand next to it, his arms folded, looking toward them.

"Malena?" he asked. She wouldn't meet his eyes. She straightened her shoulders.

"I go now. Juan is waiting."

"Let me come with you!"

"No. I must do this."

James remembered Julie's words. "Her karma. Her choices." He looked at Malena. He could stop her, physically restrain her from going. He didn't.

Malena hugged him, then pulled back and studied his face, searching for something she didn't find. Her eyes brimmed with tears. She took a long, shuddering breath and touched his cheek with a shaking hand, then dashed off to the parking lot. James watched her go, all the circuits in his mind blown and his heart pounding in his chest. Malena climbed into Juan's truck, a souped-up white pickup with expensive wheels.

James turned and saw Hector looking at him with sympathy in his eyes.

"Hector, you have a truck?" James asked.

"Sor, you should stay here." Hector's face crumpled with words he didn't want to say.

"Hector, give me your keys." It wasn't a request.

"Yes, sor," he replied, and handed them over, his eyes filled with sorrow.

They followed Juan's pickup at a discreet distance for several miles. James's mind was racing. Up wrong alleys, down corridors, into wrong buildings, and always avoiding the straight-line path. Malena was going to negotiate with Juan, say or do *something* in her self-appointed role of intermediary with the arcane and inexorable forces of *La Migra*. She was going to get Rosie released. Where were they going? To the police station? To ICE headquarters? The need for an answer, any answer, except for the most obvious one, kept him following Juan's truck.

That answer became clear when the truck turned into a Motel 6 parking lot. Juan and Malena got out, and Juan took Malena by the arm and led her to the door of a room. He unlocked it, and they stepped inside. The door closed behind them, and the world closed in on James. He couldn't breathe. He stepped out of Hector's truck and bent over, his hands on his knees, trying to get air into his lungs.

"Hey, sor. You all right?" Hector asked.

James gasped for air. "Yeah. Just a sec." He pulled himself together and, after pacing around on the sidewalk for a few moments, got back into Hector's truck.

"Let's go home," he croaked through a mouth so dry he couldn't swallow.

They drove in silence back to San Lazaro. Each minute stretched into an eternity. When they finally got there, James nodded his thanks to Hector and turned to go.

"Please, sor. Malena, she is a good woman," Hector said.

James looked at him as if he were speaking Greek and went into the trailer. Now, instead of cozy, the walls seemed to close in so claustrophobically that he was panicked to get out of there. He called a taxi and had his bags packed in three minutes. James waited, sweating, out in the parking lot under a blinking streetlight that was swarmed by a cloud of moths.

The taxi picked him up and the guy asked, "Where to?"

"Hotel Del Coronado." It was the first name that came into his mind. The place he had met Malena.

James checked in and threw his bags into the corner of the room. He stuffed all the bottles from the minibar into his jacket pocket and headed down to the beach. He turned off his cellphone, thinking that there was nothing Malena could say to soften the implosion of his world.

Under the late summer sky, Grandmother Ocean was cold and dark, sleeping fitfully, breathing in and out, her wet exhalations swirling foam around his ankles. Clouds drifted across the moon, and he waded through light and dark, swigging from little bottles, at times alone, at times with his moon shadow for company. Malena and… Juan. What the hell! The dynamics between them, the bruise on her face, the encounters he'd witnessed—in retrospect, it was obvious that Juan was fucking her. Exploiting his position of absolute power for sex. How long had that been going on? And why hadn't Malena said anything to him, James? Oh yeah, she *had* said something. She'd warned him not to ask any questions. To stay out of her business. But she'd just agreed to marry him! And gone off with Juan anyway! Marriage? That dream lay scattered across the Motel 6 parking lot like the broken glass of a car window, smashed and violated by thieves. Had he ever really known her? He was such a dumbfuck! Once again, he'd dived headfirst into unfamiliar waters, heedless of signposts and red flags that spelled out danger, and once again he'd crashed against the rocks hidden just below the surface. Why did he keep doing this?

James walked for hours along the shore, seeking answers in the dark but finding nothing but the waves that washed in and out, untroubled and unchanged by the woes of the world, woes as transient as the waves themselves. Eventually he found a large driftwood log, where he sat and dropped the rest of the bottles into the sand. Empty or full, they didn't help. His reality was as vacant as the horizon, and he wished he was out there somewhere beyond it.

"Secrets. They all have them," James whispered to the waves that flowed up the sand toward his feet, then ebbed back out to the Grandmother. Malena's secret. Nabila's secret. Sara's secret. And Charlie's and Kat's and Willow's. All women have secrets, and you never ever want to find out what they are because it always means the end of happiness. James sat for an eternity, as a million waves deposited a million different useless offerings of foam and seaweed at his feet. Eventually, the sky started to lighten, and he walked back to the hotel and crashed on his large, empty bed.

James woke with the sourness of the morning after, which only got worse when he drank a large glass of water. The light was flashing on his phone, indicating a message. James picked up the phone and heard a recorded voice tell him that an envelope was downstairs with the concierge. What could that be? Nothing good, that was sure. He took a shower, found some clean clothes in his bag, and started to make a plan. Get online and book a flight to Denver. Today. Never to come back. All the while his heart ached in his chest like it was being ground between two millstones.

He stopped by the concierge desk to pick up the envelope. It was from Mr. Abrami. James carried it into the restaurant and ordered some eggs. Then he finally looked at his phone. There were twenty voicemails and texts from Malena. The first few asking where he was; the last few begging forgiveness. In her last voicemail, she was crying so hard he couldn't understand a word she was saying. It would have broken his heart if his heart wasn't already in a thousand pieces.

He opened the envelope from Mr. Abrami. There was a handwritten note:

Mr. Wilder:

The Department of Immigration and Customs Enforcement is raiding the trailer park today. They are doing it without notice and planning to detain all illegals for deportation.

On a personal note, Agent Juan Martinez, the husband of Pamela Martinez, will be leading the raid. He has been blackmailing your friend Malena Cortez and her cousin Berenice. I thought you should know.

Kahlil Abrami
Fortress Security

Bloody hell! Berenice, too? Juan, that son of a bitch! Of course, Bere was in the country illegally, but Juan had parlayed his position of absolute power into leverage over Malena as well. She'd told James that she had a green card from her marriage! Why did *she* give in to Juan? Maybe she'd lied to James? Maybe she didn't have any recourse either? But why hadn't she come to *him*, James, *her couple*, to ask for help? *Can you slay dragons, Johnny, or are you only good with words?* He could hear again the almost dismissive, bitter hopelessness in her voice as she'd said that to him on the beach, months earlier. Had he done *nothing* to change her opinion since then? Clearly, she'd viewed him as a perfectly good escape from her problems, but not a solution. He'd offered to marry her! Maybe she was thinking that they could just get away, and…and then what? Would she have ever told him about the devil's bargain she'd made with Juan? James shook his head.

But what if she *had* told him about Juan? Yesterday, or the day before, or a month before? What could he have done? What *would* he have done? Alert the authorities that one of their own was blackmailing some illegal aliens? And get them all deported anyway? Maybe Malena was right. Maybe he was only good with stupid little words. And now *la familia*, all the people at the trailer park who'd welcomed him with open arms, were in danger, and someone needed to warn them, and James was the only person who knew what was coming. But that meant facing Malena.

James's heart ached. He weighed the idea of calling or texting her but rejected those options as cowardly. "Suck it up, Buttercup," he said aloud. "You owe her more than a shitty text." He had to face Malena, endure the full brunt of honesty.

James took a taxi to the trailer park. After paying the man, he stood and surveyed the peaceful little oasis, its residents starting a normal day. He saw Guillermo and Abuelita roasting some chilis on the barbeque grill. Guillermo waved. James waved back. He saw Xiomara over by her trailer, with Rosie and Bella, putting out water for the little dog. So, Malena had "succeeded," had convinced Juan to get Rosie "released." Had Rosie ever really been taken into legal custody, or had Juan just taken her on his own to get leverage over Malena, for one last fuck before she escaped and went off with the gringo? And now Juan was coming again, to take Rosie anyway. James smiled grimly and shook his head.

James knocked on the door of Malena's trailer. "Malena," he called. She answered, and he found her sitting in her room on her bed. She didn't look at him, just sat there, her face streaked with tears that were no longer flowing. He stood in the doorway of her tiny room, and it seemed he towered over her, made her slumped figure even smaller than normal. She held out her right hand. It was closed over something. She opened her palm. It was his ring.

"Malena—" he said.

"Take it," she replied in a low voice.

"I don't want it," he said tiredly. "Sell it, use the money for… something."

At that, she started to sob. Her shoulders shook, and her head hung over her lap, her hand still holding out the ring to him, the ring he rejected. James felt a surge of sympathy, wanted to take her in his arms and comfort her, but something held him back. She was no longer his, and he just wanted to leave, go away, and never come back.

"Malena," he said softly. "Juan is bringing *La Migra* today. Raiding San Lazaro. You should warn the others."

She didn't say anything, just kept sobbing—her long, beautiful hair shrouding her face, tears spattering the floor.

"Did you hear me? They're coming!"

Malena stopped sobbing, caught her breath, composed herself. She sat up straight and faced him. "What you want me to do for that?" she asked, finally looking him in the eyes. "I have done what I could."

"Yeah, I know what you did. With…him." James couldn't help himself. The words came out cruelly, as if he were spitting them at her.

Her face spun through shock to despair to anger. She jumped to her feet and thrust her face up into his. "What do you know, stupid gringo? That I—fuck that animal? To save my family here? To save Xiomara and Ramon and Luisa and Rosie? To save even my cousin Bere? Good for you! Now go away. Now you know our world! In our world, he has *all* the power! I fuck him before I meet you, to buy their lives here in America. I told you to stay away, but you did not.

Then I hope you would love me, but no! For you, it is more better to *judge* me!"

She shoved him backward with surprising force, and tripping over the door threshold, James fell onto his back in her tiny living room. Malena towered over him, suddenly enormous in her fury.

"That *pendejo* take my honor. Make me his…whore. But you are worse. You take my *love* and leave me with *nothing*! OK. But you will *not* judge me! I will *not* pay twice for trying to save my family!"

She stopped, gasping for breath between sobs, as she descended into despair. "I *needed* you! My couple! Where were you?"

Her sobs tore at his heart. Then she regathered her strength and fury, like a hurricane passing over heated waters. "I know you now. You run away, go hide, where I can't find you. You probably just drink, drink like a stupid, weak man! And cry because your life is so hard. Poetry about love? You know *nothing* about love! Now go! And take these *lies* with you!"

She flung his ring at him. It hit him right between the eyes and bounced across the floor. She picked up his book of poetry, the one he'd signed for her, off the bedside table and threw it, too. Then she hurled her pebble that said BELIEVE. She slammed her bedroom door, and from behind it, James heard agonizing, tearing sobs.

He got up off the floor and left the trailer, shocked and numb, skewered not by the book or her words, but by truth. He finally understood. *This* had been the final exam of the gods, a hard one, and once again, he'd failed. It wasn't about solving her problem. It never had been. The test was to *choose* between love and judgment, and he'd chosen *judgment*— of someone who was compassionate down to her DNA, who sacrificed herself for others daily at her work in the hospital, who'd done whatever she could to save her community and her cousin from an all-powerful predator. She'd warned him off against digging too deeply, asking too many questions. And then she'd let him into her life. Oh, how she'd overestimated him! His capacity to match her depth of character, her understanding of love.

As James stood outside the trailer, surrounded once again by the ashes of his world, he felt the strength drain out of his legs, and he fell to his knees, toppled by the certainty of his complete failure. Again.

Bere came running up. She was crying. "They're coming here! I asked Juan to do something, but he can't!"

James tried to turn his focus from his own despair to hers. "Bere, what? When?"

"*La Migra!* ICE! They're on their way. I was…with Juan, and… he just laughed and said thank you; it's all over now. Said anyone who's illegal is getting deported, even me! Not just criminals!"

She sobbed in his arms. "He promised to protect me, said if I…I…slept with him—"

As she sobbed anew, James held her and wished that he was holding Malena, comforting her.

Suddenly, shouts and screams rang out from around the park, and the grounds were swarming with Immigration and Customs Enforcement agents in flak jackets and helmets, with truncheons and automatic rifles, wielding militarized flashlights to bludgeon submission out of frightened, unarmed men and women. Bere screamed and clung to James as agents rushed by.

His mind spun with shock as he saw Abuelita taken down by a burly female agent. Abuelita's face was shoved into the dirt as her hands were pulled up behind her and locked into cuffs.

"*Aiee! Socorro! Socorro!*" she cried as she was dragged, her eyes terrified, toward a waiting van. James tried to pull free from Bere, but she was clinging to him, wailing with terror and despair.

He pulled Bere over to the trailer door and banged on it. Malena opened and looked out at the scene, her face still streaked with tears.

"Take her," James shouted, and Malena helped Bere through the doorway. She looked back at James, her face transformed into a wasteland of despair, and he couldn't bear her gaze. He had no place here, no standing to offer her comfort. He'd crumbled at the first blow and was no one's dragon slayer. James turned away to face the chaos and violence that was washing over the tranquil oasis that had been San Lazaro.

Time shifted to slow motion as scenes of madness flashed before his eyes. Gentle Hector, his legs kicked out from under him and body-slammed to the ground, shackled on the same spot where only hours before he'd played his drum and sung softly under the stars. The awning over Malena's patio, ripped down as Guillermo and Carmen tried to hold onto their children, who were being torn away screaming and crying. The barbecue grill, knocked over by ICE agents, sending burning briquettes flying across the scrubby ground to smolder on the dry, drought-starved grass. Ramon running, chased by three agents. James remained rooted to the spot, frozen by the violence.

Xiomara and little Rosie came running toward him, terrified, with Bella chasing and barking.

"*Señor* James! *Señor* James!" Xiomara cried. "Help!"

A helmeted agent lunged forward and tried to grab Rosie, and Bella snapped and latched onto his pants leg with her teeth. The trooper let go of Rosie and tried to shake the little dog off. Bella yelped as if in pain, and Rosie screamed, which jolted James out of his paralysis. He lowered his head and launched himself into the agent, sending him careening headfirst into the side of the neighboring trailer. The agent went down in a heap and didn't get up. James grabbed Rosie and Xiomara and hustled them into Malena's trailer, followed by Bella. He closed the door and stood there, barring entry. All around him was chaos, shouting and screams and flashing lights. *These motherfuckers!* James clenched his fists. Where was Juan? James wanted to reach through that smug face and pull out his fucking eyes. Moments later, a burly agent strode up, shouting orders to his men as he came. He stopped in front of James, his eyes hidden behind his blacked-out lenses. He was backed by two others, as large and anonymous as he.

"Where's Bere?" he demanded. James recognized Juan's voice.

"Who wants to know?" James voice trembled with suppressed rage.

"Fuck you, gringo. Is she inside with Malena?"

"Got a warrant?" James asked.

"Don't need a warrant. The owner of this trailer is a special friend of mine. In fact, I probably spend more time in her bed than you do. You aren't the only one with pussy privileges." His grin below his blacked-out lenses was wide.

Juan's words hit James like a sledgehammer right in the chest. James took a deep breath, absorbed the blow, and spit it back through clenched teeth. "Yeah, well you still need a warrant. That's the law. Go get a warrant, then come back."

The two agents behind Juan started forward at this challenge, but he motioned them back. He stepped forward, his face inches from James's, an ancient male-to-male challenge.

"Look, jackoff. She bought some time for these miserable slugs, but time's up! No pussy in the world can stop what's happening now. These fucking illegals can go back to their shithole countries. You don't like it, talk to your congressman."

That was all James needed. He launched himself at Juan, knocked him flat and held him down in the dirt, landing punch after punch on his smug face, each punch carrying with it the weight of all his failures, his frustrations, and his shame. Juan's dark glasses shattered, and blood exploded from his lips and nose. He fought back, but it was his two comrades who came to his rescue, one of them grabbing James by the arm while the other put him in a chokehold. They dragged him off, kicking and spitting with rage, and Juan pulled out his Taser and jammed it up against James's chest. His world exploded in a million sparks of white light.

* ~ * ~ *

James floated in silence above his body, which lay sprawled, face-up in the dirt. Below him, he could see the entire trailer park. Chaos, flashing lights, people running and uniformed, helmeted agents chasing. He saw Malena come flying out of the trailer, hurled by one of the agents, who also dragged Xiomara with his free hand. The elderly, bent woman was like a desiccated doll in the agent's grasp, collapsing onto her knees and being jerked roughly across the ground. Juan came out next, dragging Bere, who pulled at his arms, crying.

James saw Malena pick herself up, crawl over to his body, his unseeing eyes staring skyward. She bent over him, checking for a pulse, and then sat up and screamed for help, terror in her face. He couldn't hear her voice or any sound at all, but he knew every word she cried out as if it was echoing inside his own mind. He floated higher, paralyzed, trapped in a bubble of peaceful energy that slowly grew brighter, her frantic image getting smaller, fading, fading, washed out by brightness.

They say when you die, you meet all sorts of people. Relatives, departed loved ones, your parents and grandparents, saints and gods, even your pets. James met Malena. Somehow, she was there with him. She took his hand, and they walked down a dirt path along a riverbank edged with reeds and blooming flowers and palm trees. Rice paddies stretched to the horizon, where distant mountains rose up and merged into clouds. All was peace and calm.

Her beautiful liquid eyes shone with a golden light as she looked at him, the love in her pouring out in sweet, honeyed energy that filled his soul. They walked, their hearts as intertwined as their fingers, smiling at each other, surrounded by peace. He tried to tell her how sorry he was, to beg forgiveness, but she held her finger up to his lips. A bit farther, they came to a fork in the path. She stopped and looked at him, and tears welled up in her eyes as she smiled one last time, a smile of infinite sorrow.

She kissed him, sweetly, gently, then let go of his hand. It was goodbye. Her eyes turned back to brown, and in them he saw a deep loving sadness—for him, for their lost love, for her community, for her family. He felt her fingers pulling free just as he felt the roots of her heart tearing themselves out of his chest. He tried to cry out, "Don't leave me! Malena!" But no sound came from his mouth.

She turned and took a step down that path. He tried to follow her but could go no further. He was where he was supposed to be. She couldn't stay. She walked away slowly, and her figure got smaller and smaller, and the light around him began to fade until finally he could see her no more, and he was alone in total silence, no heartbeat, no idea of up or down, in complete darkness.

So, this was what it was like to die. Even your ability to sense darkness begins to fade. No light. Not even any darkness. You lose your sight, your body, everything and everyone you valued—you lose your love—and are left with—nothing.

Chapter Thirty-Nine

~ * ~

Compassion

When James woke, Nabila was there, with Mr. Abrami by her side. She sat next to James in a chair, holding his hand, her eyes red from weeping. Even Mr. Abrami looked shaken.

"James," she whispered, bending over him, her tears falling on his face.

"Nabila, what—?"

"Your heart stopped."

"What? Where am I?"

"You're in the hospital."

"How…how did I get here? I thought I was dead."

"Mr. Abrami got you…out of there. He was just in time."

"Malena? Where's Malena?"

Nabila's eyes welled up anew with tears. She looked up at Mr.

Abrami, unable to speak. He took a step forward and put his hand on Nabila's shoulder. His face showed real sorrow, even horror. James's heart burned in his chest, which was suddenly tightening.

"Miss Cortez saved your life," he said. "She started CPR and kept you going until I got there. Then she ran back into her trailer to rescue a little girl. It was on fire. There was a propane explosion.... She...she's in intensive care here."

Dread filled James's body. "Malena? She's hurt? How badly? And little Rosie?"

"Miss Cortez saved the girl but was struck on the head by the blast. She also suffered burns on her head and back, and a broken arm. She's in a coma. The doctors can't tell us anything yet."

James closed his eyes and wished himself back into darkness, back into emptiness. Maybe he could get a do-over, wake up to Malena's face looking down at him, her smile reassuring him that she loved him, or even her voice telling him that she hated him. As long as she was OK.

James stayed in the hospital for one more day, then moved to a hotel. His heart had stopped, shocked into arrhythmia by the Taser so soon after his heart attack. Malena had saved his life, and now he hovered near her bed, praying to every god he'd ever heard of to forgive him and bring her back.

"Please, please, please!" he begged in every language he could muster up.

The gods didn't answer, a rebuke he knew he thoroughly deserved, and Malena just lay there, breathing through tubes, a bandage wrapping her skull where she'd been burned, her eyes purpled and bruised.

While Malena lay in a coma, Pamela came to visit. She was crying.

"Oh, James, I'm so sorry! I saw Bere at the detention center, and she told me everything. Everything! About...Juan. And about Malena. Oh God, James, I had no idea! No idea! How Juan threatened to close down the trailer park, how he threatened to deport

Bere unless Malena...Oh, god, I feel sick! Ugh! That I was *married* to that...*culero cabron!*" She said some other things, but James was too numb to hear them.

Later that day, the immigration authorities came to the hospital. The tall, balding representative of the government was blunt but professional. "Mr. Wilder, we have witnesses that will testify that you interfered with the legal actions of our agents in the field. They allege that you directly assaulted two of our agents, inflicting bodily harm."

James's blood boiled at those words but he stayed calm. "Are you charging me? I'm happy to refer you to my lawyer. He's already preparing a lawsuit on behalf of the residents who were brutally mistreated by your men."

"Actually, there's no need." The representative was tight-lipped. "We've already received video and testimony from credible sources that indicate that...the leadership of the operation...perhaps did not follow our normal procedures, and we are prepared to drop all charges against you in light of your...personal injuries."

"That's nice," James replied. "But what about the residents? That was a fucking travesty."

"Those that are in this country illegally will be treated as such. The law is still the law."

"And you're still gonna hear from my lawyer." James somehow restrained himself from saying anything more.

Malena's brothers came up from Mexico, and Malena's daughter arrived from college. They were very emotional, and Carlos, her oldest brother who was a policeman in Playa Estrellita, choked on his words, "If I am there when those *pinches cabrones* attack my sister—" Tears of trembling rage filled his eyes. Malena's daughter just held Malena's hand and wept, and her sobs tore fresh holes in James's heart.

Malena finally opened her eyes on the third day. Her face was expressionless. She said nothing, to anyone. She didn't recognize James. At all. Her family decided to take her home. To Mexico.

Nabila also went home to London, but before she left, she sat with James in the hospital cafeteria.

"James, we both need to move on with our lives. You're safe and well, and that's important to me. I have a business to run with my sons. You have a woman who needs you, more than she can say right now. Stay with her, even if she doesn't recognize you. She will. The heart always knows, even if the head doesn't. Trust your heart and her heart."

His heart. It was breaking when Malena turned her bruised and bandaged face away from him without a word as she was loaded into a special ambulance for the trip across the border. It broke completely as the ambulance headed down the drive. He had no idea if she would ever recognize him, or acknowledge him if he did.

Chapter Forty

~ * ~

Forgiveness

After Malena's family took her home to Mexico, Mr. Abrami was kind enough to drive James to the airport. James was headed home to Colorado, to pick over the rubble of his life to see what was worth salvaging. "Do you know what happened to the residents?" he asked.

"Taken into custody for the most part," Mr. Abrami replied. "They'll go through the process and be deported, probably within a week or two."

"And Rosie? Do you know what happened to her, the little girl Malena rescued?"

"Sent to a detention center. In Arkansas, I believe."

"Arkansas? What the fuck! And her mother, Luisa?"

"I believe she's being processed locally for deportation."

"Separated from her own child? That's insane!"

Mr. Abrami just shook his head in what might have been agreement.

"And Bere? Malena's cousin?"

"Berenice Cortez is being held in a detention center while ICE investigates her charges against Agent Martinez."

James felt a cold wave of hatred rise up in his chest. "And him?" he asked. "What's happened to him?"

Mr. Abrami kept his eyes on the road. "Agent Martinez has not been home. Nor has he reported to work for the last five days." He spoke in clipped, professional tones.

"So, where is he?"

Mr. Abrami said nothing as he pulled the car up to the busy curb at the airport. Outside, cars were honking, policemen were urging drivers to move along, and travelers were unloading their bags from taxis and vans. The silence inside the closed bubble of the car was deafening.

"Surely you know!" James insisted.

Mr. Abrami unlatched his seatbelt and turned to look at James.

"Mr. Wilder, do you believe in karma?"

"Maybe. I guess. I'm not sure."

"Well, I do. I believe it will catch up with Agent Martinez, if it hasn't already happened." He looked James straight in the eye as he spoke, and James suddenly knew that if he ever met the angel of death, he would have those same eyes. "We all have our strengths," Mr. Abrami continued. "Yours is love and poetry. Stick to that and let other, less forgiving, entities in the universe deal with retribution."

The irony in his statement was not lost on James.

He flew down to Playa Estrellita every other weekend for three months, hoping that Malena would remember him, or at least acknowledge him. She didn't. Her eyes looked past him as if she didn't even see him. Her hair was starting to grow out again except for one place on the back of her neck where it was scarred from the burns. Her broken arm healed, and she looked almost normal except for the light that had gone out in her eyes. Even the pink lotus tattoo on her shoulder looked pale and colorless.

The trailer park named San Lazaro Estates disappeared a month after the raid. It was swarmed by bulldozers and giant diggers that attacked the site like *La Migra* had attacked the residents. The scrubby palm trees were knocked over, the parched earth where *la familia* had danced under the moonlight to *bachata* and *reggaeton* was scraped away, and the trailers were hauled off to detention in junkyards and dumps.

With Mr. Abrami's help, James located some of those who'd been deported. He found Xiomara down in a small town in Sinaloa. She'd been pretty badly roughed up and left with a broken arm and two broken teeth. James helped her move to Playa Estrellita. He rented her a small apartment and paid for her hospital bills. Rosie Gonzales was reunited with her mother Luisa after six weeks. They were both deported, and with the assistance of Malena's brother Carlos, James found them a place to live, also in Playa Estrellita. He never discovered the whereabouts of Hector or Ramon, but he did track down Guillermo and Carmen Morales. They'd left the US for Mexico City and had abandoned their shot at the American dream. Their Abuelita had been so badly traumatized that she'd disappeared into a mute retreat from the world and had to be put in a facility where she sat silently with terror in her eyes. The remaining invisibles who hadn't been deported were scattered like dandelion seeds in the breeze to other insignificant, unwanted weed patches where they sent down shallow roots, some to struggle for a while, others to wither and blow away in the unforgiving winds of financial Darwinism.

As for James, he felt like a rogue planet ejected from orbit around his sun, forced to wander through dark and empty space, frozen into an unforgiven lump of rock, no center, no heat source, no gravitational mass pulling him toward the light. He'd been there before, but at least he'd always had some tiny bit of hope. Hope that he would someday meet the part of him that was missing. His Siamese twin, cut off from birth. His sun. His couple. Now, he knew that that had already happened.

He sold his share of the company to Eliu. He had no more mental or emotional bandwidth for it. Annie and Chris were fine. They worried about him, but they also had their own lives to live. Finishing college, finding jobs and life partners. All the sorts of things young people do at the beginning of their run, when they still have a full bank account of health and optimism and energy.

He went deeply into yoga. The beauty of yoga is that it is the perfect balance of male and female energy. There is strength and stamina and perseverance. There is grace and beauty and agility. There is freedom of expression and control. There is technique and brute force. And mostly, there is the yoking of it all into peace. It seemed the only place where James found peace was on the mat. He lost twenty pounds. He became a vegetarian. Not because he believed in anything, but because he wanted less of himself. He wanted less of everything. He wanted to burn away everything but Truth, and maybe if he did that, he could find Love again. Because intellectually, at least, James believed that at the center of Truth was Love.

Rocco passed away, and James cried bitterly, but not as much as he had done for Malena. One evening on the Bobolink, James scattered Rocco's ashes in all the places he used to sniff, reading the doggie newspaper on their morning walks, and where they used to glide like feathers on the wind when James would train for miles in the heat of the day, his shirtless chest feeling the cooling of sweat and the heat of the sun and the freshness of the breeze—four miles, five miles, six miles in.

James decided to take off with nothing but a backpack and a stack of frequent flier miles. The Fool. The card with zero value. The card of starting over from the beginning, with infinite possibilities. Only this fool was no longer innocent, bedazzled by beauty, and the possibilities were no longer infinite. This fool had fallen off that cliff, and the little dog had died. But at least he was traveling light.

He put his house up for sale. The house that was finally complete, with air and space and color, the rooms filled with little pockets of beauty, like his artwork and antiques and mineral collection. A refuge that was finally serene, with his Zen garden, a modern, new kitchen and sparkling, updated bathrooms. He'd spent fifteen years working on it, believing at some level that if he could just make it perfect, his life would somehow also be perfect, and he could attract a partner, a wife, who would complete his happiness. Like Malena. But ultimately, perfection had turned out to be an illusion, and his house nothing more than a sand mandala to be blown away by the winds of karma, its perfection as transitory as an eyeblink. James let go of his fossils and his art and his Chinese antiques, giving some to his kids, selling some to strangers. A few friends and former coworkers came by to wish him luck. Where was he going? they asked. He shrugged. It didn't matter. He'd lost all interest in plans, places. He just needed to move on.

On his last night in Colorado, he stood outside under the night sky, looking up at the full moon as trees cast stark moon shadows at his feet. Clouds drifted overhead in the sharp crystal air of late November. Somewhere an owl hooted, and over the jagged silhouette of the mountains, Jupiter and Venus lingered between the black ridgeline and a few faint stars. It was the season for dying, the death of all that had seemed so green and fresh and young in the springtime of only a few months before. A cold gust of wind sent a rattling of dead leaves past his feet, and his heart felt as bare as the tree branches.

James went into the house and found his red book of poetry. He stared at it, and his heart filled with faint echoes as he felt again the crystallized moments of emotion that lay inside, framed in their gold filigree, etched onto creamy card stock. He should just burn the damn thing, he thought. No one gives a fuck about poetry. And now, certainly not him. He carried the book into the living room and lit a last fire in the fireplace. A "Burning Away" ceremony of his own. An opportunity to toss his book into the flames, just as poor Deirdre the bridezilla had done back in the Rebounders ceremony. Who'd been more deluded, she or him? Was his book of spoiled dreams any different from hers? At least she'd long since been stripped of her delusions. He'd been carrying his for far longer.

James stirred the logs of the fire, waiting for the right moment to toss in his book. The gods were whispering, but in languages he no longer understood. And as he sat there looking into the flames, he realized that he could burn the original, and that might be satisfying, but there were thousands of printed copies out in the world, and many more digital versions on the internet. His poems had escaped, taken on lives separate from his. He no longer owned them, and there was no way he could consign them all to oblivion, any more than he could consign his own pain. And why had he written them in the first place? To crystallize moments just like this, moments of soul-churning devastation or love.

James sat looking into the fire, seeking answers in the flames. The book stayed in his lap until the flames died down, leaving only glowing coals. No, he wouldn't burn it. He would write one last poem to capture how he felt, and then never write another. He was done as a poet. He rose and carried his book to his writing desk, where he poured out his feelings onto the page in one last metaphorical "Burning Away" ceremony.

~~ *Into the Forest* ~~

Alone I stand, looking back
across the ravine
at the holy spot where
my beloved had stood.
A vision, a phantom,
an impossible dream.

Had she even been real?
Only a feather
to mark the spot
where she took flight,
back to the beginning,
beyond reach,
beyond hope.

I cup my ear
for any echo
of my heart's last prayer.
Nothing.

I reach for my quiver,
but there are no more arrows.
All spent,
on words that flew
wide of the mark.
My bow, now useless,
falls from my fingers.

My heart aches,
a dry well
that pumps no water.
An empty bottle
that pours no wine.
A high-flying bird
whose wings melted in the sun.

The journey awaits,
no map,
no North Star,
no path to the end.

Just brambles,
and loneliness,
and the long dark
of a foolish journey,
to slay a nameless dragon,
to retrieve a worthless jewel,
to bring back home to no one.

Empty-handed,
I turn to the forest,
my companion desolation,
my armor despair.
My boots weighed by sorrow,
no honor, no glory, no love,
the quest has lost it grail.
Into the forest I go.

~~ * ~~

That night James dreamed that he was walking along that same mystical riverbank he'd walked with Malena. Rice paddies and palm trees and flowering shrubs stretched away to the horizon. Ahead on the path, a light floated toward him like a giant golden pearl. As it reached him, it resolved into a vision of many dancing goddesses, and he saw that they were Willow and Kat, Charlie and Sara, Nabila and Malena. Goddesses who danced separately, then merged together in a swirling celebration of feminine power. One beautiful goddess, the Divine Feminine, Shakti herself, with glowing skin that changed color from light to dark, from Malena's pale cream to Sara's brown, and a ruby *bindi*, or third eye, on her forehead that glowed like a laser beam. She had twelve arms that appeared and disappeared, each carrying a sword or a conch shell or some other ancient symbol of power. She was fire and ice, and she held out two hands to James, palms up.

She smiled, a smile that captured every smile he'd ever seen from his loves, and a necklace materialized above her palms. It was a mala, a living, breathing thing, and the beads were people and places and experiences from his life, like the beads that Hafiz had thrown into the air in front of him, and the cord that knotted them together was a cord woven from all his actions, his intentions, and his feelings. She spoke in goddess language, and James heard her words inside his head rather than through his ears.

The strongest cord is knotted with Love.
Let Love be your mantra, as you knot together the beads of your life.

Only as she said Love, her voice said all the words meaning love in all languages ever spoken or written or sung, and the resulting harmony sounded like OM, and over her head James saw the glowing symbol Kat had created in the sand out of green sea glass.

She handed James the mala, and as it passed from her to him, it sank into his palms like melting oil and disappeared. Then the vision of Shakti faded, her last words flowing like liquid smoke through his mind in colors and flavors and scents and musical notes.

Remember your purpose, your sva-dharma.
To seek, create, and enjoy beauty.

Later that morning, after the movers had left, James sat on the carpeted floor of his bedroom with his backpack. He laid out his remaining material possessions. Some shirts. Some shorts. His book of poetry and his laptop. His malas. This was it. All that remained after so much blood and sweat and tears.

James looked at the malas, arrayed next to each other. The one Kat had made for him. He felt again the echo of pain that still scarred his heart. And the one Sara had given him, the *anahata chakra* mala, the kaleidoscopic magic of mystic connection. James put those two malas into his backpack, tucked away safely, sacred memories of the gifts of love bestowed by two glorious manifestations of the Divine Feminine.

That left the six malas that he'd created to honor his feelings, his memories, his process. Six beautiful necklaces, poems crafted of bead and cord, the distilled essence of his experience of love over twelve years. Each appropriate in its own moment of time. James sighed as he remembered knotting each bead with a prayer, a mantra, a loving thought, a regret.

Willow, mysterious, beautiful, pure unstoppable chemistry. Why hadn't she chosen him? He never found out, but sometimes you aren't meant to get answers. Sometimes, you just have to accept what is.

Kat, his true friend and intellectual equal. They'd chosen each other, but the gods had determined that he needed more lessons and that she would not be the one to teach him.

Charlie, his mirror image, his reflection, perfectly imperfect and one step out of synch.

Sara, lovely, mystical Sara. Although they'd never consummated their love, he still believed that there'd been so much potential for Great Love.

Na-bi-la! James smiled at the bitter sweetness. Her lesson: to live each moment as if it were your last, because time is both infinite and finite.

And then Malena's mala, different from the others because it was a mala crafted to celebrate the beginning of a love, not to process loss. A symbol of hope, not failure. James had been planning to give it to Malena that fateful weekend, the weekend his life had changed, but not in the ways he'd expected. He'd picked:

cream-colored beryl for her skin
pink beryl for her lovely lotus tattoo
blue beryl for truth and purity
amethyst for the seventh chakra, connection to the gods
Purple silk cord and tassel for her favorite color.

At the very back, he'd placed a single red coral bead, an idea he'd borrowed from Kat, to remind Malena that he loved her. And yet, at the first test of his love, he'd failed her. Her pebble had said BELIEVE. Change a few letters, and it could have said FORGIVE. Could she forgive him? Could James forgive himself? Ever? She'd believed, and he'd judged. Maybe the final lesson was that he really *was* the scorpion, a curse to any woman who loved him, doomed to a solitary, lonely existence.

His lost loves, spread out in front of him. Six tests, six mathematical variables of the heart, feeding into a complex algorithm of Love. An equation, a calculus of fate and circumstance and learning, all lessons brought to him by the gods to see if he could learn anything. Six malas, to solve for a seventh, his life.

Make a better mala.

Hafiz's words. Did he know how to do that? Make a better mala from the beads of people, places, events of his life?

The strongest cord is knotted with Love.
Let Love be your mantra as you knot together the beads of your life.

The words of the goddess Shakti, the Divine Feminine. Could he act from pure love? Love that doesn't judge, just knots together the good and the bad, and creates order out of chaos, beauty out of both light and darkness?

You have a woman who needs you, more than she can say right now.
Stay with her, even if she doesn't recognize you. She will.
The heart always knows, even if the head doesn't.
Trust your heart and her heart.

Nabila's last words to him, before she left to go back to London. Did he trust his heart and Malena's heart? Or was he listening to his shame? James looked back at Malena's mala. Once a symbol of new love, of hope. Now, a glowing symbol of his failure to meet her love with love.

You just want to judge me!
I will no pay twice for wanting to save my family!

Judgment, the Achilles' heel of love. The final exam, the hardest lesson. Love swims upstream, battles the current of lesser emotions, but is the only pure emotion. Saayed Khan had known this, had told James in so many words, shared the secret of the final exam at breakfast. But he'd learned nothing. The gods had played for keeps on this one. James smiled grimly and cursed himself again for his failure.

Remember your purpose, your sva-dharma.
To seek, create, and enjoy beauty.

The goddess herself, the Divine Feminine, repeating back to him the six words he'd chosen as the blueprint for his life, before he really understood their meaning, their power. Before he'd truly understood *how* Love and Beauty were twin sisters. Her words rang familiar and true, even as they echoed like broken glass off the shattered remnants of his values. But what was Beauty for him anymore? Beauty for him died when Malena no longer wanted him.

And now, Malena didn't even recognize him. He'd blown his one opportunity to prove his love for her. The kind of love James wanted more than anything.

A Great Love. A love that makes time stand still, that transcends the ages, that survives war and famine and death.

His own words, hurled back at him by contemptuous memory to mock his lack of worthiness, his lack of even the most basic understanding of the cost. How arrogantly he'd assured himself that he deserved it, if only given the chance! The only thing he'd proved was his own insolvency in the only currency that mattered.

Suck it up, Buttercup!

Kat's words exploded in his head with the force of a slap across his face. Focus! Beauty for James was down in Playa Estrellita, staring at the water, no light in her eyes. She'd chosen him, had needed him. Had he done everything he could do to redeem himself?

We all have our strengths. Yours is love and poetry.
Stick to that and let other, less forgiving, entities in the universe deal with retribution.

Mr. Abrami's words echoed in his mind. Was James too focused on punishing himself, stuck at blaming himself for what happened, rather than moving on to a remedy? Was he playing the victim by martyring himself on the pyre of his own failures? Suck it up, indeed! Suddenly, James knew what he had to do. He grabbed his shorts and poetry book and laptop off the floor and shoved them into his backpack. He wrapped each mala carefully in his shirts and packed them, too, except for Malena's mala. James put that one on over his neck. He ran out the door and jumped into his car. He had to get to the airport.

* ~ * ~ *

James found Malena sitting in her chair by the ocean, staring at the water, her eyes fixed on the horizon. He sat with her, day after day, holding her hand like she'd held his, determined to hold it until she turned and looked at him, saw him. James read her every poem from his book. And when he came to the end, he started over. Poetry of Love. It was all he had. The Love Poet. The Bad Poet. The Failed Poet. The Poet Who Finally Remembered.

James wrote new love poetry and read that to her. He brushed her hair, which was growing out again, long and beautiful, dark chocolate with deep red highlights. He took her hands and had them touch each bead of her mala as he told her the 108 ways that he loved her.

She sat and watched the seagulls, listened to the waves, followed the clouds with her eyes. She gazed up at the stars and the moon in the evenings before James led her inside to her bed. He held her every night as she slept peacefully in his arms, fragile, feminine, tiny, her beating heart echoing against his skin.

Finally, one day, after seven long weeks of silence, the light came back into her eyes, and she turned to him and smiled.

"I love you, Johnny Casanova," she said, and kissed him.

~~ *The Aftermath* ~~

Over piles of bricks
and beams
they stoop,
choosing one,
leaving another.
This knotty board,
that broken curb.

Some still sound,
and straight.
Some too cracked

or completely shattered.
Some beautiful,
but no longer right.
Others twisted and yet,
perfect for what
lies ahead.

Dazed yet clear,
hearts concussed,
they survey bravely
the aftermath.
There's good stuff here,
some stalwart stuff
for rebuilding dreams,
for sheltering love.

Keystones and capstones
will rise again,
a stronger, more beautiful
temple,
built with the marble
of new hope for love.
Designed by the architect
of new heart wisdom.
Lifted into place
with the strength
of self-trust.

New windows will open
into the House of their Souls.
New altars will rise
for the praise of the Beloved.
A new roof will give shelter

from storms that
will gather.
And a new door will open
that only their
True Love
can enter.

~~ * ~~

~ * ~

Epilogue

He walks the beach in the early morning and feels the rising sun caress his face. Malena walks beside him, her hand fitting perfectly in his, her eyes alive and smiling. Brown pelicans fly in formation down the beach, skimming low over the waves and rising up on the breeze to climb unseen hills of air currents and wind eddies, and waves lap gently against the sand, the breathing of Grandmother Ocean. He gives a prayer of thanksgiving, just as he does every morning. For his love, for his couple, for the generosity and healing of the gods and goddesses.

They walk up the beach to their own little spot, *Rincon de Poesia*, the Poetry Corner. It's an open-air coffee shop in the morning, a *taqueria* at noon, and a bistro at night serving tapas, beer, and good vibes. It has a yoga studio space—a polished wooden floor with a thatched roof and no walls that looks out over the ocean, open to the breezes and the sights and sounds and smells of Playa Estrellita. It has a white stone Ganesha with orange marigold garlands that are replaced daily and an icon of Saint Francis over the door. And it has a gift shop where you can buy poetry by James Wilder. *Hafiz and I: Faint Echoes of an Ancient Heart*, in both English and Spanish, and his poems on cards, posters, and calendars. And malas. You can buy malas.

Inside, they greet their community, their family, their friends. Bere works for them now, managing the place. Xiomara is behind the counter, smiling and serving up coffees to their regulars. Little Rosie is helping, and so is her Elsa doll.

And the gods, they've gone quiet, not in abandonment, but in peace. James feels peace every day when he walks in the sunshine, every night when he looks at the stars, and every time he hears Malena whisper, "I love you, Johnny Casanova."

Maybe the Love Poet has finally learned how to make a better mala. Maybe Great Love is really about capturing the grandiose in the mundane, making the fantasy real by choosing love in every moment, setting aside jealousy, fear, anxiety, and judgment. And maybe all we can aspire to in this life is to live it fully, embracing the highs and the lows, the victories and the failures, recognizing that in the eyes of the gods, it's all the same dance, all beautiful, all part of the eternal story. In the end, it's all about love. Love swims upstream against the lesser emotions, and yet is the only pure emotion.

THE END

~ * ~

Acknowledgments

Gratitude is a blessing to the one who feels it, and due to the kindness and generosity of so many people, I am well and truly blessed.

A huge thank you to Polly Letofsky of My Word Publishing for her always upbeat and positive coaching and professional guidance. And thank you to the team of professionals who added their hard work and inspiration to the process: Victoria Wolf, cover design; Julie Kruger Photography, cover photo and headshot; Thomas Locke, proofreading; Andrea Costantine, layout; Andrew Dietrick, Website; Donna Mazzitelli, editing services.

To Roland Merullo, thank you for your encouragement, thoughtful criticism, and generosity. Your detailed input made this a much better novel, and any shortcomings are purely my own responsibility.

To the great poets Rumi and Hafiz, whose words touched me to my core, changed who I am, and loosened my tongue, I owe a deep debt of humble gratitude. And to the scholars and artists who made their works accessible to me: Coleman Barks, Michael Green, and Daniel Ladinsky. Without you, this book would not exist.

A special thanks to Coleman Barks for his kind and generous permission to use his interpretation of the Rumi poem, *"Gamble Everything for Love."* I've tried to do just that.

To my early readers who gave me such valuable feedback, every comment improved my work: Marielena Garibaldi, Mary Johnson, Julie Kruger, Guillermo Rivera, Sarah Bland, Lisa Wade, Ana Maria Hernando, Shannon Hamer Bennett, and Sandi Siegel, thank you for your time, your generosity, and your thoughtful critiques.

To all my yoga teachers and fellow students who deepened my yoga practice and influenced my worldview—especially Shannon Paige, Matt Kapinus, Steven Uvalle, Gina Caputo, Rob Loud, Steph Schwartz, and Gerry and Nicole Wienholt,—thank you for welcoming me into the tribe.

To my fellow artists who collaborated with me in public presentations of my work: Sandi Siegel, Julie Kruger, and Elaine Carter, I am grateful for your inspiration and your creativity.

To my talented and inspirational friend Sandi Siegel, thank you for inviting me to read my poetry for the first time in public. That was huge. Thank you for your constant friendship and support, and for making my words better with your music.

To Sandi McCann, my dear friend who introduced me to yoga and the poetry of Hafiz. You truly changed my life.

To Michael Franti who, at a wonderful yoga retreat in Bali on New Years Day, 2016, suggested I come up with a concrete plan to write my novel and publish my work. Thank you for your friendship and inspiration.

To James Bosley of Gotham Writers Workshop, one of my earliest teachers, and to Dede Gardner of Plan B Entertainment (and formerly Paramount Pictures): long overdue thanks for your early encouragement. You watered the seeds of this and many more works to come.

Many thanks to all those who have generously supported me and my wife in our travels, especially Cornelia Lange, Gregg Todd, Mel and Charlie Nygren, Tom and Joanne Grimes, and Nicole and Gerry Wienholt. Know that parts of the book will always be inextricably linked to the times you gave us a place to stay, a place to write and even a place to practice yoga.

Finally, a heartfelt thank you to all my family and friends who have supported me in my lifelong dream to create entertaining and inspirational stories. And most especially to my loving wife, Marielena Garibaldi, who made it possible to finish this novel.

Much love and respect and gratitude to you all.

~~ *John Leslie Lange*

~ * ~

Book Club

Have questions for the author? Invite John to connect with your book club!

As a special offer to *Seven Malas* readers, John will visit your book club either by Skype or in person.

Please contact John directly to schedule an appearance.

He can be reached at:
johnleslielange@gmail.com
www.johnleslielange.com

~ * ~

About the Author

John Leslie Lange is an author and poet from Boulder, Colorado. He's also a certified yoga teacher, a financial professional and a scientist by training. John's writing reflects his deep interest in spirituality, the natural world, human relationships and travel.

John has completed two novels, five screenplays, a book of poetry and a textbook on fixed-income and currency derivatives. He has studied at seven different universities and graduate schools in three countries, earning a bachelor's degree in science and a master's degree in international business and studies. He is also a retired Chartered Financial Analyst (CFA).

In 2017, John and his wife, Marielena, sold their house and are traveling the world. Someday they hope to find a new home, perhaps a grass shack near turquoise waters.

Look for his book of poetry: *Hafiz and I: Faint Echoes of an Ancient Heart* coming in 2019.

John can be contacted at johnleslielange@gmail.com.

Please also check out his website at www.johnleslielange.com.